CRUISE SHIP CRIME MYSTERIES

The Ghost of Dr. Edmund Netter

PAUL DAVIS MD

Blewitt Pass Publishing

Seattle, WA

Copyright © 2015 by Paul Davis MD

All rights reserved. No part of this book may be used or reproduced by any means, graphic, electronic, or mechanical, including photocopying, recording, taping or any information storage retrieval system without the written permission of the publisher except in the case of brief quotations embodied in critical articles and reviews.

This is a work of fiction. All of the characters, names, incidents, organizations and dialogue in this novel are either the products of the author's imagination of are used fictitiously.

Cruise Ship Crime Mysteries may be purchased online at amazon.com, barnesandnoble.com and booksamillion.com.

Because of the dynamic nature of the Internet, any website addresses or links contained in this book may have changed since publication and may no longer be valid.

ISBN: 978-0988579194 (Paperback)

September 1, 2015

Blewitt Pass Publishing
Seattle, WA

Dedication

This book is dedicated to my Mother who taught me an appreciation for writing at a very early age. Also to all the friends, co-workers & passengers I worked with on cruise ships over the years.

The Baroness's Itinerary:

San Francisco, Marshall Islands, Papua, Indonesia, Maldives, Madagascar, South Africa, south coast of Argentina, round The Horn, Galapagos, Ecuador, Mexican coast, San Francisco

PREAMBLE

> A U.S. Coast Guard official says the cause of the engine-room fire on the Carnival cruise ship Triumph was a leak in a fuel oil return line. In a teleconference Monday, Cmdr. Teresa Hatfield estimated that the investigation of the disabled ship would take six months. She said the Bahamas is leading the investigation, with the coast guard and National Transportation Safety Board (NTSB) leading U.S. interests in the probe. She said investigators have been with the ship since it arrived Thursday in Mobile, Ala. Since then, she said, interviews have been conducted with passengers and crew and forensic analysis has been performed on the ship. She said the crew responded appropriately to the fire. "They did a very good job," she said. In an email after Monday's conference call, coast guard spokesman Carlos Diaz described the oil return line that leaked as stretching from the ship's No. 6 engine to the fuel tank. The Triumph left Galveston, Texas, on Feb. 7 for a four-day trip to Mexico. The fire paralyzed the ship early Feb. 10, leaving it adrift in the Gulf of Mexico until tugboats towed it to Mobile. Passengers described harsh conditions on board: overflowing toilets, long lines for food, foul odors and tent cities set up for sleeping on deck. Hatfield said investigators from the coast guard and NTSB would stay with the ship until about the end of the week, then continue work at their respective offices. She said the investigation will look further at the cause of the fire and the crew's response, as well as why the ship was disabled so long.
>
> -The Associated Press, 2013

Dr. Alan Mayhew shook his head. He had read the results of the investigations following not only one, but two incidents aboard the Carnival Cruise lines. He wondered how the two could have happened. Two fires in the engine rooms of its big ships couldn't be a coincidence, he thought. From the auditors' point of view, it was statistically improbable that it could happen consecutively in a relatively short time, given the hundreds of sailings that Carnival has on a daily basis. Very suspicious indeed.

CHAPTER ONE

What is it doing there?

HIS FOREARMS RESTING ON the railing of the upper deck, Alan was watching *The Baroness* making its entrance in the port of Jayapura – the capital of the westernmost province of Indonesia. Formerly known as Irian Jaya, Papua had been the site of many pleasant memories for him. Yet, today he focused on the luxuriant forest practically descending along the flank of the mountain to the water. This tropical forest revealed many of Nature's treasures and Alan would have liked to spend a couple of days hiking its trails or discovering some of its magnificent fauna and flora. The wooden arrival pier seemed to be more appropriate for small vessels than for a cruise liner such as *The Baroness*. Although she wasn't a high-capacity ship, she was nonetheless much larger than a luxury yacht.

As soon as the gangway was lowered, Alan decided to return to the medical center and put in a couple of hours' work before going ashore himself. *The Baroness* was one of the latest ships belonging to the Gold Cruise Lines. It had been modeled after *The Contessa* – a condo-ship counting no more than 400 passengers and crew. Alan had participated in the design of *The Baroness's* medical center, but not in its construction, such as he had done for *The Contessa*. And he had to admit; he was pleased with the results. The center was nowhere as big or as spacious, but he had many of the medical apparatuses and equipment that he knew were necessary aboard ships that traveled long distances such as *The Baroness* did.

Evelyn Develon, his nurse, was at her post when Alan came in. They had worked together for some years now during various contracts, and they knew 'the routine' of the center. However, there were always surprises awaiting them at every port – literally.

"Good morning, Doc," Evelyn said cheerfully, but not lifting her gaze from her tablet where she was verifying the inventory contained in one of the medicine cabinets. This was a task she performed every day, thus ensuring that most of the drugs were accounted for and none had disappeared unexpectedly. Drug thefts weren't common occurrences aboard cruise liners, yet Alan considered it something worth watching.

"Hi, Evy," Alan replied, going to his office. Then, on second thought, he retraced his steps and went to stand beside Evelyn. "Have you heard anything from Ms. Sylvan yet?"

"No, Doc. She hasn't phoned me and I don't think I heard your phone ring since I've come in."

"That's a bit strange," Alan said, getting slightly worried. Tiffany Sylvan, apart from being his girlfriend of a few years now, was also the cruise entertainment director who was due to join *The Baroness* on the morning of her arrival in Jayapura. Tiffany had promised Alan to contact him as soon as she landed in Jakarta – which would have been the previous night – and before she boarded a flight to Jayapura. However, neither Alan nor Evelyn had heard a peep from the lovely Tiffany for the past two days now.

"Do you think she's been held up somewhere?" Evelyn asked, ending her inventory session on her tablet and turning her attention to Alan's anxious face.

"That's the only explanation I could think of, Evy. But not knowing is worse than getting bad news."

"Oh now, come on, Doc, she's probably missed her flight from Boston – that's all." She paused. "Have you checked your emails – maybe there's a message from her?"

"Good idea – I hadn't thought about that." And with these words, Alan strode back to his office, turned his computer on, and waited impatiently for it to log on to the local satellite connection. Connections at sea, even when near a decent sized city in Indonesia were not what they were on the west coast of the US. If there was an on shore Internet café or Wi-Fi area, it was much preferable. Modern telecommunications had arrived, but with the mountains and remoteness, they were not perfect.

He checked the list of unread emails quickly then more slowly, and then frowned, when he realized there was no message remotely associated with Tiffany or her assignment.

Tiffany had not been initially assigned to this cruise, but due to an unexpected fall and a subsequent broken leg, the previous entertainment director had to be flown home and replaced urgently.

"Well, anything?" Evelyn asked, coming to stand in the doorway of Alan's office.

"Nothing," he replied, caressing his beard.

Alan wasn't a man who would often worry about anything, for he thought that people's destinies were in God's hands and in the choices they made in life. Yet, in this instance, he was concerned. He was in love with Tiffany and had been for a long time before he had admitted it, even to himself.

"Maybe, you could check with Gilbert, he could probably get a passengers' list from the airlines," Evelyn suggested, trying to be helpful.

Gilbert Evans was their Chief of Security on this ship and his promptitude when responding to a request or a call for help always amazed Alan. It was as if the guy had a sixth sense or an antenna perched atop his head, which would alert him of upcoming troubles before they occurred.

"Hello, Gilbert," Alan said, when he heard the man pick up the phone. "Just a quick question if you don't mind..."

"Don't ask, Doc. She's on her way now. She's missed a connecting flight and left a message for me with the airline. So if that's what you were about to ask, you've got your answer."

Alan couldn't believe it. "Thanks, Gilbert."

"Think nothing of it, Doc. I just relayed the message. Anything else?"

"No, not at the moment…. Thanks again," Alan said, replacing the receiver in its cradle and returning Evelyn's querying gaze. "She's on her way. She had missed a connecting flight – that's all."

"There – you see, nothing to worry about," Evelyn declared, walking away and returning to her tasks.

Alan reclined in his chair and pondered about Tiffany leaving a message for Gilbert instead of him. He wasn't a jealous man, but the incident bothered him nonetheless. *Why did she have to leave a message with the airline? Why not just text me?*

Since Tiffany's flight from Jakarta would land early the next morning, Alan decided to go ashore and visit the Jayapura museum that afternoon, instead of going to the local restaurant with Tiffany, as he had originally planned. After an interesting walk from the pier through old and 'new' parts of Jayapura, he finally arrived at the State Regional Museum. When he approached the building, he was impressed by what used to be a fine old edifice, which unfortunately hadn't seen much upkeep. It appeared that twenty or so years previously, a new addition had been erected and now today -- it's in need of repair. On this section of the museum, he saw an announcement plastered near the door. It went on about needing funds for the museum due to "damage to collectables because of the inadequate budget for maintenance, the high air humidity level, and the sticky dust". It also advised the visitors that all artifacts displayed in the Antara Room on that day were subject to a final sale. Surprised, Alan read on. Apparently, the museum was in desperate need of space and had decided to put several of their miscellaneous items on sale to make room for a new collection of religious relics they had acquired from various places in the southern and western Indonesian islands. Curious as ever, Alan entered the museum wondering if this sale was going to be the subject of an auction or a straight sale to "first come, first served" type of deal.

As he began looking around at the displays – mostly old termite riddled ship relics circa mid-nineteen century – his attention rested on a framed photograph dating back to 1856, depicting the officers of a sailing ship. He did a double take – his grandmother had the very same picture and always kept it on her living room side table. She would often relate that the handsome one was Alan's great-grandfather, a ships' physician. He sailed the world as much as Alan did, but performed his duties without any of the amenities Alan had at his disposal today. Unfortunately, Alan's grandmother died long before she got to know that Alan had followed in the family's footsteps.

This couldn't be, he thought. How on earth could his grandmother's framed picture end up on the other side of the world from Palo Alto, California! Since the framed photograph was installed in a glass display case, he couldn't touch it, and asked one of the museum attendants to come to his aid.

To Alan's renewed surprise, the docent spoke impeccable English and was very illustrative when he recounted the story behind the *HMS Delmas* and why a picture of the ship and its officers was in a modern day museum. The ship was apparently part of one of the largest British shipping lines in the world at the time. They carried cargo of all kinds and had a number of upscale frigate cruise liners. Alan's great grandfather, Edmund Netter worked as the ship doctor on both types of the company's ships.

He thanked the docent for his informative talk and left him a tip before making his way to the person in charge of payment for items sold.

When he came out of the museum, the picture was securely wrapped in tissue paper in a small box, which he carried under his arm. Alan smiled and raised his eyes to the sky in a grateful but silent prayer.

Upon his return aboard ship from his little adventure to the museum in Jayapura, Evelyn summoned Alan to the medical center. She was there with Robert Ekelton, the Staff Captain, Gilbert and a Mr. and Mrs. Richards. The Richards had traveled with *The Baroness* before but specifically chose this trip so that they could meet with their son who was working in Papua as a consultant for the copper mine. The plan was for him to join them in Jayapura for the two days *The Baroness* was in port. From the worried looks on their faces, and the fact that they had been in port one day already, Alan surmised that all was not well.

Ekelton spoke first. "Doc, let me re-introduce Mr. and Mrs. Richards. They have a bit of a problem and we felt you could help. Their son Jeremy has apparently fallen and broken his leg. They are not comfortable having him taken care of at the mining site in northern

Papua. They have arranged a charter flight leaving in 45 minutes. You will go and get him and have the plane take him to the Dian Harapan hospital in Waena where your report on this part of the world indicates the best medical facility exists. You can do your thing with the other doctors to ensure that he gets the best service possible, and then get your ass back here to the ship. I am only allowing you this extended trip away from the ship because we are in port. If there are any other medical issues the nurses cannot handle, we'll have to use the local hospital here in Jayapura. Do not get yourself eaten by one of those cannibals up in the highlands. We cannot sail until you get back, and you know how head office hates delays. I am giving you this Kevlar vest to wear and this sidearm…"

"Wait just a minute," said Alan. "I am a doctor and a medical officer, you and Gilbert are the policemen. If a gun is needed, I suggest that one of you comes with us. My recollection is that bows and arrows are the weapon of choice in this country – not a sidearm!"

Gilbert said, taking back the handgun, "Okay, Doc, just be careful, this place has changed since you did volunteer work here twenty years ago. We do want you back in one piece."

Alan then turned to the parents and asked, "Does Jeremy have any ongoing medical issues like diabetes? Is there anything else I should know about him?"

Mrs. Richards answered, "Nothing that we know about. He has been working over here for a couple of years, but he has not told us about any medical issues. He does jog regularly and did mention that he has now adjusted to the higher altitude near the mine. We certainly appreciate whatever you can do to help him. If there are any 'extra costs', just let us know."

Ten minutes later, laden with emergency kit, two bottles of good whiskey, several boxes of chocolate, and a bag full of mints and balloons; Alan was en route to the mine site to retrieve the young Mr. Richards and air evacuate him to the hospital in Waena. Here he would have him evaluated and stabilized. At the airport, one of the bottles of whiskey was exchanged for rapidly going through the formalities of filing flight plans and going through the rigmarole of loading luggage, etc. Even easing the departure of a privately paid charter flight in Indonesia required the greasing of some palms. Alan's emergency kit got weighed and then Alan had to get on the scale to ensure that the plane could accommodate his weight in addition to Jeremy's approximate weight.

The view from the plane as they left Jayapura and headed to the mountains was spectacular. Lots of jungle, dotted with little villages, miniscule airstrips, and the occasional large industrial complexes. Alan could make out most of these to be mines or petroleum facilities.

The approach to their landing strip was quite an impressive ascent. It looked as if the plane was going to land on the peak of the mountain. When they got closer, it was the top of the mountain! The landing strip was an inclined gravel surface, with hundreds of feet of mountain falling off on either side. There were two grass huts and a windsock for the 'airport'. The fog was quite dense, so the pilot had to make several attempts to land.

Upon arrival, two gentlemen from the Dani Tribe greeted Alan and the pilot. They had a rather tall, well-built stature, and were wearing nothing but koteckas (penis gourds) attached to their bodies with a thin strap around the waist. Their English was quite good. They introduced themselves as representatives of the mining company. They took Alan and the pilot in what remained of a 1970's Jeep along some roads that did not seem at all passable. Alan was grateful that these guys knew the terrain as well as it appeared. They explained that Jeremy had come to this area to do a survey feasibility study of a new vein of copper that had apparently been found. He had been working on it for several weeks when he slipped on a trail and broke his leg. A couple of the local workers had found him an hour after it happened and had brought him to the local shaman.

Upon arrival at a straw and mud hut warmed from the foggy surroundings with a dung fire, Alan found Jeremy. The local shaman, with an impressive headdress put several new layers of an unknown plant on the compound fracture. After this, Alan examined him. He then used various wood strips to stabilize the several pieces of his femur bone that were extruding from the makeshift cast. Amazingly, his vital signs were stable and the blood loss was minimal. He was in no pain! That was explained because he had been given a tea containing a cocoa leaves on an hourly basis. Alan was thinking ahead as to how he would explain to Jeremy's parents that their son had been consuming cocaine and heaven knows what other local narcotic for the last two days as the reason for the smile on his face.

The main mine facility was several hours away, and the shaman was correct in not wanting to transport him there with only a basic first aid facility. Alan observed the shaman do some incantations over Jeremy with some liquids sprinkled onto the wound. They all loaded a slightly hallucinating Jeremy into the plane and off they went. Alan was grateful that he did not see the takeoff-which looked more like a run off the mountain as the pilot reversed the uphill landing to a run down to takeoff! A couple of hours of spectacular views through the clouds, imagining what Rockefeller must have seen before he met his untimely demise at the hands of cannibals, and the plane touched down in Waena. Here they were met by a proper ambulance with all the amenities Alan was used to seeing in twenty-first century medical facilities. The main difference in the greeting here, in Waena, was the fact that there were at least twenty-five children to meet the plane. Many wore the traditional dress (grass skirts for the girls, koteckas for the boys) with the added T-shirts that proclaimed the wonders of Coca Cola, Jesus, and Apple computers. *What a dichotomy*, Alan thought! The balloons and candy departed at this juncture and the whiskey soon afterward, while arranging the particulars for Jeremy's surgery and subsequent rapid transport back to the West for healing and rehabilitation.

Upon arrival back at the port, Alan showed Mr. and Mrs. Richardson pictures of their son and explained the planned procedures. Arrangements would be made for him to join the trip, when able, during his rehabilitation process.

CHAPTER TWO

A *wake-up bell*

STILL PREOCCUPIED WITH Tiffany missing a flight connection and the reason for why she hadn't texted or contacted him directly, Alan made his way back to the Sentani airport the next morning. The few times Alan had come to this airport, he always had to admire its fantastic architecture, for the various facilities were housed in buildings surmounted with brown conical structures that were perhaps a dwarfed reminder of the Cyclops Mountains crowding the horizon behind them.

As soon as the plane landed and Alan saw Tiffany descend the stairs to the tarmac in front of the arrivals' lounge, he exhaled a sigh of relief. Although he had accepted this assignment knowing that he would be traveling alone on this trip, today, he couldn't imagine being without her company during the next three months. As usual the plane and meeting lounges were over-crowded and Alan was lucky to locate quickly the big sun-hat he had seen Tiffany wear as she came off the plane.

He jostled his way through porters, taxi drivers, people of all walks of life and carts loaded with luggage before he finally planted himself in front of his lady and took her in his arms without a word, and kissed her. Somehow, he needed reassurance that Tiffany was indeed here. Again, he had to look at her to make sure.

"What's this?" Tiffany asked, looking up at him and giggling. "I've only been gone a week ... what's the matter?"

"How much luggage have you got?" Alan asked by way of a reply.

"Just my usual two suitcases," she said, pointing to the two red and blue bags coming off the ramp. "Why?"

"Nothing. I just want to get you out of here and somewhere quiet, that's all."

"Okay, Alan Mayhew, what's wrong?" Tiffany grabbed his arm when he had taken the two suitcases off the carousel.

"Nothing is wrong, Tiff – I'm just glad you're here."

"Okay, but why the worried look then?"

"I'll tell you when we get out of here."

"Okay, okay, let's go then."

Watching Tiffany walk ahead of him, Alan had to smile. *God, she'll drive me crazy,* he thought. Clad in a very attractive summer dress, her little bum bouncing rhythmically in front of his eyes was probably more than he could take at that moment. He felt hot and bothered, and tried to set all these sexual and fanciful images out of his mind for the time being – with not much success, he had to admit.

Since Tiffany had had no time to change into her uniform before boarding the ship, Alan accompanied her to her cabin and let her be, but not before getting a promise from her for them to meet at the upper deck café in an hour or so.

"What's the rush?" Tiffany asked, already unpacking one of her cases in search of her undergarments. "We've got three months."

Alan took her by the arms and embraced her. "Just come and join me as soon as you've changed, okay?" he whispered.

"Okay, but . . . "

"Please, Tiff," he insisted, releasing her. His anxiety was blatant.

"Alright, but now; you get out of here, and let me get the grime off this body of mine; okay?"

Nodding and with a smile, Alan turned on his heels and left her cabin to return to the medical center. There, he found Evelyn talking to a young woman who was obviously in pain.

"Ah, Doctor Mayhew, I am glad you've come back – just in time too," the woman said. Dressed in a jogging outfit, the light blue of which did everything to enhance her olive complexion and the silkiness of her gorgeous black hair, she pointed to her left foot.

"What's the problem, Miss . . . ?"

"Irene Walter," she replied. "It's my foot – my big toe actually, Doctor. I must have sprained it, and now I can't even get it out of my runner without suffering excruciating pain." She looked up at Alan pleadingly, while throwing a scornful glance at Evelyn.

Alan smiled at her and glanced at Evelyn. "Why don't you hop into the examining room, and let me see what the problem is, okay?"

"Sure," Irene said, getting off the chair and hopping on the one able foot in the direction of the examining room, with Alan's help.

Evelyn looked after them and shook her head before returning to her desk. *Spoiled idiot,* she thought. *Probably wants some manly attention.* In fact, Evelyn had seen many of these women come to the center under what ever pretext, just to have the doctor "examine" them. She figured they were all in need of affection or attention. Most of them thought they would ignite a romance with the doc for the duration of the cruise. *They sure don't know whom they're dealing with,* Evelyn mused.

"Okay, Miss Walter . . . "

"Please call me Irene," the young woman said, winking amorously.

"Okay, Irene, I'll need to take that shoe off your foot, if you want me to assess the damage – I'll try to be gentle."

"Oh no!" Irene cried out. "Couldn't you give me a sedative or something, so I don't suffer . . . please?" She grabbed his hand, preventing Alan from touching her foot.

"If you prefer, I could ask Ms. Develon to help..."

"No, Doctor, no, no, it's only you I want."

That strangely worded request made Alan smile. He, too, knew what this was all about. "Why don't you lie down for me, and let me see if I can cut the shoe..."

"What on earth do you mean; 'cut the shoe'? Do you know how much these cost?"

"Well, Miss Walter . . . hmm, Irene, it's either that or taking it off," Alan said firmly. "Which is it going to be?"

She stared, holding Alan's unwavering gaze. "Alright – take it off then."

All Evelyn heard was a deafening screech followed by some well-chosen swear words.

Once Irene had caught her breath and began to relax a little, she blurted, "So what is it?"

Alan chuckled and shook his head. "Have you been wearing narrow or pointy shoes lately?"

Irene stared again. "Yes, why?"

"Well, what you've got, Irene, is a simple case of ingrown toenail. And if you continue wearing the wrong shoes, or shoes that will not let your skin breathe, this toe of yours will be infected and will have to be amputated!"

"What? What do you mean, amputated? It's only an ingrown toenail for heaven's sakes!"

"Yes, Irene, and one that's going to give you a lot of problems, if I don't fix it up right now."

"What do you mean, 'fix it'? How?"

"Cut it off, that's how!" He hadn't been able to resist the teasing. "I mean cut it on the side to allow it to heal," he added, turning from the enraged Irene and getting his instruments ready on the nearby table.

An hour later, after Alan had performed a little operation on Irene's toe and had sent her away, thoroughly displeased – she was now hobbling on crutches – he was on his way to the café. Anxious as ever to hear the explanation for Tiffany missing her flight, he sat down after getting himself a cappuccino from the self-service counter.

When he saw Tiffany enter the café, he got up, pulled a chair for her to sit down and resumed his seat beside her.

"So, are you going to tell me what this is all about?" Tiffany asked, peering into the doc's eyes.

"It's just that I hadn't heard from you since you told me that you would ring me from Jakarta…"

"But didn't you get the message I left with Gilbert?"

"Yes, I did, but when he said that you left a message with the airlines, I just …"

"… You wondered if someone had kidnapped me – is that it?"

Shamefully, Alan nodded. "I just didn't know why, Tiff. That's all."

"Listen, Alan. You know very well if I had been able to contact you directly, I would have done so." He nodded, stirring his cappuccino. "And the only reason I didn't, is simply because I couldn't recharge my phone in that stupid hotel in Jakarta. So, I thought I would ask the airline to send a message to Gilbert." He took her hand. "That's all there was, and as you can see, no one kidnapped me, okay?"

"But why did you miss your flight? Was there some problem at the airport?"

"Oh that's another story. You know nobody thinks of these things when they book you on a flight in a middle of the monsoon season. The streets were literally flooded, Alan. The cabbie did the best he could to get through the city, but we got there late anyway. And as luck would have it, the flight was leaving on time for once. That, in itself, was a surprise."

Again, Alan exhaled a sigh of relief. His over-imaginative mind had churned all sorts of eventualities – one more horrid than the other.

After Tiffany got herself some tea and came back to the table, she asked, "So what have you been up to in the past week?"

"Well, nothing much really. The usual, you know," Alan replied pensively. He turned his gaze to her and finally smiled. "Except for one thing . . ."

"And what's that?" Tiffany asked, pouring some tea in her cup.

"It's still puzzling me, but anyway, let me tell you." He drank some of his coffee. "Since you weren't here yesterday, I went to the museum and they had a sale of some of their miscellaneous items – to make space for a new set of relics – and among the items they had on sale, I found a photograph of my great-grandfather."

Tiffany opened her eyes wide. "Are you sure it's him? I mean how could that be? Did you buy it?"

Alan had to chuckle at Tiffany's reaction. Her inquisitive mind must have run at full speed. "Yes, I'm sure, Tiff – it's my great-grandfather in that picture. His name was Edmund Netter. He was a physician aboard a British Frigate – the *HMS Delmas* – at the time the picture was taken. And that's one of the reasons it landed in this museum. Apparently Jayapura was one of the frigate's regular ports of call in the mid-1800s. Furthermore, my grandmother had the very same picture in her living room. She would always boast about her father being a great doctor and about him being able to travel the world aboard British ships."

"Wow, that's some coincidence," Tiffany said, all smiles. "So, you bought the picture – can I see it?"

"Why don't we go to a restaurant in town tonight, and after that, I'll ask you *to come to my place to see my picture*, Alan quipped.

A few hours later, and after a delightful dinner, Tiffany and Alan came back to the ship and Alan led his lady to his cabin. They were both tired – Tiffany had had to take over the duties of the previous entertainment director and Alan had gone through the week's planning of annual check ups for some of the crew – but looking forward to spending time alone that night.

As promised, Alan took the small box out of the closet, opened it and after taking off the tissue paper enveloping it, he lifted the framed photograph out of its nest and handed it to Tiffany.

"My God, Alan, you look just like him!" she exclaimed, peering down at the picture of Edmund Netter. "It's too bad the photo is not in color, otherwise I would bet that he's got blue eyes, just like you." She threw him a glance.

Standing beside her, he slid an arm around Tiffany's shoulders. "Do you really think I look that handsome?" he teased.

"Hungry for compliments, are you?" Tiffany asked, still holding the photograph, but still looking up at 'her man'. She, too, was in love with Alan Mayhew. She couldn't believe it at first – when she finally realized what was happening to her – and now she was thoroughly convinced of the fact.

"Aren't you going to put it on the night table or something?" she asked.

"No, I don't think I'd want the cabin attendant to finger it or damage it – it's survived nearly 160 years at sea, so I'm not about to have anyone pawing it or destroy it on this voyage." He took the picture out of Tiffany's hands and quickly replaced it in its box.

"Why don't you just leave it out for tonight?" Tiffany inquired, pleading almost.

Alan wondered why.

"Do you really want him to look at us while we're in bed together?" He smiled.

"It's not that Alan, but I don't know . . . there's something about him that is so very attractive."

"Okay," Alan relented, taking the photograph out of the box again, "let's put it on the dresser – but just for tonight, okay?"

Tiffany nodded, and before Alan could object, she took the picture from his hands, walked to the dresser and placed it in the middle of it. She took a couple of steps back, smiled and threw Edmund Netter a kiss!

"Alright, Tiff, don't go weird on me, okay?" Alan said, coming to stand behind her and lacing his arms around her waist.

"I am absolutely head-over-heels in love with your great-grandfather, Alan," Tiffany declared, turning around to face the doc. "But don't worry, I'll only make love to the live specimen!"

After a few hours of satiating love, the two of them fell asleep alone. Tiffany had gone to return to her cabin surreptitiously in the wee hours of the morning. It was 4:00 am when Alan was rudely awaken at the sound of a bell. Believing it was only a dream; he put the pillow over his head and tried going back to sleep. Yet, a minute later, he heard it again. This time he opened his eyes and looked at the clock on the nightstand. He groaned. Then he heard the bell for the third time. In utter disbelief, he got up and went to the door of his cabin, opened it and saw only the first ray of light illuminating the eastern skies. All the more puzzled, he returned to his bed and sat down. He wondered if he had been dreaming while awake. He shook his head and slid back under the covers.

As he was about to fall asleep again, some one said, "How many bells will it take to have you out of your cot, Doctor Mayhew?"

Startled beyond words, Alan turned around to find his great-grandfather towering over him. "Why? How?" he blurted.

"All very good questions, son, but none that would answer mine. So, what is it going to be? Do I have to whip you out of that bed, or are you going to stand and face me?"

"But you're dead!" Alan argued.

"An undeniable fact, to be sure."

"So, what are you doing here?"

"I'm just paying you a visit, because the voyage you're about to undertake is the same I had taken – in reverse mind you – when our frigate met with some troubles."

Now fully awake, Alan decided that if he was in the middle of an awakened dream or hallucinating, he had better play ball with this ghost. *Yes, a ghost, that's all he is*, he thought.

CHAPTER THREE

A recalcitrant door

ALAN SHOWED UP in the medical center looking extremely tired and run down, like the proverbial *cat* just dragged him in.

"Good gracious," Alice Muller said, when she saw him walk into his office. "What happened? You look like you've slept under some bridge or other – did we have some emergency?"

Alice had been a cruise nurse for some years now and since her home base was San Francisco, she had welcomed the opportunity to take the grand tour of the southern oceans when she received her assignment. She was a matronly woman who wouldn't let the likes of Irene Walter give her the run around. Her ample bosom and firm stature would have intimidated the most athletic of the crewmembers. But she was kind-hearted. Of German descent, Alice was the portrait of health. Her blonde hair tied in a chignon at the nape of her neck and her deep blue eyes inspired all the confidence many of her patients needed when undergoing any intervention.

Alan stopped in front of his desk, looked at his paperwork and plopped down on his seat. "No, Alice, we had no emergency tonight – I mean last night – I just couldn't get to sleep after I woke up from a bad dream."

Standing in the doorway of Alan's office by this time, Alice said, "Maybe you should leave all that paperwork for now and go back to your cabin for a nap. We haven't got . . . "

"No, Alice, we're leaving tonight, and I haven't got the schedule for the check-ups ready."

"I'm sorry, Doc. But if that's all that's worrying you, you'll be better leaving it for this afternoon."

Alan shook his head stubbornly. "I've got to do this, Alice." He lifted his gaze to her. "I don't want to work all night."

"Why don't I take that job off your hands then?"

Alan had to admit, Alice could certainly organize a schedule for the crew. She had done it before and she was very good at it, as a matter of fact. "What about the inventory, and the new supplies?"

"Don't you worry about all that, Doc; I've got it under control. Besides, Evelyn is on standby and if I need help in the next few hours, I can give her a ring."

Finally, Alan resigned himself to the fact that he was in no fit state to handle anything for the next couple of hours, unless he had some sleep.

Coming back to his cabin, and upon opening the door, he looked furtively around the room to see if Edmund was lurking about the place. But, he saw no one – dead or alive. Since he knew the cabin attendant wasn't going to disturb him for the next two hours, he undressed and lay down. Within minutes he was asleep.

The reason why Edmund wasn't in Alan's cabin was due to the fact that he had decided to take a tour of this impressive vessel. The first thing that he noticed was the absence of sails. He couldn't fathom how such a large ship would be able to fray itself a passage through these waters without the assistance of wind and sails. And instead of wood, its armature seemed to have been constructed of steel – another fact that amazed him. Besides which, the luxury aboard this vessel was beyond compare; everything smelled fresh, clean and new. He was used to the odors that emanated from the various common quarters, the latrines, the cooking hall, and the musty smells of old furniture and draperies. This was definitely different. Although the *HMS Delmas* was a luxury ship in its time, she still suffered from the ills of long voyages at sea. Even the best cabins were small and it didn't matter if one was rich or poor, the accommodations were certainly paling in comparison to those aboard *The Baroness*. The restaurants and taverns on this vessel were also a wonder to Edmund. The table settings, the grandeur of it all frightened him a little – truth be told. Yet, when he went down to the reception hall and the adjacent theater, he was taken aback by the openness of the foyer and the sober but comfortable-looking chairs and sofas that furnished the inviting mini-salons. He entered the theater and went to sit behind the orchestra in front of the empty stage, and his mind began traveling to the times he watched Babette's plays. On every voyage, the famous playwright from the Comédie Française would entertain the passengers with a performance she would stage especially for the particular cruise. He had been a fond admirer of the lady – and probably would never forget her. She occupied an important place in his heart. Coming out of his reveries, Edmund wondered if they would put on such excellent performances aboard *The Baroness.*

Shaking his head out of his recollection, Edmund exited the theater and made his way across the foyer to the nearest elevator. This was a piece of engineering at which he had to marvel. The glass box seemed to move upward and downward effortlessly, stopping on the upper decks whenever someone pressed a button on the panel beside the doors. Although he could have flown his way to the upper decks with ease, Edmund decided to experiment a little with this moving glass box. He entered the elevator with two girls dressed in short – very short – skirts and tank tops. Edmund had never encountered women so improperly attired. He figured that if they were going to expose themselves thus far, he would get them bare before they reached their destination. The two young ladies merely felt, but didn't see anyone doing the undressing. Only horror-stricken screams accompanied the clothes being pulled down to their ankles. Laughing whole-heartedly and enjoying the sight very much indeed, Edmund saw the glass doors open automatically on the upper deck while the two girls tried pulling up their tops and skirts in front of the astonished passengers who were ready to board the elevator.

Gasps of disgust and outrage only served to ignite further chuckles from Dr. Edmund Netter. Once re-dressed somewhat appropriately and trying to hide their shameful faces, the two girls hurried out of sight.

After that little, most enjoyable stunt, Edmund stayed in the elevator and waited for the people to step in. Among them was a rather fat, old lady. When the glass doors closed, Edmund inhaled and blew the hat off her head. If his laughter could have been heard, it would have frightened the most sedate of passengers.

Having enjoyed his ride in the glass elevators, Edmund decided it was time to see what his great-grandson was up to. He flew to the medical center's deck and entered it quietly. To his surprise, he didn't find Alan in his office or anywhere in the center – only the nurse was there. Curious as to what she was doing, he looked at the tablet in her hand and noticed that every time she pointed some sort of instrument toward the open medicine cabinet, a line of writing and numbers would light up on the tablet. Edmund was most intrigued, to say the least. The nurse didn't write anything down and yet the numbers on the far-right column of the tablet either lit up or changed automatically. And its red light would come up every time she pointed the instrument to a series of bottles in the cabinet. Again unable to touch anything physically, Edmund used his formidable kinetic powers to slam the cabinet's door shut to Alice utmost surprise and bafflement.

"What the heck!" she shouted, dropping the scanner, which she picked up and examined closely. The door closing so abruptly was less of a concern to her than the fact that she had dropped the scanner. Now afraid that she had damaged it, she opened the cabinet again, and pointed it to the last of the canisters she needed to verify. "Good, at least you're still working," she said under her breath.

As soon as she had closed the door, and was about to lock the cabinet, Edmund flung it open again and waited to see Alice's reaction. Not easily flustered, she looked at the door and at its hinges curiously, thinking that maybe one of the springs was loose. As Alice placed her head between the shelves and the open door, Edmund swung it closed on Alice's cheek.

"What on earth is going on here?" she yelled, after she had pulled her head out of the way. Rubbing her cheek, she grabbed the recalcitrant door, closed it and kept her hand on it until she was able to lock the cabinet with her key.

A little disappointed from the lack of effect he had had on Alice, Edmund went to take a tour of the examining room. He opened a few drawers on the instruments' cart. He took out some of the newest pieces of the equipment and looked at each of them curiously – trying to figure out what Alan would do with them. Edmund was in the middle of his treasure hunt, when he heard a scream emanating from Alice's mouth. She had been watching the endoscope and the other things float in the air for mere seconds before being replaced in the drawers. But mere seconds had been enough to frighten the poor woman out of her wits.

When Alan came in a few minutes later he found Alice locked in the storeroom crying her eyes out.

"Oh, Doc, thank God you've come back," she burst out, jumping out of her chair. "You won't believe what happened."

"Alright, alright, Alice, please calm down," Alan said, giving her a consoling hug. "Why are you locked in here? Did someone try frightening you?"

"Not someone, Doc, something . . ." Alice replied, wiping her eyes with a tissue.

"Okay, let's get out of here first, and then let's have a chat about the "something" that scared you, okay?"

Alice nodded and followed Alan hesitantly out of the storeroom. Somehow, Alan had no doubt that his great-grandfather was at the root of this little problem. And he was going to have a talk with the old man sooner, rather than later, he decided.

"Alright, Alice; what happened?" Alan asked again, once the two of them were sitting in his office.

She turned her head toward the examining room and pointed to it. "It was in there; I saw your instruments come out of the cart drawers and float in the air, and then all of them went back in the drawers. And, and – there was nobody in the room."

"Okay, Alice. I really don't know what could have caused this, but let's not worry about it for now. And I'm not going to try explaining it either – because I couldn't even if I tried." He paused and smiled at the gentle lady. "In the meantime, how did you get on with your scheduling?"

Feeling a little better, given that the doc hadn't thought her crazy or worse accused her of fatigue, Alice said, "That was no problem, Doc. I've got the whole schedule planned out for you. I filed it in your document folder on your computer and you just have to verify it before sending it on."

"Very good, Alice. Now, what about the inventory?"

"Oh that went well until..." She stared into space suddenly.

"Until what, Alice? Did something else happen?"

"Well, I don't know . . . but I had just finished placing all the new meds in the cabinet and registering the count on the tablet when the door was flung opened and then closed on my cheek when I tried looking at the hinges."

"You mean the door closed without you touching it?"

Alice nodded vigorously. "Yeah, and I can't really explain it. I don't think I did anything to the door for it to slam shut like that. Anyway, the inventory is done and all the drugs are accounted for."

"Well, I'm sorry to hear about all the troubles you had this morning, Alice." Alan smiled again. "Why don't you go for lunch and take it easy for an hour. I'll mind the fort while you're gone – nothing to worry about."

"If you don't mind, Doc. I'd appreciate a breath of fresh air actually."

"Then you go ahead, and please don't watch the clock – just come back when you feel like it. I've got tons to do here anyway."

CHAPTER FOUR

Irene Walter

AS SOON AS ALICE HAD closed the door of the medical center behind her, Edmund appeared. Not saying a word, he sat down in the visitor's chair, facing Alan. To get his great-grandson's attention after a few minutes of being ignored, he blew the paperwork in front of him onto his face.

"What the . . .?" Alan exclaimed, fetching the papers off the floor.

When his face popped up over the top of his desk, Edmund began laughing.

"You should see your face, boy. Hilarious, that's what it is!"

Alan was far from laughing. "What are you doing here?" He sat back in his chair, fuming, but seemingly unconcerned. "I thought you had more sense than pulling pranks on my nurse."

"Oh, that's nothing. You should have seen the girls in the glass box"—Edmund chuckled again—"they really were bare when they walked away."

"What are you talking about?" Alan advanced his body toward the desk. "Have you been playing tricks on the passengers, too?"

"Really, Alan, you can't blame an old fellow for having fun, now can you?"

"Listen, Edmund . . . "

"Granddad, please – I earned the title at great pains and I intend for you to use it!"

"Alright, Granddad..."—Alan felt funny calling a ghost Granddad—

"you've been on a ship before, and I'm sure you didn't go around teasing young girls or your own nurse, did you?"

"As a matter of fact I did, occasionally that is." Edmund crossed his arms over his chest. "Life aboard the *Delmas* was tedious at the best of times, and entertainment was meager. We had many passengers who were not amused and by no means amusing either, I can assure you."

Alan had to smile. "Well, Granddad, this isn't the *Delmas*, and as you may have noticed, we have plenty of entertainment and entertainment features aboard *The Baroness*."

"Absolutely, son. Even a fabulous theater. Did you ever read about the plays we had aboard our fleet?"

"No, not really, why do you ask?"

"I am asking because there was one lady who was somewhat of a regular passenger on *The Delmas* and being from the Comédie Française, she would organize a performance for each of the voyages she took with the fleet."

It would be too bizarre of a coincidence... Alan thought, but asked anyway, "What was her name? Do you recall?"

"Oh yes, I will never forget her – she was a splendid woman," Edmund said reminiscently.

"And her name . . .?"

"Ah yes, of course, of course. She only went by her first name, mind you. She was known as Babette."

Alan couldn't refrain from staring. "I don't know if you're going to believe this, but we have a "Babette" who travels with us regularly."

"You don't say! Could she be the great-granddaughter of *my* Babette?"

"I wouldn't know, Granddad"—still calling this ghost granddad felt awkward—"but I wouldn't be at all surprised if the two were related."

"Do you know if she has booked a passage on this ship?"

"I believe so, yes."

"Well then," Edmund said, rising from his chair, "Why don't we pay her a visit?"

Alan shook his head and remained seated. "I would not advise it."

"Even if I promise to behave?"

That sounded like a child promising to be on his best behavior when he knew pertinently well that he wouldn't. "Yes, even if you promised to behave." He continued holding Edmund's gaze. "Besides, she wouldn't be able to see you, now would she?"

"Ah-ah, yes, and all the more reason for my paying her a visit."

"But I have no reason to go and knock on her door..."

"Bah, who needs a reason to visit a patient?"

"Come on, Granddad, let's wait for a bit – maybe we could meet her during dinner tonight. What do you say?"

"I say alright, son. But . . . "

"No buts, just trust in my judgment, okay?"

The noise of the outer door opening interrupted their conversation. Irene Walter hobbled in.

"Oh my, what happened to her?" Edmund asked in a muffled voice.

"Ingrown toenail," Alan said in a mere whisper and getting up to walk over to his patient.

Gladly Edmund's guffaw couldn't be heard.

"Miss Walter, how can I help you?" Alan asked, helping her into one of the anteroom's chairs.

"You could get me a walking shoe or something else than these crutches," Irene replied, visibly annoyed. She exhaled a sigh. "I can't even think of what it's going to be like when we're at sea tomorrow – I mean I've got such a hard time going anywhere already without anything moving under my feet..."

"Why don't you come to the examining room and I'll see if your foot is healing properly first, before we do anything, okay?"

"Okay, but I am not getting out of here without a walking cast..."

"We'll see," Alan replied, grabbing Irene around the waist as she got up from her seat.

"Wow, you're so strong, Doctor; I feel as light as a feather in your arms." A broad smile appeared on her lips.

Here we go again, Alan thought.

Once Irene was lying down on the bed-table, Alan unraveled the bandage around her foot and examined her toe closely. "I don't think it would be a good idea for you to put any weight on that foot at this point,

Miss Walter; the incision has not had time to heal properly yet. You'll need another forty-eight hours before I could remove the stitches, put you in a splint, etc."

"No! No, Doctor, that's not good enough," Irene erupted, pushing herself on her elbows. "I told you I want to get out of here walking on two feet."

"Calm down, Miss Walter. Maybe, I can get you a walking boot with an open toe, so that you could take *very* short walks without moving the main part of the foot."

"That's better," Irene said, leaning back on the pillow. "And why aren't you calling me Irene? I'm sure after we've shared such an ordeal, we could be on first name basis, couldn't we?"

Deliberately ignoring the comment or query, Alan went to the storage room to get the walking boot and leaving the enamored woman alone with Edmund.

After seeing the reaction he got from Alice when he removed the surgical instruments from the cart earlier that day, he decided it was time for another examination of Irene's toe.

Within seconds Edmund had pulled the first drawer open and had taken out a couple of scalpels, which he had brought close to Irene's toe.

Alan heard a scream that could have awaken the dead – if there hadn't been a ghost already on site!

When he rushed out of the storage room, he saw Irene sitting up and beating the air with her hands as if a swarm of bees had suddenly attacked her injured foot. "Get this . . . this, out of here," she yelled. But there wasn't anything to see – the scalpels were lying beside her legs.

Well aware of what had happened, Alan approached the bed-table with the boot as if he had heard nothing of her screaming. He ignored the scalpels, and said, "Are you ready to try this on?" He showed her the boot.

"Didn't you hear me scream – there was something in here, someone was going to cut my leg off!" She pointed to the scalpels. "Look, look, the knives are still there." She stared at Alan. He didn't move.

"As you can see there's no one here, Miss Walter. And as for the scalpels, maybe my nurse had forgotten to put them back in the cart."

"No, no, they were not there when I climbed onto this bed." She returned the stare. "I'm not crazy, Doctor Mayhew."

"I'm sure you aren't, Miss Walter." He paused. "And now would you like to try the boot?"

"But don't you have to re-bandage my foot before I slip into the boot?"

"I will do that after I'm sure it will fit you properly. Shall we?" Alan added, extending an arm for Irene to step off the bed and place her foot into the boot, which he had placed on the floor.

Fifteen minutes later, Irene walked out of the examining room, a boot on one foot and a cane in her hand. "That's hundred times better, thank you." She paused and looked up at the doctor before walking toward the door. "You know that I'm not crazy, don't you, Alan? I really saw the scalpels move from the cart to my foot, you know."

"All I can say, Miss Walter, is that there is a logical explanation for everything we see, hear or feel. So, I'm sure you're not crazy, and you must have seen something – I agree." He took her arm to lead her out of the medical center – but the gesture had been a mistake, for Irene turned to him, grabbed him by the neck with her free hand and tried kissing him.

Alan pushed back as the outer door was suddenly flung opened. He ignored it. "I'm sure you'll feel better in a couple of days," he said curtly, watching Irene Walter limp out the door.

Meanwhile, Alice was having lunch in the crew's mess, sitting at a table with Gilbert. "I tell you, I had such a fright, I can't remember being that scared before," she said, finishing the last mouthful of her chicken sandwich.

"And what did the doc have to say about it?" Gilbert asked, sipping on his coffee.

"He just said that he couldn't explain any of it – that's all he said." She drank some of her juice. "And he seemed so calm about it – that's what I can't understand. He's usually so concerned about everything, but this time it was like I had told him about a fly on the wall." The more

Alice recounted the events of the morning, the more she seemed flustered.

"Just think nothing of it." Gilbert suggested.

"How can I think nothing of something like that? If we've got a ghost aboard this ship, I'll get off at the next port – that's what I'll do. Nothing good ever comes when there are weird things happening on a cruise ship." She shook her head.

"Let's not get ahead of ourselves, Alice. I'll have a chat with the doc and see what he says, but in the meantime, I suggest you keep what you saw to yourself. There's nothing like the rumor of a ghost being aboard ship to create a panic. And I'm sure you know what that would mean, don't you?"

Alice nodded. "Maybe he'll have an explanation for what I saw when you have a chat with him – let's hope so, anyway," Alice concluded, taking her sandwich wrapper and empty cup to the trash bin.

CHAPTER FIVE

A ghostly encounter

WHEN GILBERT CAME in late that afternoon, Alan was once again plunged in his paperwork. Thankfully nothing had disturbed him – Edmund had gone but not before saying he would find him before the dinner bell.

"Alright, Doc, what's going on?" Gilbert asked, taking a seat across from Alan.

"What's going on is that I still have three reports to complete before I am due to meet Tiffany at 7:00 for dinner," Alan answered, hardly lifting his gaze to look at his visitor.

"I didn't mean that, Doc…"

"What did you mean then?" Alan leaned to the back of his chair and frowned.

"I had lunch with Alice today and she told me about seeing things floating around the examining room – do you know anything about that?"

Alan grinned. "No, I don't *know* what Alice saw – I wasn't here."

"But she told you about it, didn't she?"

"Yes, she did, Gilbert, but I can't explain it since I didn't see anything." Alan riveted his gaze on the security chief. "Why are you so concerned about that anyway?"

"I'm concerned because you're not, Doc. We've been working together on a couple of contracts already, you and I, and I don't recall you ever evading the subject or not coming straight out and saying what you've got in mind."

Alan guffawed. "Yes, I can be a little forward sometimes, I admit, but really, this time, I assure you, there's nothing to tell."

"Okay, Doc; have it your way, but if someone starts spreading rumors that we've got a ghost aboard this ship, we'll all be in hot water with Captain Galveston, let alone the head office."

Alan had to consider the remark. At the moment only two people plus the girls in the elevator, had suffered from Edmund's pranks. And if he couldn't stop his great-grandfather from playing games with the passengers – Gilbert was right – he would be in big trouble. Although he knew Captain Galveston was a fair man, he wouldn't tolerate the passengers being bothered by a "friendly" ghost aboard *The Baroness.*

So, Alan decided to come clean. "Okay, Gilbert. If you want an explanation, an explanation is what you're going to get."

"Just tell me if we've got a ghost or a magician aboard and I'll deal with it," Gilbert said.

Alan got up and rounded his desk. "Come with me and I'll show you."

"Where are we going?"

"To my cabin," Alan replied, opening the office door and ushering Gilbert out of the medical center.

While Alan was on his way to his cabin, Edmund was visiting the bridge. He stayed respectfully quiet, observing the captain while he walked around and addressed a number of officers, each in turn, regarding their duties, some of which Edmund couldn't understand. Captain Galveston was still a young man, judging from his allure. His blonde hair and clean-shaven face displayed a presence of mind and a force of character that Edmund had to admire.

Apart from approving of the man himself, he noticed the care he took to speak to the crew. His officers seemed happy to be working alongside the fellow.

There won't be any mutiny on this ship, he thought. *Everyone is so well-behaved, you'd think they're all back in school.* He chuckled at the thought.

His next stop was the mess hall. There, some of the crew was relaxing in front of cups of coffee and chatting with each other.

Always happy to observe, or to take part in such conversations, Edmund sat between two crewmembers and listened.

"...And I had to wait for this guy to finish his golf game, and it was already near ten, and I still had to gather all the balls..." The crewmember drank a bit of his coffee. "Anyway, that made me think about this guy I saw out on the golf course – you'll like this one, mate – he takes a high speed ball right in the crotch. Writhing in agony, he falls to the ground. When he finally gets himself to the doctor, he says, "How bad is it, Doc? I'm going on my honeymoon next week and my fiancée is still a virgin in every way."

"The doc said, "I'll have to put your penis in a splint to let it heal and keep it straight. It should be okay by next week." So he took four tongue depressors and formed a neat little four-sided splint, and bandaged it all together -- an impressive work of art.

"The guy mentions none of this to his girl, marries, and on his honeymoon night in the hotel room, she rips open her blouse to reveal a gorgeous set of breasts. This was the first time he had seen them. She says, "You'll be the first, no one has ever touched these breasts."

"He whips down his pants and says, "And look at this, it's still in the CRATE!"

Edmund cracked up laughing and thought that men hadn't changed from the time he was on *The Delmas*. He promised himself to tell Alan what he had heard. Upon leaving the mess hall, he stopped his floating abruptly. He lowered himself in front of a woman who was walking on the promenade deck and stared into her face. He could not believe what his eyes wouldn't deny him. Babette was there in the flesh! She obviously wasn't *his* Babette but the spitting image of the lady he once knew. Edmund knew that he couldn't play any tricks on her for fear of scaring her. Above all, he would have liked for her to see him, but he thought this wouldn't have been even remotely possible.

He walked beside her, imagining they were on this ship together, arm in arm and traveling the world without a care, until Babette decided to sit down in one of the lounge chairs set along the deck leading to the pool. She gathered her dress about her legs, opened the book she had brought with her and began reading.

Standing in front of her chair, Edmund could have cried out his frustration to high heaven. And now that he had seen her, he wanted to make sure he and his great-grandson would have dinner with her tonight.

In Alan's cabin, Gilbert was looking at the picture of Dr. Edmund Netter with interest. "And you're telling me this guy is your great-grandfather and he appeared out of thin air, aboard our vessel, this morning before sunrise?"

Meeting Gilbert's disbelieving gaze, Alan nodded. "And unfortunately, it seems he is a prankster at heart. He likes to have fun and see people's reactions when he plays tricks on them."

"Do you realize what that means?" Gilbert asked, visibly concerned.

"It simply means that we have a ghost aboard *The Baroness*."

Handing the picture back to Alan, Gilbert said, "Alright, Doc, I think the only thing we can do is have him pass as a roving magician and have him wear a cape or something, so people can see him. What do you think?"

"Perhaps as a last resort, we could do that. But first, I want to have another serious talk with him."

"What if you threw the picture overboard, wouldn't he have to disappear then, or does that only happen in the movies?"

"Again, I would do that if we can't find another solution to pin him down, so to speak. He wouldn't hurt anyone, but he is not shy about embarrassing people – and that's what we've got to stop him from doing."

"And why do you think you can see him and no one else can?"

"I might have an answer for that one, but I'll have to see if I'm right first."

Gilbert bowed his head and put his hands in his pockets. "You know, Doc, I never expected to be faced with such a problem on this cruise, or even in my entire career for that matter, and it's not like I don't believe in the supernatural – fortunately – but really I am coming up empty as how to solve this one."

"Well, all we can do now is hope my great-grandfather comes to his senses…"

"Me…? Are you talking about me coming to my senses?" Alan heard Edmund say. "I hope you don't mean what I just heard you say, son."

All of a sudden, noticing Gilbert's haggard gaze, Alan put a hand up. "Hang on a minute, Granddad, Mr. Evans can see you, can't you?"

"Is, is, is that him?" an astounded Gilbert blurted. "I can't believe this! He's really here."

"Yes, Mr. Evans, and I'm very glad you've discovered how to make it possible for people to see me, because, in that case, I have a favor to ask of the both of you."

Gilbert plopped down on the bed and took a deep breath, while Alan sat in the chair beside the desk.

"Just because I touched the picture, I am able to see you – is that what it means?" Gilbert asked, still baffled by what just happened.

"Yes," Alan replied. He turned to his great-grandfather. "I was going to see if Tiffany could see you, Granddad, this evening but since Mr. Evans has proven my theory…"

"Why don't you hide the picture somewhere so no one will touch it by accident?" Gilbert interrupted.

"Maybe I should…"

"Hold on, son, please. Before you hide it, hear me out, please." Edmund was pleading now.

"Okay, what's the favor then?" Alan asked.

"First, guess who I saw on the promenade deck a few minutes ago?"

"Whomever you saw, I hope you didn't bother him – or did you?"

"It's a her, not a him, son. And she's as beautiful as I remember her…"

"Who did you see?" Gilbert ventured to ask.

"I think I know. You saw Ms. Babette, didn't you?" Alan suggested.

"Oh yes, and what a marvelous sight it was, too!"

"You mean you accosted Ms. Babette, one of our most respected passengers?" Gilbert expostulated, already afraid of what this prankster ghost could have done.

"I wouldn't say, "accosted", Mr. Evans," Edmund replied, "I just watched her, that's all."

"So, what's the favor, Granddad?"

"Since you've discovered a way people could see me, why don't you show Babette my picture so I could talk to her…"

"…And frighten her so she decides to leave the ship at the next port – are you crazy?" Gilbert shouted before Alan could answer.

"Just a minute, Mr. Evans, I think Dr. Netter has just provided us with a solution to our little problem."

"How do you mean?"

"Well, I think that having my granddad keep company with Ms. Babette would be a great idea, don't you think?" Alan said, looking at Gilbert pointedly.

"Oh yes, of course, I see what you mean," the chief of security agreed, as if a light bulb had just lit up over his head. "Yeah, I think that's a great idea."

"Alright, since you two boys seem to agree on the matter in hand, why don't we go and find the lady and hand her my picture? What do you say?"

"NO!" Alan said a little louder and a little more forcefully than he intended. "As I told you before, Granddad, I would prefer not surprising her. I do not want this to be a severe shock – we all like her too much. Let's have you meet her tonight at dinner."

"Patience has never been my forte, as you probably know from being my descendent, but if this is a better way to meet her, I'll comply with your request."

"Okay, but I'll do that only on one condition…"

"And what's that?" Edmund challenged, getting visibly frustrated.

"I want you to stop playing tricks on passengers and crew. We're leaving port tonight and we've got several days at sea before we reach the

Maldives, and I don't want to have anyone going overboard from fright – understood? I have enough work as the doctor, keeping these people healthy without extra cardiac arrests, psychotic breaks, and gastrointestinal mishaps."

"Alright, alright, I accept your condition, son. As long as I could talk to Babette and spend time in her company, whenever she allows me to do so, I will be happy with that."

CHAPTER SIX

A trip down memory lane

LATER THAT DAY, Alan was trying to finish his never-ending paperwork when Tiffany popped into the medical center.

She, too, had been working like a dog since her arrival on board. There had been so many confirmations to be sent to the various entertainers that were scheduled to appear on stage during the voyage, that she felt her head spin at the mere thought of it all.

She tiptoed into his office, putting a finger to her lips while looking at Evelyn, so to warn her not to alert Alan of her presence.

She advanced carefully toward his desk, and shouted: "BOOOO!"

About to sign on the dotted line of some document or other, Alan practically jumped off his chair, and, of course, dropped the pen onto his white trousers.

He looked down and then up – half expecting to see Edmund standing in front of him. "Oh, it's you! God, Bligh me, Tiff, I nearly had a heart attack."

"Yes, it's me," Tiffany replied, taking a seat across from Alan. "Who did you think it was?"

Fetching his pen from the floor, Alan swore when he realized that it had left a noticeable blotch of black ink on his trousers' leg. "I hope the miracle workers in the laundry can get this off my pants before the morning," he said, advancing his chair and finally looking at his lovely girl. Seeing her, in any circumstance, was always a pleasure that would have erased the most irritating thoughts from his mind. A broad grin appeared on his lips. "Sorry, Tiff, but with that trip I had to take up into the mountains…"

"What trip are you talking about?" Tiffany hadn't heard anything about Alan's MediVac flight.

"Of course, you didn't know, sorry. I had to get the Richardson's boy out of the remote area he was surveying for the copper mine where he had broken his leg. I flew with him to Waena the day before you arrived."

"Is he alright?"

"Oh yes – he will be, I mean. He was doped to the hilt when he got there, but he should be on his way back to the States by now."

"And I suppose your change of uniform is still at the laundry?"

"Yes, and with the dinner tonight with Babette, I don't have another pair of trousers…" He paused. "Do you think I could wear my shorts or my swimsuit to the dining room?"

Tiffany cracked up laughing – seeing Alan in his shorts and knobby knees attending a formal dinner was indeed a hilarious thought. "No, I don't think our good captain would appreciate it." She giggled. "But tell me, who did you expect to see when I surprised you just now?"

Alan didn't see any reason at this juncture to beat about the bush. "My great-grandfather," he replied with as a straight face as he could manage.

Tiffany stared. "You mean the old guy in the picture?"

"Yes. The "old guy" as you described, has revealed himself the morning after we took the picture out of its box."

"You mean he's a ghost? You're joking, right?"

"No, Tiff, and the only way anyone can see him is if the person touched the picture."

"Hold on a minute, Alan. Are you saying that I could potentially see him too? Because, as you remember, I touched the picture too."

"Precisely. And there's another person who can see him now…"

"Who's that?" Tiffany was quick to ask, her relaxed and carefree attitude having abandoned her by now.

"Gilbert."

"Oh God! And what did he say when he saw him?"

"At first I thought he was going to collapse from fright, but he calmed down rather quickly and was quite reasonable about the whole thing."

"What is he going to do about it though?" The anxiety in Tiffany's voice was blatant.

"Nothing…"

"Nothing? That doesn't sound like Gilbert. How come?"

"Because we've made a deal with Granddad…"

"Oh, it's "Granddad" now, is it?" Tiffany returned to her nervous tittering.

"Yes, we agreed to have Babette touch the picture so that my dear ancestor can talk to her."

Tiffany was agape now. "You're sure you haven't shared in the drugs that they gave to the Richardson's boy?" She fixed her beautiful eyes on 'her' man. "This is crazy, Alan. And why on Earth would the old goat, excuse me, old ghost, want to speak to Babette?"

"The "old goat" was in love with another Babette apparently – this one from the Comédie Française – and, as with our Babette, the lady traveled regularly between Europe and the Orient back in the mid 1800's."

"Are you serious?"

"Oh yes; and listen to this. Granddad's Babette produced plays for the passengers aboard the British ships on which he worked."

"I can't believe any of this, Alan! This is way out there, even for you!"

It was Alan's turn to laugh. He had never heard anyone assessing his behavior as being "out there" before. He liked it, too.

"And when were you planning for the two of them to meet?" Tiffany paused. "I don't believe I'm asking this."

"Well, I called her this afternoon and we agreed that you and I would go to her cabin at about 7:00 and escort her to the dining room…"

"And you plan to show her the picture before going to the dining room? That's going to be tricky, Alan. What if she's not even inclined to meet the man…?"

"You know how she is, Tiff. Her curiosity will soon get the better of her. She won't be able to resist – you'll see."

"That's all fine and dandy, Alan, but what happens when we're all sitting at the captain's table and your great-grandfather starts talking to her – what then?"

"Well, I'm quite sure that Babette will not tolerate his presence during dinner – she's much smarter than that."

"You know, Alan, we've seen a lot of things happen during the journeys we've made together – murders, treasure hunts, submarine dives, arbalest killing, to name a few – but this must be a first even for you. And I don't know how we will be able to keep this whole thing from getting out of hand."

"I agree that this is something I didn't expect, but as long as we keep the photograph away from everyone, I think we should be okay."

Alan was not about to tell Tiffany about the tricks Edmund had played on Alice or on Irene Walter – she would have been liable to go to his cabin on the double, grab the photograph out of its box and throw it overboard. And he didn't think such a move would make any difference anyway. His Granddad was "out of the picture", so to speak, and there was no way he would go back . . . or would he? *Food for thought,* Alan surmised.

Clad in freshly ironed uniform pants and shirt, with the box under one arm, Alan, Tiffany and Edmund were standing in front of Babette's cabin door, ready to knock. Tiffany was still nervous. She had first laid eyes on "Granddad" when he and Alan had come to fetch her from her cabin. She could not believe the resemblance between the two men – it was truly astonishing. Yet, her mind was still too preoccupied with Edmund meeting Babette.

"Right on time as usual," Babette exclaimed as she opened the door. "Come on in." She extended an arm toward the mini-salon of her suite. "Make yourselves comfortable." She stopped when she noticed the box under Alan's arm. "Is that for me?" She raised her gaze to him.

He smiled and shook his head. "It's only something I'd like to show you, Babette, and I think you might be interested…"

"Now, Alan, you know how I can't resist anything like that, come on, sit down and let's have a look at what's inside this mysterious box."

While Alan, Tiffany and Babette settled in the couch and chairs, Edmund remained standing. He still could not believe how this woman resembled *his* Babette. *She must be a direct descendent,* he mused. Her teasing green eyes, magnificent head of red hair, and inviting smile had probably smitten the most indifferent of men in her younger years. Yet, she was as fascinating to Edmund as the woman he knew and loved while traveling with 'his' Babette on *The Delmas* at least a century ago.

"What's this?" Babette asked once she had opened the box and removed the tissue paper from the top of the framed photograph. "It looks like you, Alan, but in a costume of the time – were you part of a play?" She looked up at the doc.

"No, Babette, it isn't me in that photograph, it's my great-grandfather."

She still hadn't taken the picture-frame out of its box. "How did you come to obtain it? Is it an authentic photo of the era?"

"Yes, and before you take it out, I'd like you to hear me out..." Alan peered into her eyes.

"You intrigue me – is there a story behind the picture?"

"Yes, Babette, and one that concerns you, in fact."

"Me...? Good Lord, what would I have to do with your great-grandfather in the 1850's, I mean these uniforms were only worn in that era."

"I guess you know your history and the costumes," Alan said.

"Yes, I would have to, wouldn't I? I write and direct plays." She turned to Tiffany. "Do you know what this is all about?"

"Yes, Babette, I do. And it's not something dramatic or dangerous – it's quite romantic actually – but I'll let Alan tell you the story." She rested her gaze on him.

"Okay here it goes...." And for the next few minutes, Alan explained – as best he could – the presence of his great-grandfather's ghost aboard *The Baroness* and Dr. Edmund Netter's obvious infatuation for the lady of the stage in 1856.

"And you're saying that if I touch the picture, I will be able to see him?"

"Yes, that's what I'm saying," Alan replied. "But it's entirely up to you. Since he's in the room…"

"You mean he's here – in my suite?" Babette sounded a little frightened now.

"Don't worry, Babette," Tiffany interposed reassuringly. "He's very friendly and well-mannered. And he certainly wouldn't want to scare you in any way."

"All right then, Dr. Netter, let's see what you look like," Babette said, taking the photograph out of the box without further ado.

In a fraction of a second, the three of them were now able to see Edmund – he looked very pleased with the fact. Without waiting for her to say a word, he went to bend on one knee and took Babette's hand.

"My sincere apologies, dear lady, if I have frightened you in the slightest, but your simple gesture, made this old soul extremely happy," he said, looking into the vibrant eyes that were peering now into his own.

"Thank you," Babette blurted, a little unsure as to what she should say at this point. "But how did you know me – I mean how did my relative know you?"

"I only knew Babette of the Comédie Française formally – and I kept my respectful distance during every one of our voyages together – but it was obvious to both of us that Eros had struck our hearts with the arrow of love."

"And did you ever say anything to this Babette back in the 1850's?"

"Oh no, milady, in those days, how could a mere surgeon like me ever hope that a lady of Babette's standing would return a gesture of affection."

"Yes, I can understand that," Babette replied, "but do you know what happened to her, where she ended up residing maybe?"

"Unfortunately no, milady," Edmund said, bowing his head in sadness.

"I'm sorry to interrupt," Alan ventured, "but we have a dinner appointment at the captain's table – and it would be bad form for any of us to be late."

"Yes, yes, of course," Babette said, getting up from her seat. She looked up at Edmund. "Why don't you and I have dinner in my suite tomorrow night?"

"Why, of course, milady, I would be delighted. Thank you," Edmund replied, visibly elated.

"However, for tonight, Dr. Netter, I beg of you to remain in Alan's cabin until he returns. You see, I would be tempted to talk to you during our dinner and it wouldn't do for a lady of my standing to address someone no one else could see, wouldn't you agree?"

Trust Babette to solve the problem with a couple of well-spoken sentences, Alan reflected.

"Yes, of course, milady. I'll do as you wish, and wait for tomorrow night with bated breath."

CHAPTER SEVEN

Death on a life raft

IF IT HADN'T BEEN FOR Irene Walter making a theatrical entrance into the restaurant when she had been sure Captain Terrance Galveston and Staff Captain Robert Ekelton had noticed her, the veritable repast their guests had enjoyed, would have been a delightful memory.

However, such as the circumstances were, Irene Walter came hobbling to the captain's table and made a point of explaining how "Alan" had saved her life by stopping a "terrible" infection from turning into an inevitable "amputation" of a limb when gangrene would have set in.

Alan was stunned. To have a passenger, who was not a close friend, call him by his first name was not only intolerable, but certainly not part of the regulations. Moreover, Ms. Walter's explanation for her foot being bandaged and in a walking boot was erroneous. The woman was obviously trying to attract attention to her person, induce Alan into making advances to her, and intrude into his personal life.

He would have none of it.

"Captain," he said, looking at Galveston, "if you would excuse me for a moment; it seems that I need to confer with my patient urgently."

"Yes, yes, of course, Dr. Mayhew. I think that would be best." Galveston flashed a thin smile toward his other guests. "And please don't be too long; we wouldn't want you to miss dessert, now would we?"

"I'll do my best, Captain," Alan replied with a raised eyebrow, getting to his feet and taking Irene by the arm to lead her out of the restaurant.

As soon as they reached the foyer, Alan led Ms. Walter to a seat near the promenade deck. "What do you think you were doing in there?" he asked her, sitting down beside her.

"I should ask you the same question, Alan," Irene replied, "Why didn't you invite me to have dinner with you? You know I would have loved to spend time with you. You are my savior," she added, raising a hand to caress his face.

Alan took the hand and brought it down to her lap roughly. "I am only your doctor, Ms. Walter, and as such, whether here, aboard this ship or anywhere in the world, I would not risk my career by having a flirtatious adventure with my patient."

"Are you saying that you would have a relationship with me if I wasn't your patient?" She paused for an instant and peered into Alan's unyielding gaze. "Don't you see what that means? I could dismiss you right now – at this very minute – and we could go to your…"

"Enough, Ms. Walter! Even if I were inclined to take you off my patients' list – which I couldn't do in any circumstances during this voyage – I am not interested in having a *relationship* with you at any time!"

"But… don't you find me attractive?"

"Very attractive, yes, but you're not my type, really."

Suddenly, something in Irene's face changed. Alan couldn't really say what was obviously glaring at him – something not human – but registered the shock nonetheless.

"You know, Dr. Mayhew, you are a fantastic doctor, but to me, personally, I find you obnoxious." She stood up with the help of her cane. "And since you seem reluctant to admit that you're in love with me, I have no alternative but to tell everyone about the knives – or scalpels I should say – that magically floated around my bed…. There is a ghost aboard this ship, Doctor, and I'm going to make sure every passenger knows it!"

Alan knew something like that was liable to happen with a patient the likes of Irene Walter. Whether it was a ghost story or anything else she would imagine being real, she would spread a rumor ignorant of the damage she could cause or the harm she could inflict. "Okay, okay, Irene," Alan said soothingly, "Why don't we go to the promenade deck and talk about us…?"

"Ah, I see that you've come to your senses. Alright then, let's go."

A half-hour later Alan returned to the restaurant and to his seat between Babette and Tiffany. All eyes were on him. "I am very sorry for the delay, Captain, but Ms. Walter was suffering from the result of taking various pain killers without observing the prescribed dosage." He stopped and looked around the table. "How was dessert?" he ventured.

"Ha-ha, Doctor, we quite understand your dilemma," Galveston said jovially, "the lady is infatuated with her physician, isn't that a better explanation?"

Alan laughed quietly and shook his head. "A little of both I suspect, yes."

"And where is she now?" Babette inquired. "Have you tucked her in bed?"

"You could say that," Alan replied with a grin.

"You didn't!" Tiffany erupted, a frown appearing on her brow.

"No, Ms. Sylvan," Ekelton said between chuckles, "I don't think that's what the doctor meant, is it, Doctor?"

"Yes, Mr. Ekelton, you're right, that's not what I meant. Ms. Walter is now sleeping comfortably in one of the medical center's beds and will probably wake up late tomorrow morning with the nurse in attendance."

"But why?" Tiffany asked.

"Because, Ms. Sylvan, Ms. Walter needed to sleep it off, as it were, isn't that right, Doctor?" Galveston stated.

"Exactly, Captain. And I thought she needed to have a rest before she did something really stupid and fall overboard accidentally."

"Well then, Alan," Babette concluded, "why don't you have a piece of that delicious strawberry gateau that we've already tasted – it's absolutely divine." She nodded in the direction of the cake tray standing in the middle of the table.

"Don't mind if I do," Alan agreed, smiling up at the waiter who had discreetly approached the table when he saw that the doctor was ready to have dessert.

Alan and Tiffany accompanied Babette back to her suite. Then, wanting to be alone for a while, made their way to Tiffany's cabin. His was off limits for the time being, since Edmund was sure to be occupying it for a while.

"Did you really give her some sedatives and put her to bed in the med center?" Tiffany asked, lacing one arm in the crook of Alan's elbow.

"You bet I did. I didn't want to go anywhere with her. And truth be told, she was "high" on something – I'm sure of it. Otherwise, even though she is a flirt, she wouldn't have made such a scene at the restaurant."

"But what if she's some sort of stalker, Alan, what are you going to do then?"

"I don't know, Tiff. But at this juncture, I want to keep her under observation. And if she is a raving lunatic, then I'll have no choice but to send her home at the next port."

Tiffany remained pensive until they reached her cabin.

"You know, Alan, there's something about the woman that still bothers me..."

"What's that?" Alan asked, opening the door for Tiffany to enter her cabin.

"I don't know, but she seems odd somehow. She is dramatizing everything in order to attract attention..."

"I agree," Alan said, closing the door behind them and taking his beautiful lady in his arms. "But for tonight, let's forget about Irene and just think about the two of us, shall we?"

"I'm all for that," Tiffany replied, kissing Alan tenderly.

A few hours later, embraced in each other's arms and fast asleep, the strident whistle of a train about to leave the station suddenly awakened Alan and Tiffany.

Startled, Alan shouted, "What? What's going on?" sitting up. Then seeing Edmund standing at the foot of the bed, he plopped down on the pillow behind him and looked into Tiffany's frightened and bleary eyes.

"Is he here?" she whispered before risking a glance over the edge of the cover.

"Yeah, Granddad is here," Alan replied, exhaling an exasperated breath. He looked up at the ghostly figure towering over him now. "What do you want?"

"Me? Nothing, son. I have kept my promise to remain out of Ms. Babette's presence until Mr. Evans told me to find you…"

"And he sent you to find me here? Why didn't he use my emergency phone number…?"

"I believe he said something to the effect that you had apparently switched it to "call the medical center after hours" – whatever that means, I frankly have no idea what these devices you carry around on your belts do."

Alan threw his legs over the side of the bed and stared at his great-grandfather before he asked, "Something has happened, hasn't it?"

"I am afraid so, son. And I think we better discuss this outside – I wouldn't want to frighten Ms. Sylvan any further than I have done already."

Popping her head over the blanket, Tiffany blurted, "You're not scaring me, Granddad, but you're annoying me no end, if you want to know."

"I am terribly sorry, my dear Tiffany, but a doctor's first duty is to his patients and not to his great-grandson's lover."

"You're impossible!" Tiffany growled, turning to face the other side of the room.

Not paying much attention to their exchange, meanwhile Alan had slipped into his trousers and shirt – ready to accompany his great-grandfather to the site of the "event".

"Let's go, Granddad," he said, "Shall we?" opening the door for Edmund to precede him out of Tiffany's cabin.

"Where should we go?" Alan asked once they were outside.

"Lower deck, son. On the starboard side, near the life-rafts."

"Okay then, you get down there and tell Mr. Evans, I'm on my way. I'll have to go to the center and grab my medical bag…"

"I don't think you'll need it," Edmund declared somberly.

"What are you saying?"

"I'm saying your ministrations will not be needed."

"Is there a dead body...?"

Edmund nodded. "And I think you'll be surprised to find out who it is."

"Stop being so cryptic, Granddad. Who is it?"

"The lady with the ingrown toenail."

Agog, Alan stared at his ancestor. "But that's impossible! I've given her two lorazepam – she should be asleep until..."

"What ever you gave her, son, had no effect on her apparently, or let me rephrase that – your medication may have struck her dead."

"Don't be funny," Alan retorted hotly. "This is no joke." He paused and waited for a moment. "Okay, why don't you go ahead and I'll join you in a minute."

When Alan arrived on the lower deck, the eerie silence that enveloped the ship seemed to pervade his thoughts. In fact, he couldn't speak. He was thinking of all the ramifications this situation could have.

"Hi, Doc," Gilbert said quietly, "Dr. Netter alerted me first..."

"How? I mean he wasn't supposed to roam the ship; he had promised to stay in my cabin..."

"Yes, he explained all that. But according to him, he had promised to keep away from Ms. Babette tonight – which he did – but he saw no reason for him to remain in your cabin while we were all asleep."

"Alright. And where is he now?"

"I think he said he was going back to your cabin."

"Okay. Anyway, what are we looking at?" Alan asked.

Gilbert turned toward the railing. "She's fallen over and landed on the tarp covering one of the life-rafts. Have a look."

As they bent over the banister, Alan wondered if Irene was injured and unconscious or really dead. "Okay, we need to get her up here and into the center before morning, Gilbert. Do you have a couple of your men who could go down there and bring her back on a gurney?"

"Sure, I thought that's what you'd be asking and they're on their way already."

"By the way, did Evelyn contact you?"

Gilbert stared. "No, why would she?"

"Because, I put Irene Walter under observation tonight and gave her a couple of sedatives…"

"You mean she was sleeping in the medical center…?"

Alan nodded. "Okay, let's get up there and see what Evelyn has to say." He was already hurrying toward the nearest elevators.

"What about my guys getting the body…?"

"Don't worry about them; I'm sure they'll know what to do."

"But they'll need a gurney…?"

Alan stopped and turned to face Gilbert. "I've got a bad feeling about this, Gilbert. So, please stop asking questions for a minute and come with me to see if Evelyn is okay."

"What on Earth…?"

"No time… Gilbert… let's go."

Bewildered, but suddenly realizing what Alan meant, Gilbert followed the doc to the elevator and up to the medical center.

As soon as they reached the door, they both saw Edmund standing on the threshold. "I thought you would never get here," he said, unfolding his arms from across his chest. "Your nurse needs you."

That's all his granddad had to say for Alan to push past him and literally run into the ward where he found Evelyn on the floor, bleeding from a nasty wound on her head."

"I just came in here when I saw the door ajar, son. I didn't touch anything…"

"How long ago was this, Granddad? I mean when did you find Ms. Walter's body?" Alan crouched down beside Evelyn and felt for her pulse. It was strong, but he was still worried.

"I'd say a little under an hour ago, why?"

"Because that means Ms. Evelyn here has then been unconscious for that long, since I would guess that Irene Walter knocked her over the head to get out of here."

CHAPTER EIGHT

Cloak and cowl?

SOON AFTER THE BODY OF Irene Walter had been properly stored in the morgue for the night; Alan and Gilbert went to the chief's office to discuss the incident. Alan was still wondering what happened. Evelyn, when she had regained consciousness, had only been able to explain that when she had gone to check on Ms. Walter, the patient had been asleep – "or pretended to be I guess" – and that everything had appeared fine. But when she had been about to leave the room, she had been knocked on the head and couldn't remember anything else after that.

"Okay, Doc, this isn't looking good for you…"

"I know, Gilbert. I'm the one who gave her the sedatives – but I doubt these were the cause of her reaction. In fact I can't be sure that she actually swallowed the meds. They're very small pills and if she had decided to stay awake, it would have been easy for her not to swallow them."

"But the thing that's going to be harder to explain is the fact that you were not in your cabin when the incident occurred. You and I know where you were, but I don't think it would be a good idea to tell anyone that you were sleeping elsewhere last night, now would it?"

"Sorry to contradict you, Gilbert, but I think it would be better for me to admit that I was with Tiffany, so that she could vouch for my being at her side from the moment we left the restaurant until you woke me up with the news."

"Maybe. But at this point, I would prefer concentrating on finding out whether Irene Walter died from jumping over the railing and hurting herself upon landing or if she was pushed over that banister."

"Or if she was hit over the head before being thrown over…"

"Did you see any evidence of a wound on her head before we put her in the morgue?" Gilbert asked, lifting his gaze from his note pad.

"No, not that I recall, but I need to have another look when I perform a preliminary autopsy," Alan replied, looking down to his lap. "You know, Gilbert, this whole thing is far too strange for me to understand at this point."

"Why don't we sleep on it for a couple of hours before we have to confront our captain with our reports – How's that?"

"Good idea," Alan agreed, getting to his feet.

This sure is going to be tricky, Alan mused, as he returned to his cabin. He didn't want to return to Tiffany's room and wake her with such troublesome news. As he opened his door, he saw Edmund waiting for him, sitting on the chair beside the desk. Alan was in no mood to discuss anything with his great-grandfather at this point. He wanted to lie down and think about everything that had happened since the moment Irene entered the restaurant. Yet, of course, Edmund had other ideas.

"Aren't you going to ask me where I roamed last night?" he asked, crossing his arms over his chest.

Alan sat on his bed, took his shoes off and lay down over the covers. "Why ask; you are going to tell me anyway, aren't you?"

"Very well then; I'll consider your answer as a yes." Edmund got up and went to sit beside his great-grandson. "As you know, I promised Babette to remain out of sight…"

"No, Granddad," Alan snapped, "you promised to stay in my cabin – that's what the lady asked you to do."

"Precisely. And I did so for a while until I thought it wouldn't do any harm if I had a stroll along the promenade and observe people…"

"And what did you observe then?" Alan asked, sitting up and pulling the pillow up to support his back against the headboard.

"Well, not much at first. In fact, apart from being dressed scantily, most of the passengers seemed relaxed and carefree, enjoying a leisurely walk along the deck – such as the passengers on *The Delmas* would."

"Did you observe anything out of the ordinary then?"

"Yes, but only one or two curious occurrences."

"Oh, and what was that?" Alan pressed, knowing what his granddad must have seen.

"I saw you coming out of the foyer of the restaurant in company of Ms. Walter and standing with her by the railing."

"Did you hear what was said?"

"No, not really, son. I didn't want to come too close to you – I didn't want you to see me."

"Yes, that would have been awkward – for me at least."

"Exactly. Yet, I was close enough to hear snatches of your conversation." Edmund shook his head. "And you didn't sound too pleased with Ms. Walter's statement. What ever she said to you obviously irritated you."

"That's right. Ms. Walter was trying to impress upon me that unless I took her to my bed, she was going to declare your presence aboard this vessel."

"Ah-ah; she was threatening you then?"

"Me and everyone working on this ship, Granddad. Telling anyone aboard that there is a ghost roaming the ship would see the passengers leaving in droves, the cruise company losing its reputation and, of course, most of the officers and crew being dismissed for misconduct or some such excuse."

"Do you realize that you have given yourself a motive for committing murder?" Edmund frowned but kept his eyes on his great-grandson.

"Don't I know it, Granddad," Alan replied. "The only way out of t his situation is for me to ascertain the approximate time of death and admit that I was in Tiffany's cabin all night."

"Except for the fact that you do not want to endanger Tiffany's reputation, you are possibly correct in your surmise."

"Do you see another way out of this mess?"

"Perhaps, son. Since I saw what happened to Ms. Walter, I could certainly attest to the fact that her killer wasn't you."

Alan chuckled quietly. "I knew you would have observed the whole thing since you were the one who alerted Gilbert. But how could I implicate you in this affair – you're not a very believable witness are you?"

"Do you doubt my word?" Edmund blurted in a huff.

"Of course not, Granddad, but you yourself must realize that your testimony would be worthless in any court of law since you're a ghost and you're not supposed to be here."

Edmund paused for a minute before he asked, "But do tell me something; how did you get Ms. Walter to the medical center? Given the fact that what the lady wanted was only to go to your cabin and spend the night with you."

"Ah yes; I think that requires an explanation, but one I will only be able to confirm once I have ran some blood tests."

"Let's not go into the confirmation at the present moment, and just give me the reason for which Ms. Walter ended up in a bed of the medical center, if you please?"

"Alright. As you saw and gathered accurately, Ms. Walter was menacing me, and prior to that conversation, I had seen her sudden and inexplicable mood swings. Those, as you know, are typical symptoms of mental instability or of someone being under the influence of a powerful drug."

"Do you mean she had been taking some alchemist's potion or some opiate perhaps?"

Alan sniggered. "Something like it, yes. But these days, some drugs are chemically altered to provoke hallucinations…"

"That's the answer, son!" Edmund cut-in. "She must have been hallucinating when she supposedly saw the scalpels traveling to her bed…"

"Yes, I thought of that, Granddad, but the point is I lured her into the medical center under the pretense that *we would be more comfortable and away from prying eyes if we went to the center.*" And not visualizing much of reality at that point, Ms. Walter accepted the invitation readily and even lay down on the bed of her own accord."

"However, didn't you say you gave her some sedatives? Did she think they were opiates?"

Alan nodded. "She probably did, but the point is that she must not have swallowed them, otherwise she would have been asleep right now." He paused for a moment. "Since you saw what happened, could you tell me who committed the crime then?"

"I don't know who the person is – not by name, of course – but it was a man."

"Alright; and how was he dressed? Would you say it was a crew, or a passenger?"

"I couldn't say, son. It was the middle of the night remember? And I only happen to see the two of them when I was on my way down to the engine room..."

"The engine room...?" Alan blurted. "What on Earth would you want to go down there for?"

"Well, you must admit that such a large vessel seemingly navigating the ocean waters with ease and without sail or even rowers, must be intriguing to an old seafarer the likes of me. I wanted to see for myself what made this vessel tread water – that's all."

"So, because it was dark you can only describe the assailant as a man..."

"Yes," Edmund interrupted, "but as for his attire, I must not forget to mention he was wearing a cloak and cowl."

Alan stared. "Did you say "a cloak and cowl"? Are you sure? I mean I don't doubt your word, but we generally do not wear cloaks of any sort these days, Granddad. Some young people wear jackets with a hood, yes, but not a cloak with a cowl. Was it something like a monk's habit perhaps?"

"Yes, yes; that's precisely the comparison I made at the time. I even wondered if Ms. Walter had gone to the chaplain, but we wouldn't have a monk ministering the flock aboard a vessel, even in my century."

Alan slid down from his pillow to lie on the bed. "Okay, Granddad. Let me get some shut-eye, and in the morning, we'll do the autopsy and see what sort of drug Ms. Walter had ingested, shall we?"

Unable to go back to sleep right away, Tiffany had spent the rest of the night reading. The result was obvious – her usually radiant face was pale and showed all the signs of fatigue when she reached the café the next morning. After fetching a strong coffee, a couple of toasts and an orange from the counter, she went to sit down at a table near the open deck. The fresh breeze was invigorating and it managed to restore her a little. As she was eating, she couldn't help but overhear a conversation from two young fellows who seemed to be very busy playing a game on their laptops.

"You know, Jeff," the younger of the two began, "we were talking about frogs and how intuitive they are…"

"Yeah, so what?" the other fellow replied. "It's not like we could experiment with some bullfrog around here, is it, Nathan?"

"No, but I heard from Robert the other day, and he was telling me about this frog that he almost ran over when he was driving to the lab…"

"Oh yeah, did he capture it or something?" Nathan asked, visibly interested now.

"He sure did, and then the frog told him…"

"You're putting me on, right?"

"No-no, just listen to this: The frog piped up, "I'm really a beautiful princess and if you kiss me, I'll stay with you for a week". Robert shrugs and puts the frog in his pocket. A few minutes later, the frog says, "Okay, okay, if you kiss me, I'll give you great sex for a week." Robert nods and puts the frog back in his pocket.

"Since the offer didn't seem to appeal to Robert, the frog says, "Turn me back into a princess and I'll give you great sex for a whole year!" Robert smiles and returns to his car.

"Finally, the frog says, "What's wrong with you? I've promised you great sex for a year from a beautiful princess and you won't even kiss a frog?"

"I'm a programmer," Robert says, "I don't have time for sex…. but a talking frog is pretty neat."

Upon hearing the punch line, in a jerk of laughter, Tiffany spilled some of her coffee onto her uniform. "Oh God," she erupted, "this is going to be one of those days!"

CHAPTER NINE

Ecstasy

BABETTE WAS TYPING FURIOUSLY on her laptop when she suddenly felt a presence in her room. She stopped and reclined against the back of her chair. Still dressed in her bathrobe, she gathered the collar about her chest, smiled and turned around. Edmund was there, standing beside the door and smiling.

"Alright, Dr. Netter, I know you can appear and disappear at will, but the next time you decide to pay me a visit, I would appreciate a knock at my door or even a word thrown into space to forewarn me of your presence. Do you agree?"

"Of course, my dear lady. Far from me to intrude on your time when I am not wanted, however, the current situation forced me to come into your cabin surreptitiously. In fact, I didn't want you to open your door to an invisible guest…"

"And what situation are you referring to, Dr. Netter?" Babette asked, rising from her chair. "Why don't we have a seat," she offered, stepping to the sofa and sitting down.

Edmund followed her and sat down in the chair facing her. "Yes, yes," he said, slightly hesitant. "The situation to which I alluded concerns my great-grandson."

"I see, and what has he done?"

Edmund raised an eyebrow. "He has done nothing untoward, I am sure. Nevertheless, the situation in which he finds himself at present may become difficult…"

"I am sorry to interrupt, Dr. Netter, but could you be clearer and tell me what happened?"

"Hum... simply put, my great-grandson might be accused of murdering Ms. Irene Walter last night and if found guilty will be facing the noose."

Babette gasped. "What on Earth are you saying, Dr. Netter? How? I mean how can Alan be accused of murder? And who is making such outlandish accusations?"

"Yes, yes, of course, you are not aware that Ms. Walter had made advances to my great-grandson..."

"Sorry, Doctor, but I was aware; actually quite a few people were aware of such being the case. So, how could anyone conclude that it led Alan to murder?"

"Let me explain then, my dear lady..."

"Yes, I think you better," Babette said, preparing herself mentally for what was sure to be an elaborate discourse.

When Edmund concluded his narrative, he stopped abruptly and waited for Babette's reaction.

"Have you... I mean has Alan performed the preliminary autopsy yet, do you know?"

"I was there this morning, yes, but even if the blood tests prove conclusively that Ms. Walter had been drugged, it doesn't make his case any easier to handle."

"How do you mean?" Babette asked, getting to her feet. "Let me warm some water for some tea..."

Edmund followed her to the mini kitchenette hidden in a closet.

"I meant that my great-grandson might be accused of giving opiates to Ms. Walter to prevent her from spewing non-sense at every turn."

"Ah-ah, now we come to it; you have been playing games and she would have been liable to tell everyone and sundry that there was a ghost aboard *The Baroness*, is that the assumption?"

"Yes, Ms. Babette, and even though she was sure to have taken opiates before last evening, her words could have been misconstrued or taken as truth. Therefore, she had to be silenced."

"No, Dr. Netter. Even if Alan wanted to silence anyone, as you say, he would not recourse to murder to accomplish his goal. He would have more likely sent her to a hospital at the next port."

"You are correct, Ms. Babette, but what would have prevented her from spreading the word that this ship is haunted?"

"You are playing the devil's advocate, Dr. Netter..."

"Please, dear lady, call me Edmund. I'm well past the age of practicing medicine, don't you think?" He chortled.

Babette, too, had to laugh at the rejoinder. "Yes, you are, Edmund. But then, I'll ask you to call me Babette, and to do away with the Ms. Too formal for my taste."

Captain Galveston leaned against the back of his chair when Gilbert finished recounting the events that led he and Alan to be seated across from him.

"So, Dr. Mayhew, you have ascertained that Ms. Walter must have consumed a large amount of a street-drug called "ecstasy" prior to her little performance at the restaurant last night, have you?"

"Yes, Captain. And I will add that her blood tests revealed that she was a regular user of such drugs."

"Good, good." Galveston turned his attention to Gilbert. "And have you received any reply to your correspondence with Interpol yet?"

"No, Captain. But it's not surprising since we're not receiving reliable communications for the last day or so. I am hoping to receive details about Ms. Walter's background by the time we reach the Maldives. But, based on the information we have on file, Ms. Walter had been traveling regularly from Mumbai to Bangkok and back to the States every six months or so."

"Was she flying between these cities or had she taken a cruise, do you know?"

"It's not clear, Captain. But she most likely flew between these destinations."

"And do we know where she resided in the States?" Galveston asked, twiddling his pen between his fingers.

"San Francisco, sir. But her address has still to be verified."

"What about next of kin – do we have that info on file?"

"Yes, sir. She has a sister who also resides in San Fran. We have tried contacting the woman, but without much luck so far."

"Alright then," Galveston said, advancing his chair to the desk. "And you, Dr. Mayhew, you said that you observed a man dressed like a monk at the corner of the deck as you were making your way to the crime scene – would you be able to describe this man in more detail?"

Alan shook his head. "No, sir. I only caught a glimpse of him. His attire is what attracted my attention, but other than that, I couldn't be more precise."

"And you're sure it was a man?"

"Yes, Captain, of that I'm sure. And now that you mention it, there is a detail that may be relevant or help us; he was wearing a signet ring on the little finger of his right hand."

Gilbert turned his face to Alan with raised eyebrows. "You didn't see his face but you saw the signet ring?"

"Yes, I know that sounds odd, but he was poking his head around the corner and clasping it with his right hand as he was observing Gilbert and I..."

"Why didn't you say anything of this at the time?" Gilbert demanded, visibly annoyed by Alan's omission.

"Because, if you remember, I was more worried about Evelyn's condition when I realized that she had been in charge of keeping Ms. Walter under observation."

Although Alan, personally, hadn't seen anything of what he had just described, Edmund's description of the assailant had to be recorded somehow. As for noting the signet ring, his granddad had remarked about it during a further conversation he had with Alan at breakfast.

"Even though we can't very well go around checking every passenger's hand," Galveston said, "this is a detail, which might be important later on." He paused. "And what do you think would be the motive for killing Ms. Walter?" He riveted his gaze on Gilbert.

"At this point, I couldn't say, Captain. But if I were to make a conjecture, I'd say Ms. Walter was probably a mule for some drug lord and had done something wrong – either wanting to keep the profits for herself or attracting too much attention – she had to be eliminated."

"But that would mean we have some sort of henchman on board, wouldn't it?"

"Or a vigilante," Alan put in.

Two pairs of eyes turned to the doc.

"What do you mean by vigilante?" Galveston asked.

"Well, some people consider themselves self-appointed law-enforcers when justice doesn't take the right course or is not exacted upon the person who has done them wrong."

"Yes, I see what you mean," the captain agreed with a nod. "However, in either case – vigilante or henchman – we have a person with murder in mind aboard my vessel, and the sooner we clear this up, the better it will be for everyone concerned."

After a moment spent in silence, Gilbert asked, "Would there be anything else, Captain?"

"No, Mr. Evans, thank you. Just keep me informed as soon as you have received a response from Interpol, okay?"

"Yes, of course, sir," Gilbert replied as he and Alan got up from their seats.

"...And you said you saw a cloaked figure push Ms. Walter over the railing...?"

"Yes, Babette, I did. That's what I saw."

"Did you try following the man to wherever he went after committing the crime?" Babette was steeping the tea and looking up at Edmund.

"Unfortunately no. I was taken aback by his actions, of course, and my first thought was to alert Mr. Evans. And even if I had followed him, I don't think the man would have led me to his cabin or hiding place."

"What makes you say that, Edmund?" Babette asked, pouring some tea in a cup.

"To my understanding, a man the likes of him would probably mingle among the crowd..."

"At three o'clock in the morning...?" Babette interjected. "Come now, Edmund, just admit that it was an error on your part not to follow the man."

"Alright, my dear lady, I confess; it was an error of judgment on my part. But I did observe his wearing a signet ring on his right hand..."

"Did you really?"

"Yes, I did." Edmund peered into Babette's eyes. Her gaze was so lovingly penetrating that he couldn't look away. He was mesmerized. "It was only a glimpse mind you, but enough for me to recognize that hand anywhere, if I should see it again."

"Well, at least that's something," Babette said, taking a sip of her tea. "But, you know, the cloak is what intrigues me. As it is, I know one place where such attire would be readily available."

"The theater – of course!" Edmund exclaimed. "I should have thought of that. Thank you, dear lady. Thank you."

"Oh don't thank me just yet, Edmund. This was just a thought that crossed my mind. On the other hand, I will check the costumes stored back stage as soon as I can. But, if the man has borrowed it and wore it in the commission of a crime, I would think he wouldn't have replaced it on the hanger for anyone to find."

A knock interrupted them. Not wanting to be seen, Edmund was quick to fly into Babette's bedroom before she answered the door. When she opened it, she found Alan standing in the doorway.

"Ah, there you are," Babette said, "come on in and have a seat." She stretched a hand toward the chair Edmund had just vacated.

"Thank you, Babette," Alan began, sitting himself down. "I'm sorry to disturb you so early…"

"Oh don't you worry about that; besides, you're not my first visitor of the morning." She giggled. And then turning toward her bedroom, she added, "Come out, Edmund. Your great-grandson is here."

Taken aback, Alan stared in the direction from which he expected to see Edmund. But when no one answered Babette's summon, he got up, ready to blast his granddad for having bothered the playwright.

"He's probably gone," Babette said with a shrug of her shoulders.

"So, what did Granddad have to say for himself?" Alan queried, returning to his seat.

"Not much about himself, but a lot about you," Babette replied to Alan's frown. "You've got yourself into a mess, haven't you?"

"I was for a while, yes. But now I think we can safely say that someone else will be burdened with the suspicion of murder."

"You mean the cloaked fellow Edmund saw?"

"Yes, and although there's a reasonable assumption to be made in regards to Ms. Walter being a carrying drug mule, I suggest we're not looking at a drug lord seeking repayment of some debt or other, but for a vigilante."

"A vigilante?" Babette was all ears now. "How did you come up with that?"

"Two things: first, a henchman would probably kill any disobedient mule, execution style – with a gun perhaps – and secondly, I don't think he would disguise himself with a cloak and cowl or wear a signet ring."

CHAPTER 10

A *"clipper" of a different sort*

ON HIS RETURN to the medical center, Dr. Mayhew thought a little further about his discussion with Babette and the matter of the cloaked man. This merely confirmed what Edmund had related about the incident. He had asked Babette to verify if such a costume would have been available among some of the apparel kept backstage in the theater.

In the anteroom, he found a lovely woman waiting for him. Ah, Dr. Mayhew, so nice to see you again," she said, getting up from the chair. "I'm sorry to interrupt your day, but I thought I could be of some help."

Alan thought he had not heard the woman correctly. "I'm sorry, Miss...?"

"Oh, I am so terribly sorry; where are my manners? I am Mrs. Clipper." She extended a hand for Alan to shake. Her strawberry blonde hair simply glowed under the powerful clinic spotlights, while her radiant smile was nothing short of enticing. Alan took her well-manicured hand without his eyes leaving her beautiful alabaster face.

Mrs. Clipper went on to say, "As I said, I must apologize for interrupting your day, but I wish to offer you my assistance."

Alan had not been mistaken – Mrs. Clipper wasn't sick; she was offering him assistance. *Assistance to do what,* he wondered. "Won't you come in the office," he said, stretching an arm in that direction. "We'll be more comfortable to talk."

"Oh, yes, yes, of course," the young woman replied, shouldering her capacious leather bag and following Alan into his office. "But it'll only take a moment."

Alice, who had been observing the little exchange from her desk, wondered if this was going to be another one of those flirts. When she had heard what happened to Ms. Walter, she had only been sorry she hadn't been on duty when the doc had put the woman under observation. *I wouldn't have let her clobber me so easily,* she remarked to herself, still watching the newcomer enter Alan's office.

"Won't you have a seat, Mrs. Clipper," Alan offered, rounding his desk and sitting down.

When the lady had gathered her long, flowery dress about her, she deposited her bag beside the chair and said, "Thank you, Dr. Mayhew." She paused and fixed her gaze on him. "I'll come straight to the point," she then went on decisively, "I knew Ms. Walter and although I can not apologize for her unforgivable conduct at the restaurant last night, I was wondering if you could tell me if you have seen her since she left the captain's table in your company?"

Alan was taken aback, but didn't want to show it. "If you saw Ms. Walter leave with me last night, Mrs. Clipper, you must have seen me coming back to the restaurant, or did you?"

"Well, that's just it, Doctor, I left soon after you both did, actually I wanted to go to her cabin and perhaps see if she was alright. You see, we're... I mean we're acquainted, and I was afraid that she might have had a little too much to drink. Anyway, I thought you might know where she is."

"But didn't you say you wanted to offer your help – what did you mean by that?"

Mrs. Clipper seemed uncomfortable all of a sudden. "Well, if you knew where she is right now, I could tell you that if she's made advances to you... it's not her fault, really."

Alan was getting confused. Yet, one thing was clear; Mrs. Clipper was on a fishing expedition. She obviously had been looking for her "acquaintance" for some reason, and not having found her, she wanted to see if she had spent the night with the doc.

"Alright, Mrs. Clipper, let's be clear about this," Alan suggested firmly, "You are looking for Ms. Walter, correct?"

"Yes, yes, that's what I said. I'm just worried about her, that's all."

"And why would that be, Mrs. Clipper?"

"Well, she's not been herself lately, and I was worried that she had met with an accident or something, that's all."

"And how long have you known Ms. Walter, if I may ask?"

"Oh just over a year, I suppose."

"I see; then you were acquainted with her before this cruise, were you?"

"Well yes. As a matter of fact we are neighbors in Pacific Heights, San Francisco. You do know San Francisco's better neighborhoods, don't you? Anyway, although we didn't see much of each other, one day at Wilma's annual elegant extravaganza – only for the neighbors, we were talking about taking a cruise together one day, and the rest is history as they say."

"Alright, Mrs. Clipper. You were right; Ms. Walter has met with an accident yesterday evening and unfortunately died as a consequence of that fall."

Mrs. Clipper was aghast. "You mean she fell overboard? How awful!"

"No, not exactly. Suffice to say that she had a very bad fall and broke her neck in the process."

"My God! I really don't know what to say," Mrs. Clipper blurted, getting to her feet. "This is terrible. I'll have to phone her sister…"

"Do you know her sister then?" Alan thought he better keep this woman in his office until he could give Gilbert a call.

"Oh yes, yes…. That's how we met actually." She replaced the bag over her shoulder and was about to turn to leave when Alan stopped her.

"I'm sorry, Mrs. Clipper, but I need to ask you to remain here, in my office, until I can contact our chief of security." Alan stood up and came to her side from around his desk.

"But why? Why would you contact the security officer? I've done nothing wrong…!" Fear suddenly reddened her cheeks as she eyed Alan.

"I'm quite sure you haven't, Mrs. Clipper." He pointed to the chair she had just left. "Have a seat, and I'll phone Mr. Evans – it won't take long." He smiled as the young woman sat down, visibly reluctant to do so.

Yet, she obviously was uncomfortable with the idea of being

interviewed. "But I've told you all I know, I don't see why I should stay here," she argued somewhat vehemently as she stood up and strode toward the door of the medical center decisively.

Alan couldn't stop her without using due force. He didn't want to turn up the heat under this stewing pot. He looked after her as the door closed behind her and shook his head.

Gilbert was chuckling as he was reading a sheet of paper his assistant had just handed him. "Where did you get this, Freddy?"

"Just came with my girlfriend's email," Freddy replied. "It's good isn't it?"

"Sure is," Gilbert said, as he continued reading:

> 1. Only in America . . . can a pizza get to your house faster than an ambulance.
>
> 2. Only in America . . . are there handicap-parking places in front of a rollerskating rink.
>
> 3. Only in America . . . do drugstores make the sick walk all the way to the back of the store to get their
>
> prescriptions while healthy people can buy cigarettes at the front.
>
> 4. Only in America . . . do people order double cheeseburgers, large fries, and a diet coke.
>
> 5. Only in America . . . do banks leave both doors open and then chain the pens to the counters.
>
> 6. Only in America . . . do we leave cars worth thousands of dollars in the driveway and put our useless junk in the garage.

> 7. Only in America . . . do we use answering machines to screen calls and then have call waiting so we won't miss a call from someone we didn't want to talk to in the first place.
>
> 8. Only in America . . . do we buy hot dogs in packages of ten and buns in packages of eight.
>
> 9. Only in America . . . do we use the word 'politics' to describe the process so well: 'Poli' in Latin meaning 'many' and 'tics' meaning bloodsucking creatures'.
>
> 10. Only in America . . . do they have drive-up ATM machines with Braille lettering.

He was still laughing when he picked up the phone. "Evans here," he said. "What can I do for you, Doc?"

"I think we might have a material witness aboard," Alan replied.

"You mean somebody saw the murderer?"

"No, I don't think she did, but this Mrs. Clipper came to see me and told me that she knew the deceased."

"Is she still with you?"

"No. Unfortunately, she left before I could convince her to stay. Anyway, I think it would be worth your while to track her down and have a word with her."

"Right you are, Doc. I'll check her cabin number and I'll go and see her…"

"Hold on, Gilbert, before you hang up…"

"Yes, what is it?"

"It's just that I've got a funny feeling about the woman. I don't think she's who she says she is."

"You mean she's going under a false name?"

"Well, maybe. She said she is "Mrs." Clipper, yet I didn't see a ring on her finger. And then she came in pretending that she wanted to offer her help regarding Irene Walter's conduct – or something to that effect – when, in fact, she was looking for information from me."

"Okay, sounds like she's looking for the woman. Did you tell her where she ended up?"

"Yes I did. And before you blast me for telling her, I wanted to see her reaction to the news…"

"And how did she react then?"

"I think she was genuinely shocked. She might be a great actress mind you, but somehow I don't think so. What's more plausible to me is that she may have had something to do with the drug shipping and she wanted to know where her contact was."

"Yeah, sounds like it," Gilbert agreed. "Anyway, let me have a look into it, okay?"

"Absolutely. I'll be in my office if you need me," Alan said before hanging up. When he did, he reclined in his chair and sat there, pensive, for a while. *Those green eyes of hers are unbelievable,* he mused, smiling to himself before returning to his ever-mounting paperwork.

Babette and Edmund were looking through the racks of costumes backstage when Tiffany popped her head through the doorway. "Are you two planning to put on a play for us?"

"Oh hello, Tiffany, how are you, my dear?" Babette said, shifting hanger after hanger without looking up.

"Good morning, Ms. Tiffany," Edmund rejoined, smiling gently. "Have you slept well?"

"No, Granddad, I haven't – thanks to you!" Tiffany said, walking into the room. "What on Earth are you looking for that could not be discovered during a routine crew cabin inspection? You know, those invasive checks where the security staff and officers ply through your undies and try and discover if you have stolen anything from the ship or are hiding drugs"

"A long cloak with a cowl," was Babette's answer. "But what are you doing here?"

"A monk's habit you mean?"

"Yes, my dear. Have you seen such a costume among these

apparels?" Edmund asked.

"But why? Why would you want a cloak? Is that for you, Granddad?"

Edmund guffawed. "Oh no, Ms. Tiffany, not for me. Yet, we would like to find such attire if possible."

"Are you going to tell me what this is all about?" Tiffany was a little more than curious by now.

Babette stopped what she was doing and turned around. "Has Alan talked to you this morning?"

"No, I haven't seen him since last night – why?"

"Well, then come with me, my dear, I think it's time to update you and tell you what's happening on the ship today."

The three of them went to sit in one of the dressing rooms and after Babette had brought Tiffany up-to-date, she said, "And this is why we were hoping to find the cloak the villain used."

Tiffany's gaze shifted from Edmund to Babette. "But he wouldn't have brought it back, now would he? I mean any forensic specialist could identify him if they found even a hair on that cloak." She stopped and seemed to be lost in thought for a moment. "Maybe we should check the dry-cleaning department. He might have left it with the steward with instruction to have it dry-cleaned, what do you think?" She looked at Babette.

"Yes, that's a possibility, but somehow I don't think he would have bothered. I rather think that he'd be keeping the cloak in his cabin for further use."

Tiffany gasped, putting a hand to her mouth. "Do you really think he's intending to eliminate or hurt someone else?"

"As a matter of fact, Ms. Tiffany," Edmund interposed, "if my great-grandson's assumption is correct, and we have a vigilante aboard this ship, he might strike again, yes."

"But why?" Tiffany argued. "If Ms. Walter was the subject of his anger, and he's now done away with her, why would he go after someone else?"

"I believe that Ms. Walter traveled on this cruise for a reason," Babette said, "And that reason might be to find someone else – a contact perhaps."

"I think you're right, Babette," Alan interposed as he came into the dressing room. He had seen the door open and had heard their conversation. "And I think we've found the contact in question."

"You did?" Tiffany blurted. "How?"

Alan took a seat in the fourth chair. "Actually, she found me. She was looking for Ms. Walter and wondered if I had spent the night with her since she saw me walk out of the restaurant in her company."

"Ha-ha," Edmund laughed. "Women were always seeking refuge with the doctor, in my day; it was a great time to treat the broken hearted."

Alan frowned but then cracked a smile. "And for once I'm glad this Mrs. Clipper did…"

"Is that her name?" Babette asked. "Has she given you any indication as to her involvement in this affair, though?"

"Nothing that would stand up in court, no. Yet, I've got a feeling that we haven't heard the last of Mrs. Clipper."

CHAPTER ELEVEN

A bull he is not

INTERPOL'S REPORTS ON Ms. Walter were not quite what Gilbert had expected. She had been suspected of being a drug mule for a few months, according to the CIA, but she was never arrested – "insufficient evidence" was the reason given for not apprehending her. Gilbert surmised that the real reason might have been quite different. He had heard that in similar cases, the suspect would be used to lead the authorities concerned to the "big fish" at the end of the line. As for getting more information regarding her life in Pacific Heights, Interpol hadn't fared any better. She had lived in the neighborhood for some three years; she held a part-time job at some real-estate agency; wasn't married and had no children. Wilma Simpson, Irene's sister, on the other hand, was the wild card. She was married to some successful investment broker, lived in a big house with her husband and their two children. Although, Wilma seemed to carry on the life of a stay-home mom, she took somewhat regular trips to cities like Chicago, Miami, Dallas and Seattle. She had no other family than her sister, Irene, and didn't seem to have friends on record in those cities. Whether she was linked somehow to the drug trafficking ring was a question Interpol or the FBI might have to answer – if an investigation into Irene Walter's death was to be carried out.

The other item that bothered Gilbert at this point was the manner in which Irene Walter died. The doc's report and death certificate mentioned the cause of death being a broken neck. Moreover, there was no sign of struggle, such as bruises or abrasions on the body. This would have proven that Irene had fought with her assailant before plunging over the railing and landing on the top of the life raft. With such lack of evidence and only Alan's report that someone had been watching him from the corner nearest to the scene of the crime, the final report would read: "death by misadventure". And that would be the end of it.

Yet, Gilbert felt uneasy about it. What's more, there was Mrs. Clipper to consider – how did she fit into this picture. Was she just a neighbor and friend of Irene, or was there more to the friendship? Then there was the matter of the cloaked man – with the signet ring – who was he? Did he really push Irene Walter over the railing? According to Dr. Netter, their friendly ghost, this had been the case. Could he have been mistaken? Somehow, Gilbert didn't think so.

At the end of all these this, Gilbert got up and walked out of his office. He wanted – no, needed – to find the mysterious cloaked figure. If the man was deranged and helped his prey on their way to the *other side*, he needed to know who he was and why he did what he did.

The next morning they would reach the Maldives and although there were many items still to be checked off on his "to do list", Alan felt somewhat restless and wanting to escape with Tiffany somewhere – anywhere. The presence of his great-grandfather was beginning to bother him. He was uncomfortable with the idea that he could appear at anytime at any moment, day or night. He felt as if he had a surveillance camera constantly hovering around him and watching his every move. What disturbed him the most was his granddad being capable of intruding on his private nights with Tiffany. He couldn't accept the idea that his great grandparent could be in his cabin at the very moment he wanted to make love to Tiff. Yet, if someone was going to be able to locate his vigilante aboard *The Baroness*, it was his great-grandfather.

Ruminating these thoughts and incapable of concentrating on his work, he decided to leave his office for a while and find Tiffany. He had left her, Babette and his granddad to resume their search of the cloak, which would be a futile pursuit as far as he was concerned.

He was about to pass the threshold of the center when he saw Tiffany come toward him.

"Ah, just the man I wanted to see," she announced, a broad smile coming across her lips.

"Have you found the cloak by any chance?" Alan asked, returning the smile.

"No, as you probably expected, but I've had a wonderful idea." She looked up at Alan.

He closed the medical center's door behind him and fell in step with Tiffany. The mere fact of being at her side restored his good humor.

"And what idea was that?"

"I think we've got enough costumes backstage to have a party..."

"You mean like a costume party?"

"Yes, exactly. We could invite all the passengers into the ballroom and have something like the *Rio Carnival* as a theme..."

"And why would you do that? I mean there's nothing on the entertainment schedule..."

Tiffany grabbed his hand discreetly and squeezed it. "Think about it. If you want to find a butcher's apron, you go to a butcher shop, and if you want to find a monk, you go to a monastery, don't you?"

"And you hope the cloaked fellow would show up dressed as a monk, is that it?"

"Don't you think it's a good idea?"

"Yes, I think it's a fantastic idea. At least it would give Granddad the opportunity to see everyone in one place and search for that hand with the signet ring."

"Exactly what I thought."

"Have you asked him about it?"

"Oh yes – and he agreed. He thought he would be able to examine every one closely."

Alan laughed quietly. "I bet he will do more than that... but since he's not only a prankster but in reality, a responsible fellow – I mean was – he'll probably take the task to heart."

As they were waiting in front of the elevator and as the doors opened, Gilbert came out. "Ah," he said, "just the man I wanted to see."

Alan and Tiffany erupted in laughter.

"Did I say something funny?" a bewildered Gilbert asked, looking at Alan and Tiffany with a frown.

Alan shook his head. "No, you didn't – but it seems that I am the man everyone wants to see this morning." He paused. "Anyway, what did you want to see me about?"

"The cloaked man," Gilbert replied, getting a titter out of Tiffany in turn.

"Sorry, Gilbert, but it also seems that everyone has the same goal in mind."

"Okay, guys," the chief of security said, "why don't we go to the café upstairs and talk about this – what do you say?"

Alan and Tiffany exchanged a glance and a smile. "This is exactly where we wanted to go," Tiffany said. "Talk about a meeting of the minds." She pressed the elevator button. "But I can already tell you that "we're on the job"," she remarked, crossing her arms over her chest.

"Oh yeah, and how's that?"

"Just wait until we're sitting in front of a cappuccino – then we'll tell you," Tiffany added as they boarded the elevator.

In the meantime, Edmund and Babette had returned to the playwright's cabin for a pow-wow. But Edmund's intentions were not quite the same as those of Babette.

"But do tell me, Babette, how did you end up traveling aboard this ship?"

Babette laughed as she took a seat across from Edmund. "As I end up on every cruise ship," she replied. "You see, my work requires a lot of peace and quiet. I cannot get into the characters I am describing unless I can travel into their world in my imagination. And I can't do that when I have people intruding into my silence or my surroundings."

"How did you come to America? Where were you actually born, in what country?"

"Why the questions, Edmund?" She fixed her gaze on him. "Why are you so interested in my background?"

"My dear lady, I can assure you I meant no offense. Yet, the resemblance you bear with the woman I knew and admired more than a century ago is absolutely uncanny. Besides, my curiosity has gotten the best of me since I have met you."

"Alright then," Babette said, bending her head and looking down to her lap. "And to answer your question; yes, I was born in the USA – in San Francisco actually. But, when I was four months old, I was taken to my father's homeland of France. He was called back after the Second World War to attend political meetings in Geneva.

"Since he was so busy with these, I soon found myself living with an uncle in Paris. I made friends with a group of theater people in my teens while I was still living with my uncle's family in a lovely old flat in Montmartre. After that I saw the insides of the Comédie Française and learned my trade as a playwright.

"I believe, although I am not sure, that my grand-mother had been born to a French family, whose parentage had some "difficulty", shall we say, before leaving Europe."

"What sort of difficulties; do you know?" Edmund asked.

Much against herself, Babette blushed. *Most becoming*, Edmund thought.

"Let's just say that my great-grandmother was born on the wrong side of the cover. Her mother had apparently fallen in love with the son of the Conte de Crillon and my great-grandmother's birth was hushed up." She looked at Edmund for a moment, a soft smile parting her lips. "Anyway, as it happened, the uncle's family with whom I grew up in Paris took care of the little girl. And very much like I did, she was encouraged to pursue a career on the stage. The Comédie Française became her second family and since her talent resided more into writing plays than acting, she wrote stage plays for the Parisian theaters."

An awkward silence fell between them.

"It's quite amazing how history repeats itself, don't you find?" Edmund said feeling a little embarrassed to have pried into Babette's past. "And is that also the reason for which you bear the same name as the playwright I knew and who traveled aboard *The Delmas*?"

"I suppose it is. Actually, I am quite sure it is the sole reason for being called by a single name. You see, my uncle didn't know all of the details of my history, but one thing of which he was sure, was that I had none of my mother's character traits."

"And who was the woman who gave you birth?"

Babette shook her head. "Truth be told, I know very little about her. I remember her being a typical American woman; always interested in the arts, until my father was sent to Switzerland on that diplomatic mission…"

"And that's when your parents dropped you on your uncle's doorsteps, so to speak," Edmund finished for Babette.

She nodded and smiled at her ghostly friend. "And now, how about a spot of tea?"

"By all means, milady. I won't have any, you understand, but I will enjoy the company nonetheless."

"And Tomorrow or so, you can tell a little more of your history, leaving no stone unturned, of course. A ship's Doctor must have a few good stories for this playwright!"

After Tiffany told Gilbert about her idea to hold a costume party to attract the cloaked man into a trap of some sort, Gilbert sat pensive for a moment before he said, "You know all this 'ghost stuff' reminds me of a story…"

"Oh, and what story is that?" Alan asked, relaxing into the back of his chair. He felt better somehow. Tiffany's idea would probably put an end to the hunt for their vigilante and he could then resume somewhat of a 'normal' life – if Granddad would agree to stay out of the way when he was with Tiffany.

"Do you believe in reincarnation?" Gilbert asked in reply.

Tiffany and Alan exchanged a curious glance.

"Not particularly, no," Alan answered.

"Okay, well in a way we all do reincarnate into our progeny somehow, don't we?"

"If you're talking about our DNA…"

Gilbert held up a hand to stop the doc. "Hold on, Alan, this is no medical discourse, just a little story."

"Okay, Gilbert, let's have it then," Tiffany said, getting impatient.

"Alright here goes it: There were two lovers, who were really into spiritualism and reincarnation. They vowed that if either died, the one remaining would try to contact the partner in the other world exactly 30 days after their death. Unfortunately, a few weeks later, the young man died in a car wreck. True to her word, his sweetheart tried to contact him in the spirit world exactly 30 days later. At the séance, she called out, "John, John, this is Martha. Do you hear me?"

"A ghostly voice answered her, "Yes, Martha, this is John. I can hear you."

""Martha tearfully asked, "Oh, John, what is it like where you are?"

"It's great. There are azure skies, a soft breeze, sunshine most of the time, the grass is so green and the cows have such beautiful eyes."

"What do you do all day?" asked Martha.

"Well, Martha, we get up before sunrise, eat some good breakfast, and there's nothing but making love until noon. After lunch, we nap until two and then make love again until about five. After dinner, we go at it again until we fall asleep about 11:00 pm."

"Martha was somewhat taken aback. "Is that what heaven really is like?"

"Heaven? I'm not in heaven, Martha."

"Well then, where are you?"

"I'm a high priced bull, living on the plains of Montana."

"Very good," Alan said between chuckles. "But I personally prefer my great-grandfather the way he is today – a ghost. Can you imagine him coming back to me as a bull as soon as I touched his picture?"

Unable to control the laughter, Tiffany almost spilled her coffee all over her uniform, again!

CHAPTER TWELVE

Uncle Vladimir

THE ARRIVAL TO THE SOUTHERNMOST atoll of the Maldives was a little surprising for the passengers of *The Baroness*. The Addu Atoll is a circle of small string-like islets forming a luxuriant ring of forest and palm trees, skirting an ocean of the deepest blue one could rarely have the opportunity to observe in other parts of the world. The contrasts of green foliage, sparkling sand and royal blue waves crested with white caps under the blazing sun was superb. Somehow, as if invited to this welcoming fare of colors, the white terns of the Indian Ocean graced *The Baroness's* arrival with an impressive circle of joyous cackles, as the ship was about to lower anchor near Addu City.

"Have you ever seen a more splendid sight?" Babette asked Mrs. Clipper once the playwright had succeeded in cornering the elusive friend of the deceased.

"Perhaps not as vivid as this, no," Mrs. Clipper replied, turning her face to Babette. "But when I visited Australia and took a yacht to the Great Barrier Reef, I saw several of these kinds of colorful sceneries." She paused and smiled. "What about you? Have you been here before?"

"Oh no, my dear, never been quite this far west of San Francisco before – I mean I've visited the Far East, yes, but not the islands."

"Do you take cruises like these often?"

I should be the one asking questions, Babette thought. "I'd say so, yes. You see, I'm a writer and as writers often require silence and solitude to accomplish their tasks, I do find these cruises to be most convenient in that regard."

"You must be very wealthy to afford to travel like this so often," Mrs. Clipper remarked, shaking her head a little. *Prying into someone's life and gossiping is perhaps this girl's forte,* Babette reflected silently. "As for me, I was tempted to do it – with Irene urging me to come with her – that in the end I couldn't resist. I had planned a big holiday in Paris, but here I am circling the world – by myself now." The dismay and perhaps a little sadness were quite audible in the young woman's voice.

"I guess your friend's death has been hard on you, hasn't it?"

"More than you can imagine." Mrs. Clipper returned her gaze to the ocean.

Babette turned around and leaned her back against the railing. "She was more than a neighborly friend then?"

"Oh, I wouldn't say that, no. But it was someone to talk to, to go shopping with and all that sort of thing. You see, I'm separated and my family lives out of town, so besides my work colleagues, I don't have many friends."

The morose tone in her voice didn't abate.

"Do you have any children?"

"Oh no – thank goodness. Otherwise, I don't think I could have survived a custody battle after my very painful separation." She turned her head to look at Babette again. "What about you; are you married?"

"Oh good Lord, no, not anymore." Babette tittered at the thought. "What on Earth would I do with a man at this stage of my life? I've got enough trouble sorting out the lives and loves of all my characters, without having to bother with a "real" man about my place."

The remark finally brought a broad grin to Mrs. Clipper's lips. "Yeah, they can be cumbersome sometimes, can't they?"

"You said it. I've got one of my characters – a troublesome man, you have no idea – who's always fretting about his wife's well-being and I think I was a little overzealous when I began describing him in my latest play…"

"Oh, you write plays as well then?" Mrs. Clipper asked, seemingly interested.

"Actually most of my work is dedicated to writing plays these days. I haven't got the patience to write entire volumes. I've tried my hand at it when I was much younger, but failed miserably." Babette paused at the recollection. "As I said, I was too impatient. I wanted my story to get to the end before I even started writing the first line."

"Is "Babette" your nom de plume then?"

Babette laughed. "No, it's actually my first name, and as for a last name, let's just say that only the IRS and occasional customs' officers have a chance to look at it. I think Babette is enough." She looked at Mrs. Clipper fixedly. "And Clipper; is that your maiden name?"

"No, since I'm not divorced yet, it's my husband's name. But why don't you call me Lizzy?"

"Short for Elizabeth?"

"Yep. I couldn't stand "Elizabeth" when I was a kid. My friends always called me "Queen E" until the day I put my foot down and told them that Lizzy would do fine"—she shot an amused glance to Babette—"I was quite a spoiled brat in those days and that's perhaps why the kids saw fit to call me Queen E."

"Okay then, Lizzy, why don't we go to the restaurant and have a bite to eat?" Babette offered.

"Good idea. I'm starving actually."

As the two women left the promenade deck and made their way to the elevators, someone – a man – kept his eyes fixed upon them. He passed his hand over his beard, the signet ring reflecting in the sunlight. As if he had suddenly changed his mind, he decided to follow them and caught the elevator, as its doors were about to close
on the two ladies.

"Sorry," he said, throwing them a smile full of mischief, "I just remembered I am hungry."

Babette raised a questioning eyebrow. She was never a person to intrude on someone's reflections or remarks, but this time she couldn't help herself. "Did you say you "just remembered" that you were hungry?"

The man chortled. "Yes. But first let me introduce myself; I'm
Vladimir Romanov. And to answer your question, you see, hunger, such as so many other human sensations, calls you to attention every so often

during the day. However, I choose to ignore the signal and eat or drink when I decide it is a good time to do so."

"How very interesting," Babette remarked. "And what made you decide to eat at this particular time of the day?" *This is another weird one.*

For her part, Lizzy was switching her gaze from the strange bearded fellow to Babette, as if she were watching a tennis match.

"The mere fact that hunger pains can only be tolerated or ignored for so long before you succumb to dizziness and lack of strength."

"Is it one of these times then?"

"Yes, Madame, it is. I was watching our arrival when I felt uneasy and remembered that I had forgotten to remind myself to eat."

This time, Lizzy burst out laughing.

Vladimir raised one eyebrow toward the young woman. "Have I said something so funny, mademoiselle, that you have to laugh at me?"

Lizzy shook her head and lowered it. When she raised her amused gaze to him again, she said, "I'm very sorry, Mr. Romanov, but you must admit that regulating one's body functions the way you do, is quite funny to someone like me."

The elevator doors opened at that moment, letting them exit onto the upper deck and the terrace restaurant.

"Someone like you? Why should that be, Mrs. Clipper?"

Upon hearing her name out of the lips of someone she obviously had never met, Lizzy stopped walking. "How do you know my name, Mr. Romanov? I don't remember meeting you before."

"Ah-ha, very good question, my dear," Vladimir said, having turned to look at the young woman. "I must confess that I had been listening to you two ladies talking on the promenade deck." He shot a glance toward Babette. "And you are Ms. Babette, the playwright, correct?"

"Yes, Mr. Romanov, you are correct," Babette replied, visibly obfuscated. "But why would you eavesdrop on our conversation? Quite rude for a man of your standing, wouldn't you say?"

Vladimir crossed his arms over his chest and chortled again. "Yes, it is, Ms. Babette, but truth be told, I was desperate to make your acquaintance. You are the playwright of my ancestors." Babette giggled, recalling Edmund's *Babette* who wrote plays for the aristocracy living in

Paris. "I am sorry – I didn't mean you personally, of course, but perhaps someone whose name you have adopted in this century. And as far as my great-grand uncle remembered, Babette of the Comédie Française was quite famous in her time."

Vladimir was wearing an elegant suit, tailored to perfection. His jovial and debonair attitude seemed to match the attire perfectly. But that wasn't the only thing that Babette – and possibly Lizzy – had observed as she had looked at the man a little closer. His signet ring was quite distinctive. Babette didn't want to stare at it, but the question was menacing to breach her parted lips at any moment. And it did. "Would that be the Romanov family crest on your ring?" She pointed discreetly at the man's little finger.

"Yes, it is, Ms. Babette…"

"But I thought the Romanov's were all dead," Lizzy put-in.

"Oh no, not all of them died during the Russian Revolution. One of the brothers survived and was, shall we say, a frivolous ladies' man." He chuckled. "There are members of my family everywhere – if one would care to look for them." Vladimir's laughter receded into a smile.

"Actually, I have heard of your family's tribulation," Babette interposed. "You, or perhaps your cousins or uncles, are famous on the Parisian scene – even today."

"Glad to hear you are aware of that fact, Ms. Babette." Vladimir paused and then extended a hand toward the restaurant's opened doors. "I think I have just time to reach a seat before I swoon like a young maiden," he added, chuckling at his own silly comparison and stepping ahead of Babette and Lizzy. "Please join me for lunch or brunch, as you Americans call this mid-morning meal, won't you?"

As soon as the brunch was over, Babette excused herself under the pretext that she wanted to return to her writing, and went to the medical center. There, she found Alan deeply absorbed in his report writing. She knocked on his office door – which was opened – and as he lifted his gaze to her, a broad smile appeared on his lips.

"You have no idea what a relief you are," he said, pointing to one of the chairs opposite his desk.

"And what sort of "relief" would that be, my dear Alan?" Babette asked, sitting down. "I hope you're not about to compare me to one of your sedatives."

Alan had to laugh at the rejoinder and shook his head. "Oh no, not at all. The relief I had in mind was actually a "break" from this horrible tedium. Writing reports will be my downfall – you'll see. Even with everything being computerized these days, I still have to write (or type) the darn things. And, believe me, sometimes I wish I had chosen a private practice rather than all this"—he waved a hand over the paperwork covering his desk—"It never seems to end." He paused to look at his favorite passenger and long-time friend. "But do tell; what brought you here? Aren't you going to take a trip around the atolls?"

"Maybe later, Alan, but for now, I want to tell you that I have probably found our man…"

"You mean the cloaked man?" Alan stared, as if the news had shocked him, which it had.

"Exactly. You told me that he was wearing a signet ring, according to your great-grandfather's observation, right?"

"Yes, I did say that, yes." He continued staring. "And you have found a man wearing a signet ring. But how can you be sure he's our cloaked fellow?"

"I couldn't say I'm sure, but my instinct tells me that Vladimir Romanov is connected to this story – somehow."

"Did you say, "Vladimir Romanov" as in the Romanov Brothers?"

"Yes. And more than that, Mr. Romanov's great-grand uncle was surely an acquaintance of my great-grandmother, as far as I can conclude from his account."

"Are you serious?"

"Absolutely, Alan. And it makes all the sense in the world. Vladimir Romanov and I are probably related or even "kissing cousins"."

"That's quite a story!" Alan said. He was astonished. "Have you told Granddad yet?"

Babette shook her head. "No, and that's the problem. I don't know how to call on him. He always appears on the scene – out of nowhere – and for once I would like to be the one making *my* presence known to him, instead of the other way around."

"And you want him to locate Vladimir to look at his signet ring, I suppose?"

"Yes and maybe – that is if you would agree – have Vladimir meet Edmund."

"Do you think that's wise?" Alan wasn't sure he wanted another person, especially one the likes of Vladimir Romanov – another prankster perhaps and a "coureur de jupons" as the French say – running around the ship.

"As I said, it would be entirely up to you, Alan. However, we could kill two birds with one stone in putting the two men together…"

"How's that?"

"Well, if Vladimir, in fact, pushed Irene Walter over the railing – not intending to kill her, mind you – we would have our culprit. On the other hand, Edmund, while questioning Vladimir, could perhaps shed some light on my ancestry. Although, as I have explained to Edmund, I have been told that I was the offspring of my great-grandmother's indiscretion with the Conte de Crillon. So, I'd like to know which is the true story." She paused. "It is not of great importance, for what is done is done and the past can't be undone, but the thought of having some Russian blood flowing through my vein would be quite exciting to me."

Alan had to think about this. He couldn't possibly refuse to satisfy Babette's curiosity, yet Vladimir if he was the vigilante he personally thought he was; his friend would be in mortal danger.

"Why don't you and I talk this over with Granddad first, what do you say?"

"Yes. I think that would be for the best," Babette agreed.

CHAPTER THIRTEEN

We've no teeth

AS THE TOUR MINI-BUS DRIVER was taking a small busload of the senior passengers along the causeway linking the atolls, he was tapped on the shoulder by one of the little old ladies. She offered him a handful of peanuts, which he gratefully accepted and munched up. Fifteen minutes later, she tapped him on the shoulder again and handed him another handful of peanuts. She repeated this gesture about five more times. When she was about to hand him another batch, he asked her, "Why don't you eat the peanuts yourself?"

"We can't chew them because we've no teeth," she replied.

The puzzled driver then asked, "Why do you buy them then?"

"We just love the chocolate around them!"

Stunned, the driver stopped the bus, stepped out and began throwing up on the side of the road under the surprised gazes of the passengers.

When Alice came back to the ship and told Alan the story, he burst out in loud laughter.

"I don't think it's funny, Doc," she said, obviously surprised at Alan's reaction. "These old folks don't see any harm in some of the things they're doing sometimes."

"I'm sorry, Alice, but I think some of these local drivers are often too quick to accept a hand-out and will get in trouble for it every time."

"I guess you're right. Anyway, since I was the nurse on the bus, I checked that the driver was okay and we finished the tour without further incident."

"Did you enjoy the scenery anyway?" Alan asked, still smiling.

"Sure did. It's amazing to think that these islands have evolved naturally from living organisms. And everywhere it's so clean – it's like traveling through a postcard."

"Well, I'm glad to hear you've enjoyed a bit of time off. Escorting the tours is definitely one of the perks of our jobs." He paused, looking at his nurse. She seemed to have something else on her mind. "Is there anything wrong, Alice?"

"Well, nothing that you'd call wrong, Doc, but I've been thinking about my seeing your scalpels float in the air, I mean I can't get it out of my mind."

"I wouldn't worry too much about it, Alice. I'm sure you've seen something – no question – but how it happened, I truly have no idea. Actually, I wish I had been there to catch the culprit. Because I still think this was some prankster's trick – nothing else."

"Like in one of the onboard magic shows, you mean?"

"Yes, exactly like that. I can't tell you how it's done, but if we had another magician aboard to tell us how he could do that, I'd be sure to ask him."

Finally Alice got up from her seat, perhaps reassured somehow. "Yes, I guess you're right. It was weird though..." she added, putting her capacious bag over her shoulder. "I'll be in the store room if you need me."

"Okay," Alan replied to Alice's back, watching her leave his office.

Then, looking at his wristwatch, he suddenly realized that he had just enough time to meet Babette in her cabin for a meeting with his great-grandfather. He got up and was about to make his way out of his office when Mrs. Clipper burst through the door of the medical center.

Alice caught sight of her as she was coming back from the storeroom. "May I help you?" she asked.

"Oh, no-no, thank you. I'm just here to see the doctor," Mrs. Clipper replied, planting herself in the doorway of Alan's office and ignoring Alice's presence altogether.

Alan repeated the question: "Can I help you?"

"I don't know that you can, Doctor. Actually, I'm just here to inform you that we have a descendent of the Romanov Brothers aboard this ship."

"And how would that concern me, Mrs. Clipper?" Alan asked, rounding his desk, while making it obvious to the lady that he intended to leave his office.

"Well, it's just that Irene told me that she had a Russian friend and that she was hoping to meet him on this trip."

"Did she now?" Alan said, pushing past Mrs. Clipper intending to exit the medical center. He didn't want to show her that he was interested – for the moment anyway.

"She sure did. And maybe your security chief would do well to *interrogate* the man. Don't you think?"

Alan stopped in front of Mrs. Clipper and riveted his gaze on her. "I'm sorry, Mrs. Clipper, but our security officers do not "interrogate" passengers under any circumstances. And if you have some concerns regarding this particular passenger, or reasons to believe that your safety is in danger, I suggest you address these concerns with Mr. Evans, Chief of Security directly."

"Is that it then?" she asked, visibly offended by Alan's offhand attitude. "Is that all you're going to do about it?"

"Yes, Mrs. Clipper, that's all *I can do* about it. And now if you'll excuse me, I am due to visit one of our passengers." He had his hand on the doorknob and looked at the obtrusive lady for a moment before opening the door. "Shall we?" he then said, holding it open for her.

"Oh alright then. I'll have a word with Mr. Evans if I must."

"I think that will be best," Alan concluded, bowing slightly. "Have a good day."

Instead of heading straight for the elevators as he first intended, Alan veered off toward the bow of the ship and took the crew elevator opposite to the one Mrs. Clipper would use to go to the security office. He breathed a sigh of relief before knocking on Babette's cabin door.

His friend met him with a broad grin as soon as she opened it. "Come on in, Alan. You're right on time." She trotted to the sofa of the small lounge room and sat down. "I'm anxious as a girl on a prom date," she added while Alan took the seat facing her. "I can't help it, but Edmund is stirring some strange feelings in me. It's as if I have known the man all my life."

Alan had to smile. Was his friend falling in love with a ghost? However improbable, the thought amused him. "That's interesting. And I hope you won't be disappointed if he decides not to show himself this evening."

"Oh no, Alan. It's just that it's all too intriguing for me to resist the temptation of knowing more about my ancestry and this woman who is likely to be my great-grandmother."

"Well, let's just call his name and see if he shows up, shall we?"

"Hold on a moment," Babette said unexpectedly, arranging her dress about her and passing a hand through her hair. "Do I look alright?"

Alan chuckled. "Yes, you do, Babette. You look gorgeous as you always do."

"Okay then... go ahead," she said, sitting upright – her attitude regal.

"Alright, Granddad, I'm sure you've been following our every move in the past while, so why don't you show yourself to discuss the matter of Ms. Babette's ancestry – please?"

"Ah-ah, the magic word, son, will do it every time," Edmund said, appearing near the door of the cabin. "I've been waiting for your call, since I knew you didn't want me to intrude in your life..."

Alan looked up. "How did you know what I thought...?"

"Never mind that, and don't let me be rude," Edmund said, taking the few steps separating him from Babette. He bowed. "How are you, dear lady?"

"I am just fine, Edmund," she replied, smiling. "Why don't you have a seat beside me?" She padded the sofa cushion.

"By all means, dear lady." He sat down. "And to what do I owe the pleasure?" He looked at Alan fixedly. "Or should I ask my great-grandson?"

"No-no, Edmund," Babette said quickly, "this is about me – I mean *your Babette* and the Romanov Brothers. Do you know them?"

"By George! Don't tell me, you've met that philanderer?"

Babette burst out laughing. "I'm sorry, but no, I have not met either of the brothers in person, yet I have reasons to believe that my ancestor met one of them before the Russian Revolution. Would that be possible?"

"It's more than possible, my dear lady. You see, at the time I was traveling the high seas Russia was in turmoil already. There was more than one child born into the Romanov family before the Revolution. The one I knew"—Edmund stopped for a second—"his name was Nicholas Nicolaievich. He was a military man and a flirt. I met him once or twice when I chose to take leave for a few days and meet Babette in Paris."

"Are you telling me that you saw Babette in company of that Russian prince?"

"Yes, I did. But I don't think she was too enthralled with him or his manners. She always referred to him as the "crazy Russian"."

Babette giggled. "That's perhaps the way I'd like to describe Vladimir…"

"Are you saying there is a Romanov aboard this ship?"

"Hold on, Granddad," Alan cut-in when he saw that his great-grandfather was getting irritated at the mere mention of the Romanov's name. "The reason our Ms. Babette had a conversation with this man was that he was wearing a signet ring."

"You don't say?" Edmund blurted. "And he says he is a Romanov?"

"As far as I could ascertain, yes, that's his name."

"And where is he located? I mean does he occupy a cabin or is he working in some capacity aboard the ship?"

"No-no, Granddad, he is a passenger, and his cabin is actually located on this deck."

"Well then, what are we waiting for? Why don't we go and confront the blighter?"

Alan shook his head. "We can't confront anyone, Granddad. I could be facing severe reprimands if I went about accusing a passenger of felony murder just because he's wearing a signet ring."

Edmund reclined on the sofa, apparently reflecting on the problem at hand.

Babette looked at him intently. "What if we waited until the costume ball and you meet him then?" she suggested.

"What costume ball are you referring to, my dear?" Edmund asked, turning his head to Babette.

"The one Tiffany is organizing for the passengers," Alan replied for Babette. "You see, we needed a means to find the cloaked man without examining every man aboard to see if he wore a signet ring…"

"I see," Edmund said, "And you were hoping that I could recognize the hand, and in turn the man who pushed Miss Walter over the railing, is that it?"

"Yes, originally that was the plan…"

"And now this plan has changed, has it?"

"No, not really, Edmund," Babette interposed, "But now that I have met Vladimir Romanov and ascertained that his ancestor apparently knew my great-grandmother, it would just be a matter of confirming our suspicions in regards to his presence on deck at the time of Irene Walter's demise."

Edmund groaned. "Hmm, yes, but will he be wearing that cloak?"

"That's what we're hoping he will do, yes," Alan said, and then paused. There was something that bothered him still. "There is something else that we would need to clarify, Granddad."

"Oh yes? And what would that be?"

"The fact that she broke her neck in the fall. She was not knocked on the head, as you know from performing the preliminary autopsy with me."

"But you do agree that she must have been pushed in order to fall over the railing, do you not?"

Babette, meanwhile, had been looking at Edmund with the eyes of a woman in love. His white shirt, vest and elegant breeches together with his leather boots were more than the romantic picture a girl would paint in her mind of her prince in disguise. She was smitten all right, Alan had to admit, chancing a glance at her a couple of times during his conversation with his granddad.

"Yes, I do. But our assumption, or shall we say your inadmissible evidence of such happening, will make it difficult for us to find a motive or a reason for the authorities to suspect the man."

Still visibly pensive, Edmund asked, "And you think this man is to be considered our vigilante – but why would you think that?"

"Originally, it was because of his strange attire. But now I have further reasons to think so."

"Oh? And what would that be?" Babette asked, suddenly coming out of her reveries.

"Just as I was leaving to come here, Mrs. Clipper paid me a visit…"

"That's interesting," Babette said, "and what did she want?"

"To tell me that Irene Walter was hoping to meet a Russian fellow on this trip."

"Wow, did she really?"

"Yes, Babette, she did, and what's more, she is probably talking to Gilbert Evans right about now."

"And what did she hope to accomplish by telling Gilbert about Vladimir?"

"She wanted him "interrogated" – that's what she said anyway?"

"The little vixen!" Babette declared. "If that isn't a ruse, I don't know what is."

Edmund was staring at Babette by now. "I will hate myself for saying this again, my dear, but you react precisely as Babette aboard *The Delmas* would have done, and very typically French."

CHAPTER FOURTEEN

The Grand Duchess of Luxembourg

TIFFANY WAS ABOUT TO ENTER the ballroom to organize the final details of the costume party when she heard Staff Captain Robert Ekelton call after her: "Ms. Sylvan... I'm sorry to intrude on your day," he said, holding the door open for her, "but I was wondering if you could give me some pointers...."

"Sure, Mr. Ekelton," she replied in a rush – her arms laden with cardboard boxes – and walking into the ballroom, "But, if you don't mind, I'd like to get rid of these..."

"Oh, why don't I give you a hand," Ekelton offered, taking the boxes off her arms. "Where do you want them?"

"Just by the stage. Thank you. They're just some stringers to finish decorating the room."

Ekelton deposited the boxes on the floor and straightened up. "As I said, I'm sorry to interrupt you in the middle of the preparation for the ball, but Captain Galveston thought it would be a good idea if we organized a costume party for the crew." *I hope he's not going to ask me to organize another party,* Tiffany thought, and frowned. Ekelton smiled. "And don't worry, the captain doesn't want you to feel that you need to be involved in any way with the organization of it – he's asked me to do it – and that's why I need your help." He stopped and looked at the entertainment director expectantly.

Tiffany had to giggle. The poor man didn't know what he was in for. "I'm sorry, Mr. Ekelton, I don't mean to laugh at your request; it's just that it might involve a little more than stretching stringers across the room... By the way where is this party to be held?"

"Captain Galveston thought we would have it in the officers' mess hall. Do you think that's going to be big enough of a place?"

Tiffany nodded. "Yes, that should be okay. But are you intending to serve liquor?" She was already thinking of the disaster they would find in the officers' mess after such a party.

"Just beer, wine and maybe some whiskey I suppose," Ekelton answered, "or is that not recommended?"

"Oh, I'm sure that will be fine. It's not like we've got a bunch of winos and drunks working on this ship, have we?"

Ekelton chuckled and shook his head. "Besides, we'll only have officers and executive staff members or engineers – not everyone will be invited to this one. We'll have another one for full crew out on the forward deck soon."

"Okay," Tiffany said, sounding relieved, "Why don't we meet a little later today, when I've got this ballroom decorated and the staff organized?"

"Sure thing, Ms. Sylvan. Just tell me where and when and I'll make sure to be there."

"Okay then, let's meet at the upper deck restaurant around five."

"Perfect."

"And now I better get my assistant to give me a hand." She smiled at Ekelton.

"I'll see you later – and please don't fall from any ladder, okay?"

Tiffany laughed and watched him leave the ballroom. *Nice guy,* she thought.

One could have called the crew's costume party an "appetizer" to the main course that was to be the passengers' fancy dress ball. The mess hall had been appropriately decorated for the festivities, and it took only a half-an-hour for the officers and staff to begin enjoying the exhilarating atmosphere. All until Simon, the sanitation engineer, made a grand entrance. Everyone stopped talking all at once. The six-foot tall, broad shouldered, muscular man usually attracted the eye of every young woman aboard the ship. He was often the subject of wagers among the crew to see how long it would take him to lead another woman to his bed. He even claimed to keep a scorecard in his cabin. As long as they were good-looking and flirtatious, he would succeed in seducing his prey in no time flat. Although he looked as straight as an arrow, and appeared to have no trouble getting the best looking girls on the ship into bed and have mad, passionate sex, there was a rumor that he had the same passion for the good looking guys.

Tonight, however, it was not his success with the ladies which came to the forefront of the mind of the officers and crew attending the party; it was his costume – a glass jar held by a string around his penis-sort of a modern version of a Kotecka (the penis gourd worn by many of the locals in Papua).

Half of the crew dropped their drinks or gagged trying to swallow the drink they had in their mouths. Alan thought for sure someone would either choke or have a heart attack from laughing. Alan and Tiffany certainly had a good laugh.

This appearance with no shame whatsoever at walking confidently into a party, dressed only in a glass bottle, made a few of the doubters get confirmation.

Leon, the 'sweet' spa manager on the ship asked Simon, "What are you?"

"I'm a fireman," Simon replied proudly.

"But you're only wearing a glass jar?" Leon, one of the new crew assigned to the fire brigade, objected. "What's that got to do with firefighting?"

"Think about it, Leon." Simon chuckled. "What do you do in an emergency? You break the glass, pull the knob and I'll come as fast as I can!"

To this, Leon, Ekelton, and several dozen crewmembers of various nationalities, cracked up with renewed laughter.

Later, when he had changed into a more appropriate costume – that of Clark Kent, the investigative reporter – Simon pulled Alan aside, presumably for a medical question. Alan always had the crew asking medical advice or questions; one of the things Alan enjoyed giving or answering in his position. However, Simon didn't have a medical question, but just happened to have a couple more clues for Alan; he had overheard a conversation and seen something while checking one of the septic tanks.

Although quite intrigued by Simon's latest discovery, Alan wanted to focus on the matter at hand, which was to see if Edmund could recognize Vladimir during the passengers' fancy dress ball. His granddad had agreed that if he thought the man was indeed the person who had pushed Irene Walter to her death, he would be willing to talk to him. Babette, for her part, had decided to let the chips fall where they may.

On the night of the ball, she had made a grand appearance, dressed as Madame de Pompadour, strolling amid the crowd of passengers and officers as if the entire world was to fall at her feet. Even though Babette was more often behind the scenes, she had from time to time stepped on the stage professionally. She was an inveterate actress. It took very little for anyone talking to her to not imagine they were in Madame de Pompadour's presence. She played her role to perfection. And someone other than Alan was observing her. He had not approached her yet, nor had he made any move to interrupt her conversation with any of the passengers until she found herself standing in front of the cocktail bar. Dressed as a Russian Cossack, Vladimir bowed to her before taking her hand and kissing it gently. "May I have this dance?" he asked, fixing his gaze on Babette.

"Vladimir – how lovely of you to ask, but…"

"No buts, my dear, I insist," Vladimir said, taking her arm and leading her to the middle of the dance floor.

Tiffany and Alan, who had been watching the two of them ever since Vladimir had approached the cocktail bar, smiled at each other.

"She is such a beautiful woman, Alan," Tiffany remarked, "I wonder; has she ever been married?"

Alan nodded, while watching the couple waltzing around the ballroom as if the world around them didn't exist. "Yes, I believe she was married, but the man was a difficult character apparently and it wasn't long before they divorced."

"It's just that she never speaks of her past – I was just wondering," Tiffany said, her eyes riveted on Vladimir. "And was Granddad able to give her some answers regarding her ancestry?"

"Yes. And furthermore, he seems to know a lot more about Babette's great-grandmother than he originally let on."

Tiffany turned to him. "Why, what did he say?"

"Well, everyone seems to place Babette's great-grandmother in Paris, writing plays for the aristocracy – that appears to be factual. However, Babette had been told that her great-grandmother was the illegitimate child of the Conte de Crillon…"

"You mean the man who owned the now Hotel de Crillon on the Place de la Concorde in Paris?"

"The very same, yes. But Granddad tells a different story. And I would have a tendency to take his account as true…"

"Oh my, do tell, this is interesting," Tiffany said, all ears now.

"Okay, but why don't we go and have a seat somewhere a little more quiet?"

"Sure; you lead and I'll follow," Tiffany replied, putting her empty glass on the nearby table.

As soon as they were sitting in the foyer, Alan began recounting Babette's great-grandmother story, as told to him by his granddad.

"Grand Duchess of Luxembourg, Babette was of royal blood, with a long, proud family history. However, she fell in love with her English teacher; a private tutor. Given that their marriage was forbidden, they eloped to America in the early 1790s. All Babette's great-great-grandmother knew to do were ladylike things; lace making, sewing, reading, singing, etc. He, of course, was an English professor and was promised a job teaching at Williams & Mary College in the New World. Unfortunately, he got consumption on the ship going over to America and couldn't manage the rigorous duties of a full professor. Therefore, after he healed enough to travel, they went west to Wisconsin, where he ended up teaching in a local school. To pass the time, Babette made lace for all the ladies in the town, taught singing, English and French grammar. She was banished from the family, but made a name for herself with the stories she would write about the Wild West – the Mid-West really. Wisconsin was considered as far west as one would want to go in those days. After her husband's death, she returned to Europe and found her brother-in-law in Paris. Within months she gave birth to a little girl, which she named Babette. Unfortunately, she died soon after the child was born. The great-grand uncle raised the infant. As she grew up, she made friends with a group of theater people in her late teens while they lived in Montmartre. After that, same as our Babette, she saw the insides of the Comédie Française and learned her trade as a playwright, which led her to write plays for the new Parisian aristocracy." Alan paused. "And that's about all Granddad knew of Babette's ancestry."

"So our Babette would have legitimate blue blood flowing through her veins – amazing," Tiffany said, sinking in the sofa and looking up at the ceiling. "Does she know now?"

"Oh yes. And I believe that knowledge is going to make a difference in Babette's life."

"Such as what?"

"Well, for one thing, I think she will go to Luxembourg as soon as she has completed this cruise."

"And do what?"

"I don't know, Tiff," Alan replied, chuckling. "Yet, I would be surprised if she didn't pay a visit to his Royal Highness the Grand Duke of Luxemburg – his name is Henri, by the way, and he has auburn hair, same as Babette."

"Good God!" Tiffany exclaimed. "Do you think she would be welcomed?"

"Perhaps not officially, and she would have to prove her assertion, which might be a difficult thing to do, but, to my way of thinking, she is a grand duchess, no question, Tiff."

"But why did they tell her some story about the Conte de Crillon then?"

"I think it's because the Conte de Crillon's family has no heir or relatives still alive today. So, Babette wouldn't have been tempted to stir old family issues – she couldn't."

After a moment of silence, Tiffany said, "Do you think she'll continue writing plays after being told a truth like this?"

"Oh God yes, Tiffany. This has only re-ignited her desire to write historical comedy – that's what she told me anyway." Alan got up. "I think we better go back in there and see if Vladimir has captured more of Babette's time and attention. Shall we?"

CHAPTER FIFTEEN

Bags and bags of the stuff!

AS *THE BARONESS* LEFT the Maldives and reached the high seas for the longest part of her journey without lowering anchor until reaching Madagascar, "all hands had been on deck" – literally. This was to ensure that nothing untoward would happen to her, the passengers, officers and crew. Once the crew and officers had resumed their regular duties and chores, such as he considered his report writing, Alan called on Simon, the sanitation engineer, to come in for a "check-up" at the end of the second day at sea.

"Hi, Doc," Simon said cheerfully, appearing at Alan's office door at the appointed time. "Did you want to see me?"

Alan raised his head to the man and smiled. He threw his pen on the desk and got up. "Yeah, and if you don't mind, let's take a walk – I've had enough of this place for one day." His eyes roved around the paperwork. "It's getting crazier by the minute." He looked up at Simon. "Okay with you?"

"Sure, Doc, what ever you say. As long as I don't have to go through another physical, I'm fine with what ever you suggest."

Leaving Evelyn to 'hold the fort' for a while, Alan and Simon left the medical center and took the elevator to the upper deck promenade – away from eyes and ears.

"Tell me something, Simon," Alan began when they found a couple of vacant lounge chairs in the shade of the nearby transom, "why are you guys so afraid of going through a physical? I've yet to meet a crew that likes having a check-up."

Lacing the fingers of both hands at the nape of his neck, Simon grunted before replying, "It's not the physical, Doc. Most of the time, none of us mind one bit paying you a visit; it's the needles. See, every time you get those big vials out on the tray and poke a hole in my vein, I feel like a hog ready for the slaughterhouse. It's like you need a pint of the red stuff to tell me that I'm okay." He chortled. "And you know, the other thing that bugs us, it's having to undress for the nurses..."

Alan had to raise an eyebrow. "But you're a magnificent specimen of a man, why would you be shy taking your clothes off in front of my nurse?"

"Thanks for the compliment, Doc. But I'm still shy to show it all off when it's for a woman and when there's only the two of us in the cabin."

"I guess I can understand that. I wouldn't like to have to undress in front of some other woman than my girlfriend either."

"Ah yes – Ms. Sylvan – I bet she's a wonderful lover, ain't she?"

"Let's not kiss and tell, Simon, okay?"

"Okay, okay, Doc. No problem. And I guess you haven't called this little meeting to talk about our individual love-lives either, have you?"

"No, I haven't, Simon." Alan laughed. "As a matter of fact, it's about what you told me at the costume party – do you remember what you said?"

"How can I forget? I'm down there every bloody day and all I can see is me getting those bags out of the shit. I smelled to high heaven for days afterwards..."

"Did you say, "bags"?" Alan cut-in. "Bags of what?"

"Well, let me first tell you how I happen to notice them. As you probably don't know, every day, when I make my rounds, I've got to check the sump-pump to make sure there's no obstruction – otherwise our pax might have problem with "irregularities" as you
might say. If you get my meaning."

Alan couldn't stifle the laugh that erupted out of his mouth. "I guess that would be a problem, yes," he had to admit.

"Well, as you say, it might be a problem, especially for us guys – our cabins are closest to the tanks and we'd suffer the effect of the back-flush right first."

Still grinning, Alan asked, "So what happened when you discovered there was a plug in the system?"

"Ha-ha," Simon laughed and turned to Alan. "It's like this, Doc, if we've got a plug, as you said, in the tanks, I'm the one who's got to fish it out, ain't I?" He paused. "And so, here I went, down in the tank and pulled out the first bag – it was an old garbage bag and I thought right away that it was strange, 'cause we get all sorts in there like nappies or the odd condom, or maybe a toilet sponge that might have found their way down there by accident like, but not a whole great big plastic bag."

"And was it full of something – like garbage, maybe?"

Simon shook his head, swung his legs off the chair and placed his elbows on his knees to face the doc. "No, this one was empty. But the others were not."

"And how many were there?" Alan asked, baffled.

"About five at the last count."

"And did you open one of them to see what was in them?"

"Sure did, Doc. Because, if they'd be filled with garbage I would have gone to the kitchen and have it out with the chef. He'd probably end up in the tank himself – I tell you."

"Okay – and what did the bags contain then?"

"Pure cocaine!"

Alan stared for a long minute before he said, "How can you be sure it was cocaine, Simon? Did you taste it? And where are the bags now?"

"Ah yes, I mean yes, Doc, it's cocaine alright. There may be a dozen packets of the stuff in each bag. And once I had the whole mess cleaned up, including myself, I got the bags into my locker and since that was the morning before the costume party, I just made sure I told you about it..."

"But that happened a couple of days ago; are you sure the bags are still there? And what about the guys in your crew – do they know about this?"

"Yeah, the bags are still under lock-and-key and no worries about my guys, given that I make my rounds at five in the morning, no one knows what I've found."

Alan stood up. "Okay, Simon, let's get the bags into the security office's safe and discuss this with Mr. Evans, okay?"

Ever since Babette had discovered the truth about her identity, she had retreated to her cabin to begin writing another play – this one was going to make it to the Broadway stage, if she had anything to say about it, and she had. She was in the middle of writing furiously on her laptop when she heard a knock at the door. She groaned but didn't get up from her seat. However, when the rapping became more insistent, she rose from her chair in a huff and strode to the door, intending to send the caller on his way immediately, if not sooner. Yet, when she opened it, she was surprised to find Mrs. Clipper facing her with a broad smile adorning her lovely face.

"I'm terribly sorry to disturb you…"

"No, you're not," Babette snapped, in no mood to be charming, "but do come in and tell me why you wanted to interrupt me?"

"Well, yes… thank you," Lizzy replied, stepping indoors while Babette closed the door behind the woman.

"Have a seat," Babette offered, sitting down herself on the sofa. "What can I do for you, Lizzy?"

"Well, I thought you might have some information about Vladimir. I haven't been able to find him since the night of the fancy ball. Has he called on you?"

"No, he has not," Babette replied tersely. "And what would you want with him anyway?"

Lizzy put her bag on the floor beside the chair and seemed to hesitate. "It's just that he's Russian and that Irene wanted to meet him…"

Babette held up a hand to stop the young woman's insinuations – which they were sure to be – from spilling into her ears. Babette hated gossip with a passion. "Let me stop you right there, Lizzy. How do you know Irene wanted to meet Vladimir? Before he accosted us, you didn't even know the man. So what makes you think it was him she intended to meet?"

"It's just because he's Russian and…"

"But there must be a half dozen Russians aboard this ship – maybe more – so why him?"

"Because he's the one who approached us – not the other way around. Don't you see...?"

"No, Lizzy. All I see is that Vladimir approached us because he wanted to make my acquaintance – not yours." That was a bit blunt, but there was generally no other way to deal with a false premise.

"How do you mean?" Curiosity laced Lizzy's every word.

"I mean, Vladimir's family was acquainted with my family some time long ago, and he wanted to meet me and talk about our great-grand parents. That's all. And he was surely not interested in Irene Walter – not in the least, in fact." She paused to observe Lizzy's reaction. "Besides, you wouldn't be knocking at my door if he had contacted you personally – now would you?"

Lizzy shook her head, grabbed her bag from the floor and stood up. "Whether you believe it or not, I'm sorry to have disturbed you," she said, visibly disappointed. "But if Vladimir ever mentions Irene, would you let me know?"

Babette stood up too, and walked her visitor to the door. "I sure will, Lizzy. And I am sorry for the cool reception I gave you, but I am in the middle of writing something for my producer, which sends all of my manners by the wayside."

Lizzy smiled as Babette opened the door for her. "Well, goodbye then. I hope we can have tea sometime..."

"Yes, yes, we'll do that – plenty of time for it," Babette replied, "See you then," and closed the door.

While Babette and Lizzy were having their short conversation, a couple of decks below, Simon and Alan were sitting in Gilbert's office. The chief of security had already put the five bags of cocaine in the safe and was about to ask a few questions after he had heard Simon's story.

"Okay then, Simon," he began, "To your knowledge, these bags were not there the day before you discovered them, is that right?"

"Yes, that's right. As I said to the doc here, I make my rounds every morning and check the septic tanks carefully 'cause of the problem a blocked sump pump could cause, besides, I would have noticed them before that morning 'cause, they were floating on the surface like."

"But aren't these tanks sealed?" Gilbert asked, looking up from his notepad.

"Oh yeah, they sure are, but they've got three windows around the lid sort of thing, and that's how I saw them."

"Okay." Gilbert paused. "What about the door to that area, who's got keys?"

"Only the chief engineer and myself. And before you ask, we both keep our keys on our belts. They don't leave our side, as you might say."

"And what happens at night, where are your keys then?"

"In my locker with my clothes. I don't sleep with them under my pillow, if that's what you're asking, Chief." Simon chuckled.

"Yeah, I don't suppose you do. But did you entertain any ladies lately or before the day you discovered the bags?"

Simon lowered his head and wringed his hands. He was visibly reluctant to say.

"I think it's time for you to kiss and tell," Alan suggested, throwing him an encouraging smile.

"Okay, if I can be sure what I say stays in this room," Simon said, looking directly at Gilbert.

"Well, that will depend upon if the lady is involved in this situation, Simon. If we can ascertain that she's in no way responsible for putting these bags in the tanks, then we'll all forget about it. But, if she is involved, then her identity will have to come out."

"Will she be facing prosecution like?" Simon asked. "I mean I don't want to get her in trouble with the law or anything."

Gilbert shook his head. "Well, unless you want to face the music yourself for possession of illegal drugs, her name is what we need."

"Okay, Mr. Evans. I think she said her name was Lizzy – like in Elizabeth – and I'll never forget her last name. It's like the name of some old boat; it was Clipper."

CHAPTER SIXTEEN

Odds and Ends

AND HOW DID SHE END UP in your cabin?" Gilbert asked. "And how did you two meet in the first place? It's not like the passengers mingle with the engineers and other technical staff too often, do they?"

"Oh no, Chief, we sure don't – that's against regs as you know," Simon replied, "But in this case, I was taking a bit of a break outside on deck, while me and the guys were busy decorating the mess hall and she was looking at the ocean yonder, like in a daydream or something." He paused, hesitantly. "It's like she was waiting for me – though I know that's not likely – and I started talking to her."

"I see," said Gilbert, "and what happened after that?"

"Well, I showed her the mess hall – like it was very nice with all the lights and other decorations – and we got talking a little more and... well, anyway, we ended up in my cabin for a bit that night... Please don't tell staff captain...."

"And the next morning, that's when you found the bags in the tank, right?"

"Yeah, Chief, and like I said, she's a nice lady, and very hot..."

"What about the keys, did you notice them missing the next morning?" Alan asked.

"No, none was missing like. As I said, I get on my rounds at five, but one thing I did notice was that I had a blasted headache when I woke up. The alarm clock kept ringing in my ears, like if I had got a hangover or something."

Alan frowned. "Did you have something to drink before you got into bed with her?"

"Yeah. Actually, she brought this fancy wine with her, and we got just to the second glass when I kinda passed out for a bit." He smiled at the chief. "That's not my usual performance, you understand. I don't like to leave my ladies 'high and dry' as they say."

"And did you know, or are you aware of Mrs. Clipper…"

"You mean she's married?" Simon erupted, interrupting Gilbert.

"Separated I'm told," Alan put in.

"Wow, that's a relief – I wouldn't like to face a husband of hers – never do actually. I mean I don't usually get it on with the married types anyway."

"That's okay, Simon," Gilbert said, "but to come back to my question; could you tell me when this lady left your cabin then?"

"Actually, I fell asleep like right after we had the wine – and that's all I remember," Simon said, shaking his head.

"I would venture to say that you were drugged, my friend," the chief said, "and the fact that you fell asleep has nothing to do with your ability to perform I'd say." He looked at Alan.

The latter smiled. "I'd say you're right, Gilbert." Alan turned to Simon. "I wish I had known of this much sooner, because we could have tested your urine for drugs within a few hours of having ingested it, but now whatever it was, is probably gone from your system, as I suspect it was short acting."

"Would it have made a difference if I had told you about it the morning before the party?"

"I believe it would have, Simon. But we can't worry about that right now – it's water under the bridge so to speak – and we can only hope that our Mrs. Clipper shows her cards another way."

"What about the bottle of wine and the glasses?" Gilbert asked, "Did she leave anything behind?"

"No, nothing, Chief. I believe she took the lot back with her when she left."

"Okay then," Gilbert said, reclining in his chair. "I think you need to be careful from now on Simon, because someone is bound to be looking for these bags and who ever it is, may not be coming to your cabin with a nice bottle under his arm."

"That's not a problem, Chief," Simon said, chuckling. "Anyone gunning for me will have to contend with my fist first."

"Yeah, but you should be careful anyway." Gilbert paused and looked at the sanitation engineer fixedly. "You go on your way now, and if anything happens, you let me know right away, okay?"

"You got it, Chief," Simon replied, getting up. "I'll be seeing you all then," he added before closing the door behind himself.

As Alan was making his way back to the medical center, he heard his name called. "Oh, Doctor Mayhew…?"

Alan turned around to see two older gentlemen – soberly dressed, both sporting mustaches and beards – sitting on a couple of chairs along the deck, and one of them waving to him. "Sorry to catch you unawares, Doctor, but my friend and I had a little discussion and maybe you could help us solve our little quandary."

Stepping toward the two men, Alan searched his memory to recall if he had ever seen or met them. Nothing came to mind. "Hello, gents," he said, "So, what's that little quandary you mentioned?"

"Oh, I'm so sorry, but let me introduce us first," one fellow said, dragging a third chair toward him. "And why don't you have a seat?" Alan did. "I'm Doctor Sigmund, a psychiatrist by profession, retired mind you. And this is my good friend, Doctor Lanugos – he's a proctologist," he added, nodding in his friend's direction.

Alan wondered what this was all about, but made a mental note of Sigmund's name – he would have loved to consult a psychiatrist from time to time with some of the weirdoes he would inevitably encounter in his travels.

"Nice meeting you both, Doctors," he said perfunctorily. "How can I help?"

"Well, it's about our sons," Sigmund began. "You see, they both graduated from medical school at the same time…"

"They've been friends since prep-school," Lanugos put in, "and they wanted to follow in their fathers' footsteps sort of thing."

"That's right," Sigmund said, nodding. "And now they've decided to open a practice together, along with other things they do together, and believe it or not, they had the hardest time describing what they did." He chortled.

"And now we're at a loss to suggest something to them," Lanugos added.

"But let me tell you first how it went," Sigmund went on. "So, my son, Dr. Sigmund, the psychiatrist and Dr. Lanugos's son, the proctologist put up a sign reading: *Dr. Sigmund and Dr. Lanugos: Hysterias and Posteriors*. The town council was livid and insisted they change it. Then our sons changed it to read: *Schizoids and Hemorrhoids*. This was also not acceptable so they again changed the sign to read *Catatonics and High Colonics* – no go. Next they tried *Manic Depressives and Anal Retentives* – thumbs down again. Then came *Minds and Behinds* – still no good. Another attempt resulted in *Lost Souls and Butt Holes* – unacceptable again! So they tried *Nuts and Butts* – no way. *Freaks and Cheeks* – still no good. *Loons and Moons* – forget it. Almost at their wit's end, our sons finally came up with: *Dr. Sigmund and Dr. Lanugos - Specializing in Odds and Ends*. Everybody in town loved it. But what do you think as a fellow professional?"

Alan was out of suggestions but not out of laughter. "Are you serious? Or were you pulling my leg, Doctors?" he asked after he caught his breath.

In a chorus of hearty chuckles the two doctors nodded.

"A bit of both, Dr. Mayhew," Sigmund said, still visibly amused. "I'm sorry about this, but we couldn't help it after what we've heard about your latest exploits…"

"And what *exploits* might those be?" Alan asked, intrigued now.

"The magical scalpels," Lanugos replied, practically whispering. "I mean, everybody is talking about it."

Alan's eyebrows shot up. *Has Alice been talking again,* he wondered? "I'm afraid you've been misinformed," he blurted. "I'm sorry, perhaps I've been the butt of a joke, but I can assure you I don't practice any magician's tricks – never have."

"Now, now, Doctor, don't be offended. I'm sure the story was just passed around in good fun," Sigmund said, patting Alan on the arm.

Alan smiled for the benefit of the two men, but inside he was seething. "Yeah, that's probably what happened." He got up. "And now, if you'll excuse me, Doctors, I think I've got several reports to do before the day is over."

"That's right – a doctor's duty doesn't stop with the sun setting, does it?" Lanugos remarked.

"It sure doesn't," Alan said, "Sorry, but I have to leave you. Have a good day, gents," he concluded, walking away.

Sigmund looked after him. "He probably will need to perform a lot of magical tricks before we get back to San Francisco," he remarked pensively.

"What makes you say that?" Lanugos asked.

"That man is very preoccupied right now, my friend, and something is definitely bothering him."

Sigmund was right. Alan was indeed preoccupied. This latest news of him performing magical tricks had him more annoyed than troubled. He couldn't think how that gossip spread so fast. Yet, there was something else on his mind that was trying to jostle its way for first place in the forefront of his brain: How was Lizzy Clipper involved? And why was she hiding bags of cocaine in the septic tanks when she must have known that they would be discovered at the first sign of a blockage problem. Nothing made sense at the moment.

As he entered the medical center, he found Babette waiting for him in his office. *What's the matter now*, he asked himself. *I would love for people to leave the poor woman alone.*

"Ah there you are, Alan," Babette said cheerfully, turning her head as he rounded his desk to sit down. "How are you?"

"I'm better now that I have you sitting across from me," Alan replied, a broad smile appearing on his lips.

"That bad, eh?" Babette tittered. "Well, maybe what I have to tell you will cheer you up a little."

"And what's that?"

"It's about Lizzy…"

"Don't tell me; she's paid you a visit," Alan interrupted.

Babette nodded. "Yes, she did indeed. And unfortunately I was in no mood to cajole her into a lengthy conversation, but what she told me was enough to drag me out of my concentration." She paused. "Actually, I couldn't write another word on my new play after she left."

"And what did she say that disturbed you so?"

"Well, it's not so much what she said that bothered me, but what she implied by it. You see, when we met Vladimir, it was all about him and me getting to know each other and talking about our ancestors. Yet, Lizzy now insists on Vladimir being the person Irene Walter wanted to meet before her death."

"I see," Alan said, playing with a paperclip that he found lying on his desk. "And did she say why she thought he was the man Irene wanted to meet?"

"The only reason she offered was because the man is Russian," Babette replied.

"And do you think he's involved in Irene's death then?"

Babette shook her head vigorously. "Absolutely not, Alan. I had a chance to talk to him at length during the costume ball, and I can assure you, the man was not interested in the least in Irene."

"What about the signet ring then? Did Granddad confirm it was the same ring?"

"No. The last time I spoke to him about that, he told me that even the hand didn't resemble the one he had noticed that night. So, by all accounts, Vladimir is not involved in any of this, as far as I can tell."

Alan's head bobbed up and down. "Alright. And now let me tell you what our Mrs. Clipper has been up to, off the record, of course." He smiled when he saw a spark of curiosity lighting Babette's eyes.

"Oh do go on, this is better than my drama plays," Babette pleaded.

"Okay, here goes ...." Alan then recounted Simon's misadventure with Lizzy and his finding the bags of cocaine in the septic tanks.

When he finished, Babette was staring at him. "Are you saying these two women were running a trafficking ring using this ship?" She sounded amazed.

"Yes, Babette. And now that one of them is dead, and that the drugs have been impounded, it appears that the other one is trying to divert the buyer's attention to our sanitation engineer as the one who had the drugs all along."

"But that's terrible," Babette exclaimed, visible disgust marring the multiple character lines of her face. "And Lizzy thinks Vladimir is the buyer, is that it?"

Alan nodded. "Or the courier perhaps. Yet, since he doesn't seem to have any interest in Lizzy, I suggest we need to find the quarry before he finds Simon and does away with him. Alternatively doing away with Mrs. Clipper for having double-crossed him."

CHAPTER SEVENTEEN

Some PR!

MEANWHILE THE CAPTAIN had been alerted of the cache of drugs that had been found aboard his ship. He was none too pleased when he had heard Ekelton's report, obviously. After getting over the shock, he had told Gilbert that he wanted Mrs. Clipper locked up in the brig. "If she doesn't admit to her involvement, you will have no other choice. Do you understand me?" he had said before slamming the receiver down in Gilbert's ear.

So, a couple of days later, and after he had received some Intel from Interpol regarding Irene Walter's antecedents and another set of info on Lizzy, Gilbert decided it was about high time that he interview 'the lady'.

"Have you got any news for me, Mr. Evans, regarding Irene's accident?" Lizzy asked innocently as she took a seat across from Gilbert.

He reclined in his chair and played with his pencil before he replied with, "Do you think it was an accident then, do you?"

"Well, what else could it be?" she asked with a slight shrug of her shoulders.

"For one thing, you, yourself have advanced the idea that she had been pushed over the railing, didn't you?"

"That's because I had heard something like that, yes."

Gilbert rolled his chair to his desk and advanced his body to place his forearms on the blotter. "Yes, quite. And I hate these kinds of rumors myself, Mrs. Clipper." He smiled. "It's like the one I heard about you, seducing our sanitation engineer into spending the night with him, in his cabin. You do know it's strictly against the rules for any crew member or officer to be involved with our passengers?"

"Did he tell you I went to his cabin? Because if he did, he's a liar!" Lizzy flared. "What would I want with such a clown like Simon, who gets stark naked to impress his friends at a costume ball?"

"Oh, I see that you've heard about his little 'mooning' stunt. How did you hear about that?"

She shook her head, visibly annoyed. "I really don't remember, Mr. Evans. And what has that got to do with Irene's death?"

"That particular event has nothing to do with Ms. Walter's death actually. You're right. But the fact that you can describe our sanitation engineer and the fact that you even know his name, has a lot to do with this case."

"How's that?" Lizzy asked, opening her eyes wide.

"Well, for one thing, you've met and you've seduced one of our crew to lure him into his cabin under the pretext of spending the night with him, do you see what I'm getting at now?"

"Not at all, but do go on; I love a good story," she said, daring Gilbert.

"Yes, and it's getting even better." He paused to look at the tigress in the seat opposite him. It was as if she was shedding skins of innocence one after the other. "You see, we know you went to Simon Albertson's cabin with a bottle of wine. He drank a glass or two with you and promptly fell asleep."

"Well, I don't see anything wrong with that," Lizzy interposed, "except for the fact that – if I had been there at all – I would have left the man's cabin without getting what I came for."

"Not quite, Mrs. Clipper. As far as we can gather you got exactly what you came for when you went to Mr. Albertson's cabin."

"And what was that?"

"The keys to the sanitation room and the key to the lid of the septic tanks."

Lizzy stared before she said, "And what on Earth would I do with these keys, Mr. Evans?"

"Well, we know… I mean, at this point we have considered the possibility of you hiding some two and half kilos of cocaine in one of the septic tanks."

"Well, doesn't that beat all?" Lizzy exclaimed. "I've never heard such poppycock in all my life." She got up from her chair. "And as soon as we reach Madagascar, I'll be sure to leave this cruise and write a letter of complaint to your head office."

"Oh, I'm sure you will be able to write all of the complaints you want – from prison that is." Lizzy sat down again. "Yes, Mrs. Clipper. You see, before I called you to have this little chat, I received confirmation from Interpol that you have been involved in a couple of thefts – misdemeanors really – when you were in school…"

"But that's all in the past," Lizzy tried arguing.

Gilbert lifted a hand to stop her. "Oh it is, no doubt of it. However, in both cases, these involved people whom we now suspect to have been involved in much greater endeavors. We also understand that they have called on your services to be their PR, for a lack of a better word. Now we suspect that Ms. Walter was, in fact, transporting drugs aboard this vessel, intending to sell them to someone either in Europe or the states."

"And how does this fanciful story involve me as a PR, to use your description?"

"The buyers don't care who comes knocking with a package really, and you would be the perfect stand-in for Irene. She probably had told you about the drugs and you decided to take over."

Lizzy got to her feet again. "Well, that was a very interesting story, Mr. Evans, but until you have any proof of your assertion, I don't think you'll be able to obtain a warrant from any authority abroad or in the States. So, if you'll excuse me, I'll continue enjoying this cruise until we reach the next port."

She was about to reach the knob on the door, when Gilbert stopped her with, "We have lifted your prints from the inside of Mr. Albertson's cabin and that's enough for me to ask you to remain at my disposal until we have obtained all the proof we need to arrest you as soon as we reach Madagascar."

"That's fine," she replied, before slamming the door behind her.

That evening Babette was locked up in her cabin finishing her latest play

– the one she intended to produce and present to the passengers later during the cruise, when a knock at the door took her out of her concentration, once again.

"Why don't you people address your queries and your thirst for company to someone else," she groaned, as she opened the door. "Oh my goodness, what on Earth are you doing here at this hour?" she asked, looking at the man standing before her. "Come in, come in," she invited.

Edmund did. "I'm sorry to disturb you at such a late hour, my dear, but I needed to see you…"

"What about?" Babette stopped and lifted her hand. "But before you explain, could you tell me how you were able to knock at my door and why you did."

"Simple, dear lady. I have some kinetic powers which enable me to move objects from one place to the other, as you know, and in this instance, I took a golf ball from those strange, artificial links on the upper deck and bounced it a couple of times on your door." He paused and smiled. "And as to why I did; I remember you saying that I would have to announce my presence, if it was unexpected, before appearing… am I not correct?"

A broad smile draped over Babette's lips. "You are perfectly correct, my friend. And I am grateful for your attention to my requests." She sat on the sofa and pointed to the chair opposite her. "And now do tell why you needed to see me, as you put it?"

Edmund slipped into the chair and advanced his body to peer into his friend's eyes. "I have been listening to some of Mr. Evans's conversations with a couple of people, and these brought me to the conclusion that we have some dangerous individual still at large and wanting to do harm."

Babette gasped. "How did you come to that conclusion?" She returned Edmund's gaze.

"You have also heard what happened between Mrs. Clipper and Mr. Albertson…"

"Who?"

"Mr. Simon Albertson, the sanitation engineer – you do remember, don't you?"

"Yes, yes, of course. Alan told me." Babette paused. "And of course the situation where someone may have helped Irene Walter over the railing, but the fall that broke the poor woman's neck, was surely an accident. I don't see where or why we should worry."

"Yes, my dear. Yet, we have to contend with the fact that we can't be certain that someone didn't push Ms. Walter intentionally. Perhaps, that someone is now after the people who have knowledge of these incidents."

"And you've had a look at Mrs. Clipper's hand have you?"

"Precisely. And she definitely doesn't have a man's hand. Her dainty hand was surely not the one I observed protruding from the cloaked figure."

"Then, I will have to agree with you. Perhaps Mrs. Clipper has an accomplice who is in charge of clearing her path. According to what we now suspect, the people, who knew Irene Walter's motives on this cruise, are in danger."

"And that includes you, Babette," Edmund declared. "Although I would love to have you at my side for all eternity, the Good Lord, who has graciously allowed me to be in your company at this time, would not forgive me if anything should happen to you."

"But how, Edmund? I mean I have absolutely nothing to do with this whole affair. I have only talked to Mrs. Clipper on a couple of occasions…"

"Too true, my dear," Edmund interrupted, "but you have been informed of where the drugs have been stored in the first instance, and you are now aware of where they are, are you not?"

"Yes, but what would any of these drug dealers, or who ever these people might be, want with me? It's not like I could go to Mr. Evans's safe and open it, now could I?"

"But someone might use you…"

"You mean abduct/kidnap me?" Babette said, before putting a trembling hand over her mouth.

"Perhaps, my dear. It is definitely a possibility, given the circumstances."

"And what circumstances are those?"

He put his elbows on his knees. "You're famous, Babette, and you're traveling on this ship. Anyone who knows anything about you, and what you do besides writing plays, would use you as leverage. The price of which –when compared to the street value of a couple of kilos of cocaine – is nothing."

"Goodness, Edmund, do you really think these people would go to that extreme just for a couple of kilos of cocaine as you put it?"

He nodded. Babette rose to her feet.

"Well, that is making my decision a lot easier," she declared.

"And what decision is that, my dear?" Edmund asked, raising his gaze to her.

"I was going to ask you to stay with me…" She raised a hand and smiled. "Let me re-phrase that; I was going to ask you if you wouldn't mind remaining in my company for a while…kind of like cabin mates of sorts."

"Great minds think alike," Edmund said, grinning. "And yes, I would be delighted to remain with you." He paused. "But why did you intend to do that before you knew of the peril lurking about this vessel?"

"Firstly, you are quite the gentleman and a pleasure to be around. Furthermore, I have this play to produce, and since it's staged in the nineteen century, I wanted your help to ensure I wasn't making any mistakes."

"Oh but that is an excellent idea. Working with you is really a dream come true, my dear lady."

Babette then went to her desk and took the sheet of paper on top of one pile. Bringing it to Edmund and holding it in front of his eyes, she asked, "Why don't you read this and give me your first impression."

Edmund looked up at her and then smiled, returning his gaze to the sheet of paper.

A Cat Named Hoodoo Voodoo
A three-act play by Babette

This play takes place in the home of Marie Laveau in New Orleans in the nineteen century.

Prologue

The chief investigator is standing on the stage in the dark; on the apron on the stage we have a dance. The dance is a counter-clockwise dance in a circle. The one to be possessed begins by clapping his hands, nodding and tapping his feet to the rhythm of the drums. Like the others, soon the eyes of the one possessed become fixed, his eyes become glassy, his movements become faster and faster, his head is thrown back, his arms thrash about. He falls to the ground in the center of the circle, then jumps up and down, then he rolls around and around. He speaks in tongues saying words he had never said before. Other worshipers move around in a circle about him, always counter-clockwise. He faints finally, exhausted, the drums become fainter and fainter and stop. Then dancers exit during a blackout and the chants that accompanied the dancers' ritual die down.

Visibly uncomprehending, Edmund shook his head. "This sounds like the "*Danse de St. Guy*" in a group performance, he remarked, lifting his gaze to Babette, as she removed the piece of paper from in front of his face, laughing.

"Yes, it does a bit, doesn't it? But perhaps I should describe the plot to you before I let you read the whole play."

Edmund reclined in his seat. "Is that the city we referred to as "*Nouvelle Orleans*"?

"Yes. And the whole play revolves around the intricacy of those who believe in the powers of voodoo...."

And for the next few hours, late into the night, in fact, Babette and Edmund immersed themselves in reviewing the play.

Meanwhile, someone was reviewing a play of an entirely different sort...

CHAPTER EIGHTEEN

She just sank

TAKING A BREAK FROM the usual toils of the day, Staff Captain Ekelton was entertaining a couple of friends in the officers' mess when one of his colleagues asked if he remembered his trip to Java. At a loss for a moment to recall what Elias was talking about, he said, "You mean the day she just sank?"

"Yeah, that's the one. I told the guys about it – or tried to – but I think it'll be better coming from the horse's mouth." Elias chuckled.

"Okay, okay. Here it goes then," said Robert, taking a sip of juice before beginning to tell the tale. "There were two twins, Joe and John Gladstone. Joe was the owner of an old dilapidated boat that I, and a few of the crew, had rented for the day in Carita. This was on the coast of Java. It just so happened that John's wife died the same day Joe's boat sank – the day we had rented it. A few days later a kindly old woman saw Joe, and mistaking him for John, she said, "I'm sorry to hear about your loss. You must feel terrible."

"Joe, thinking she was talking about his boat, said, "Fact is, I'm sort of glad to get rid of her. She was a rotten old thing from the beginning. Her bottom was all shriveled up and she smelled like an old dead fish. She was always losing her water; she had a bad crack in the back and a pretty big hole in the front, too. Every time I used her, the hole got bigger and she leaked like crazy. I guess what finished her off was when I rented her to the staff captain and those four guys looking for a good time for the day in port. I warned them that she wasn't very good, but they wanted to use her anyhow and were willing to pay. The fools all tried to get in her at the same time and split her right down the middle." Elias, along with his friends were practically in tears from laughter, when Ekelton concluded, "The old woman fainted!"

"True story!" Elias confirmed. "I was there. And I can tell you, the poor thing – the boat just sank beneath our feet."

The following day, Alan was still thinking about the rumors that had been going around the ship regarding the "floating scalpels". He really felt he needed to have a chat with Alice. He called her into his office and asked her to close the door before sitting down.

"What is it, Doc?" Alice asked, visibly at a loss to know why Alan had called her in.

"It is about you seeing floating scalpels in the emergency room…"

"But, Doc, I've told you *I saw your instruments,*" Alice flared.

"Yes, Alice, I know what you said, and I do believe that's exactly what you saw. I don't believe you have some kind of a fertile imagination to the point of having hallucinations. I do believe that you have told some people about your experience, haven't you?"

Alice sank in her chair. "Well, yes. I've told a couple people. But everyone told me that it was probably a magic trick of some sort."

"Precisely, Alice. And now passengers are calling on me and asking if I perform magic tricks in the medical center."

"Do they really?" Alice's hand went to her mouth. Her eyes told of the smirk she was trying to hide.

"Yes, they do, and I don't like it, Alice," Alan said sternly. "I don't want our passengers to think that they have a "medicine man" performing some magic tricks to cure their ailments – do you understand me?"

"Yes, of course, Doc. But I don't see how my remarks got so out of proportion and such gossip started."

"I guess you're not one to blab or given to spreading rumors, yet we now need to redress this situation."

"Okay; what can I do then?"

"I think it might be a good idea to tell the people you talked to in the first place that I was just playing a joke on you. You think you can do that?"

"Sounds silly to me after telling everyone how frightened I had been, but I guess I can do that, yes." She paused for a minute and fixed her eyes on Alan's unwavering gaze. "But, Doc, did you really play a joke on me?"

"No, Alice, I didn't, but someone did. And after I explained to the young man that he was not welcome to perform his tricks in the medical center, he said – promised actually – that he wouldn't do it again, at least not here."

"Do I know him?"

"I'm sure you don't, Alice, but he's the next Kris Angel, I'm told. He supposedly moves things through walls and can transfer himself from one room to another apparently. So, if he's true to his word, we won't have to worry about he or his tricks anymore."

"Okay then," Alice said, sounding relieved. "I'll talk to my friends and tell them that we've both been victims of some magician's trick – that'd be a bit closer to the truth, wouldn't it?"

"Yes, it will be – just as long as you don't end up passing another rumor about the ship, okay?"

"Of course, Doc." Alice paused, while getting up. "And I'm sorry about the trouble…"

"That's alright, Alice." Alan looked after her as she went to the door and opened it. "Tell you what, why don't we have breakfast together with Ms. Sylvan tomorrow morning?"

Alice spun on her heels, practically agape. "You mean it – I mean I'm sure you mean what you say, Doc, and that would be wonderful. Thank you."

"Okay, okay, on your way then."

As soon as Alice had closed the door of his office behind her, Alan picked up the phone and dialed Gilbert's number.

"Hi, Doc, are we okay for lunch," Gilbert asked as he picked up the receiver on his desk.

"Yep, no problem," Alan answered, a smile appearing on his lips. "But I have just one question for you…"

"Okay, shoot."

"Have you gotten anywhere with Mrs. Clipper?"

"No, not much further than I was yesterday, but she just about admitted to being in Simon's cabin – nothing more."

"Did she admit taking the keys then?"

"No, but she must have talked to Simon or a member of crew after the costume party, because she mentioned not being interested in "that clown who got stark naked" – which meant that she had some contact with the engineer after the party."

"I know you want to talk more about this at lunch, but I would prefer if we talked about it over the phone…"

"Why? Do you think the walls have ears, as they say?"

"Let's just say that I would like to keep everything about Mrs. Clipper quiet for now."

"So you think there is actually someone other than our tigress involved with this drug trafficking?"

"Don't you?"

"Yes, as a matter of fact, the thought had crossed my mind. You see, I believe our Mrs. Clipper went to Simon's cabin, but when she got the keys, she gave them to someone else, and that someone else put the bags in the tanks for her."

"But then that means she's got an accomplice to do her dirty work, doesn't it?"

"Yes, and that's because your great-grandfather couldn't recognize her hand as the one who pushed Irene Walter over the railing. Furthermore, Irene would have recognized her before being pushed and would have probably fought with her, or even argued with her. And lastly, Mrs. Clipper would not have had the strength to push Irene the way our murderer did."

"All good assumptions, Gilbert," Alan said, "but what is this mystery guy up to right now, that's what I'd like to know."

"You and me both, Alan. And as far as we can tell, there were no prints left on the lid of the tank, or anywhere else, to make a positive ID at this point."

Alan reflected on what he had just heard for a moment before he went on to say, "Do you think anyone is in danger right now?"

The question surprised Gilbert a little. "Whom do you have in mind?" he asked.

"Well, let's just say that I have an over-imaginative granddad…"

"I'd say that runs in the family," Gilbert remarked jocularly.

"Well, maybe…. But anyway, he came up with a possible scenario whereby our Ms. Babette would be grabbed and ransomed for the drugs in your safe. How does that sit with you?"

"Not very well, Alan. And I must remind you the guy is a lone ranger against an army when it would come to Ms. Babette's safety. I think the captain himself, would stand in the front row to protect Babette."

Alan had to laugh at the picture he was quickly drawing in his mind's eye. "Yeah, I believe you're right, besides which, we're still at sea and there's no means of escape for that would-be abductor."

"Good point, Alan, but we need to be vigilant anyway – assuming your granddad is correct in his conjecture."

"Oh absolutely. By the way, I have to tell you that granddad is already camped out in her cabin and is not about to leave her side."

"That would be one for the record books if our culprit would attempt to lay a hand on Ms. Babette." Gilbert laughed in his turn.

While Babette was finishing her writing, and he was sure she was safe for the next while, Edmund decided to leave her cabin and make his way to the theater where he was sure to find Tiffany. As he expected, she was sitting at a small desk backstage, flicking a finger over her tablet. When she lifted her gaze and saw Alan's great-grandfather standing beside the table, she gasped.

"Good Gracious, Granddad, you do know how to scare a girl, don't you?"

He laughed. "I am terribly sorry, Tiffany, but saying, "BOO" is not in my repertoire, I'm afraid."

Tiffany shook her head and smiled up at him. "That's good, besides, I do prefer to see my ghosts in person, so to speak, rather than hear them." She paused. "So, what can I do for you?" She switched off the tablet.

Edmund stared at the disappearing picture, visibly intrigued. "I've seen a couple of people using these framed pictures; what do they do exactly?"

"Well"—Tiffany switched it on again—"come and see for yourself," she said.

Edmund moved and went to stand and look at the tablet from over her shoulder.

"You see, when I press the tablet screen here, the scene I'm working on for Babette appears."

Edmund couldn't believe his eyes. There, on that little screen was a perfect picture of Mrs. Laveau's boudoir. It looked as if he could step into the frame and be in the room. "That's extraordinary," he exclaimed, enthusiasm audible in his voice. "I have seen my great-grandson's nurse using one of these things to count the medicine bottles, but I didn't imagine it could do such a thing as painting a theater backdrop."

"Oh yes, Granddad. And that's the beauty of this 'little machine' – it can do all sorts of things, like getting the cast to move about and the lighting to be directed where it should be…" Tiffany went on to demonstrate the cartoon figures moving about Mrs. Laveau's boudoir.

Edmund was stunned, amazed and astonished all at once. "As I said, this is extraordinary." His eyes didn't leave the tablet, until Tiffany turned it off.

"But I'm sure you didn't come here to look at my tablet, did you?"

Shaking himself out of his stunned state, Edmund replied, "Hmm, no, no, of course not, my dear. I came to see you because I wanted to know where Ms. Babette usually stands when she directs her plays, or during the performance."

"Oh, I see. Well, she is here every day during rehearsal – backstage or sitting in one of the orchestra seats if she wants to visualize the scene or listen to the actors. But why do you ask?"

"Hmm, it's a bit complicated, my dear, but I think our beautiful playwright might be in grave danger…"

"How do you mean," Tiffany demanded with a shocked look.

"Let me tell you then," and Edmund went on explaining what he had overheard and the possible peril that the conversations could bring upon Babette.

CHAPTER NINETEEN

Lukewarm coffee and burnt toast

WHEN TIFFANY ARRIVED AT the upper deck café the next morning, she found Alan practically in tears from laughter.

"Wow! That must be a good one," she said, throwing a glance at the newspaper still folded in Alan's hand.

"That... surely... was," Alan replied, handing her the paper. "Have a read of this."

Already smiling, Tiffany began reading. Soon her smile turned into giggles as her eyes traveled down the page.

STELLA AWARDS:

It's time again for the annual 'Stella Awards'! For those unfamiliar with these awards, they are named after 81-year-old Stella Liebeck who spilled hot coffee on herself and successfully sued the McDonald's in New Mexico, where she purchased coffee. You remember, she took the lid off the coffee and put it between her knees while she was driving. Who would ever think one could get burned doing that, right? That's right; these are awards for the most outlandish lawsuits and verdicts in the U.S. You know, the kinds of cases that make you scratch your head.

SEVENTH PLACE
Kathleen Robertson of Austin, Texas was awarded $80,000 by a jury of her peers after breaking her ankle tripping over a toddler who was running inside a furniture store. The storeowners were

understandably surprised by the verdict, considering the running toddler was her own son.

SIXTH PLACE

Carl Truman, 19, of Los Angeles, California won $74,000 plus medical expenses when his neighbor ran over his hand with a Honda Accord. Truman apparently didn't notice there was someone at the wheel of the car when he was trying to steal his neighbor's hubcaps.

FIFTH PLACE

Terrence Dickson, of Bristol, Pennsylvania, who was leaving a house he had just burglarized by way of the garage. Unfortunately for Dickson, the automatic garage door opener malfunctioned and he could not get the garage door to open. Worse, he couldn't re-enter the house because the door connecting the garage to the house locked when Dickson pulled it shut. Forced to sit for eight, count 'em, EIGHT days and survive on a case of Pepsi and a large bag of dry dog food, he sued the homeowner's insurance company claiming undue mental Anguish. Amazingly, the jury said the insurance company must pay Dickson $500,000 for his anguish. We should all have this kind of anguish.

FOURTH PLACE

Jerry Williams, of Little Rock, Arkansas, garnered 4th Place in the Stella's when he was awarded $14,500 plus medical expenses after being bitten on the butt by his next door neighbor's beagle --even though the beagle was on a chain in its owner's fenced yard. Williams did not get as much as he asked for because the jury believed the beagle might have been provoked at the time of the butt bite because Williams had climbed over the fence into the yard and repeatedly shot the dog with a pellet gun.

THIRD PLACE
Amber Carson of Lancaster, Pennsylvania because a jury ordered a Philadelphia restaurant to pay her $113,500 after she slipped on a spilled soft drink and broke her tailbone. The reason the soft drink was on the floor; Ms. Carson had thrown it at her boyfriend 30 seconds earlier during an argument.

SECOND PLACE
Kara Walton, of Claymont, Delaware sued the owner of a nightclub in a nearby city because she fell from the bathroom window to the floor, knocking out her two front teeth. Even though Ms. Walton was trying to sneak through the ladies room window to avoid paying the $3.50 cover charge, the jury said the night club had to pay her $12,000.... oh, yeah, plus dental expenses. Go figure.

Ok. Here we go!!

FIRST PLACE
This year's runaway First Place Stella Award winner was: Mrs. Merv Grazinski, of Oklahoma City, Oklahoma, who purchased a new 32-foot Winnebago motor home. On her first trip home, from an OU football game, having driven on to the freeway, she set the cruise control at 70 mph and calmly left the driver's seat to go to the back of the Winnebago to make herself a sandwich. Not surprisingly, the motor home left the freeway, crashed and overturned. Also not surprisingly, Mrs. Grazinski sued Winnebago for not putting in the owner's manual that she couldn't actually leave the driver's seat while the cruise control was set. The Oklahoma jury awarded her, are you sitting down? $1,750,000 PLUS a new motor home. Winnebago actually changed their manuals as a result of this suit, just in case Mrs. Grazinski has any relatives who might also buy a motor home.

While Tiffany was continuing to read the article, Alan's attention was drawn to a gentleman who had called the waiter to his table – presumably to place his breakfast order. Reading from the menu the man said, "I'd like one under-cooked egg so that it's runny, and one over-cooked egg so that it's tough and hard to eat. I'd also like grilled bacon which is a bit on the cold side, burnt toast, butter straight from the freezer so that it's impossible to spread, and a pot of very weak, lukewarm coffee."

"That's a complicated order, sir," said the bewildered waiter. "It might be quite difficult."

The passenger raised his gaze to the waiter. "I frankly don't see where you would have any difficulty with this order, young man, because that's exactly what you brought me yesterday!"

Alan shook his head and grinned, and watched the young waiter leave the passenger snickering. He turned to Tiffany. "So, what do you think of our justice system?"

"Well, the Lady Justice wears a blindfold, doesn't she?" Tiffany replied, throwing Alan a devilish smile.

"Yeah, and I wish somehow that she would find someone to get that blindfold off her eyes sometimes."

"What's that about, Alan? Apart from laughing your head off at the article, you look and sound quite preoccupied. Are you worried about Babette?"

"Yes, Tiff, I am. But how do you know about that?" Alan asked just as he saw Alice approach their table.

"Oh, good morning, Alice – is there an emergency?" Tiffany asked, surprised to see Alan's nurse join them.

"Good morning to you too, Ms. Sylvan," Alice replied, taking a seat. "The doc invited me to join you, and here I am!"

"Okay then," Alan said, getting to his feet, "why don't we all go to the buffet and help ourselves?"

"Good idea," Alice said, "I'm starving."

Still wondering why Alan had invited Alice to have breakfast with them, Tiffany rose to her feet and followed them to the serving counters. The spread of every imaginable breakfast fare was quite a sight. From kippers to fruit, to calabashes of cereals, to eggs and crepes with strawberries, or yoghurt and baskets upon baskets of bread and rolls or croissants – one couldn't deny that the choice would be difficult.

"That is surely a far cry from toast and jam," Alice remarked, helping herself to a variety of fruits and cereal.

"Glad you could come," Alan remarked, choosing quite a few items to fill his plate that were not all low calorie in content.

Once they had returned to their table and had started eating, Tiffany couldn't help but ask Alan, "What's the occasion?"

"If you mean why I invited Alice to have breakfast, it's simply because I wanted the two of you to help me uncover the identity of our criminal."

Tiffany and Alice stopped eating and stared at the doc.

"How? I mean who?" Alice was the first to ask.

"Well, as you are aware, Alice, Ms. Walter died under mysterious circumstances. We don't know if she was pushed deliberately over the ship's railing or if her fall was the result of an accident. And now, we have discovered that Ms. Walter was trafficking drugs from Asia to the States, and some of these drugs have now been safely stacked in
Mr. Evans's safe."

"I'll be damned," Alice said, returning to eating her cereal, "but what do you want us to do – it's not like we're investigators or anything like that?"

"But there's something else that you might not be aware of either," Tiffany interposed, "Ms. Babette is now in danger…"

"You mean our famous playwright? That's a real shame. She's such a nice lady. But what would somebody want with Ms. Babette?"

"That's where I think you might be able to help, Alice," Alan replied.

"Me? How?"

"Let me explain something first though…" Alan then proceeded to explain what led to how he and Gilbert came to the conclusion that the trafficker might want to abduct Babette.

"Good grief!" Alice exclaimed, finishing her cereal. "How can I help – just say what I should be doing and I'll do it!"

"Okay, but it's not going to be simple and I don't want to put you in harm's way, so if you think you can't do it – no problem."

"Why don't you spell it out, Doc? Let's have it!"

"Alright. I'd like to move Babette to another suite and for you to take her place."

A silence fell among the three of them. Tiffany switched her gaze from Alice to Alan and back again. "But why Alice?" she asked. "That's a lot to ask…"

"Don't you worry about me, Ms. Sylvan. I've seen my share of combat in my time, and I'd make mince meat of any of these thugs."

"But what if someone menaces you with a gun – what will you do then?"

"That too, Ms. Sylvan, I'm an excellent marksman – or should I say "markswoman with various types or armaments.""

"What about me then?" Tiffany asked, turning her face to Alan. "What can I do? I am no marksman for sure."

"Once we've made the switch with Mr. Evans's assistance, I'd like you to show Alice what Ms. Babette does when she goes to the theater for rehearsals and transmit all of your tablet's files to Babette's computer…"

"That's what we do anyway," Tiffany interposed. "That's not a problem." She paused. "But what about Babette's wardrobe? Will she be willing to lend her clothes to Alice here?"

"Oh yes. I talked to her last night, and she's all set," Alan replied, returning his attention to Alice. "All you have to do is to be sitting in the orchestra seat and listen to the actors rehearse the play. Ms. Babette will actually see the same thing as you do, but on her computer screen. If there's anything that needs changing, or repeating, you'll have an earpiece through which Ms. Babette will tell you what to do."

"Sounds fine to me," Alice said, her head bobbing up and down. "And Mr. Evans will arrange all the communication devices, will he?"

"Absolutely. He's working on that this morning." Alan looked at the two women in turn. "Anything else?"

Alice asked, "Just one question, Doc."

"Sure, what is it?"

"What about Evelyn? Is she aware of what we're planning to do?"

"Not yet, Alice. But now that I have your approval, I'll let her know."

"And what about the shifts – who's going to fill in for me?"

"I'll get Evelyn to take the day shifts until we get to Madagascar in three days' time, and I'll take evenings and early mornings."

They finished eating in silence.

Alice seemed utterly pleased. In fact she displayed a radiant smile when she said, "You know, Doc, I only did one short tour in Afghanistan, but the training before that is what I enjoyed the most. And I am glad to be helping."

CHAPTER TWENTY

Cocaine wine?

BABETTE WAS ALL IN a flutter. She had accepted the plan to switch cabins. The one she was going to occupy was actually much nicer than her own – but moving wasn't on the top of her favorite "to do" lists. Edmund was there, watching her while she packed her clothes.

"You look a little perturbed, my dear," he remarked, "is something bothering you?"

"Perturbed? Perturbed you say?" Babette groaned in response. "No, I am not perturbed or even disturbed, Edmund, I am darn right furious!"

"Do you want me to leave?" he asked tentatively.

"Don't you dare move a muscle!" she ordered, folding another summer dress in her suitcase with less care than usual. "You're supposed to guard me against any attacker – so do your job!"

Edmund stood up – he had been sitting in the chair beside the bed in Babette's bedroom – and went to stand beside her. "Will you just calm down." She looked up at him, tears lining the rim of her eyes. "Think of the reasons why you're doing this, my dear. We want to catch a killer and I, for one, do not want to put you in harm's way."

"And I suppose this was all your idea, was it?"

"No, it wasn't entirely my idea, no. You see, Alan and Mr. Evans have no idea who we're dealing with. We don't know if Mrs. Clipper is an assassin or just a pawn in this horrid game. We don't know if the cloaked man was her accomplice, or if the two of them even know each other."

Babette paused before she said, "And I'm the bait that will assist you in finding out answers to your questions, is that it?"

Edmund shook his head. "No, Babette, you're not. Ms. Alice is – remember that. She is the one taking your place…"

"How could you hope for a nurse to fend off attackers the likes of the one that threw Ms. Walter over the railing?"

"Oh but she's much more than a regular nurse, my dear; she is a qualified military trained individual, I have been told."

"Really?" Babette said, resuming the folding of her clothes in her case. "I guess I'll just have to hope that the fine French clothes I've set aside for her are not damaged with bullet holes then, won't I?"

If Edmund could have turned Babette around to look at him, he would have done so. Her remark about the clothes was something he had never expected coming out of her mouth.

"Please, look at me," he asked.

She did.

"Do you realize how cold that statement was?"

She bent her head down to look at the suitcase. "I'm sorry, Edmund. It's not me. I'm not ready for any of this." She shook her head in dismay. "All I want to do is to be left in peace to write plays that can lift up the spirit of the sick, enlighten those feeling down, and use the Bible to help people come closer to the beauty of a spiritual world. Be it little children with leukemia in Seattle or multi-millionaire passengers on a ship; love and humor will always cure problems and lead people in the right direction." Unable to control the tears, she began crying in earnest.

That evening, Babette, with the help of her steward, moved her luggage to a larger suite, only two doors down from hers. Having recovered from her battle with the 'blues', she seemed quite happy with her new lodgings.

She even asked Alan when he came by to see if everything was okay, if she could stay in that cabin on a more permanent basis.

"I'm sure that won't be a problem, Babette. One move for this trip seems to have been enough for you, hasn't it?"

"Oh yes, Alan, more than enough I can assure you. I can't even begin to understand people who spend two days here, two days there, and have to pack, unpack and repack their luggage at every stop. And they call that a holiday. I sure wouldn't! Of course, I travel with more than a t-shirt and jeans. Don't I?"

"I hear you," Alan said smiling. "Have you had a chance to see if the communications are okay between you, Tiffany and Alice?"

"Not yet, and to tell you the truth, Alan, tonight, I'm going straight to bed. I've got a hard enough time dealing with these gadgets and computer things when I'm wide awake. I don't think I'll be good for anything technical of that sort tonight."

"That's fine, Babette – no pressure," Alan concluded, turning toward the door. And then as an afterthought, before leaving, he asked, "Have you seen Granddad yet this evening?"

"Yes. Just briefly mind you." She paused. "I think he said he wanted to see you before taking up his post in the living room for the night."

Alan smiled. "Is he howling at the moon during the night by any chance?" he asked, a smirk drawing across his lips.

"Oh, do go away, will you?" Babette retorted, all smiles now. "I'll let you know if he does," she added, pushing him out the door, tittering.

Walking toward the elevators, Alan was still smiling. *Those two are definitely a pair made in Heaven,* he thought. A few minutes later he opened his office door to find his great-grandfather waiting for him.

"Ah, you've finally decided to return to your post, have you?" Edmund's reproach was jocular, judging by the grin on his face.

"Yeah, and Babette is ready to retire for the night…"

"Yes, yes, of course she is. Poor woman. This whole thing is much too hard on her," Edmund remarked, taking a seat across from Alan.

"What can I do for you, Granddad?"

"Just a little bit of information is what I'm after, son."

"Oh, and what's that?"

"I know that everyone described these packets of cocaine as illegal drugs, but are you or Mr. Evans sure of your facts?"

"Why, wasn't cocaine illegal in your days?"

"No, not entirely."

Alan stared at his grandparent. He recollected his university professor in the History of Medicine, a Dr. 'von...' something. He was such a captivating educator. Alan and the other students learned a great deal about the Systems Theory, the belief that the body had various 'Humors' that regulated what we did, etc. But specifics of the use of cocaine were not high on his list of interests.

"What was their use as drugs back then?" he asked.

"Oh lots!" Edmund replied and then paused. "Let me give you a few examples of some of the popular medicines of the day, including cocaine containing potions."

Alan waited – this was sure to retain his interest.

"Alright, here is one.... *Bayer's Heroin*. I didn't have a chance to prescribe it myself since it came on the market well after I retired. But it was advertised, as I recall, as a strong non-addictive substitute for morphine."

"And was it a potion of some sort?" Alan asked.

"Yes. Actually I've been told that some practitioners would prescribe it for children who suffered from hacking coughs."

"Really? Amazing!"

"Yes, isn't it?" Edmund said matter-of-factly.

"Anything with cocaine itself?"

"Oh yes. In fact there was a plethora of medicines that contained varied amounts of cocaine. We even had some medicinal wines fermented with cocaine."

"Do you recall any of them?" Alan asked, trying not to laugh in the face of his very serious granddad at the thought of modern day doctors prescribing wine fermented with cocaine! Loss of license came to mind very quickly.

"Well, I can't readily recall all of them, but two of them were certainly hitting the markets in a big way. The one was the Mariani wine, which was really famous at the time, because Pope Leo XIII used it and the Vatican even awarded its Gold Medal to Angelo Mariani, the producer." Edmund paused and lifted his gaze to the ceiling. "It was suggested that you should take a full glass with or after every meal. Children should only take half a glass. I must say it was quite effective medicine – no depression among the patients I prescribed it to, I am happy to report."

Alan had no doubt of it; they were all high as kites. "What about the second wine you mentioned, what was it prescribed for?"

"That one was Metcalf's Coca Wine. Everybody used to say that it would make you happy and it would also work as a medicinal treatment."

"Any others?" Alan's curiosity was mounting.

Edmund nodded. "C.F. Boehringer & Soehne in Germany were proud of being the biggest producers in the world of products containing Quinine and Cocaine. Back then we also used opium to treat asthma: It had 40% alcohol plus 3 grams of opium per dose. It didn't cure you... but your respiratory tract was completely relaxed and you didn't care about the carbon residue coming from the smoke stack of the ship," Edmund remarked, the smile returning. "The cocaine tablets, as I recall, came much later. But we had cocaine drops for toothaches. Very popular for children in 1885 and even opium for newborns..."

Alan looked at his granddad open-mouth. He wasn't sure he wasn't joking. "...I'm sure this would make them sleep well. Not only the Opium, but also the 46% alcohol."

Edmund returned his gaze to Alan and chuckled. "I can see that you think I might be joking, son. But I can assure you, I'm not. You see everything revolved around what we learned along the way. It was a 'trial and error' type of medicine that we practiced most of the time. We took a stab in the dark more often than not, and were often right. We did not have to have the controlled studies you mentioned to your nurse one day. The government did not look over your shoulder all the time. We did not have malpractice suits. Our human rights' laws meant laws to help people, not cripple them. And when I see the restrictions that you have, I wish I could return to my medical room aboard *The Delmas*, and treat those sick bastards with some proper medicine."

There was a tone laced with some sorrow in Edmund's voice. "Anyway, this was the reason for my asking if the cocaine our engineer found in the tanks was, in fact, illegal."

"Well, Granddad, all I can tell you is that now, we don't use any heroin or cocaine in our regular medicine. Morphine is given to patients who have undergone serious operative procedures, and derivatives of cocaine are used in the fabrication of codeine tablets – that's another strong painkiller. Many studies that we have done in recent years have shown that cocaine, heroin, and codeine are very addictive. Therefore we try not to give our patients these medications unless there is an absolute need for it. We have other meds with similar pain relief and without the addictive qualities. NSAIDS for example."

The night had arrived, and with it, a silence that Alan enjoyed. He knew he usually wouldn't be disturbed for the few hours that it would take him to finish his reports and, as far as he knew, everyone was asleep. But he was wrong – someone was awake and knocking at the medical center's door.

He frowned, shook his head and went to answer the insistent rapping.

"Hi, Doc, may I come in?" Harold asked when Alan had opened the door wide for him. Harold Salter was the Second Officer aboard *The Baroness.* In his forties, he was a jovial fellow and very quiet generally. You couldn't fault his conduct even if you tried.

"What's the matter, Mr. Salter?" Alan asked, directing the man toward his office. "Are you sick?"

"Oh no, Doc. I'm well enough, but I've put my brain through the grinder lately and since I saw the light on, I thought you might have a few minutes to talk."

"By all means. How can I help?" Alan reclined in his seat, ready to listen to the troubled fellow officer.

"It started out innocently enough," he began. "I started to think at parties now and then – just to loosen up and be a part of the crowd. Inevitably, though, one thought led to another, and soon I was more than just a social thinker. I began to think alone – "to relax," I told myself – but I knew it wasn't true. Thinking became more and more important to me, and finally I was thinking all the time.

"That was when things began to sour at home. One evening I turned off the TV in our cabin and asked my wife, who was visiting for two weeks, about the meaning of life. She spent that night at another crewmember's cabin. I began to think on the job. I knew that thinking and employment don't mix, but I couldn't help myself.

"I began to avoid friends at lunchtime in the mess so I could read Thoreau, Muir, Confucius and Kafka. I would return to the office dizzied and confused, asking, "What is it exactly we are doing here?"

"One day the Captain called me in. He said, "Listen, I like you, and it hurts me to say this, but your thinking has become a real problem. If you don't stop thinking on the job, you'll have to find another job."

"This gave me a lot to think about. I went back to my cabin early after my conversation with the captain. "Honey," I confessed, "I've been thinking..."

"I know you've been thinking," she said, "and I want a divorce!"

"But, Honey, surely it's not that serious..."

"It is serious," she said, lower lip aquiver.

"You think as much as college professors and college professors don't make any money, so if you keep on thinking, we won't have any money!"

"That's a faulty syllogism," I said impatiently.

"She exploded in tears of rage and frustration, but I was in no mood to deal with the emotional drama. "I'm going to the library," I snarled as I stomped out the door.

"I headed for the crew library, in the mood for some John Locke. I roared down the hall and ran up to the big glass doors. They didn't open. The library was closed. To this day, I believe that a Higher Power was looking out for me that night. Leaning on the unfeeling glass, whimpering for Emerson, a poster caught my eye. "Friend, is heavy thinking ruining your life?" it asked.

"You probably recognize that line. It comes from the standard Thinkers Anonymous poster. This is why I am what I am today: a recovering thinker.

"When I am home, I never miss a TA meeting. At each meeting we watch a non-educational video; the week before we left San Fran, it was "Porky's." Then we share experiences about how we avoided thinking since the last meeting.

"I still have my wife, job on the ship, and things are a lot better. Life just seemed easier, somehow, as soon as I stopped thinking. I think the road to recovery is nearly complete for me.

"Today I took the final step...I joined a political Party."

Alan didn't know if he wanted to laugh or console the guy, but laugh he did. "You're pulling my leg, aren't you, Harold?"

The Second Officer nodded and cracked up laughing. "I thought you might enjoy a little diversion. See, I was talking to Gilbert at dinner tonight and he told me a bit about what you guys are doing to get that trafficker off our ship, and I thought since you're camping out here for the night, I'd provide the entertainment." Harold got up.

Getting to his feet too, Alan replied, "Thanks, Harold – I sure appreciated that. It's food for thought, indeed," he quipped.

CHAPTER TWENTY-ONE

Buttered bread

LIZZY CLIPPER WAS FAR from happy; she was down right worried. She had known this deal was rotten since day one. When she had met Irene Walter, months ago now, her 'little voice' had told her to be leery of the woman. And once again her instincts had proven right. Lizzy had been tempted to come on this cruise because of that darn separation – she needed to get away from the incessant phone calls. If it wasn't the lawyers, it was her mother, her sister, and of course her ex. He wanted back in, but Lizzy would have none of it. Finding him in the arms of another woman had been enough to deter her from entertaining any thought of getting back together with the man.

And at first, the cruise seemed to be the perfect way to escape the troublesome situation on the home front. Once they had left the coast, what should have been a dream holiday turned into a nightmare. Irene kept to herself most of the time. She only let on that she was carrying some packages for a friend of hers that she was supposed to meet on board. But this so-called 'friend' seemed to be invisible. In fact, he never showed up until one night, after Irene had fallen to her death. It was then that this illusive guy came to Lizzy's room.

"I'm sorry to disturb you, Mrs. Clipper, but I wonder if I could have a word?" he had asked when she had opened the door to this nondescript, average everything man. Truth be told, if Lizzy was ever asked to describe him, she would have a hard time doing so. He had brown hair, brown eyes and a face that could have been anyone's face. Nothing remarkable about him, except perhaps for his voice. Lizzy remembered the grating tone, the subdued speech – almost as if the guy was speaking into a microphone – hard to describe really.

And when she had let him in, he had simply sat down, without being asked, and had begun to recount this fantastic story about having to hide some packages somewhere on the ship. Then he asked if Lizzy could help him do just that.

"Well, I truly don't know if I should, sir," she had replied. "Are you the friend Irene was supposed to meet?"

"Yes, Mrs. Clipper, but given the circumstances of her unexpected demise, I am surely at a loss to know where I could hide the packages she was going to entrust into my care…"

"So, you did meet her then?"

"Oh no, I only saw her going to the deck and when I was about to go to her, I saw someone push her."

"And where were the packages then? Did you find them?"

"Oh yes. I found them in her cabin, but now, I don't want to keep them with me…"

"But what's that got to do with me?" Lizzy had asked, getting a little leery about this whole story and where the man was going with it.

"Plenty, Mrs. Clipper." The man had smiled. "You see, I need you to get the keys to the septic tanks…"

"Before you go any further, sir, let me ask you, why me? Why should I get involved?"

"Because, Mrs. Clipper, you're an accessory to a murder, and I could make life very difficult for you, if you didn't cooperate."

And that was that. Lizzy, afraid of being implicated in a murder case that was sure to diminish her chance to get her hands on her ex-husband's money, had accepted to play ball with the "brown man".

Now, even after she had done what the "brown man" had asked, she had ended up being questioned regarding her involvement in getting the keys from that idiot, Simon Albertson. How could she get out of this stupid situation unscathed, was the question. The only possible and reasonable answer was to go back to Mr. Evans and explain what really happened. But then what would the "brown man" do? Would he kill her too? Besides, how will he get his packages back now that they are in Mr. Evans's safe?

"Or maybe he doesn't want them back?" Lizzy said aloud. "Maybe that's where he wanted them in the first place."

She shrugged – out of answers and out of courage. She would have to resign herself to her fate and see what happened.

Yet, something told her, that wasn't the right course of action, if she wanted to find herself with some buttered bread at the end of this trip.

The next morning Babette was ready to tackle the first day of rehearsal of her play, sitting in front of her computer, instead of being comfortably ensconced in one of the orchestra chairs in front of the stage. Alice, who had no idea of what she would be asked to do, had decided to pay a visit to the playwright before the rehearsal started.

Seeing that Babette was quite distracted and unable to maneuver the computer images the way she wanted, Alice decided to give her a little diversion of her own at the same time giving her some computer tips.

She said, "You know, Ms. Babette, I'm really glad for this opportunity..."

"Well, that makes one of us," Babette replied dryly. Then realizing how aggravating that sounded, she shook her head, and added, "I'm sorry, Alice, but this is so unnerving for me. It's not like I'm the spring chicken everyone seems to think I am. I feel like I'm in high school facing a difficult exam. We did not have computers, tablets, and the like in our schools!"

Unexpectedly, Alice burst out laughing.

Babette stared. "I don't think that's funny."

"Oh no-no, Ms. Babette. I quite understand how you feel, but what you said reminded me of a dental visit I made a short while ago..."

"Now, that's better, I always like to hear a good story. I hope it has nothing to do with computers, though," Babette said, turning to the nurse, who was now dressed in one of her own dresses and shawl.

"No, nothing like that. Have you ever been guilty of looking at others your own age and thinking, surely I can't look that old?"

"Sometimes, yes," Babette replied.

"Well... you'll love this." Alice paused. "I was sitting in the waiting room for my first appointment with a new dentist. I noticed his DDS diploma on the wall, which bore his full name. Suddenly, I remembered a tall, handsome, dark-haired boy with the same name who had been in my high school class some 30-odd years ago. Could he be the same guy that I had a secret crush on, way back then, I asked myself. Well, upon seeing him, however, I quickly discarded any such thought. This balding, pot bellied, gray-haired man with a deeply lined face was way too old to have been my classmate.

"After he examined my teeth, I asked him if he had attended Morgan Park high school.

""Yes. Yes, I did. I'm a *Mustang*," he gleamed with pride.

"When did you graduate?" I asked.

"He answered, "In 1975. Why do you ask?"

"You were in my class!" I exclaimed.

"He looked at me closely.

"Then, that ugly, old, bald, wrinkled-faced, fat-assed, gray-haired, decrepit, son-of-a-bitch asked me, "What subject did you teach...?"

Babette's laughter resonated so loudly throughout the cabin that Edmund came out of the bedroom to see what was happening. He smiled when he saw the two women laughing their hearts out.

And so the ice was broken, so to speak. Babette returned to maneuvering the computer images with much more ease and Alice was now able to follow her directives without her initial qualms troubling her.

An hour later Alice, a scarf around her head and sunglasses on the bridge of her nose, made her way to the theater to attend the rehearsal while listening to Babette's instructions through her earpiece. When she crossed the foyer, she noticed a passenger looking at the framed posters of some of Babette's previous plays displayed along the far wall. She paid him no mind until he came to sit two rows behind her in the theater. Not wanting to attract attention by questioning this unknown intruder, she spoke softly once she had switched on the earpiece's connection, "Ms. Babette, please contact Mr. Evans. There's a man sitting behind me."

"Right away, dear," she heard Babette reply before being

disconnected for a minute or so.

It didn't take five minutes for Gilbert and two of his men to burst through the doors of the theater and come to stand beside the man. "I will have to ask you to leave, sir," Gilbert said quietly, "this is a private rehearsal…"

"Mr. Gilbert Evans, isn't it?" the man interrupted, getting to his feet, "Just the man I wanted to see." He smiled amicably. "Let me save you the trouble…"

"Please, follow us, sir," Gilbert said, "We can talk about this outside," not wanting to question the guy before they left the theater.

Once they were in the foyer, Gilbert went on, "May I ask who you are, and how do you know my name?"

"Well, Mr. Evans, I make it my business to know everything there is to know about the people I am due to contact." He paused and smiled at the three puzzled faces looking at him. "Yes. My name is Edward Chulbridge – MI5."

"May I see some ID, Mr. Chulbridge?"

"By all means, my dear man," he replied, taking his ID wallet out of his breast pocket and brandishing it in front of Gilbert's eyes. "As you can see, I am an accredited agent of Her Majesty, and here on a particular mission, which might require your assistance…"

With raised eyebrows, Gilbert cut-in firmly, "That may be so, Agent Chulbridge, but I would appreciate you contacting me in my office before I find you gallivanting aboard our ship in places where you're not wanted."

"Alright, alright, mate. Let's go to your office then and I'll explain."

As the four men were walking down toward Gilbert's office, Lizzy was coming toward them from the other direction.

She stopped for a fraction of a second and then hollered, "That's him! That's the guy who forced me…"

Chulbridge smiled, while Gilbert grabbed Lizzy's accusing finger and brought it down, asking, "Please, Mrs. Clipper, let's go to my office and you can then tell me *quietly* what this is all about."

Lizzy nodded, still staring at the "brown man".

"Alright then," Gilbert began when he, Chulbridge and Lizzy had taken a seat, "why don't you go ahead and tell me what this gentleman is to you, Mrs. Clipper."

"Well, that's why I wanted to see you, Mr. Evans. You've been accusing me of putting Irene's packages inside the septic tank – but I didn't do it!"

"So what did you do?" Gilbert asked.

"I did what this man"— she pointed to Chulbridge —"told me to do. He said he found the packages in Irene's cabin after she'd been killed. He wanted me to get the keys from Simon for him. After that, I don't know what happened. And that's the truth!" She nodded vigorously under Chulbridge's smiling gaze.

"And you think that's funny?" Gilbert asked the MI5 agent.

"Well, it's got a humorous side to it, you must admit?"

"No, Agent Chulbridge, I don't see the humorous side of it, as you say – not at all, in fact."

"And you accusing me of murdering Irene is not funny either," Lizzy stated in a huff, addressing Gilbert.

"I've never accused you of murdering your friend, Mrs. Clipper; I simply mentioned that we were considering the possibility of you taking over her duties as a "PR"."

"There you go again with that stupid PR business. I don't even know what a PR really does. So, I'd appreciate if you would retract your inference and start questioning this guy here"—she pointed to the MI5 agent again—"and ask him what HE knows about this horrid business."

"I'll do that, Mrs. Clipper – not to worry – and yes, I apologize for mentioning your participation in a proposed trafficking ring. Yet, you have stolen – I'm sorry, borrowed – the keys to the sanitation room from Mr. Albertson, didn't you?"

"Yes, but I only did it because he told me to do it?"

"Oh I see, and if someone tells you to do something, you always do it, no matter what it is, do you?"

"Of course I don't! But he told me that he could make trouble for me as an accessory to Irene's murder." She turned her face to Chulbridge. "That's what you said, didn't you?"

The agent still had his arms crossed over his chest. He looked at Lizzy and started laughing. "Yes, Mrs. Clipper, I did. And I'm grateful for what you did actually. You've saved me the trouble…"

"Alright, Agent Chulbridge, enough with the play-acting," Gilbert said, and turning his head to Lizzy again, he added, "Thank you, Mrs. Clipper, for your cooperation, but now, you'll have to excuse us, I need to clear this matter up. You can be sure we won't be bothering you any further, unless you remember anything else that could help us close this case."

Lizzy got to her feet. "Thanks for nothing, Mr. Evans. I just hope that you or your staff won't be coming around to my cabin anymore – I only want to finish this cruise in peace!" And with these words, she walked out.

CHAPTER TWENTY-TWO

Call me Chubb

THE WHOLE INTERVIEW seemed to have amused Agent Chulbridge to no end. He was still grinning when Gilbert said, "Okay, Agent Chulbridge…"

"Please call me "Chubb", everybody does," the MI5 agent cut-in.

"Okay, Chubb, I'm glad you find this whole thing funny, but I don't." Gilbert paused, riveting his gaze on the man. "You see, I've got the powers-that-be on my back to clear this up. Now you come out of the shadows having forced our Mrs. Clipper to 'borrow' Albertson's keys to open the septic tanks in order to stash Irene Walter's cocaine in there. You knew full well they'd be discovered and brought to me. Could you at least tell me why you did that?"

"Alright, Mr. Evans, I can appreciate your concern, but there's really nothing to it…"

"Nothing to it? I beg your pardon, Chubb, but I can't set your actions aside when I have a possible murder to solve. So, what's your involvement in this affair?"

"Let's just say that Ms. Walter had been working undercover for us for a few months now and the cocaine was her latest haul. She followed her contacts through Asia for several weeks and foiled a few deals – not very smart these Asian dealers if you ask me. Then it appears that her "Asian boss" assigned her to take this cruise and collect the cocaine in Papua. The stash, which you've got in your safe now, was to be brought down to Madagascar to some unknown other contact."

"I see," Gilbert said, "and someone interrupted her trip by pushing her over the railing, is that it?"

Chubb nodded.

"Okay, that part I understand, but why this elaborate act of involving Mrs. Clipper in this affair and forcing her into borrowing keys…"

"That was just a test to see if the woman was really involved with the gang Irene was following, or if she was just the "friend" who happened to come along for the ride."

"But you could have come to me and avoid all this – wouldn't it have been simpler and much more professional?"

"Not really, Mr. Evans. You see, you still have a murderer to catch, and I still have a ringleader to rope in. If I let you know what was going on and did not involve Mrs. Clipper, the "boss" in San Fran might have "smelled a rat", as you say in the States, and Irene's cover, even in death, would have been blown."

"But isn't it the reason for which she's been murdered – her cover being blown I mean?"

Chubb shook his head. "I don't think so. By my way of thinking, someone – probably a Malagasy – is interested in carving himself a piece of the pie. This bloke wanted the cocaine to take to Antsiranana and perhaps open shop for himself. Madagascar is quite a ways out from San Fran and our "boss" may not have that long an arm to reach across oceans and continents."

"Okay, I'll buy that," Gilbert said, feeling a little more at ease with this Chubb character. He seemed to display all the phlegmatic characteristics of the typical Englishman. The chief hoped he was a little more adept when it came to catching criminals. "So, if we find our murderer, we'll find your person of interest, is that what you're thinking?"

"Precisely. I think we should join forces and, if possible, apprehend our perpetrator before we reach Antsiranana."

"That's a tall order, and you know it," Gilbert said, reclining into the back of his chair and starting to play with his pencil.

Chubb chuckled again under Gilbert's surprised gaze. *Maybe it's some sort of nervous tic,* he thought. "I'm sorry, Mr. Evans, but I can't help but think of the many "tall orders" your Doctor Mayhew has been able to fill in his career." Gilbert's surprise melted into a frown. "You see, your good doctor has been involved in quite a few international cases in the past few years, and MI5 as well as Interpol are well aware of his past good deeds. He's quite famous in our circles you might say, even though he is not a paid agent."

"And what would you expect him to do to fill this particular "tall order" then?" Gilbert asked, still puzzled.

"Oh I don't expect anything from the doctor at this point; you see, he's already organized a scheme to protect your playwright, which is exactly what needed to be done, and now I suspect he's planning his next move to uncover the identity of our cloaked man in spite of what us professional sleuths do."

"How did you know about him?"

"Observation, Mr. Evans, is part of my trade, and since I was there when Ms. Walter was pushed overboard, I saw the cloaked fellow."

"You didn't happen to see his face by any chance, since "observation" is your trade, did you?"

Chubb guffawed. "Don't give credit where it's not due, Mr. Evans. And no, I did not see the person's face, unfortunately."

And Agent Chulbridge was right. Now that Babette was 'covered' as one might say; Alan was trying to devise a plan by which the cloaked man would show his face or, at least, his hand – with the signet ring. The costume party had been a great idea on Tiffany's part, but the alleged culprit had not showed up in a cloak. Now Alan wondered, for the umpteenth time, how he was going to draw him out.

Truly out of ideas, and looking down at the reports that littered his desk, Alan decided to make his way to the bar and have some juice. Maybe a change of atmosphere would focus some of his thoughts out of the confusion.

Since the place wasn't too crowded – it was still early – he thought he would have a chat with Eric, the bartender. There was a chance, how ever slim, that Eric could have observed a hand with a signet ring grabbing a drink.

"What will it be, Doc?" Eric asked as Alan sat down on one of the stools.

"Just an orange juice, Eric, thanks," Alan replied, looking at the alluring woman sitting two stools away from him. She was nursing what looked like a martini and seemed lost in thought. Alan, knowing the feeling, returned his attention to Eric. When he deposited a tall glass of juice in front of him, Alan asked, "Tell me something, Eric, recently have you noticed anyone wearing a signet ring?" Seeing Eric's quizzical face, Alan smiled. "I know, it's a bit of a strange query, but a passenger left his ring in our washroom and since I wasn't there, I can't place the man. Even Evelyn can't remember who it could be. As you know, we have had a bit of a rush of passengers with gastroenteritis lately," Alan lied.

"And you thought since people grab drinks around here that I would have noticed it, is that it?"

"Something like that, yes."

"Well, sorry to disappoint you, Doc, but I haven't seen anyone – a man I gather from your description – wearing any signet ring, no."

"Okay then, it was just a thought," Alan said, drinking a bit of juice.

As he was about to look around at the men sitting at the tables behind him, a fellow came to sit beside the gorgeous woman sipping her martini.

Smiling at her, he said, "May I sit here – or is the seat taken?"

"You can sit all you want," she replied curtly to his undoubted question, "but you're wasting your time. I'm only interested in women."

Not taking 'no' for an answer, the man pressed on, "Oh, come on, I bet I can change your mind, a good looking guy like me…"

Alan smiled and wondered where this conversation was going to end. He drank his juice while he listened. After ten minutes of the bloke pestering the young woman, it was obvious she had had enough.

"Okay," she said, "I'll sleep with you if you can do anything for me that my vibrator can't!"

"Okay, barman, get this lady another drink," he said. "Let's see your vibrator do that?"

Shrugging, and dismissing the annoying fellow with a wave of the one hand, the lady grabbed her drink with her other hand and stood up. "Sorry, but not tonight, dear," she told him, walking toward a nearby table.

Alan stared into space – the space the hand around the stem glass had occupied seconds ago – like a stunned deer in the headlights. The woman wore a signet ring!

When he recovered from the slight shock – he couldn't be sure it was the same ring or the hand his granddad had seen – he finished his juice, thanked Eric and made his way out of the bar, heading directly for Babette's new abode.

Surprised to find the door opened, he walked in and looked around. No one was there. Panic-stricken, he rushed to the bedroom, rapped his knuckles on the bathroom door and then realized that his friend was nowhere in the cabin. He stood in the middle of the living room wondering what happened to her. He then turned to the computer, put the headset on and tried to log in. Of course, the system was password protected. He swore under his breath.

Where did she go? Could she have been abducted after all? Such thoughts were roaming his mind as Alan pulled his phone out of his pocket and called Tiffany. It rang a couple of times and went to voice-mail.

"Where the hell is everyone?" Alan yelled, still standing in the middle of the empty suite.

"You called?" he suddenly heard his granddad say from behind him.

"Why did you leave the door wide open?" was Alan's first question, turning around to face him. "Anyone could have come in here…"

"And you're wondering where our friend has gone in such a hurry, aren't you?"

"You could say that, yes. So, what's the answer?"

"Let's just say, we're tempting the devil," Edmund answered, grinning.

"What does that mean?" Alan frowned. "Do you mean to tell me, you want someone to come in here, the same way as I did and catch the culprit in the act?"

"You summed it up pretty well, son. And, yes, that's the general intention."

"And did anyone take the bait yet?"

"No one, except you, of course."

"Okay, but where is Babette now?"

"Backstage talking to the actors; something she couldn't do with these gadgets," Edmund replied, pointing to the computer.

"Fine then," Alan said, suddenly impatient. "But I came here to find you actually..."

"You did? And why would that be?"

"Because I found 'the' signet ring – at least I think I did."

"And you want me to identify it and the hand wearing it, right?"

"Right, Granddad, except the hand belongs to a woman..."

"I don't think it was the hand of a woman that I saw that night, son..."

"I know, I know, but just humor me, and come with me, will you?"

"Alright then, show the way young man, and I'll follow."

When Alan arrived at the bar, his gaze honed in on the table where the lady had taken a seat after her bothersome conversation with the fellow still sitting on the same stool. He shook his head, swung on his heels and walked toward Eric who was clearing some of the tables at the back of the establishment.

"Oh, hi, Doc, forgotten something?" Eric asked, wiping the table nearest to him with a sponge cloth.

"No, not really, but I wonder if you could help me..."

"If it's about the man "without" the signet ring, I still can't recall..."

"No, it's not that, and I'm sorry to bother you again, but could you tell me if you know the name of the lady who was sitting at the bar when I was here earlier today?"

"Oh, yes, of course. That's Miss Pilkington. She comes here every other day and always orders the same thing: vodka martini. Why?"

"Nothing in particular, it's just that she reminded me of a friend of mine back in San Fran," Alan replied, "But Pilkington was not my friend's name."

Putting his cloth on the tray, Eric smiled. "You should watch your step, Doc. Don't you let Ms. Sylvan catch you running after another woman – could be dangerous to your health."

Following Eric to the bar, Alan went on asking, "Do you know if she was waiting for someone?"

Eric dropped his tray carefully under the counter and fixed his gaze on Alan. "May I ask what this is about, Doc? You're not usually asking all these kinds of questions – can I help?"

"It's just curiosity, Eric. I'm trying to find someone and I'm having a hard time of it – that's all."

"Is the person sick or something?"

"That I'm not at liberty to tell you, but if you see Miss Pilkington again, could you ask her to swing by the medical center when she has a chance?"

"Sure will, Doc. And don't worry, in the meantime if anyone is asking after that ring, I'll send the fellow to the lost and found, okay?"

"Yes, Eric, you do that," Alan concluded. "And thanks," he added, as he walked out of the bar.

CHAPTER TWENTY-THREE

Miss Pilkington

AS SOON AS ALAN and Edmund went back to the medical center, and after checking that Evelyn had left for the day, Edmund said, "Can you find out where she's located on the ship?"

"Sure," Alan replied, sitting at his desk and logging in onto the passenger locator.

Edmund watched him. He was still amazed. These small screens, without visible way to connect to each other, which transmitted all sorts of information across untold distance, were a wonder to him.

A few seconds later, Alan raised his eyes to his granddad. "There she is – Miss Sarah Pilkington," he said. "She's got an inside cabin on the fourth deck and boarded in Papua."

"Didn't I hear you say that's the new name for Irian Jaya?"

"Yeah, that's the place. It seems that all roads do not lead to Rome in this case but to Papua – too much of a coincidence, wouldn't you say?"

Edmund guffawed. "And you don't like coincidences, do you, son?"

"Not at all, Granddad, especially when they involve women and cocaine. To my way of thinking the two don't mix."

Then switching to his email account distractedly, he saw a notice from one of the drug companies that announced that Viagra will soon be available in liquid form, and will be marketed by Pepsi Cola as a power beverage suitable for use as a mixer. The friend who sent it added a note to the forwarded email saying, "It will now be possible for a man to literally pour himself a *stiff one*. Obviously we can no longer call this a *soft drink*, and it gives new meaning to the names of *"cocktails"*, *"highballs"* and just a good old-fashioned *"stiff drink"*. Pepsi will market the new concoction by the name of: MOUNT & DO. Thought for the day: There is more money being spent on breast implants and Viagra today than on Alzheimer's research. This means that by 2040, there should be a large elderly population with perky boobs and huge erections and absolutely no recollection of what to do with them."

Alan erupted in loud laughter under his granddad's curious gaze. "What have you seen?" he asked.

"Just hold on, I'll print it for you," Alan replied, pressing the 'print' digit on his keyboard. Within seconds he put the sheet of paper on the side of the desk where his granddad could read it.

Edmund smiled. "I guess this Viagra thing has something to do with male organs, has it?"

"I'm sorry, Granddad, I should have explained. You see, in this century men are so busy trying to be more powerful than the next man, they want to use these drugs to enhance their physical prowess with women."

And what's this "Pepsi Cola" they're referring to?" Edmund asked, pointing to the name on the sheet. "Is that another pharmaceutical company?"

Alan had a hard time keeping a straight face. "No, Granddad, that's what we call a "soft drink" company. They mix all sorts of chemicals and add sugar to their concoction and then sell it in cans and bottles."

"But aren't these chemicals dangerous to one's health?"

"Long term, yes, absolutely; responsible parents these days try to have their kids drink more natural juices rather than these so-called "soft-drinks"."

"So they mix these potions for children, too, do they?"

"Well, let's say that's their principal market, but some adults are really addicted to the taste also. It is as addictive as cocaine-in a different way. Pepsi Colas' predecessor, Coca-Cola actually did have cocaine in it originally."

Edmund fell silent for a moment, and then said, "What about our Miss Pilkington, are we going to pay her a visit?"

"Why don't we?" Alan replied, logging out of the program and getting to his feet. "She's in cabin 405. Just one deck above us."

Since Edmund was invisible to everyone, except to the few people who had touched his photograph, as they reached the cabin in question, Alan asked, "Would you mind taking a tour of her suite before I knock?"

Edmund smiled and disappeared through the door. Alan didn't hear anything for the couple of minutes his granddad was inside the cabin and wondered if he had found her in various states of undress and was watching the show incognito. Leaning his back against the wall, he crossed his arms over his chest and waited. Finally his granddad reappeared, a broad smile on his lips.

"She or I should say "he" is in there alright…"

"What do you mean "he"," Alan cut-in, staring at his great-grandparent.

"Just as I said, son. "He" was getting ready for bed and I watched the man shedding the underwear, some malleable substance for breasts and all those things that he used to appear as a female when you observed 'her' in the bar."

"He's a transvestite or cross dresser then," Alan concluded.

"If you mean a man who dresses as a woman, I think you're right."

"That's bizarre," Alan remarked, frowning.

"Why is that bizarre, son? There have been these sorts of *inadaptable* humans throughout the ages, even a few kings and other nobles – nothing new or extraordinary with this particular chap."

"I would suggest that you don't refer to these people as "inadaptable" in mixed company, Granddad; that's what we call being politically incorrect."

"I see," Edmund said reflectively. "But then why did you say it was 'bizarre'?"

"Sorry, I should have said that I can't but wonder why I didn't catch on to that before. We doctors pride ourselves in being very observant."

"But you only saw "the woman" in the dim light of the bar, so no wonder you couldn't…"

"No, Granddad. You see, when she stepped off the bar stool and walked to the table, I watched her, and her calves looked like those of a woman, I could swear to it."

"Well, all I could say is that the person in that cabin is definitely a man – his genitals are all there and accounted for!"

Alan had to chuckle quietly.

"And you say Miss Pilkington is in bed now?"

"Yes... or should be by now."

"What about the hand with the signet ring, was it the one you saw?"

"I can't be sure, son."

Alan stared. "What do you mean? You said you saw the hand..."

"I know what I said, but I can't be sure because he took the ring off and it was on the dresser when I went through the room. I believe it's the same ring, yes. Yet, when I looked at both hands, the white band of skin where he usually wears the ring was on the left hand – not the right one."

"And you're sure it was a right hand that you saw wear the ring?"

"Yes, son. I'm definite on that score."

"And that's another thing that bothers me – when I observed his hands handling the glass, they were those of a woman not those of a man."

"Alright then; what's your conclusion?" Edmund asked, as the two men were walking back to the elevators.

"She was a woman at birth and she's had a sex change later in life."

"You mean some surgeons have given her the organs of a man? Extraordinary!"

"Yes. These sorts of procedures are not uncommon these days, but that doesn't solve our problem, does it?"

"If you mean whether it's the hand I saw, no it doesn't, since I am quite sure it's not the hand we need."

"Okay, Granddad, I think it's time for you to return to Babette's cabin. She should be back by now. And please, make sure she's safe, okay?"

"You can count on me, son. That woman is far too precious to me to let anything happen to her."

When Babette returned to her suite, she found the door wide open.

Afraid to go in, and thinking that someone had gone through her cabin and was perhaps still inside, she stood on the threshold, uncertain as to what she should do. Arming herself with all the courage she could muster, she took a tentative step inward, then another, and another. Once in the middle of the living room and seeing that nothing had been disturbed, she exhaled a sigh of relief and shook her head. However, she wondered where Edmund was. She went to her bedroom and looked around her – there again, nothing was out of place.

It's only when she went to the bathroom that she froze in horror in front of her mirror. There, written in red, bold letters was a message:

**DON'T PUT YOUR NOSE
WHERE IT DOESN'T BELONG!**

She put a hand to her mouth and gasped. "Edmund!" she screamed as soon as she was able to put her mouth back in motion and utter his name.

Babette wasn't a woman who would swoon easily under any circumstance, but this time she had to hold herself up with her hands gripping the edge of the sturdy sink.

Seconds later, she was still holding herself upright when Edmund appeared beside her. He looked at the mirror and said, "Dear Lord, how evil can people be?"

"Where were you?" Babette blurted reproachfully. "I thought you were waiting here to catch…"

"Come, milady, please, you need to sit down," Edmund said, ruing the fact that he couldn't help her physically, such as offering his arm for support.

Babette nodded, turning away from the mirror, releasing her grip on the sink, and walked slowly back to the living room. She slumped into the nearest chair, visibly exhausted and pale from shock.

"So, where have you been?" she repeated, her voice returning to normal.

"I was helping Alan. He thought he saw a woman wearing the signet ring…"

"A woman? But I thought you said it was a man's hand that you saw?"

"Yes, and it's still true…" Edmund peered into Babette's eyes, having taken a seat across from her. "But that's not important for the moment, dearest. Either you ring Alan right now and get him to alert Mr. Evans of what's happened or I will – what shall it be?"

"You're right, and maybe someone is going to be able to lift some fingerprints from the mirror," Babette replied, getting up and grabbing her cell-phone from her desk.

As soon as she had Alan on the line, she said, "I'm sorry to disturb you at such a late hour, Alan, but I think you should come to my cabin as soon as you can…" She paused. "No-no, I'm fine… no damage…" She listened again. "And please bring Mr. Evans with you…" She raised her eyes to the ceiling. "No, Alan. You're worse than a child – you know that?" And with these words, Babette hung up.

Returning to her seat, she said, "He's really a child at heart, Edmund. He was asking me a dozen questions when all I needed him to do was to call Mr. Evans and come to my cabin." She shook her head and then smiled.

"He has an analytical mind, my dear. That's all I can say in his defense," Edmund said in reply.

"Yes, but he should use that mind of his only once he's in possession of all the facts. I should think it'll be much more productive that way."

When Alan hung up from talking to Babette, he punched Gilbert's cabin number and waited for the fellow to pick up the receiver.

"Yeah, Evans here…" he groaned, obviously awakened from a deep sleep.

"Sorry to get you out of bed, Gilbert, but I think something has happened to Babette…"

"Is she okay?" the chief asked in a rush, flinging his legs out of bed. "Did you talk to her?"

"Yes, on both counts, but you need to come up to her cabin… I'll meet you there."

Alan was about to hang up when he heard Gilbert holler over the line, "Hold on... Alan? Alan?"

"Yeah, what?"

"I'll get Chubb out of bed, shall I?"

There was a moment of silence over the line.

Alan then asked, "Who's Chubb? Is that one of your guys?"

Wiping his eyes, Gilbert suddenly remembered that he hadn't told Alan about the MI5 agent. "No, he's MI5. I'll explain later."

"Do what you think is best, Gilbert," Alan replied, quite puzzled by this time. "One way or the other, hurry up!"

CHAPTER TWENTY-FOUR

A fleeting shadow

ALAN REACHED BABETTE'S CABIN before Gilbert and Chubb. *What is MI5 doing here,* he wondered; ready to knock on the door.

"Come in! The door is open," he heard Babette say.

As soon as he stepped in, he noticed the playwright slumped in the sofa – she was visibly upset. "How are you?" Alan asked, taking her wrist and palpating her pulse. Her hand was warm but not clammy and no irregular pulse, which told him that Babette was probably over the initial shock.

"I am as well as can be expected," she replied and paused, looking up at him. "Why don't you have a look at the bathroom mirror and tell me what you make of it."

Turning to Edmund, Alan asked, "What is it? What..."

"Why don't you just do as the lady asked, Alan – go and see for yourself."

Hesitant, and not knowing what he would find, Alan went to the bathroom and stared at the mirror. He was stunned. He couldn't fathom what the perpetrator was trying to accomplish. He looked at the writing closely and saw that the message had been written with Babette's lipstick. He shook his head and returned to the living room.

"That's quite a threat," he said, taking a seat beside Babette.

"Yes, my dear Alan, it is," she replied, patting his hand, "But what I don't understand is why address the message to me? I haven't been prying into anyone's business, as far as I know."

Another knock on the door interrupted them.

"Come in," said Alan, "it's open."

As Gilbert walked in, he looked at Edmund for a fraction of a second before addressing Babette, "I'm so sorry, Ms. Babette, but Alan tells me you've been... assaulted...?"

"No, not assaulted, Mr. Evans." She turned her head to Alan. "Our good doctor here has a tendency to exaggerate a little." She smiled and then planted her gaze on the man standing behind Gilbert. "And who might you be?" she asked.

"Edward Chulbridge, ma'am. Pleased to meet you," the agent replied, a smirk on his face.

"Same here, I'm sure," Babette said, frowning. "But may I ask what you're doing here? Or are you one of Mr. Evans's men?"

"Oh no, ma'am. I'm with the MI5 in Britain."

"Are you really? My goodness – what would the illustrious British Agency want with me?"

"Not with you, ma'am, but with the case we're trying to solve..."

"I'm sorry to interrupt the introductions," Gilbert cut-in, "but could you tell us what happened, Ms. Babette?"

"No need to tell you – just go to the bathroom and see for yourselves."

Chubb didn't wait – he was already staring at the mirror by the time Gilbert passed the threshold. "What do you make of this?" he asked the chief.

"At best, it's a bad joke. At worst, it's a threat," Gilbert replied.

"And is Ms. Babette a nosy-parker?"

"Far from it," Alan interjected from behind the two men. "She has no time for that sort of thing and abhors gossips."

Turning to Alan, Chubb asked, "Are you two related?"

"Perhaps we are," Edmund said. He had come in and was now standing in the bathtub, arms crossed over his chest.

Hardly able to refrain from exploding in loud laughter, Gilbert turned not to look at Edmund, while Alan, trying hard to keep a straight face, replied, "No, we're not, Agent Chulbridge, but Ms. Babette is a frequent passenger on our cruises, and we consider her presence aboard a privilege and family."

Returning to the living room, Chubb was quick to ask, "And you were obviously not in your cabin when the person intruded on your privacy, were you?"

"No, Agent Chulbridge..."

"Call me Chubb, everyone does," the agent interposed.

Babette cracked a smile. "No, Chubb, I was back stage with the cast..."

"Oh, I see, you were among lots of people then?"

"What's this?" Babette flared. "If you think for one minute that I left my door open for someone to come in and attract attention on my person – you've got it all wrong, Agent Chulbridge!"

"I am sorry, ma'am, but I just thought it would have been difficult for anyone to come in if your door was locked..."

Alan had enough. "Okay, Agent Chulbridge, perhaps you don't appreciate, as you should, that Ms. Babette here was and is in danger – she is not to be considered as a suspect in any way or means."

"Yes, yes, of course..."

"What's more," Gilbert piped-up, "we don't need to interrogate our esteemed passenger at this juncture. We just need to return to my office and review the surveillance camera tapes."

"Well, why didn't you say so sooner," Chubb demanded, once again demonstrating that he was used to being in control of any given situation.

Babette got up. "Well, in that case, gentlemen, I'll ask you to leave and let me go to bed. I am really tired and have lots to do tomorrow."

"Yes, of course, Ms. Babette," Gilbert agreed, already turning toward the door. "But we'll need to lift some prints from the bathroom and the door if we can..."

"Don't bother, Gilbert," Alan said, "I'll do that. I have a latent print kit in the medical center and I'll get what ever I can"—he shot a glance at Babette—"in the morning."

"That will be fine, Alan," Babette said. "I don't think I would want to look at my tired face between now and then anyway."

It was late when Tiffany finally returned to her cabin. She and Alice had parted ways when she had exited the elevator on her deck. She knew Alan wouldn't be able to come to stay with her for the next couple of nights since he was on call and taking over the night duties for Evelyn until they reached Madagascar. She got undressed and went to the bathroom to take a shower. That's when her gaze rested on her mirror. She screamed when she read:

DON'T PUT YOUR NOSE WHERE IT DOESN'T BELONG!

Clasping the collar of her bathrobe, she rushed back to her room, grabbed her phone and called Alan.

"Hi, sweetheart," Alan said cheerfully. "What can I do for my lovely girl?"

"You... you can come to my cabin... that's what you can do!"

"What's the matter? What happened?" Alan asked, standing up and rounding his desk already.

"I don't know if it's someone's idea of a bad joke, but some idiot wrote an awful thing on my mirror..."

"What does it say?"

"It says that I shouldn't put my nose where it doesn't belong. Just come and see – it's too awful for words, Alan."

"I'm on my way," he replied, switching off the line and calling Gilbert while walking out of the center. "Yeah, Gilbert," he said as soon as the man had the phone to his ear. "He's written another one – in Tiffany's cabin this time." He paused. "Yes, I'm on my way out there now. See you there."

Within minutes, Tiffany opened her door to Alan and said, "It's in the bathroom..."

"Yes, I gathered that..."

"How did you know?" Tiffany demanded, following him.

"Babette got the same message," he replied, turning to her and taking her in his arms consolingly.

"What's happening here, Alan?"

"I don't know yet, honey, but I am going to find out – and that's a promise," he replied, releasing her when they both heard the knock at the door of the cabin.

"Come in, Gilbert," Alan said, "it's the same as in Babette's room."

"Sorry for the intrusion, Ms. Sylvan, but I'll just take a couple of photographs and be on my way."

"Sure, no problem," Tiffany said, and then asked, "What's happening here, Mr. Evans? Why is this person attacking us like that?"

"To add fuel to the fire, Ms. Sylvan. He, or she, wants to create havoc so that we stay away from the real problem."

"Have you told Chubb about this?" Alan asked unexpectedly. He hadn't seen the MI5 agent come in with Gilbert and wondered where the man was.

"No, Alan, I haven't." He looked away from the mirror and turned to face Alan. "I sent him back to his cabin for now." He paused. "Frankly, I don't like his methods, and I don't like what he did to Mrs. Clipper either."

Alan frowned. "I guess you'll put me in the picture sooner rather than later, won't you?"

"Sure will, Alan. Actually, if you wouldn't mind coming to my office and looking at the tapes with me that would be helpful."

"No problem, the reports will have to wait," Alan replied. Then glancing at Tiffany, he added, "I think you're safe for tonight, sweetheart. Just lock your door and I'll check on you later, okay?"

Tiffany nodded. "I don't think I'll sleep… but what do I do with that crap on the mirror then?" she asked as she followed the two men to the door of her cabin.

"Just wipe it clean, Ms. Sylvan," Gilbert replied. "We'll get what we need from Ms. Babette's room."

"But what about prints…?" Tiffany inquired. "Don't you need to check?"

Gilbert shook his head. "No, I don't think I'm going to spend any more time with this joker. As I said, he's got other plans and he's trying to divert our attention. And throwing a wrench in the works won't cut it with me!"

And with these decisive words, Gilbert walked out and left Alan to kiss Tiffany before he too left the cabin.

On their way down to Gilbert's office, the chief explained what Chubb had done in order to have the cocaine taken from Irene Walter's cabin and his subsequent interview with Mrs. Clipper. "That's why I don't like the guy," Gilbert added as they reached his office.

"And what is he hoping to accomplish now?" Alan asked, following the chief to the back office where Raphael was already examining the couple of screens that were displaying the activities in the corridors adjacent to Babette's cabin.

"Hi, Raph," Gilbert said, taking a seat beside the young man. "You remember the doc, don't you?"

Raphael turned his head up to Alan. "How can I forget – he's taken at least three pints of my blood since I've come aboard." He smiled. "I swear, Doc, you must have a vampire in your family, did I guess right?"

Alan laughed. He liked the young Raphael. The poor guy had survived a couple of surgeries due to arthritis in his wrists, but since he had returned to duty on this cruise, Alan had kept an eye on him as he suspected that he had an underlying rheumatological disease.

"I don't think I have, Raphael, but I like drawing blood from brainy people like you. You never know, one day maybe I could drink some of it and understand how computers work."

Raphael shook his head and returned his attention to the screens and keyboard. "Alright, Chief," he began, "I've reviewed the corridor tapes near Ms. Babette's cabin between the time she left and the time she returned…"

"And what have you found out?" Gilbert asked.

"Let me show you," Raphael said, typing something on the keyboard.

The camera had captured a couple of scenes of interest. The first was when Babette left her cabin, closed her door and went on her way – she was hardly recognizable. One could not swear it was Babette – or Alice. Alan thought the two figures could look identical. The second scene was the one that Raphael couldn't understand. A few minutes after Babette had left; the door of her cabin was opened, seemingly by itself. No one entered or came out. Yet there was a fleeting shadow that floated past the camera for a fraction of a second and then disappeared.

"What do you make of that, Chief?" Raphael asked, switching his gaze from the screen to Gilbert.

"I don't know, Raph – I have no idea," he replied, although he was well aware that the only thing that could have created such an "apparition" was Edmund. "But what's important here is not that shadow but the fact that the door has been opened and has remained opened after Babette left." He looked up at Alan behind him. "Do you know anything about this?"

"No, I have no idea," Alan lied. He didn't want to say anything in front of Raphael. "Anyway, can we roll the tape slowly up to the time Babette returned to her cabin – maybe we can see the person entering her suite. And they did. A cloaked man appeared entering and exiting Babette's cabin."

Still pondering what he had seen on the tape and the reason for which this person would want to leave such upsetting messages on Babette and Tiffany's mirrors, Alan returned to the medical center to finish the last of his paperwork. He sat at his desk and after logging on; he went to check his inbox. A broad smile drew on his lips when he saw an email from his friend, Calvin.

It said, "I thought you'd like to know some current statistics…"

The Transportation Safety Association has disclosed the Airport Total Body Screening

Results:

June 2012 Statistics On Airport Screening from the Department of Homeland Security

TERRORISTS DISCOVERED	1
CROSS DRESSERS	133
HERNIAS	1.485
HEMORRHOIDS	3,172

ENLARGED PROSTRATES	8,239
BREAST IMPLANTS	59,350
NATURAL BLONDES	3

It was also discovered that 535 politicians had no balls.

"And these are food for thought:"
- How is it possible to have a civil war?
- One nice thing about egotists: they don't talk about other people.
- Do infants enjoy infancy as much as adults enjoy adultery?
- If one synchronized swimmer drowns, do the rest drown too?
- If you ate both pasta and antipasto, would you still be hungry?
- If you try to fail, and succeed, which have you done?
- Whose cruel idea was it for the word 'lisp' to have 's' in it?
- Why are hemorrhoids called "hemorrhoids" instead of "assteroids"?
- Why is it called tourist season if we can't shoot at them?
- Why is there an expiration date on sour cream?
- Can an atheist get insurance against acts of God?
- Why do shops have signs, 'guide dogs only', the dogs can't read and their owners are blind?

"Enjoy!"

Laughing despite the evening's events, alone in his empty office, Alan didn't open the next message until he had stopped laughing....

CHAPTER TWENTY-FIVE

Two reports – one answer

THE NEXT E-MAIL WAS quite disturbing for Alan. He read it twice before he grabbed his phone and dialed Gilbert's office again.

"Don't tell me, you've got another one? Whose mirror is it this time?" Gilbert asked, sounding exasperated.

"Yeah, but this time it wasn't on any mirror. I just received an email with that same message."

"This is insane, Alan. Let me send Raphael to your office to search the IP address. Maybe we can find out who the sender is."

"But, wouldn't it be the same person as the one we saw on that tape?"

"Yeah, but all we saw was the cloaked man again. But maybe Raphael can find out who this guy is once and for all."

"Let's hope so," Alan said, "because I am getting tired of this joker."

"You and I both, Alan." He paused. "But, tell me something, was it Edmund we saw on the tape opening Babette's door?"

"I believe it was."

"What was he doing leaving the door of Babette's cabin open? Do you know anything about that?"

"Yes, actually Edmund was trying to catch our cloaked man in the act."

"That was a great idea; except he wasn't there when the man came in. Do you know where he was?"

"He was with me in my office."

"What was he doing there?"

"Just discussing the use of Viagra and comparing notes on this case." Gilbert had to chuckle.

After he had attended that troublesome meeting with Agent Chulbridge in Babette's cabin, Edmund made himself scarce and decided it was time to see what this "Chubb" was up to. His presence and his actions didn't make any sense. Edmund was not au fait with the latest methods the British Intelligence Agency would use in similar circumstances, yet he knew when someone was trying to pull the wool over his eyes – and Chubb was that someone, in this instance.

In the wee hours of the next morning, Edmund entered Chubb's cabin and went through his suite like a breath of cold air. He entered the guy's room and watched him snore with some intermittent breath holding that he found unusual (sleep apnea had not been defined in the medicine of his day). He smiled. Then, using his kinetic powers, he lifted the pillow next to his head and plopped it down on the man's face. He waited. Shoving the thing away, Chubb grunted and turned on his side.

"That's better," Edmund said, "at least I won't have to listen to your snoring while I check what's under the bed." Joining action to words, he slid under the boxspring and, using his kinetic powers, he pushed the briefcase out of its hiding place. Fortunately, it was unlocked. Edmund stared at the clasp for a moment until the flap was released and the case was opened. He then began leafing through the papers and folders. What seemed inconsequential, he tossed aside. Towards the end, two reports caught his attention. Unable to carry the sheaf of papers, he sent them flying across the room, through the living room, to have them land beside the cabin's door.

Next, he went to his great-grandson's cabin and howled him awake.

"What...? What the hell...?" Alan yelled, sitting up in bed, startled.

"Don't call on the devil, son, or he will appear," were Edmund's first words when he saw that his progeny was awake.

"What are you doing here at this hour? Has something happened to Babette?" Alan rushed to inquire, getting out of bed.

"No, nothing of the sort. I just need your help with something."

Still stunned, Alan slipped into his trousers and then his shirt, and asked, "What? What time is it?" He turned to the alarm clock. "At this hour?"

"Yes, and it's most urgent in fact."

"What is?"

"Stop asking questions, will you, and follow me to Agent Chulbridge's cabin…"

"What for…?"

"Let's just say that you'll find your answers in the papers I left inside his door."

"You've been in his cabin?"

"Does that surprise you?" Edmund asked, chuckling.

"No, I guess not." He looked up at his granddad and shook his head. "Just tell me; were these papers reports of some sort?"

"You'll see for yourself. All you need to do is get in there…"

"How should I do that do you think?" Alan asked, stopping before opening the door of his cabin.

"Don't you have a pass key?"

"No, only Gilbert has one…" Alan paused and frowned. "But didn't you open Babette's cabin door earlier tonight? Why can't you open this one then?"

"Don't know, son. I tried every way I could, but for some odd reason it wouldn't budge."

"Well then, I think we better get Gilbert up and get him to open Chulbridge's door," the doc said, taking his cell-phone out of his pocket.

With only a couple hours of shut-eye, Gilbert arrived in front of Chubb's door, his hair frazzled and his face still attesting to his lack of sleep.

After Edmund explained briefly what he had discovered in the briefcase of the MI5 agent, Gilbert grunted and slid his keycard in the slot. The door wouldn't budge. He looked at both Alan and Edmund and grunted some more. He repeated the exercise, and again the door wouldn't open.

Alan asked, "Now what?"

"Just knock on that door as hard as you can and I'll do the rest," Edmund replied.

"But... he'll grab the," Gilbert said.

"Will you do as I say, and trust me," Edmund cut in, visibly impatient.

Gilbert shook his head and rapped his knuckles on the door, gently.

"That will not do, Mr. Evans! Bang on that door, will you?"

Gilbert did.

Moments later, Chubb opened the door wide, groaning his displeasure in the process and picking up the two reports from the floor. "What do you want, Mr. Evans... Doctor? Has someone died?"

Not waiting to hear either man's answer, Edmund moved the reports out of Chubb's hands and transferred them into Alan's opened palms.

"What the...?" Chubb hollered, trying to retrieve the papers from Alan's hands.

It was too late though. The reports were already floating away out of reach in the direction of the security office several decks below.

"Sorry for the disturbance, Agent Chulbridge – it seems we have the wrong cabin..."

"Wait a little minute here, Mr. Evans..."

Before Gilbert or Alan could react or say anything, the door slammed shut in Chubb's face.

"I'm sure we'll hear about this in the morning," Gilbert said to Edmund while he was photocopying the reports in his office.

"Don't you worry about a thing, Mr. Evans. No one will hear anything about this little escapade."

"What makes you so sure?" Alan asked.

"When you two read these reports, you'll understand," Edmund replied and then added, "I'm still wondering why we couldn't open that door."

"That's probably because he's installed electronic interference on the lock. Sometimes when we need to keep a door closed to prevent anyone from entering a cabin, Raphael sends a signal to the locking device so that no one, even somebody with a passkey, can enter the room," Gilbert explained.

As soon as Gilbert sat down facing Edmund and Alan, and began reading the first of the two reports, he understood. He passed the sheaf of paper to Alan, shaking his head.

In short, Agent Chulbridge was no agent at all. He was a paid "collaborator" assigned to safeguard the cocaine that Irene Walter had "stolen" from a Columbian cartel. What better way to ensure the safekeeping of the loot than having it kept in Gilbert's safe? The next step in the plan was for Chubb to retrieve the cocaine soon after their arrival in Madagascar, disembark and disappear.

In the second report, they discovered that Chubb was the "cat amongst the pigeons" – such as Gilbert had deduced – and had painted the messages in both Babette and Tiffany's cabins. As for the email Alan had received, nothing of the sort had been mentioned in the reports.

But why write reports for someone to find, Alan wondered. Edmund had explained where he found the briefcase – unlocked – and that fact had Alan more curious than ever.

It was about 6:30 am by the time Gilbert had gone over the reports again. He then had placed them and their copies in the small safe beneath his desk, locked it and had returned to bed.

As for Alan, when he left the chief's office he decided to go up to Tiffany's cabin. He wanted a cuddle before starting another day of drudgery along with all the unanswered questions flying through his mind.

Gilbert, Tiffany and Alan were sitting at the pool café having breakfast with multiple cups of espresso a needed part of the repast, when Gilbert asked, "So, we're back to square one, aren't we?"

"Not quite," Alan replied, taking a bite of his toast, "Chubb has confessed to writing the messages on Babette and Tiffany's mirrors, but he didn't mention sending a similar email to me."

"Yeah, I noticed that," Gilbert said, scooping a wedge of his grapefruit. "And the other thing that's bothering me is the fact that we only saw our cloaked man going into Babette's cabin. Are we then right in assuming that Chubb is our cloaked villain?"

"Why?" Tiffany piped-up, looking up from her cereal. She had read the reports, too. "Anyone could get a cloak from anywhere or even a blanket over their head and appear like a cloaked man."

"True, Ms. Sylvan," Gilbert agreed, "but when we searched our fake agent's cabin this morning, there was no cloak or dark blanket that could have been used as a disguise to be found." He drank some juice. "So, as I said, it's back to square one."

"And we still have to protect Babette and Mrs. Clipper – even though we've found out about Chubb," Alan added.

"Have you seen Ms. Babette this morning?" Gilbert asked Tiffany.

"Sure did. I went to see her first thing. The play is scheduled for tomorrow night, and she's nervous as ever about it."

"Why's that?"

"Because, I don't know if you realize it, Chief," Tiffany went on, "but putting on such a complex performance as this one – with dancers and special effects – is not simple. The choreography alone takes three-quarters of the organizational time. And Babette needs to attend the dress rehearsal tonight; otherwise she's liable to cancel the whole thing."

"But isn't your nurse assisting her with all that?" Gilbert asked, glancing at Alan.

"Sure, but she's the body-guard sort of thing and doesn't know the first thing about choreography or theater performances."

"Well, I'll have someone look after Ms. Babette for the dress rehearsal – no problem."

"What about Mrs. Clipper, is she okay?" Alan asked.

Lifting his gaze toward the pool, Gilbert nodded. "Look for yourself."

Tiffany and Alan turned around to see Mrs. Clipper, clad in a see-through dress with only an itsy bitsy, very small bikini underneath it. She waved at them from the other end of the pool.

"Wow, talk about being discreet," Tiffany remarked, returning the wave with a smile.

"Real nice display," Alan said, chuckling and getting a slap on the shoulder from Tiffany.

"And who's the guy with her?" Tiffany asked, looking at the fellow who was rubbing some sunscreen on Lizzy's back.

"That's one of my guys," Gilbert answered, buttering his toast.

"Lucky guy!" Alan exclaimed teasingly, and looking at Tiffany.

She returned the smile and winked.

They were about to leave when Raphael came rushing toward their table.

"Chief, I think I've got it," he said, sitting down beside Gilbert and putting his laptop on the table. Looking up at Tiffany and Alan, he added, "Good morning, Doc. Ms. Sylvan…"

"Good morning, Raphael," Alan and Tiffany replied in unison.

"What have you found out?" Gilbert asked, glancing at the screen that Raphael had turned toward him.

"I think Agent Chulbridge is on the level, sir."

Three pairs of eyes turned to the technician.

"What are you saying?" Gilbert queried, visibly surprised.

"Just this, Chief: The message that Doctor Mayhew received was in fact sent via Interpol…"

"You're kidding?"

"No, Chief – look for yourself." Raphael typed a few keys and suddenly a world map showed up on the screen with lines crisscrossing three continents. "This is the path the message took before it landed in the doc's computer." He then pointed to Washington DC. "And that's the point of origin."

"May I see?" Alan asked.

"Sure," Raphael said, turning the screen to him. "And when I saw that the message issuer was located in the Interpol's office, I figured Chulbridge must be some sort of undercover agent, working for Interpol."

"That's sounds logical," Gilbert agreed, "but before we release the man, I want to receive confirmation from my contact in Washington, okay?" He looked at Raphael.

"Sure, Chief. But to my way of thinking, Agent Chulbridge should be okay."

"We'll see," Gilbert said, obviously not convinced.

On his way back to the medical center, Alan decided to stop by the barbershop. A passenger was already settled in one of the chairs so he decided to wait. He sat down in the waiting alcove and soon his attention was drawn to the passenger explaining his last experience with a barber in Papua.

"I told the man that I couldn't get all my whiskers off because my cheeks are somewhat wrinkled," the passenger began, "And then the barber goes to a shelf in his shop, gets a little wooden ball from a cup on the shelf and tells me to put it inside my cheek to spread out the skin. When he'd finished, I told him that was the cleanest shave I had in years." He paused. "But then I wanted to know what would have happened if I had swallowed that little ball." The passenger looked up at the barber and then turned to Alan. "And you know what he said? He said that I should bring it back in a couple of days, like everyone else does!"

"Good Lord!" the ship's barber said between bursts of laughter. "I can assure you I don't dispense any little balls to my customers," he concluded, throwing a quick smile in Alan's direction.

CHAPTER TWENTY-SIX

A "Charlie Drill"

HOURS LATER, WHEN EVERYONE had returned to their regular duties, Tony burst into Gilbert's office. "Chief, she's gone!" he blurted, out of breath.

Gilbert raised his gaze to the man. He had been trying to concentrate on writing a comprehensive report for Galveston before the captain would be confronted with difficult, if not embarrassing questions from the authorities in Madagascar, from the head office and, of course, Interpol. "What's up? Who's gone?"

"Mrs. Clipper, sir." Tony said, still gasping for air.

"What do you mean Mrs. Clipper is gone – gone where?" Gilbert got up and rounded his desk to face the guard. "I saw you slathering her with sunscreen at the pool just this morning…"

"Yes, Chief, we were there alright, but after that she went to the spa and never came out. I've questioned the staff and the spa manager, but no one has been able to give me a straight answer."

"Okay, let's go and talk to Eileen Flounder and hear what she's got to say," Gilbert said, putting his cell-phone in his shirt pocket.

Eileen Flounder had been working as a spa manager for a couple of years already. The buxom lady knew the 'spa business' inside out. She had managed her own establishment for some fifteen years before deciding to 'retire' to a contract on cruise ships. Her iron-fist-in-kid-glove attitude had seen her through the difficult and sometimes impossible situations of pleasing clients that were never to be satisfied.

"Hello, Eileen," Gilbert said cheerfully as he and Tony entered the salon. "How are you this fine morning?"

"I've seen better days, Chief," Eileen replied, taking off her cap to let her dark hair fall to her shoulder. "One of the new sign-ons has just waxed off half of one of our regular client's eyebrows, and then there is your Tony"—she shot an angry glance in the guard's direction—" coming in here, in *my salon*, accusing me of hiding a Mrs. Clipper..."

"No one is accusing you of anything, Eileen," Gilbert argued.

"That's what it sounded like to me, Chief," the spa manager retorted, going behind the reception desk. She looked down at the girl who was still talking on the phone. "See, here, Chief"—she put the appointment book on top of the counter—"Mrs. Clipper was scheduled for a manicure at 9:30 this morning. And that's what we gave her." She fixed her gaze on Gilbert, whose eyes were traveling down the register's page. "After that, she got ready and left, and no one in here has seen her since."

"Who gave her the manicure?" Gilbert asked, raising his gaze toward Eileen.

"Cynthia did. And Tony here questioned her already. There's nothing more we could tell you, Chief." She took the appointment book back and replaced it in front of the receptionist.

"And you haven't seen her leave?" Gilbert asked the young lady.

Putting down the phone, the girl said, "Sorry about that, Chief, but while I was busy taking down an appointment, Mrs. Clipper could have easily slipped out of here unnoticed."

"And you've searched the change rooms, have you?" Gilbert asked Eileen.

"Of course we have, Chief. And the room she used was spotless – nothing left behind. I'm sorry."

"Alright then, we'll take it from here," Gilbert concluded, turning toward the door – Tony in tow.

Once they were outside, Gilbert shook his head. "And you haven't seen her come out of here, have you?"

Tony looked down to the floor beneath his feet. "Well..."

"Well what, man?" Gilbert demanded, more than annoyed now.

"It's just that I went for a drink of water and by the time I got back, she was not there. First, I thought she hadn't come out yet, so I went in and asked. And that's when Ms. Eileen told me she had finished her session about fifteen minutes before."

"Did you go to her cabin?"

Tony nodded emphatically. "First thing I did after I knew she had left."

"Okay, maybe she's just gone shopping in the stores, or went back to the pool – did you look for her in-and-around those places?"

Tony nodded again. "Sure did, sir." He hesitated. "The only places I haven't looked are in the officers or crew's areas."

"Well, we'll do that next then," Gilbert concluded.

It was two o'clock in the afternoon when Gilbert returned to his office. He and Tony had not seen hide-or-hair of Mrs. Clipper. Although *The Baroness* was far from being a huge ship, it was still large enough to make it practically impossible for the two men to search the vessel discreetly from prow to bow thoroughly. His mind filled with apprehension – fearing that the worst may have happened to the woman – Gilbert decided it was time to alert the captain of this latest development.

He found Galveston in the middle of roaring laughter with Epstein Silver, the cruise director. Before Gilbert could say anything, the captain handed him a sheet of paper, saying, "Have a read of this, Mr. Evans."

Gilbert took the one page of typed notes and began reading:

The 10 Most Stupid Questions and Answers the Pursers Heard Aboard a Cruise Ship:

1. Does the crew sleep on board? Actually no, we fly in by helicopter every morning.
2. Does the ship generate its own electricity? Of course not. Didn't you see the long extension cord at the back of the ship?
3. Which elevator takes me to the front of the ship? Elevators go up and down, not from one end of the ship to the other, sir.

4. Is the water in the toilets salt water or drinking water? I haven't really tasted it but if you do please let me know.
5. What do you do with the ice carvings after they melt? I'll let you in on a secret; we make ice cubes out of them and put them back in your drinks.
6. How do I know what pictures are mine? I'd take the ones that you are in.
7. Is this island surrounded by water?
8. What language do they speak in Alaska? Probably Alaskan, don't you think?"
9. How high above sea level are we? Well, there are several ways to find out....
10. And the most stupid question ever asked on board a cruise ship is: At what time is the midnight buffet?

Gilbert looked up from the sheet and only smiled. "Is that part of some of your comedy lines?" he asked Epstein.

This was Epstein's first entertainment contract on a luxury ship. Unlike what happens on large holiday vessels, *The Baroness* catered to high society, high paying passengers who expected classic entertainment, such as piano or violin recitals, Broadway dance performances, operatic performances, theatrical plays and the like. Nothing like the crass type of comedy shows you could expect to hear on other cruise liners.

"Well yes," Epstein replied, his enthusiasm deflated. "I don't think it would fly on this cruise, as a show in the main theater, but I was just asking Captain Galveston"—he turned his face to him—"if we could put on a tasteful comedy hour in one of the bars, that's all."

"We certainly could think about it, Mr. Silver," Galveston interposed, "but for now, I'd like you to concentrate on helping Ms. Babette with her play. As I told you, she's got an extremely complex show to present tomorrow night and your assistance will not be ignored."

Epstein got up. "Thank you, Captain. I'll have a chat with Ms. Sylvan about it."

"You do that, Mr. Silver," Galveston concluded, nodding and returning his attention to Gilbert. "Now then, Mr. Evans, what can I do for you?"

Once Epstein had left the captain's office, Gilbert sat down, visibly uncomfortable. "I'm afraid we've got some complication regarding our cloaked man, sir."

"The captain reclined in his chair. "What else could be happening with that infernal fellow," he asked, almost grumbling the words. "I thought you had your man Raphael on a full shift observing the main cameras live. Has he noticed something unusual?"

"No, sir, not yet." Gilbert hesitated before saying, "I'm afraid Mrs. Clipper has slipped out of the net, Captain."

"What?" Galveston exploded. "What do you mean 'slipped out of the net'? I thought you had your men guarding her 24/7…"

"We have, sir, but she slipped out of the spa when one of my men had gone to the 'john' – and we've searched most of the main areas, but I'm afraid we've lost track of her."

Pondering this latest turn of events for a moment, the captain then said, "I think it's time to take the proverbial bull by the horns, Mr. Evans. Frankly, I have had enough of this silliness. First we have a Ms. Walter who is found dead, presumably pushed over the railing; then we have a fellow dressed in a monk's habit, scaring one of our most respectable guests, and members of our crew; next we discover an Interpol agent undercover, playing games with a Colombian cartel, wearing an MI5 badge, and now you're telling me that one of our passengers has gone missing – does that sum it up, Mr. Evans?"

"Yes, sir. And I'm afraid of finding Mrs. Clipper…"

"What do you mean 'afraid of finding her'?"

"What if the cloaked man finds her first and… well, you know what I mean."

"Yes, Mr. Evans, I can put two and two together as well as you can. And that is the very reason for which I will instigate a "Charlie Drill" at 1600 hrs. this afternoon…"

"A Charlie Drill, sir? But what about our passengers…"

"No one is to be above suspicion at this point. Besides, I don't think you and your security staff could visit every cabin and every room of this vessel in less time than our entire staff could, do you, Mr. Evans?"

"What about head office, sir...?"

"Leave those idiots to me. They'll be only too happy to congratulate us when we solve this problem before we reach Madagascar, don't you think?"

"I'd say so, Captain," Gilbert replied, although none too sure that finding a solution was going to be possible before their next port of call.

A Charlie Drill was usually implemented when there was a bomb threat or any other event that could endanger the passengers and crew's life. The exercise was conducted in two distinct phases in accordance to the Safety of Life at Sea (SOLAS) and each phase demanded a thorough search of the vessel to locate the offensive or dangerous item. During the first phase of the exercise, the crew would search the areas where they work and then report to their department heads. If the threat (or as in this instance the person) was not located by the end of the first phase, the officers and staff would then get involved and go through every single part of the vessel – from bridge to engine room. Only then, and if the person or item wasn't located, would the captain alert the authority at the next port to have a bomb squad (or in this case the CIA) called aboard the vessel to finalize the search. A Charlie Drill generally took hours to complete and most often brought positive results. In this instance, Galveston hoped that Mrs. Clipper would be located, preferably alive and well.

"So, I will make an announcement over the departments' internal PA system, so not to alert our cloaked fellow, and get the drill started." Galveston fixed his gaze on Gilbert.

The latter was not happy about the decision, but they needed to locate Mrs. Clipper as soon as possible and a Charlie Drill was the only way to do it, he had to agree.

As soon as Alan was alerted of the captain's decision, he swore under his breath. Gilbert had phoned him regarding Mrs. Clipper's disappearance before he had gone to meet with the captain.

Evelyn was busy with a passenger.

The older fellow had a swollen leg and after careful examination, Alan had given the man a big tablet – big enough to choke a horse – saying, "Evelyn will get you some water for Mr. Rimsky," and had left the fellow to return to his office. Evelyn had gone to the storeroom and had only returned a few minutes later to find her patient drinking from the fountain in the waiting room. He cleared his throat, straightened up and returned to his chair, throwing a curious gaze at the nurse.

Unaware of what Mr. Rimsky had done, Evelyn deposited a bucket of warm water in front of him, saying, "Okay, after the tablet dissolves in the water, soak that leg for at least 30 minutes."

"You mean that tablet you gave me...?" Mr. Rimsky asked, realizing what he had done.

"Yes." Evelyn stared. "Oh no! You didn't swallow it, did you?"

"I'm afraid I did, Ms. Evelyn..."

Not losing her nerve, she strode to Alan's office and told him what happened as he was putting the phone down from talking to Alice in the theater.

By 4:30 pm, the poor Mr. Rimsky was now resting comfortably in the emergency room, his leg up and his stomach emptied of the offensive tablet.

CHAPTER TWENTY-SEVEN

Mrs. Clipper?

SINCE THE FIRST PHASE of the drill had not been successful, all executive staff and officers took turns to search the vessel once again. This time, however, the general crew was not participating in the search and had returned to their duties. It was about seven o'clock in the evening when Alan was called down to the sanitation department. *I bet they found her,* he thought.

As soon as he arrived in front of the septic tanks, he saw Simon waiting for him. Gilbert was there together with Captain Galveston and Staff Captain Ekelton.

"I think we will leave the rest up to you, Doctor," Galveston said. He pointed to the inside of the tank. "As you can see, we have a corpse in that tank, and judging from the protruding hand, I would say it's probably the body of Mrs. Clipper."

Alan bent down over the edge of the tank. The captain had been right; that hand was definitely that of a woman. "We'll have to get her out of there," he said, looking up at Simon. "Can we do that?"

"Yes, Doc. No problem, except I can't guarantee that we can get all of her out of there in one piece."

"You mean the chemicals could have eaten through the flesh already?"

"Well... we'll leave you to your duties, Doctor," Galveston interrupted, turning to his staff captain. "Let's get back to the bridge, Mr. Ekelton, we've got work to do."

Alan and Gilbert looked after the two officers as they were climbing the stairs and then returned their attention to Simon. "So, you think we're going to have to take her out piece by piece, do you?" Alan asked him.

"That's my guess, Doc. See, these chemicals and bacteria are designed to eat up whatever is in the tank. Except for plastic containers or some forms of metal, a corpse would completely disappear and be liquefied in a matter of hours."

"And that's probably why our murderer has chosen to put his victim in the tank," Gilbert put in. "He was hoping that no one would discover her before reaching Madagascar."

Alan had to agree. He nodded. "Okay then, let's get a bag from the morgue and put the pieces you can recover in it," he suggested to Simon, as he took his cell-phone out of his pocket. He called Evelyn and one of the attendants to bring the stretcher and body bag down to the sanitation room. Closing his phone, he said to Gilbert, "You know, I hate to say this, but Galveston was right in calling for a Charlie Drill. We wouldn't have found her otherwise."

"You're right, but that still leaves us with the same question mark: Who's the cloaked man?"

"I think I'll have a chat with Edmund tonight," Alan said pensively. "He can go through every stateroom, suite and cabin in no time..."

"But, Alan, we've just done that..."

The doc shook his head. "No, what we've done is searching for a woman. In this instance, I'd like my granddad to look for that cloak, and that signet ring."

When Evelyn arrived in the sanitation room, she gasped at the sight of Lizzy's hand protruding from the surface of the green liquid, with freshly painted fingernails. "Oh Good Lord," she exclaimed, "the poor girl." She then turned to Simon, who was just coming out of his change room dressed in some sort of space suit, and started giggling. "I'm sorry, Simon, but you look picture-perfect. You should make the yearbook!"

Gilbert and Alan couldn't help but laugh with her.

"Why don't you suit up too, Doc? You could come with me and experience first hand what it feels like..."

"No thanks, Simon, another time maybe... but I would like some gloves and something to cover myself so that I don't get any of that stuff on me when you hand me the body parts."

"Yeah. I have just what you need in the change room," Simon replied, pointing to a small cabin on top of a set of stairs. "You'll find three sets of aprons, masks and gloves up there – just go and help yourselves while I get in *my* tank."

A few minutes later, Gilbert, Evelyn and Alan emerged from the cabin looking like surgeons from an old Frankenstein movie. And before anyone noticed him doing it, Gilbert had snapped pictures of Alan, Evelyn and Simon dressed for the next horror show, which this particular exercise turned out to be.

Two hours later, Gilbert, Evelyn and Alan were looking down at Mrs. Clipper's body parts laid out on the autopsy table in the morgue. The stench of decomposition was permeating their every pore, so much so that Gilbert turned as white as a sheet and had to sit down with his head between his knees. "I'll have myself cremated when I go," he declared. "I wouldn't want anyone to smell me," he added, igniting laughter from Alan and Evelyn.

"Okay, Gilbert," Alan said, "Why don't you go to your cabin, take a hot shower, drink plenty of water and try resting for a bit."

"No-no, I'll be fine in a minute," Gilbert objected from his chair.

"Actually, that's doctor's orders, Chief. You've inhaled enough chemicals to fumigate your entire body inside out – so you go and do what you're told. Okay?"

Reluctantly, Gilbert got up and left the center without another word. He knew the doc was right.

After a grueling night in the theater, going through the dress rehearsal with Babette and the cast, Tiffany entered her cabin to find Alan and Edmund waiting for her. "Good grief, you two, can't you give this girl a break?"

"We know you are tired, my dear…"

"You have no idea how exhausted I am, Granddad, but I can see I'm not about to lay down for the night yet, or am I?"

Alan took a seat beside her and was rubbing her shoulder when he s said, "We won't be here long, Tiff, but we wanted your opinion about something we're planning to do..."

Tiffany turned her head to Alan abruptly. "Why ask my opinion now? You're the one who called that Charlie Drill on us...without asking anyone."

"No, my dear," Edmund cut in, "don't exact blame where it's not due. Captain Galveston is the one who came up with the idea..."

"Really?" Tiffany looked up at Edmund. "And did you find her?"

"Unfortunately we did," Alan replied.

"Is she okay?"

"No, Tiff, she's dead."

"Oh God. That man must be a maniac," Tiffany said, letting Alan return to massaging her neck and shoulders.

"Yes, Miss Tiffany, he is that and much more," Edmund said, crossing his arms over his chest.

"So, what are you going to do about him?" she asked.

"Well, I wondered if you could direct Granddad to the people you think would be the most likely suspects..."

Tiffany opened her eyes saucer-wide. "How should I do that? I'm not a chief of security or anything like that..."

"No, but you are a very good judge of character and perhaps you've noticed some people's behavior, especially members of the cast..."

"Oh I see what you mean now. You want me to tell you if I've seen anyone among the cast members behave strangely since we began the rehearsals, is that it?"

Alan and Edmund nodded in unison.

"Okay... well, right now no one comes to mind. But maybe if I could sleep on it, I'll have a better idea in the morning."

"Okay, you've got it, Tiff," Alan said, standing up. "We're going to leave you now, but I'll come back in the morning to see if you want to have breakfast on the upper deck . . . okay?"

"Yes, that will be great, except my day will start early again – if that's okay?"

"No problem, Tiff," Alan agreed, kissing his lovely girl on the forehead before leaving her cabin with his granddad.

Not wanting to leave his granddad alone to perform his ghostly task of visiting every stateroom on the upper decks; Alan sat down in one of the lounge chairs by the pool and waited. Within minutes he was asleep. For some reason, his dream took him back to the *HMS Investigator,* the sunken ship he and some archeologists from Parks Canada had visited a year and half ago during his latest cruise across the Northwest Passage. He saw himself once again looking through the porthole of the submarine and observing a sealed recess in the physician's room. Next, he was aboard the *HMS Investigator* moving planks away from the front of the recess and extracting a monk's cloak.... His laughter woke him up with a start. He was still stretched on the lounge chair. He looked around him. At this hour of the night, there was no one around except for a couple of security personnel "walking their beat" along the deck.

Alan sat up, wiped his eyes and was about to call his granddad, when he appeared before him, looking downcast.

"Any luck?" Alan asked him, lifting his gaze to him.

"I'm afraid not, son. If our monk is one of our passengers, he's stashed his cloak somewhere where no one will find it."

"And yet, I think I know how we could find it," Alan countered, smiling.

"Have you been "inspired" while I was gone?"

"Yes, Granddad, I believe I have." Edmund frowned. "You see when I visited an old sunken ship last year during a cruise through the Arctic Circle, the archeologists that were assigned to catalogue the relics aboard that vessel, found the treasure chest in a sealed recess inside the physician's room..."

"Would that be the *HMS Investigator* by any chance?" Edmund queried.

"How did you know?" Alan asked, getting up.

"Well, there was a lot of talk about the ship and its disappearance at the time. The news even traveled as far as India where I was spending a few months on shore."

"So, you knew about the treasure then?"

"No, not really, son. I thought there was something about the story that didn't sound right, but didn't pay much attention to it." He paused.

"So, what are you thinking now – maybe the cloak is hidden in the medical center, is that it?"

"Actually not only the cloak, but the man wearing the cloak is hiding somewhere other than a regular cabin…"

"Somewhere such as a closet of some sort?"

"Yes, Granddad," Alan replied, already walking back in the direction of the elevators. "You see, many closets in this vessel are only opened in case of emergency or during safety drills. And these are announced over the PA system well in advance."

"And you think all the man has to do is to come out during the drills and mingle with the passengers or crew until the drill is done…?"

"Yes. In fact, I think our man is nothing more than a stowaway, besides being a murderer, of course."

"But tell me something else, son; why would he go about killing these two young ladies, what could be his reason?"

"That I don't know yet, Granddad." Alan shook his head and paused while he stepped into the empty elevator. "Yet, there's something else that bothers me about this Chubb character."

"What's that?" Edmund asked.

"Why did he say he went to Babette and Tiffany's cabin to write the messages on their mirrors when the only figure we saw on the tapes was that of the cloaked man?"

"Perhaps the two know each other," Edmund suggested as Alan stepped out of the elevator.

"Maybe…" Alan said musingly. "But for now, I think it's best for you to stay in Babette's cabin and accompany her everywhere she goes. She is still in danger, by my way of thinking."

"No problem, son. Meanwhile, you try to think which closet would be the best one to hide," Edmund concluded, suddenly disappearing before Alan's eyes.

CHAPTER TWENTY-EIGHT

A Cat Named Hoodoo Voodoo

WHEN TIFFANY WOKE UP the next morning, she was still tired. Too much on her plate and not enough sleep – it was starting to take its toll on her. While she showered, she thought of what Alan had asked her the previous evening. *There isn't any one person that I could think of as being "suspicious". Those people and their voodoo, all behave suspiciously.*

Once she was dressed and ready to go, she put a call through to Alan.

"Good morning, my lovely, how are you today?" Alan asked as soon as he noticed her name on the call display.

"As well as can be expected with only five hours' sleep," Tiffany replied testily – although she didn't mean to sound that way.

"How about you sleep in my arms tonight?" Alan asked, trying to cheer her up.

"That would be lovely, except I don't think I'll be getting to bed before three or four am. It took us almost three hours yesterday to get the forward platform ready for tonight." She paused. "Anyway, you had asked me to think about the cast's behavior – do you remember?"

"Yes, I do. And have you thought of anyone in particular?"

"No one jumps to mind – they're all weird, Alan," Tiffany said. "That play is fantastic, and it really intensely draws you into its theme…"

"How do you mean?"

"Well, it's voodoo at its best. It's haunting actually."

"Wow, that sounds like a tour-de-force on Babette's part. Can hardly wait to see it."

"And I can hardly wait to hear the passengers' reaction – they'll bring the roof down – it's really that good, Alan."

"Okay then, are you ready to have breakfast now?"

"Sure am. I'm starving actually."

"Okay. Let's meet at the café by the pool in ten. And I'll tell you what Granddad and I deduced last night."

"Did he find the cloak?" Tiffany asked.

"No, but I think I know where to find both the monk and his habit."

"Sounds great. See you in ten," Tiffany said before she hung up.

Alan looked at the receiver before replacing it in its cradle. *That woman definitely needs a restful vacation like many of us working on these ships,* he thought.

After breakfast, Alan's entire day was spent writing reports to head office regarding the autopsy he had performed on Lizzy's corpse. The poor woman had obviously been clobbered over the head with the all too common "blunt instrument", which had left a deep gash in her skull. But the most surprising pathological finding was the remnants of a fresh fracture of her left tibia. Alan had deduced that she must have been forced to take a tumble – as if someone had tripped her with some kind of cane or other stick. He also observed an old fracture on the right ulna, which he attributed to a fall. He couldn't be sure.

Once he had sent the report, he looked at his wristwatch – 5:00 pm. He figured he would just have time for 15 minutes of cardio in the gym, have a bite in the officers' mess, take a shower and change before going to the theater. This promised to be a performance he didn't want to miss.

By 7:30 that night, the foyer of the theater was already full with passengers enjoying a glass of champagne with their partners and friends while the captain was making his usual rounds. When he saw Alan, he made a beeline for the doc and grabbed him by the arm. Leading him outside onto the promenade, he asked, "What have you concluded, Doctor, was she killed before being put in the tank?"

"I believe she was tripped first, sir." Galveston frowned. "Yes, you see, in order not to attract attention, when Mrs. Clipper came out of the spa, she was whacked on the legs, she tripped and fell down. The killer must have offered her some kind of assistance and then killed her on the way to her cabin…"

"How did he kill her?" Galveston asked, quite curious.

"He smashed her skull."

"Oh! But then there must be traces of blood somewhere – perhaps in her cabin? Has someone checked?"

"Not yet, sir, but the CIA's forensic team will be all over that cabin as soon as we reach Madagascar. Yet, how can we be sure that's where she was killed?"

"Alright, let's talk again in the morning, shall we?"

"Of course, Captain," Alan replied, relieved. He didn't want to spend any more time having to think about this murder tonight.

At eight o'clock the bell called the audience to their seats and within minutes of the second bell, the curtain rose to the *Prologue to "A Cat Named Voodoo"*.

Isidor, the chief investigator is standing on the stage in the dark; on the apron. In the center of the stage we have a dance. The dance is a counter-clockwise dance, in a circle. The one to be possessed begins by clapping his hands, nodding and tapping his feet to the rhythm of the drums. Like the others, soon the eyes of the one possessed become fixed, his eyes become glassy, his movements become faster and faster, his head is thrown back, his arms thrash about. He falls to the ground in the center of the circle, then jumps up and down, then he rolls around and around. He speaks in tongues saying words he had never said before. Other worshipers move around in a circle about him, always counter-clockwise. He faints finally, exhausted, the drums become fainter and fainter and stop. Then dancers exit during a blackout and the chants that accompanied the dancers' ritual die down.

On the riser of the apron there is a pole. It is a night scene.

Chief investigator, ISIDOR mumbles, looking at his watch. He is waiting for an informer – ISABELLE.

ISIDOR: Where is that woman? She's 15 minutes late already. How would it look for the chief investigator to be caught in this neighborhood and to be talking to a prostitute? The police board could hang you for that one. (He raises his hat). Oh, it's you (Isabelle stands left stage)

ISABELLE: You asked me to meet you here; right at this very spot. (Touches the pole)

ISIDOR: Why are you so late?

ISABELLE: I have my skirt

ISIDOR: Don't tell me, I don't want to know. (Starts to leave)

ISABELLE: Come back here! First you asked me to come, then you yell at me. Do you know what you want?

ISIDOR: I want you…

ISABELLE: Me? When you could have any girl in New Orleans…

ISIDOR: I want you to do something for me.

ISABELLE: What sort of things did you have in mind? I do only normal…

ISIDOR: Nothing like that.

ISABELLE: Oh?

ISIDOR: Do you know Marie Laveau?

ISABELLE: Sorry I came… (Starts to leave).

ISIDOR: (pulls her back) I must have a complete dossier

ISABELLE: Huh.

ISIDOR: I must know everything about this person. Where she was born who her parents were, her background, and what she does. Who does she spend time with, etcetera…

ISABELLE: Don't you know?

ISIDOR: Not enough. That's where you come in. You fill me in with all the details.

ISABELLE:	Only for a price.
ISIDOR:	Of course. What is a gris-gris?
ISABELLE:	I don't want to get mixed up with no gris-gris.
ISIDOR:	You don't have to. All you have to do is to go here and there…
ISABELLE:	I do that all the time… go here and there.
ISIDOR:	See how easy it is. As you go here and here you find out everything about her. You understand?
ISABELLE:	Yes, sir. It could be dangerous for my health. What did you plan on paying me?
ISIDOR:	Nothing.
ISABELLE:	I don't work for the love of it. I am a professional.
ISIDOR:	There will be some money for you.
ISABELLE:	(holds out hand) How much?
ISIDOR:	(under breath) As little as possible.
ISABELLE:	That won't be enough.
ISIDOR:	I'll make it enough (slaps her hand) after you give me my information. I must have the minute details on her life
ISABELLE:	She has very powerful friends, the blacks, mulattos. And even in the white community. If I do this job for you, I want protection, but I don't want any of your boys following me. All right?
ISIDOR:	How do I give you protection if nobody is to follow you?
ISABELLE:	Pay for my protection.
ISIDOR:	That will cost me.
ISABELLE:	Whatever it is.
ISIDOR:	Report back to me right away. You do understand?
ISABELLE:	For the right price, I can understand almost anything (exits).
FR. CYRIL:	(Religious leader) enters the scene.
FR. CYRIL:	Is that who I think it is? (pats Isidor on the

back.) What are you doing out so late – and in this area?

ISIDOR: Business. And you?

FR. CYRIL: Business.

ISIDOR: A man of the cloth?

FR. CYRIL: It's the nineteenth century, my man. May I walk a ways with you?

ISIDOR: I'll see you to your home. What do you know about hoodoo voodoo?

FR. CYRIL: You're asking the wrong person.

ISIDOR: Surely you've heard about it?

FR. CYRIL: Yes, from what some of my congregation tells me. You know. They confess to me. And you know that the churches, all Christian churches, are opposed to black magic and voodoo, gris-gris and the like. But of course, I know it goes on all over New Orleans, in the countryside and elsewhere in big cities like New York, Chicago, and the like.

ISIDOR: You said gris-gris. Exactly what is it?

FR. CYRIL: Gris-gris comes in many forms; curses, love potions, love charms. A young parishioner of mine was told to get a glove from her would-be lover. They then filled the glove with a so-called magic mixture. The lady was advised to sleep with the glove under her mattress, and after a very short time she would gain the young man's affection.

ISIDOR: Who believes in that stuff?

FR. CYRIL: Too many, I'm afraid. (The two of them stop in front of a door.) Here I am at my destination. Thank you for walking me home. I say if you're going to get involved in investigating this sort of thing, I'll give you this cross. It might help you at least stop and think what direction to choose.

ISIDOR:	Don't they have symbols, (pause) too?

(Lights * * denote time)

ISABELLE:	I have some things for you that you wanted to know about. Marie Laveau. She was probably born right here in New Orleans.
ISIDOR:	Don't you know for sure? I'll pay only for facts.
ISABELLE:	Her father was a wealthy white planter and her mother a mullato with a strain of American Indian blood, she is (pause) was married.
ISIDOR:	Which one is it?
ISABELLE:	If she is married to him? If he is alive...? If he is dead...? Do you want to hear what I have to tell you?
ISIDOR:	If I am paying for it, yes.
ISABELLE:	Jacques Paris, her husband, he was a carpenter. But then I guess that makes him...dead
ISIDOR:	Being a carpenter makes him dead? (Shakes his head.) Yes, yes, I heard of the disappearance of one Jacques Paris.
ISABELLE:	That's the one. So, he's dead -- now, pay me.
ISIDOR:	For what?
ISABELLE:	I gave you valuable information.
ISIDOR:	What else? It's getting chilly out here.
ISABELLE:	(under her breath) that's all I have except this. (Hands him something wrapped in paper) there's something inside that will protect you from harm.
ISIDOR:	Here, you'll need it more than I.
ISABELLE:	I have mine (opens coat – all kinds of symbols are visible on the lining).
ISIDOR:	Add this to your collection (hands her a cross. Walks off)
	(Throws some money after it, Isabelle runs and

picks it up, chews on the coin. She exits the stage.)

The curtain came down under applause. The sound of drums accompanied the passengers to the foyer for the mini-intermission.

Knowing that Babette would probably make an appearance during that half hour, Alan waited for her at the stage door.

When she came out – with Edmund – she was radiant. No one would have guessed this wonderful lady had just spent one of the most difficult weeks in her life. Dressed in a beautiful emerald green gown, she looked as if she had just come out of a picture book.

"Alan, how are you...? Tiffany and Edmund"—she shot a quick glance in his direction—"have kept me informed of all that you've been doing. And I deeply regret Mrs. Clipper's absence tonight. She would have enjoyed the play, I'm sure."

"I am sure we will have plenty of time to catch up when we reach Madagascar, Babette, but for now I am here to make sure you enjoy the night."

Walking toward the foyer to the awaiting crowd, Babette said, "Just one thing, Alan..."

"What's that?"

"I feel more secure when Edmund is with me. Knowing that he's beside me at all times is more reassuring than any body guard."

Her pleading eyes said it all, Alan reflected. "I'll ensure that I will not distract him with anything else, I promise," he said before they reached the foyer.

In no time everyone was back in their seats, anxiously waiting for the curtain to rise on the first act.

ACT I

CURTAIN UP

This is Marie Laveau's home. Marie is crying. Isabelle (the informer) is listening.

MARIE: What can I do? I am but a poor widow without any money. I work all day and sometime even at night in the homes of rich, white ladies. Fixing their hair this way and then that. And all that I get is… "No, no, that way, don't you understand… girl (sighs) the other way, girl."
ISABELLE: They pay you very well, don't they?
MARIE: Generally, comme ci, comme ça, especially the French husbands, they seem more generous than the others.
Speaking of husbands: there's a Dr. Kraut.
ISABELLE: He's French?
MARIE: Who said he is. Come on now, even you know he's not French. One evening he left his wife at home saying he had to go out on business. Ha, ha, some business. He visited six different women in one night.
ISABELLE: That's what hurts my profession. Non-professional women. At least in your work you get gossip, while in mine, for the most part, I get beaten up.
MARIE: Then change your profession.
ISABELLE: I don't know anything else. Except today I learned that the police department pays very well for certain kinds of information.
MARIE: That's dangerous.
ISABELLE: Not if you work for the chief inspector of police.
MARIE: What have you been up to?

ISABELLE: Nothing, really, nothing at all.
MARIE: Then how do you know so much about it? And the chief inspector (laughs, points a finger at her) you're too dumb to be an informer. That's something I'll never do.
ISABELLE: I could get you a few men.
MARIE: That's another thing you'll never find me doing. I might have a lover but I'd care about him. And I'd have to care a lot about him, but never, never other men. Anyway, as an informer, I could go to jail, and if I did…what you do, I would positively go to jail very quickly. I don't want to hear any more about your shady ideas. I'm a very religious woman.
ISABELLE: Me too. Look (she shows the cross).
MARIE: You stole it. Do you realize what would happen to you…? You idiot.
ISABELLE: No, no, you're wrong; it was a present…
MARIE: From a man?
ISABELLE: Yes.
MARIE: (looks at it, reads aloud) The *Holy Scriptures Christian Religious Store.* (Starts to laugh.) Priests and ministers pass them out (laughs) all the time.
ISABELLE: (laughs with her).
MARIE: (hands the cross back to her).
ISABELLE: (puts her coat back on again with all the symbols). You could blackmail people better than anyone in the whole world.
MARIE: You could leave before I'm accused of collaborating with you. Out, out. Go before I get someone to cast a spell, on you
ISABELLE: I might never come back (exits}
MARIE: All you can think of is, (pause) yes, I see it here in your tea leaves. Jail! She has a good point. If

there was only a way to use blackmail, and do it subtly within the law and have it pay off. Well it's a nice dream...

(Knock on door)

(Marie goes to the door. Dr. John is at the door)

MARIE: Yes?

DR. JOHN: May I come in? I'm Dr. John. You do know who I am.

MARIE: Come in please. So you are Dr. John the most important voodoo leader of the nineteenth century. Are you the real Dr. John?

DR. JOHN: I am indeed.

MARIE: Please (motions him to a chair to sit down) may I offer you some tea?

DR. JOHN: (waves hand – no) You've heard of me (taking off gloves).

MARIE: Everyone has. You sell gris-gris, you heal, and you give advice.

DR. JOHN: (waves his hand again – no) Let us get to the point (looking at his pocket watch) I perceive that you are an intelligent young woman and that you are one of the finest hair dressers in all of New Orleans.

MARIE: Well, I wouldn't go that far.

DR. JOHN: Well, I would. Now, we both work for the same (laughing) rich and influential lady. You do her hair, while I am removing a curse placed upon her. I am also advising her on romance, etcetera.

MARIE: Who is this lady you are interested in?

DR. JOHN Her name is to remain anonymous until you have agreed to be of professional assistance to me.

MARIE: Are you a real doctor?

DR. JOHN: I give potions and advice, but no, I'm not a physician.

MARIE:	I won't do anything against the church or anything that would put me in jail.
DR. JOHN:	(stands) I'm deeply hurt that you could harbor such an idea; (crosses to door) really, a man of my reputation, to . . .
MARIE:	Please, I didn't mean it like it sounded. If it's legal and there's money in it, I am your coworker.
DR. JOHN:	Fine. I'll have that tea now.
MARIE:	(brings him a fresh cup. Teapot is sitting on the charcoal burner).
DR. JOHN:	This, Madame Rousseau, tell me all about her as I am sure she speaks freely to you about all the most intimate things in her life.
MARIE:	I know a great deal about her and her friends.
DR. JOHN:	Good, (holds up money) for each piece of information you give me, I assure you this information shall be kept in professional confidence. I am prepared to pay you grandly (laughs) and it's perfectly legal.
MARIE:	Of course, I feed you information and you use it along with your potions, fortune telling and advice.
DR. JOHN:	To our best advantage. Shall we drink on it, my dear?
MARIE:	(They raise their cups and drink.) I read tea leaves like Dr. Jack taught me. .
DR. JOHN:	Dr. Jack, indeed, (puts down his cup) he just took the name Dr. Jack to cut himself into my practice. All he can do is love potions, simple voodoo. How close are you with this Dr. Jack?
MARIE:	I haven't seen him in years, he knew my late husband.
DR. JOHN:	Accept my deepest sympathies for your late husband.

MARIE:	Thank you. I wonder if as part payment to me you would consider teaching me fortune telling, gris-gris and...
DR. JOHN:	One thing at a time (pauses). If thinking you might be a very good asset to the profession, (he stands up) one moment, I'll be right back. (Exits. Returns with a cat.)
MARIE:	(She has followed him to the door) Dr. John, when may I see you again?
DR. JOHN:	Lesson one: never appear too anxious. It is not professional. (Pause) Second lesson: this is Hoodoo Voodoo.
MARIE:	(Taking the cat from Dr. John) What a beautiful cat. Are you giving her to me?
DR. JOHN:	One never owns a feline, but if Hoodoo Voodoo adopts you, it's your friend as long as she desires to stay with you. This is a very special cat with a very special name. Appropriately, as I said, it is Hoodoo Voodoo.
MARIE:	Hoodoo Voodoo? Stay with me, I am so lonesome.
DR. JOHN:	She will be your assistant in your new work. She lived with a witch and was taught many things pertaining to witchcraft and voodoo.
MARIE:	Why has the witch and Hoodoo parted?
DR. JOHN:	The witch returned to Europe and Hoodoo Voodoo decided she did not wish to cross the water on a ship. I don't blame her. So many weeks on the Atlantic Ocean can be very rough and unpleasant. I want you to get to know hoodoo very well. When you are friends, you may send her, at first, on small errands.
MARIE:	What kinds of errands?
DR. JOHN:	To begin with, by taking potions to our ladies. The delivery will be made to their threshold by

	Hoodoo Voodoo. She is adept at going to the second and even third story windows to deposit whatever…
MARIE:	How do I communicate with her?
DR. JOHN:	You'll find a way. It's usually to talk to her, to chant, whatever. Remember two things, first, if the cat likes you, and she will if you're good to her, and secondly if your magic is genuine if you believe in what you are doing, there will be no problem. So now, I leave you. Practice makes perfect. I must go (kisses her hand).
MARIE:	When shall I see you again?
DR. JOHN:	Number one – when I need more information. Number two: when Hoodoo Voodoo can bring me a message from you. For now, I want you to only communicate your information through hoodoo voodoo. This is my address. This is your way of becoming rich and famous.
MARIE:	This is gentle blackmail. Who's to know where the intimate details of a person's life come from? (Laughs) One question…?
DR. JOHN:	(looking at his pocket watch) I have time for only one – quickly, please.
MARIE:	Does Hoodoo Voodoo understand English?
DR. JOHN:	(exits laughing. Can be heard off stage)
MARIE:	(To cat, petting it) You really are a different cat. Your coloring, and those blue, blue eyes. (Knock on door.) (Marie goes to the door)
MARIE:	Please come in. I'll get a fresh cup so we can have some tea.
FR. CYRIL:	(Religious leader) (counting cups) I see you've already had company today.
MARIE:	Yes, the famous Dr. John. It's so exciting
FR. CYRIL:	Do you think it wise to be seen with him?

MARIE:	The most aristocratic ladies of New Orleans go to him and just think, he came to see me.
FR. CYRIL:	Marie, you are a good, hard working woman. I should hate to see you compromise your good principles and…
MARIE:	Why do you say that? What's the difference between that man and a religious leader? He helps people in the here and now, and you help them in the here after.
FR. CYRIL:	Have you heard of heaven and hell and of Satan?
MARIE:	Yes, in church, which reminds me, I have (she crosses over to Fr. Cyril) money for the church. And here is some more for the poor. (Fr. Cyril puts a hand out and takes the money)
FR. CYRIL:	Bless you, my child.
MARIE:	I'll need plenty of blessings (laughs and pours some tea in Fr. Cyril's cup)
FR. CYRIL:	Thank you, I wonder if you could do me a small favor. I have to leave town today and I thought perhaps you could bring this cross to Madame Rousseau. I went by her home, but I was told she would not return until much later today. So, I thought you could deliver this cross for me. That would save me another trip way across town.
MARIE:	Of course I'll do it for you. But why didn't you leave the cross with one of the servants?
FR. CYRIL:	That's a good question, Marie. You could always see right through a person, almost like you could read their minds (stands). Today the chief investigator of police – chief Isidor, mentioned your name to me. Rest easy, I told him nothing. I wonder if you want to tell me something.
MARIE:	There is nothing to tell.
FR. CYRIL:	No matter what it is, you know you can talk freely with me. I am your friend and I do want

	to help.
MARIE:	If I need you, I'll call on you. Right now I'm looking through rose-colored glasses. That's better than before. Now I have new hope, new horizons.
FR. CYRIL:	Remember, the devil speaks with a sweet and double-edged tongue. Be careful, you are judged by the company you keep.
MARIE:	That's why I always like to be with you.
FR. CYRIL:	What can I say (exits) (leaves the cross on the table).
MARIE:	(to cat) Make yourself right at home. Relax (pushes the cat outside). I've got to hurry and get over to Madame Rousseau…
	(There is a knock on the door)
	(Marie opens the door. Chief Inspector Isidor is at the door.)
ISIDOR:	My card, Madame. (Marie runs her fingers over the card) I am Chief Inspector Isidor.
MARIE:	Come in, please. (Pause) I can read.
ISIDOR:	So many do not in these times – maybe in a few hundred years, if the teachers do their work.
MARIE:	Would you like to have a cup of tea?
ISIDOR:	Thank you, I take sugar…
MARIE:	I'm sorry I'm out of sugar, but I have some honey.
ISIDOR:	Too sweet. I'll take it plain.
MARIE:	(Pouring tea in Isidor's cup) it's really hot. Please do be careful.
ISIDOR:	Thank you. (Clears throat) What I have to ask you is very personal.
MARIE:	It must be, otherwise you would have made me come to you at the police station.
ISIDOR:	From what I have heard, you are a person who can carry gossip from one patron to another.

MARIE:	If I did that I'd be out of business immediately.
ISIDOR:	Therefore, I would expect you to keep our conversation between the two of us totally private.
MARIE:	(Picks up the cross).
ISIDOR:	Swear on the cross.
MARIE:	I swear.
ISIDOR:	I am investigating a Dr. Kraut – k.r.a.u.t.
MARIE:	What has he done?
ISIDOR:	You know who he is. Tell me about him – in your own words.
MARIE:	Let me see. Old Kraut. He's passé (giggles) I'd say he's a high stepper.
ISIDOR:	By that you mean…?
MARIE:	He steps from one bed to another. Don't misunderstand me -- he's quite harmless.
ISIDOR:	Quite harmless, you say? (Writing everything down.)
MARIE:	(Motioning to Isidor to continue writing) He's too old – can't really do anything, physically, you know.
ISIDOR:	Have you ever visited him professionally?
MARIE:	I don't fix men's hair.
ISIDOR:	No, of course not. But I meant as one of Dr. Kraut's patients?
MARIE:	No. He's some sort of surgeon, but very old fashioned. I wouldn't go to him.
ISIDOR:	Now, we're getting somewhere.
MARIE:	What else, is there to say?
ISIDOR:	Has he ever lost a patient?
MARIE:	How would I know?
ISIDOR:	Women talk. Is he popular?
MARIE:	He was, yes.
ISIDOR:	Let's leave his age and popularity for a while. Is he an honest man? I know you don't know him

	professionally or otherwise, but what do the ladies, say?
MARIE:	He'd cut anybody's throat for a price.
ISIDOR:	What about he and a certain Doctor Carre from the Bayou…
MARIE:	Sorry, I never heard of him.
ISIDOR:	It's been in all the newspapers… the duel…
MARIE:	I never read the newspapers. I can't afford it.
ISIDOR:	Do you know Dr. Alerson?
MARIE:	Only by reputation. It's getting late, and I have an appointment to do a lady's hair, and it's way out on the other side of town. I have to walk over there.
ISIDOR:	I'll take you in my carriage.
MARIE:	Would you? How very kind of you. I'll get my cat.
ISIDOR:	No cats, I detest the little beasts.
MARIE:	You won't even know she's there. I'll put her in a basket (touches his arm), please?
ISIDOR:	If you insist. We still have a little time. What about this Dr. Alerson person?
MARIE:	There's a frightful scandal brewing around him, I just love scandals. Don't you? It seems that the doctor left his wife of a trillion years for another man's wife. There is talk about a duel!
ISIDOR:	Before hand, could you, would you find out more about the duel?
MARIE:	Before hand?
ISIDOR:	Who the seconds are going to be, and when it's going to be held?
MARIE:	The seconds are Dr. T and Dr. F. When it's going to be held, I don't know. But why this sudden interest in duels?
ISIDOR:	I could ask you the same thing. Like why your sudden interest in cats, especially this one.

MARIE:	I think we are beginning to understand each other…
ISIDOR:	Quite well indeed, my dear. (Laughs) (They exit.)

(CURTAIN – END OF ACT ONE)

CHAPTER TWENTY-NINE

Madagascar

GILBERT ORGANIZED HIS CREW to protect Babette and Tiffany, and they cleared a passage for them through the throng of admirers. It felt like a multitude was crowding the playwright as she exited the theatre. At the end of the made-up corridor, Captain Galveston was waiting near the elevator to congratulate their famous passenger.

"Ms. Babette, let me be one of the first to say how much I admire your talent. This play is the best I have seen in a long time." He took Babette's extended right hand and kissed the top of it lightly.

"My dear Captain, thank you so much, but congratulations are perhaps a little premature; we still have two more acts to perform after all."

"Dear Lady, if they are as good and as well choreographed as this first one, then I would personally recommend having this play produced on Broadway."

"I am quite sure, Captain, that my producer would be very receptive to your complimentary comments. And again thank you for allowing the cast to perform aboard this wonderful vessel."

"My pleasure, Ms. Babette." Galveston paused. "And now let me accompany you to your cabin…"

"Thank you, Captain, that would be lovely."

Alan, in the meantime, had grabbed Tiffany's hand and had led her away from the ever-inquisitive passengers.

"You were right, Tiff," Alan said, "This is one of the best – if not the best play Babette has ever written and produced aboard one of our cruises."

A broad smile adorning her beautiful face, Tiffany lifted her gaze to her handsome man. "I know. But it's been so hard on Babette. You can't imagine what a production such as this one takes. This is not a simple performance with some actors moving from one room to another or reciting lines; there are drummers, dancers, singers, special effects, light changes, and costumes, my God, Alan, the costumes…"

"Did you have a dresser for all these costume changes?"

"Oh yes, and I think Babette herself had her come on this trip especially for this play."

"Do you know her name?" Alan asked, his curiosity peeked slightly.

"Sure. I think it's Pilkington, Sarah Pilkington."

Alan's mouth fell open. He couldn't believe it. "I think I met the lady briefly a few days ago," he remarked.

"Oh? And where was that?" Tiffany asked; eyebrows arched.

"I was just having a break and went to the bar on the second deck for some juice, --- she was there having a drink…"

"Did she introduce herself then?"

Alan shook his head. "No, not to me anyway, but she did to another fellow who was sitting on the other side of her," he lied. Alan didn't want to divulge what he and Edmund had found out about the woman, or why.

"I guess she had to take a break from being on that sewing machine all the time. Seems like there was a rehearsal or a fitting practically every day since the cruise started."

"Well, let's leave this lady's sewing and entertainment aside for now, shall we?" Alan suggested, passing an arm around Tiffany's waist. "Do you remember what I promised you?"

"When?"

"This morning, if my memory serves me."

"Oh yeah – you mean spending a night in your arms, is that it?"

Alan nodded, grinning.

"Well, let's go and get that promise fulfilled, shall we?" Tiffany said, already walking in the direction of the elevators, which were quite empty by now. Most passengers had retired either to their suites or to the buffet restaurant on the upper deck.

The arrival into the port of Antsiranana, the northernmost seaport on the island of Madagascar, was a splendid sight. The bay fronting the coast seemed to embrace every vessel that passed between the idyllic islands punctuating its waters. As in most seaports of the world these days, the captain doesn't maneuver his ship to the pier. The seaport authorities send a pilot to board the vessel, and it's this expert who steers the ship to port. In this case, *The Baroness* was to be driven to her berth by an English fellow – a seafarer of long experience by the name of Julian Bainbridge. Well into his fifties with a handsome beard adorning a square and decisive jaw line. When the pilot boat came to the starboard flank of *The Baroness*, to Galveston's slight, but not totally unexpected surprise, Julian climbed aboard with two other men.

"Captain Bainbridge," Galveston said genially when Julian made his appearance on the bridge, "How nice to see you again, my friend."

"Permission to come aboard, Captain," Julian replied quite formally in his British accent.

"By all means, dear chap, by all means, permission granted," Galveston replied, returning Bainbridge's salute. Then looking at the two fellows behind him, he asked, "You brought company, I see?"

"Yes, Captain, but they are not part of the port authority – they are CIA agents."

Galveston looked the two fellows up and down. He knew he had no choice but to grant them coming aboard his vessel. "Welcome aboard, gentlemen," he said stiffly. "May I have your names for the record, please?"

The first agent was a young and brash-looking man in his mid-thirties perhaps, who showed every sign of ultimate boredom with formalities. His brown eyes were leading his traveling gaze to every corner of the bridge until it finally rested on Galveston. "I'm CIA Agent Fredrick Chalkstone, sir."

"Thank you. And you are?" the captain asked the older of the two men.

"I am Agent Simeon Mallard, Captain." Simeon was non-descript. Everything about him was average – average height, average looks, average face – no distinguishing features at all. He was probably perfect in any sort of job.

"Very good. Now that I know who's who, let me show you two agents to my office while I leave the maneuvering to Captain Bainbridge and my First Officer. Shall we?" He stretched an arm in the direction of the door that would lead them to the bridge deck's private office of the captain.

As they entered Galveston's quarters, again, Chalkstone looked around him, like a squirrel making sure there were no hidden acorns, before he responded to the captain's invitation for both men to sit down in the visitors' chairs facing his desk.

"Well then, Agents Chalkstone and Mallard, am I to presume correctly that you're here to question some of our passengers and crew about what they saw or heard at the time of Mrs. Clipper's murder?"

Mallard was the first to open his mouth. "Yes, Captain, you presumed correctly. On the other hand, our task will not be restricted to those interviews only, we have to take another look at Ms. Walter's murder – confirm if, in fact, she was murdered or if it was an accident. And furthermore, we are expecting a team of forensic scientists to come aboard – with your permission, of course – to examine the crime scenes and the cabins that had been occupied by Ms. Walter and Mrs. Clipper." He paused. "I suppose these cabins have remained sealed, have they?"

"As per the CIA's instructions, yes they have," Galveston replied, leaning to the back of his chair.

It was Chalkstone's turn to speak now. "We have a list"—he pulled an iPhone out of the inner pocket of his leather vest—"of passengers and officers that we would like to interview." He passed it to Galveston's extended hand.

The captain took a few moments to scan the names. "I see that you want to see Doctor Mayhew first; any reason for this?"

"No particular reason, Captain," Mallard answered, "as you know, Dr. Mayhew has assisted Interpol in the past and we would be interested in his expertise from speaking to him. We would like to have a summary of what he knows about both cases, before we question anyone else. That's all."

"And what about Agent Chulbridge?" Galveston asked, already wondering why he hadn't seen the man's name listed on the iPhone.

"He's out of our field of purview, Captain. As far as we know, he's an undercover Interpol agent and we have copies of his reports on file. No need to go any further with him." Mallard seemed to be adamant about not approaching Chubb.

"You have to understand, Captain," Chalkstone added, "that Agent Chulbridge is probably the lynchpin in blowing this drug trafficking operation out of the water. We don't want to upset his work at this point."

"Yes, of course," Captain Galveston agreed concertedly. "However, Mr. Gilbert Evans, our chief of security, may ask you to clarify a few points regarding the fellow's movements…"

"What movements are those?" Mallard asked.

"I can only refer you to the fact that our "cloaked man" was seen entering Ms. Babette's cabin while she was out and Agent Chulbridge later confessed that he was the person in question. Should we then deduce that Agent Chulbridge is our "cloaked man" – that's my question."

Mallard and Chalkstone exchanged a glance.

"We might see what the best course of action would be, once we've talked to Mr. Evans," Mallard said, although his answer was as indecisive and as politically correct as it could have been at this juncture.

Playing it close to the chest, Galveston reflected silently. "Very well, gentlemen," he said, indicating the meeting was over by getting to his feet. "I'll have Mr. Ekelton show you to the cabin we have reserved for the time you'll spend aboard *The Baroness*."

"Thank you, Captain," Mallard said, standing up together with Chalkstone.

The latter looked around at the bookcases lining one of the walls, and the comfortable décor of this small room before he and Mallard walked to the door of Galveston's private office.

"Robert Ekelton," the staff captain said, introducing himself to the two men as they emerged onto the deck.

"I'm Agent Simeon Mallard, and this is Agent Fredrick Chalkstone," Mallard replied, shaking Ekelton's extended hand.

"Let me show you to your temporary quarters, gentlemen. This way…" Ekelton said, stepping in front of the two agents.

Everyone was on the promenade deck, watching *The Baroness* making her way ever so slowly through the bay. The cell-phone and digital cameras were clicking at the sight of the rising sun illuminating the hills bordering the coastline. The scenery seemed almost unreal. The green of the forest, the multicolored roofs of the city and the pink of the hillside were veiled in a blue morning haze rising from the ocean.

"Incredible sight," one passenger said to a gorgeous young lady standing beside him against the railing. Her long, black hair did everything to accent her clear and beautifully made-up face, even at this early hour of the morning.

"You said it, quite fantastic in fact," she replied. "And steering such a large vessel seems much simpler than driving a car…"

The man laughed. "My name is Henry Duchesne," he said, turning to the lady.

She smiled. "I'm Miss Avonlea – just call me Avon," she said, winking.

The laughter returned. "You're "Avon calling" then?"

"I suppose I would be if I were to call on anyone." She grinned this time.

"What were you saying about steering a ship…?" Henry asked.

"Yes," Avon said, turning to face the fellow. "You see, I love driving and I always like to be prepared. So, when I come to a new city, I like to get oriented to everything and know where I'm going before I stop at the hotel."

Henri nodded. "And you travel much?"

"Not so much now – not since I had a flat not so long ago."

"A flat? Did the tire blow out on you?"

"A flat, not a blow out, but it was just a big misunderstanding…"

"Did someone help you change the tire...?" Henri couldn't fathom what could have happened to Avon.

"That's just the point" – Henri stared – "of what happened. I had a flat tire on I95; so, I pulled over, got out of the car and opened my trunk. I took out my cardboard men, unfolded them and stood them at the rear of my car, facing oncoming traffic. They look so lifelike you wouldn't believe it! Just as I had hoped, cars started slowing down, looking at the men, which made it much safer for me to work on the side of the road. People honked and waved. It wasn't long before a police car pulled up behind me. The officer wanted to know what the heck I was doing, so I calmly explained that I was changing my flat. He told me he could see that. He demanded to know what the heck my cardboard men were doing standing at the rear of my car. I couldn't believe he didn't know! So I told him: 'They're my Emergency Flashers!' I go to court in May. Damn Police. No sense of humor."

Exploding in roaring laughter, Henri almost burst a vein on his ruddy face. "And you carry flashing cardboard men in your trunk?"

"Not anymore I don't," Avon said, shaking her head. "Far too dangerous!"

CHAPTER THIRTY

Forensics galore

WHEN THE FORENSIC TEAM, composed of two men and a woman, boarded *The Baroness,* Alan was near the top of the gangway to meet them.

"Good morning," he said, "I'm Dr. Alan Mayhew. Welcome aboard *The Baroness.*"

"Very pleased to meet you, Doctor, my name is Dr. Francis Rivers, and these"—he turned to his companions—"are my assistants, Ms. Jenny Ashton and Mr. Daniel Richard."

Alan shook hands with the three of them. "Stevie, your steward"—he put a hand on the man's shoulder—"will show you to your quarters, and then escort you to the medical center where we can discuss the situation."

"Very well, Dr. Mayhew," Rivers said, looking at Stevie, "Let's get going then."

Alan watched the three of them as they were walking away toward the elevators and wondered why a doctor would have been assigned to this case. *Perhaps he's a forensic pathologist,* he reflected as he made his way toward his cabin.

Dr. Francis Rivers was, in fact, a forensic pathologist of some note. In his fifties, with a clean-shaven face and intelligent hazel eyes, he seemed to take everything in stride. He had seen more than one dismembered corpse during his career and the body parts of Mrs. Clipper were probably going to be of great interest to him. *We'll see,* he thought, as he followed the steward to their suite.

Jenny Ashton was another story altogether. She usually accompanied Dr. Rivers on his assignments with the CIA. She was his sounding board, his "devil's advocate". Her short ash-blonde hair and brown eyes accentuated her sober facial features. She was a no nonsense woman and a very critical one at that. She also had a degree in forensic science, same as her colleague, Daniel Richard. He, on the other hand, was the quiet and reserved fellow that made good use of his analytical mind. No detail, however minute, would escape him. He was known to spend hours in the lab analyzing a microscopic piece of evidence and come up with the strangest, but usually correct, deductions.

"Here we are then," Rivers declared genially as soon as he deposited his case on the luggage rack of the bedroom. "Let's not keep Dr. Mayhew waiting," he added as his companions extracted two body suits out of their cases.

They were about to follow their mentor when Jenny said, "Don't you want to take a suit with you?"

"Yes, yes, of course," Rivers replied, turning back to his luggage. "Can't *leave home without it*, now can we?" He guffawed.

Mallard and Chalkstone were waiting for Alan as soon as he reached the medical center. *They don't waste any time, do they,* he remarked to himself as he stepped inside to welcome the two agents.

"Doctor Mayhew, is it?" Mallard asked as he got up from the waiting room chair and advanced toward Alan, a hand extended.

"One and the same," Alan replied, shaking the man's hand. "And you must be Agent Mallard."

"Yes, Doctor, and this is my partner, Agent Chalkstone." The latter nodded. "May we have a word?" Mallard asked.

"Yes, of course. Do come in, gentlemen, and have a seat," Alan invited, stretching an arm toward the visitors' chairs across from his desk.

They sat down.

"Okay," Mallard began, "We've received and read your reports, Doctor, and we only need you to answer a few questions, if that's okay with you."

"Sure, what would you like to know?"

Chalkstone looked at his partner before he said, "We know very little about life aboard a cruise liner, Doctor, but it seems to us it's very much like a floating hotel with no door to escape onto the streets."

Alan grinned. "Yes, it is similar to a hotel as you say, except for another fact that I think is very pertinent to this case; we are totally self-contained. Nothing and no body comes in or gets off the vessel when it's at sea; unless, of course, they are tossed off."

"What about when the ship is at port?" Mallard inquired.

"Ah yes, and that's where it gets tricky when it comes to keeping track of our passengers in particular. We have an electronic system that controls their comings and goings, and several guards on dockside and at each end of the gangway. You must have noticed them yourselves."

"Yes, we did, Doctor, and so it would be fair to say that our person of interest – or the "cloaked man" as you call him – came aboard in Papua, is that correct?"

"Yes, that's my contention. Since the first incident occurred before we reached the Maldives, we assumed that our cloaked fellow was already on board before then."

"That is if we assume our fellow was the one who pushed Ms. Walter over the railing. Right?"

"Absolutely, Agent Mallard. But your own man – or I should say Interpol's own Agent Chulbridge – was a witness to that incident…"

"Yes, yes," Chalkstone interrupted, "but he only saw a cloaked figure at the time – it could have been another man in Mrs. Clipper's case, couldn't it?"

"And that would mean that someone else, dressed as a monk, drove Mrs. Clipper to her demise," Alan rejoined. "That's a possibility, I suppose," he added.

At that moment the three men turned their heads to see Dr. Rivers and his assistants come into the medical center.

"Hello, hello, everyone," Rivers said with a broad grin accompanying his loud voice. "I see the "duck" and the "chalk" have arrived," he remarked, advancing toward Alan. "Doctor Mayhew, how are you, my dear fellow. I've heard so much about you, I feel we've known each other for years..."

"Welcome, Dr. Rivers. Why don't you have Mr. Richard pull three chairs from the waiting room for all of you to have a seat?"

"Yes, yes"—Rivers turned to Richard—"why don't you do that, dear boy."

"You know, Dr. Rivers, since we've worked together last," Mallard said, "you haven't changed – taking charge everywhere you go, don't you?"

"Well, can't very well leave you nincompoops bungle the job, can we? The boss wouldn't like that, now would he?"

All the while this was happening, Alan smiled to himself. *This Dr. Rivers is sure a character, just like many pathologists.*

"But don't let us interrupt your interview of the good doctor here," Rivers added, "I always like to listen to those, Ducky." He laughed. "And as for you, Chalky, make sure you listen closely to Ducky here – he's going to teach you a thing or two about investigative work..."

"I'm sorry, Dr. Rivers," Alan cut in, "but I think we need to concentrate our efforts on the matter at hand and as Agent Chalkstone remarked before you arrived, we may have two perpetrators aboard."

"Hmm, that would be very interesting indeed, wouldn't it, Ducky?" Rivers said, as Richard and Jenny came back with three chairs, which they placed beside those of Mallard and Chalkstone. "Thanks, Jenny," Rivers added, sitting himself down.

"The first one," Alan went on, "would have hidden under a cloak to avoid detection from the surveillance cameras on deck, but the second perpetrator, would have simply taken his cue from the first man. Is that what you're advancing, Agent Chalkstone?"

"As you said earlier, Doctor, it's a possibility worth exploring." Mallard turned his face to Rivers. "And that's where you and your team come in, Dr. Rivers. You see, the first incident occurred on the open deck, but the second one occurred somewhere else, presumably in closed quarters – perhaps Mrs. Clippers' cabin – before the woman was brought down to the sanitation department in the bowels of the ship to be dropped into one of the septic tanks."

Daniel Richard sat up. "We could follow her traces from the tank back to wherever she was killed," he suggested.

"Why don't I call Simon Albertson, our sanitation engineer," Alan interposed, "and he can take you down there as soon as you want?" He looked at the five faces staring at him.

"Yes, of course, Dr. Mayhew," Rivers said, "But as for me, I'd like to see and start working on Mrs. Clipper's body, if you don't mind."

"Okay then," Alan said, "why don't we resume our little chat, Agent Mallard, later this afternoon once Dr. Rivers and his team have been introduced to the various scenes of the crimes."

Mallard nodded in reply. "Yes, I think that's best. Perhaps we could interview the playwright in the meantime…?"

"Yes," Alan answered, "but she's had a very long night and if you wouldn't mind interviewing her in my presence, I think that would be better."

"And why would that be, Doctor?" Chalkstone asked, suspicion lacing his words.

"Because, Ms. Babette is one of our most esteemed passengers, and she is not a young woman either."

"But we have no intention of frightening the dear old thing," Mallard said derisively, smiling. "We just want to have a friendly chat with her."

"Then if that's all you want, you wouldn't mind if I attend "your friendly chat", now would you?"

Mallard shook his head and chuckled. "Okay, Doctor, have it your way. We'll follow your lead – no problem."

Meanwhile, Dr. Rivers had been listening to the little exchange with interest. He now lifted his gaze to Alan expectantly.

Alan nodded and lifted the telephone receiver. As soon as he got Simon on the line, he said, "Mr. Albertson, this is Doctor Mayhew. Would you mind coming up to the medical center to escort the CIA forensic team to your department?"

"Be right there, Doc," Simon replied before hanging up abruptly.

"He'll be right up," Alan said, signaling the meeting was over by standing up.

"Okay, we'll check back with you at lunch, after we've had a chat with your chief of security," Mallard said to Alan.

"No problem, Agent Mallard. Take my mobile number in case I'm still in the morgue with Dr. Rivers." Alan handed the man his cell-phone for him to take the number.

A half-an-hour later Alan was facing Dr. Rivers across the autopsy table in the morgue.

"The poor woman," Rivers said, as soon as Alan had unzipped the body bag. "I hope she was dead before lowering her in that tank."

"As far as I could tell," Alan began, "she was struck on the right tibia"—he pointed to the exposed bone—"which caused her fall, and then she was struck on the head, probably with the same weapon."

"And you have examined the skull and determined perhaps what sort of weapon was used."

"Yes," Alan said, moving toward the woman's head. "You see"—he took the skull in his gloved hands and turned it over—"there is a deep, elongated indent at the back of her head, which indicated to me that she was struck by a cane or a pipe."

"Ah yes, I see what you mean," Rivers agreed, looking at the wound closely. "I think we should scrape the skull and tibia in and around the wounds and give the tissue to Daniel Richard to examine. And if our killer indeed used a cane, he will soon tell us."

"But wouldn't he need a powerful electron microscope to determine what sort of weapon was used?"

Rivers shook his head. "Although you're right, his findings couldn't be conclusive until we go back to the lab, he could at least tell us if the wounds either on the leg or on the skull were caused by a metal or wooden object."

"Well then, let's get to work," Alan concluded, pulling the surgical instrument trolley closer to the table.

When everybody had left the medical center, Alice and Evelyn exhaled a heavy sigh of relief. They looked at each other and started laughing.

"Wasn't that Dr. Rivers something else?" Alice said.

"He sure was. And did you see that Ms. Ashton – she looks like the perfect spinster, doesn't she?" Evelyn added.

Their exchange was soon interrupted when a strange male passenger came in. Evelyn and Alice looked at each other and smiled, the fellow unzipped his fly as soon as he came through the door.

"Sir," Alice said, "Why don't we go to the emergency room before you demonstrate or show me what's wrong, okay?"

"Sure," the old man replied, holding his hand in front of his pants, "but there's sure something wrong with my fellow today."

As soon as Alice and the man were out of sight, she asked, "Okay then, tell me what's wrong."

"It died today," the old guy said, exposing his penis.

"What do you mean it died today?" Alice asked, trying to keep a straight face.

"Well, look at it – it's not moving, is it?"

"Sir, I'm sorry but there doesn't seem to be anything wrong with it," Alice said, lifting her gaze to the man's face now.

"Oh don't tell me I've made a mistake? I've already arranged a private showing and a bunch of flowers for its funeral!"

"You're pulling my leg, aren't you?" Alice said, trying not to laugh.

"No, not at all, Ms. Alice. Actually I was hoping you'd do me the honor to accompany me to that private showing…"

Now laughing outright, Alice said, "Not a chance, you old goat. But I sure thank you for the compliment in that pick-up line!"

CHAPTER THIRTY-ONE

A second cloaked man?

AS CHALKSTONE AND MALLARD entered Gilbert's office, once again Chalkstone looked around him, his eyes darting from one corner of the room to the other.

"Chief Evans, very nice of you to spare time for us," Mallard said when Gilbert stood up to shake hands with the man.

"Not at all," Gilbert replied, "I'm the one who's grateful for the CIA coming all the way from Washington to take over this case." He looked at Chalkstone who still hadn't said a word. "And you must be Agent Chalkstone?"

"Yes, Mr. Evans. Nice, but claustrophobic office you've got here."

"Thank you," Gilbert said. "Why don't you have a seat, so we can begin reviewing the cases?" He pointed to the two chairs facing his desk.

"Thanks, Chief," Mallard replied, while Chalkstone nodded, sitting down.

"Okay, as you probably know from reading the reports," Gilbert began, "we've got two unresolved crimes."

"Not exactly," Chalkstone interrupted, "we've got one unconfirmed case of manslaughter and one confirmed murder."

"Yes, you're right. Although we have a witness that places a perpetrator at the scene of Ms. Walter's accident..."

"Agent Chulbridge you mean?" Mallard asked.

This is going to take longer than I thought if these guys don't stop with the interruptions, Gilbert thought. "Yes, exactly. He's only identified the person – man or woman – as a cloaked figure who pushed Ms. Walter over the railing. Unfortunately, she hit the edge of one of our rescue vessels and broke her neck in the fall."

"So, from the witness's account you've deduced that Ms. Walter was either pushed with intent to harm, or pushed as a result of an altercation that occurred previously, correct?"

"Yes, Agent Mallard. Yet, either way, as you will see for yourselves, she couldn't have fallen by accident. These railings are high enough that a person intending to jump would have to climb over it before anything could happen to them."

"And Agent Chulbridge could not confirm whether it was a man or a woman dressed in that monk's habit, could he?"

"Precisely. As you read in my report, Agent Chulbridge didn't stay around to provide any assistance to the victim or even alert us of the accident. Instead he chose to run to Ms. Walter's cabin, take possession of the cocaine she was hiding in her room, and subsequently involved Mrs. Clipper and our sanitation engineer in a scheme, whereby the packets of cocaine ended up in my safe."

"Yes, yes, that's what we've read," Chalkstone uttered somewhat impatiently. "And we have no intention of intervening in Agent Chulbridge's assignment at this point…"

"Something to do with him being undercover, I gather," Gilbert remarked.

"Exactly. And all we will ask is that he be permitted to take the drugs to Antsiranana when his contact gets in touch with him."

"I can appreciate your position, Agent Mallard, and I will be pleased to put these drugs into Agent Chulbridge's hands when two things are clarified."

"What two things are you talking about, Mr. Evans?" Chalkstone asked.

"Well, first we have an Interpol agent who put Mrs. Clipper in grave danger when he involved her in his scheme to hide the drugs, and that plan ultimately resulted in her death."

"But he's by no means responsible for her death," Mallard cut-in, visibly annoyed.

"We do not know that for a fact, Agent Mallard," Gilbert snapped.

"We only took his word for it as soon as we knew he was undercover. But it wouldn't be the first time that an undercover agent has gone over to the other side."

"Yes, of course, but I don't think it's the case here."

"We'll see," Gilbert replied. "And what's more, when it comes to our cloaked fellow, no one has been able to locate anyone wearing a signet ring – or *a man* wearing a signet ring."

"And what's that second item you mentioned, Chief?" Chalkstone asked.

"When I show you the security camera tapes you'll understand." He paused. "You see, Ms. Babette and Ms. Sylvan have been victims of a bad joke, whereby Agent Chulbridge went into their cabins and wrote a threatening message on the mirror of their bathrooms. When we examined the tapes, we saw a cloaked figure enter Ms. Babette's cabin shortly before she returned from the theater on the night in question."

"And so you think our cloaked figure is none other than Agent Chulbridge, is that it?" Mallard inquired.

"Well, what other deduction could there be?"

"I see what you mean. But why kill Mrs. Clipper, when it's the last thing an undercover agent would want – like attracting attention, I mean."

"I must agree with you, Agent Chalkstone, it was not the best of plans if you want to pass unnoticed. However, you must also admit that everything Agent Chulbridge is alleged to have done was designed to attract attention. First, we have him take the drugs from Ms. Walter's cabin after he probably helped her to her death, then we have him writing silly messages on Ms. Babette and Ms. Sylvan's mirrors, and finally we have this elaborate killing and dismemberment. If I wanted to keep away from anyone prying into my work, I would certainly find a more discreet way of doing it, wouldn't you agree?"

Mallard and Chalkstone exchanged a nodding glance.

"What if someone used the cloaked figure scheme as a cover for murdering Mrs. Clipper?"

"Then I would have to ask, where's the motive, Agent Mallard?"

Meanwhile, Jenny Ashton and Daniel Richard were down in the sanitation department examining the tank in which Mrs. Clipper's body had been found.

"And how long was it between the time she was introduced to the tank and the time you found her, Mr. Albertson?" Daniel asked.

"I couldn't tell you for sure, Mr. Richard. It's thanks to Captain Galveston that we were able to locate her before the evening check, actually. You see, I check the tanks twice a day and she wasn't in there that morning."

"What time was that?" Jenny interrupted.

"Five every morning, Miss Ashton, as usual."

"Okay, and what time was it when you found her?" Daniel asked.

"Well, let me see..." Simon replied musingly. "It was about 6:30 or 7:00 pm during the second phase of the Charlie Drill."

"What's a "Charlie Drill"?" Daniel asked, frowning.

"That's when we're looking for something aboard ship, Mr. Richard. Crew search every where during the first phase, and the staff and officers search again during the second phase."

Daniel and Jenny nodded.

"So, she must have been dropped in the tank at around 10:00 am after she left the spa," Jenny said to Daniel.

"Sounds accurate." Daniel returned his attention to Simon. "And where were you around that time of the morning, around 10:00 am, Mr. Albertson?"

"Not anywhere around here, that's for sure," Simon replied. "See, I've got other duties associated with sanitation, like filtering garbage, compressing all recyclables and verifying all water regulators."

"So, you are not anywhere near this area after the check at 5:00 am and 7:00 pm, is that correct?"

"Yeah, that's right. See, these tanks take care of the crap – excuse my French – all by their lonesome. No one needs to watch over them."

"Okay then. I think we'll need a couple of hours to go over everything around here, if that's okay with you?"

"Sure thing, Mr. Richard. And if you need me in the meantime, I'll be in my cubbyhole"—he pointed to his office—"up the stairs there."

"We know you said that you weren't around here during the morning," Jenny said, "but if you had been in your office, could you have observed the perpetrator lower the victim into the tank?"

Simon shook his head. "No, Ms. Ashton. As you will notice there's only a small window in the door, and when I'm sitting at my desk, the window is at my back."

"And you couldn't hear anything either, or could you?"

"No, not a thing, Mr. Richard. The lid slides open without as much as a squeak."

"Do you have a cell-phone?" Jenny asked.

"Oh yes. Here, take the number from it." Simon took his phone out of its case on his belt and handed it to Jenny's extended hand.

"Well, thank you, Mr. Albertson." Daniel paused and looked at the tank. "Would it be possible for you to open it for us to examine it?"

"No problem," Simon answered, taking a set of keys out of his pocket, and turning one of them into the lock on the lid. Half of the lid swung open and slid beneath its counterpart silently. "See, you need a key to open the lid. So unless the killer's got a duplicate key, I don't know how he could have opened it." Jenny looked at the lock closely. "And if it's prints you're looking for, Miss Ashton; sorry, we didn't think we'd find anybody in there when I opened the tank that day, and my crew do daily cleaning of the tank's casings."

"Well, okay, Mr. Albertson. Thanks again for your help," Daniel said, his tone dismissive.

And that's that, Simon thought as he turned away with a nod. *I'll be curious to see what they find.*

Once they had completed their review of Mrs. Clipper's autopsy, Dr. Rivers and Alan parted ways. Rivers went back to find Daniel and Jenny in the sanitation department while Alan returned to the medical center. He was just about to settle down to writing his report to the head office when the door of the center opened. As soon as they came through, Alan recalled Mr. and Mrs. Roberts' first visit. They were in their nineties and both were having some problems remembering things. Alan had suggested that they write things down to help them with important things like medicines.

And today they were on their way to visit Antsiranana and wanted to see if Alan was going ashore. He wasn't planning on it, so he asked if they were both okay – especially with the "little memory problem."

"Oh sure," said Mr. Roberts. "We're writing everything down now."

"See, we had to, Doctor." Mrs. Roberts nodded to her husband. "That night you told us about writing things down, we didn't…"

"Let me tell the Doc, Dorris – you don't remember it the same," Mr. Roberts cut in decisively. "We were watching a movie in our cabin, when Dorris asked me to order a bowl of ice cream from the room service…"

"Love ice cream," Dorris noted.

"And then you said"—Mr. Roberts turned to his wife—"you wanted strawberries, didn't you?"

"Yes, and whipped cream, too." She nodded emphatically. "But I asked you if you wanted to note it down…"

"And I said: Of course not – you want ice cream, strawberries and whipped cream."

"And then he went to the phone," Dorris explained, "and I wasn't listening to what he ordered…" She smiled at her husband. "And you know what I got when the tray arrived?"

Alan didn't have any idea.

"Well, we got bacon, eggs, toast and coffee for two – at 10 o'clock at night!" Dorris said, erupting in laughter.

"And that's why we write everything down now, Doctor," Mr. Roberts concluded. "Now, did you say you were coming with us to visit the island?"

Alan didn't reply right away, but took his pad and wrote down:

SORRY, CANNOT COME WITH YOU TODAY, and handed the slip of paper to Mr. Roberts.

"Thank you so much, Doctor," Dorris said, after she read the one-liner note. "We'll check back with you tomorrow then!"

As they were walking out, Alan smiled to himself.

All the while this was happening aboard *The Baroness*, the dozens of passengers, who had booked a tour of the city or a trip to the surrounding areas, had already disembarked and had gone on their guided tours. Babette and Tiffany – with Edmund in their shadow – were among those who had decided to visit some of the older parts of the city on their own.

"These houses are so similar to those we can see in New Orleans, it's quite remarkable," Babette said, lifting her gaze to the corner two-story mansion in front of which they were standing. "The wrought iron balconies, the ornate windows and arcades are so well preserved, amazing!"

"They were quite new in my time," Edmund rejoined, "and I'm very happy to see that they've been restored properly."

"Apparently, some of them are open for visitors," Tiffany put-in. "Would you like to go inside?"

"Oh sure, that would be wonderful, my dear," Babette replied. "But do you know which ones are open?"

"Yes, I think our tour director said it was the one across the street just down the block from here." Tiffany pointed to the house in question.

Not waiting for the two ladies to cross the street, Edmund flew to the house, entered it through the balcony door and reappeared a few seconds later in front of the door on the ground floor.

"I hate when he does that," Babette remarked quietly to Tiffany as the two ladies crossed the street.

"Why is that?" Tiffany asked.

"It reminds me that he's only a ghostly figure and even if I wanted to, I couldn't nestle in his arms."

Tiffany giggled. "That must be frustrating," she said, refraining from laughing out loud.

"I wish the same," Edmund said to Babette as the women were in earshot.

"You heard me?!" Babette sounded taken aback.

"Absolutely, my dear. I don't miss a word you say – even a murmur will reach my ears."

"Well, in that case, I think you should shut your loud-speaker when we have our 'ladies' chat'," Babette said jocularly. "There are some things you shouldn't be allowed to hear."

"Alright then, but for the time being and while you're still under my protection, I beg of you to let me hear every sound you make," Edmund pleaded.

"As you wish," Babette said, a broad smile coming across her lips. "But do tell us, are there many people visiting the house right now?"

"Not at the moment, milady. It seems that most of the tour group has gone farther down the street." He paused and pointed to the upstairs balcony. "I just saw a couple admiring the bedroom furniture and one other person looking at the bath tub with some great interest." Edmund laughed.

Tiffany and Babette exchanged a smile. "Well then, let's see the inside of this intriguing house," Babette invited, walking ahead of Tiffany and Edmund.

"How perfectly wonderful," Babette said, as she entered the parlor off the foyer. "It looks almost the same as the décor I had chosen for Marie Laveau's parlor in our play."

"Doesn't it just," Tiffany agreed. "Look at the sofa and chairs – they're almost the same."

"Not quite, Ms. Tiffany," Edmund countered. "These are carved in redwood and upholstered with some local cotton cloth. Your décor furniture, although only reproductions, were better associated with the era in which Marie Laveau lived."

"Well, not everything was the same, I suppose, there are continents separating them after all."

"But it's gorgeous all the same," Tiffany remarked, following Babette up the stairs to the bedrooms.

As they entered, Edmund immediately noted that the couple who had been examining the four-poster bed was nowhere in sight. He planted himself in front of Babette. "Let's get out of here, ladies," he whispered to them.

"Why?" Babette asked – her voice down to a murmur.

"I can sense someone here, milady."

"Where?" Tiffany blurted, looking around her. "There's no one here…"

By the time she had uttered the last word of her reply, a cloaked figure rushed out of the huge wardrobe and lunged at Babette with a knife directed at her throat, pushing her down to the parquet floor and under him. In a wave of kinetic fury, Edmund sent the knife flying out the open window while Tiffany straddled the figure as if he were a bucking horse.

"Get off me!" Babette screamed, wiggling her body from under the man.

Her entire body fueled with rage and adrenalin, Tiffany grabbed the fellow by the shoulders and pulled him away, both tumbling backward to the floor. Aghast, the attacker jumped to his feet and ran down the stairs, out the front door and across the street, to disappear in a side alley.

Out of breath and quite shocked, Babette got to her knees and then Tiffany helped her up to her feet. "I need to sit down," she said, gasping for air.

"Yes, of course," Tiffany replied, leading the playwright to the chair near the dresser.

"Thank you both," Babette said, "I'm so glad you were here, Edmund. He would have killed me, if it hadn't been for you getting the knife out of his hands."

"And for Ms. Tiffany pulling him back," Edmund added modestly. "I'm sorry I couldn't do more…"

"Are you serious?" Babette blurted. "If it weren't for you, I would be standing beside you right now – I would be dead!"

Having regained her breath and having calmed down a little, Tiffany asked, "Did you see his face?"

Babette shook her head. "Not his face, Tiffany, no. He was wearing some sort of white stocking over his head, so I couldn't recognize him."

"But there was something I noticed," Edmund added.

"What's that?" Tiffany and Babette asked in unison.

"He was wearing a signet ring on his right hand."

CHAPTER THIRTY-TWO

Chubby Chubb-Chubb

AND THAT'S ALL EDMUND said before he suddenly exited the room, flying through the balcony door and over the alleyway where the three of them had observed the cloaked man disappear.

"Where is he going?" Babette blurted, looking up at Tiffany who was still standing beside her.

"I think Edmund feels a lot more than we could ever imagine, Babette. And I bet he's gone after the cloaked man."

"But he couldn't stop him anyway," Babette argued, "so why go after him?"

"I'd say he's hoping the man would take that stocking off his face and he'd be able to identify him that way."

"Yes, of course, Tiffany. Very clever of you, my dear," Babette said, getting up from the chair.

"Are you sure you're okay?"

"Yes, yes, I'm sure, dear. It would take a little more than a rough tumble about the bedroom floor to get me off my feet," the playwright replied with a broad smile. "But the curious thing to me is that Edmund mentioned three people being up here moments before we came into the house. What do you suppose happened to them?"

"No idea, Babette. Perhaps they left the house while we were downstairs in the parlor."

"Yes, I suppose that's a possibility, but I'd say the man who was looking at the bathtub stayed behind."

"And you think he's the one who attacked you?"

"Yes, Tiffany. It would be nothing for him to hide in the wardrobe after the couple had left the room and put on his cloak and balaclava to emerge as soon as we were up here."

"That sounds like a strong possibility," Tiffany agreed. "But then it also means Edmund saw the man before we arrived, doesn't it?"

Babette nodded. "Let's get out of here," she suggested, heading for the door and down the stairs. "I think I prefer writing about these sorts of things than living them."

After receiving a call from Tiffany on his cell and after she had told him what had happened at the old house, Alan was waiting for Babette and Tiffany at the top of the gangway.

"We should have sent one of Gilbert's men with you," Alan said as soon as Tiffany and Babette were close enough to hear him.

"I totally agree with you, son," Edmund said as he landed beside the three of them. "But as it is, I know the man who attacked you, Babette."

"And who's that?" Babette demanded, looking up at Edmund.

"Let's not talk here, shall we?" Alan suggested, "These cameras"—he looked up at the surveillance cameras above the door—"have eyes. No use alerting the culprit, okay?"

Babette and Tiffany nodded, and preceded Alan and Edmund into the foyer. Agents Mallard and Chalkstone were waiting for them.

"We've heard that you had a frightening experience, Ms. Babette, and we're sorry about that."

Babette stopped in front of Mallard and glowered at the man. "Yes, my young man, I did have a 'frightening experience' as you say, and if you kept a closer eye on the possible victims rather than questioning everyone, maybe none of this would have happened."

"I understand what you're saying, Ms. Babette, but we needed to have all the facts…"

"Yes, Agent, what ever your name is…"

"Agent Mallard, ma'am."

"Yes, well, Agent Mallard, if all of those reports I'm sure you've been receiving from our various officers aren't sufficient for you to gather all the facts, I suggest you go back to training school!"

"She's not happy," Edmund whispered in Alan's ear.

The doc smiled and nodded almost imperceptibly.

"Why don't we follow you to your cabin where you could tell us all about it?" Agent Chalkstone suggested mildly.

"And who are you?" Babette snapped.

"I'm Agent Chalkstone, Ms. Babette."

"Right you are, Agent Chalkstone, it's about time we had a chat as you said."

A few minutes later, the two agents went into Babette's cabin ahead of her to ensure that no one was waiting for the dear woman.

"There's no one here," Chalkstone confirmed, stepping aside to let Babette, Alan and Tiffany come inside.

"Alright, gentlemen, have a seat," Babette said, indicating the sofa as the place where the two agents should sit together.

Once everyone had taken a seat, Babette began, "We went on a tour…"

"Did you book the tour in advance with the purser?" Chalkstone asked.

"Okay, gentlemen, I appreciate you've got a job to do, but I won't tolerate any interruption from you while I am recounting this morning's events. Afterward, you can ask anything you want. Is that understood?"

"Yes, ma'am," Mallard answered, elbowing his partner and turning his head with a slight smile on his lips.

"She's definitely not happy," Edmund repeated to Alan. He was standing beside the doc's chair, his arms crossed over his chest.

"And I may be old and tattered, but I have all my faculties, Agent Mallard. And your snickering will only delay these proceedings."

Mallard bowed his head and looked down to his lap.

"Alright then, as I was saying," Babette went on, "Ms. Sylvan and I decided to follow a tour of the old city this morning. And no, I hadn't booked anything in advance. I have been far too busy with Hoodoo Voodoo…"

"Hoodoo what?" Chalkstone couldn't refrain from asking, lifting a questioning eyebrow.

"Hoodoo Voodoo is the play I have been writing and producing on this cruise."

"Voodoo, did you say? Are you practicing sorcery?" Mallard inquired, visibly baffled.

"Do you want to hear what I have to say or not?" Babette said, quite angry by now.

"Sorry, ma'am," Mallard was quick to say, "by all means, go ahead."

It took the better part of ten minutes for Babette to tell about the tour, the attack and being unable to recognize the man's face.

"What about the knife?" Chalkstone asked. He looked at Babette and Tiffany in turn.

"Ms. Babette, you said that Ms. Sylvan grabbed the knife out of the man's hand"—Mallard turned his face to Tiffany—"Do you remember what you did with it?"

"Yes," Tiffany replied assertively, "I remember throwing it out the window."

"And did you find it when you got out of the house?"

"I did," Babette said, grabbing her capacious bag from beside her chair. "I've got it here…" She retrieved the weapon from its hiding place and handed it gingerly to Mallard.

"I'll get some tissue to preserve the prints," Alan said, standing up and going to the desk. He pulled a handful of Kleenex from the box and handed it to Mallard.

"Thank you, Doctor," Mallard said, returning his attention to Babette, while he wrapped the knife carefully and put it inside his breast pocket.

"Anything else you would want to add, Ms. Babette?" Chalkstone asked.

"No, but I think Ms. Sylvan noticed something else about the man, didn't you, dear?" Babette turned her gaze to Tiffany and shot a sideway glance to Edmund.

"The ring with an E and a C inside a circle," Edmund said quietly to Tiffany.

"Oh, yes, of course. When I grabbed the knife off the man's hand, I noticed he was wearing a heavy signet ring on his right hand."

"Ah yes. I recall our witness to Ms. Walter's attack noticing that same ring," Mallard remarked. "Do you remember anything particular about the ring, Ms. Sylvan?"

"No nothing really, except that I think it wasn't a blazon or emblem on the face of the ring, but a couple of initials."

"Can you remember what these initials were?"

"I can't be sure, Agent Chalkstone, but I think there was an E and a C carved inside a circle." Tiffany shook her head. "It's all a blur really. It all happened so fast, I couldn't be sure of anything."

"That's okay, Ms. Sylvan," Mallard said, getting to his feet, "And if either of you ladies think of anything else, please call this number." He handed Babette a card. "The office will relay all important calls directly to my cell."

Babette looked down at the official-looking card, nodded and put it on the coffee table. "Thank you, Agent Mallard." She turned to Alan. "Would you mind seeing these gentlemen out?"

"Of course, Ms. Babette," Alan replied, escorting the two agents to the door of the suite and opening it for them. The ring tone on Mallard's phone interrupted their parting words.

"Sorry, I've got to take this," Mallard said to Alan. "We'll talk soon. And thanks again for alerting us."

As the two agents walked away, Alan closed the door and leaned against it. "Are you sure about the ring?" he asked his great-grandfather.

"Yes, son, I am. At first, I saw it when I took the knife out of this maniac's hand, but then, when I observed him in the alley, I distinctly saw the two initials, yes," Edmund confirmed.

"Well, that's good," Babette declared, looking up at Edmund. "Now would you mind telling us who you saw admiring the bathtub in the bedroom?"

"Sorry, my dear, at that point I only had a fleeting glance at the fellow, but later when I followed him in the alley, he took the white stocking off his face and I saw Agent Chulbridge catch his breath while leaning against the outside wall of one of these old houses."

"What about the ring you saw in Miss Pilkington's room then?" Alan asked.

Babette and Tiffany stared up at Edmund. He smiled in reply.

"Did you say Ms. Pilkington's room?" Babette asked, befuddled.

"Yes, Babette, and I'm sorry to have to tell you that I think Ms. Pilkington may be involved in this affair."

"But I've known Sarah for years, how could she be involved in this treachery?" She paused. "Have you told anyone about this?"

Alan shook his head. "Since Granddad only saw the ring on the dresser of her room, we couldn't be sure it was hers."

"And did you see her wearing it at any time?" Babette asked. "Because I sure never noticed her wearing any jewelry."

"Granddad never saw her wear the ring," Alan answered, "But I noticed it when she handled a drink at the bar where I first saw her."

"Oh, is that why you two went through her cabin?" Tiffany asked.

"Yes," Edmund put in. "But I can assure you, Tiffany, that Ms. Pilkington's hand was not the one that would usually wear that ring."

"Okay, let's leave it at that then," Babette suggested.

Edmund went to sit on the sofa. "I am so sorry for what happened to you, milady."

"Don't say another word about it, Edmund," Babette replied. "At least we now know who's after me. But what I'd like to know is why. What motive could an Interpol agent have for wanting to kill me?"

"It's not like you've witnessed anything," Tiffany added. "Maybe you've heard something you shouldn't have..."

"No, Tiffany, I don't think that's it," Babette countered. "But ever since I've started investigating my ancestry and my relationship to the Grand Duke of Luxemburg, it has become apparent that things have started to happen to me."

Tiffany, Alan and Edmund exchanged a glance.

"Just because you're a lost relative, you think someone would want you out of the way?" Tiffany queried.

"It's a possibility such as any other you've advanced thus far, my dear," Babette concluded. "But for now, I need some rest. So, if you don't mind leaving me for a while?"

"Of course, Babette," Alan replied. "I've got reports to attend to anyway."

"And I have the stage to reset for Act II," Tiffany added. "Would you like to join us for dinner?" she asked Babette.

"Yes, that would take me out of my brooding mood – thank you." She smiled at Edmund. "And as for you, Edmund, I'll have something else in mind."

At these words, Alan and Tiffany burst out in laughter, while Edmund grinned.

"Oh do get out of here," Babette said, waving at the two of them, toward the door.

When Mallard snapped his phone shut, his partner asked, "What was that all about?"

"That was Mr. Evans asking us to go down to his office – Mr. Clipper has apparently boarded the ship."

"You mean the woman's ex-hubby is here?" Chalkstone asked, visibly surprised.

"Oh yeah. And he wants to take the body of his wife back with him to San Francisco."

"But we're not finished. I mean Rivers and his crew have hardly began their investigation."

"I know that, Chuck, but we've got to keep the man happy, otherwise the shit will start flying."

"What about Chulbridge; what do we do about him?"

"I don't know yet. We've got to send an email to the chief in Washington though. He'll have to decide on that score," Mallard answered. "I wish we had been there in that house this morning, though. We could have grabbed Chubby, Chub-Chub before he fled."

"Are you sure it was him who attacked Ms. Babette?"

"There's very little doubt of it, Chuck. You heard Ms. Sylvan describe the ring, didn't you?" Chalkstone nodded. "Besides, we'll have him dead-to-right when we confirm the set of prints on the knife." Mallard padded his breast pocket. "But we should have gone with her."

"Well, you could blame Dr. Mayhew for that; he's the one who wanted to attend our interview, wasn't he?"

"Yeah, but he was right. That lady's got some heavy pull in high places," Mallard said.

"How'd you know?"

"I just asked for a background check on her, and believe me, we're not going to bother her anymore, especially after this morning's little episode."

Moments later the two agents were sitting on either side of Mr. Clipper and facing Gilbert.

Mr. Leonard Clipper was a man of presence. He commanded and retained his interlocutor's attention. His assertiveness and striking demeanor were noticed as soon as he walked into a room. With a pleasant, clean shaven face, a white head of hair, and blue eyes that wouldn't miss a detail or a movement around him, he was perhaps the perfect picture of a highly paid, highly regarded – if not feared – professional man.

After making the introduction, Gilbert began, "Mr. Clipper, thank you for coming all this way to accompany your wife's body…"

"Ex-wife," Clipper corrected, "unfortunately."

"Yes, yes, of course, I'm sorry," Gilbert backtracked. "But there are a few formalities to complete before we can release the body to you, sir."

"What sort of formalities, Mr. Evans?"

"Well, there's the autopsy for one thing, and then Agents Mallard and Chalkstone here, need to complete their investigations of Mrs. Clipper's murder."

"And how long is that likely to take?" Clipper demanded, crossing his arms over his chest.

"I don't really know, sir."

"I'm sorry to interrupt here, Mr. Evans," Mallard piped up, "But at this point, it appears that Mrs. Clipper was the victim of a gross misconduct on the part of an Interpol undercover agent…"

"How on Earth did she get involved with such things?"

"That's just our point," Mallard replied, "Mrs. Clipper came on this cruise with a neighbor, hoping to have a restful vacation. However, the neighbor was heavily involved in drug trafficking and was also an informant for Interpol, which activity cost her dearly."

"Are you telling me that my ex was involved in drug trafficking?"

Chalkstone shook his head. "No, sir, not at all. However, the Interpol agent is alleged to have drugged her and forced her into participating into a scheme, which ultimately cost her her life."

"I see," Clipper said, unfolding his arms and looking down to his lap. "So, you're saying Lizzy was an innocent by-stander, is that it?"

"Exactly, sir. She didn't know anything about her neighbor's trafficking and we are currently investigating the Interpol agent's activities. There are now some doubts as to his integrity."

"Are you implying this man is a rogue agent?"

Mallard nodded. "Yes, sir. And we are going to pursue this investigation as far as we can go with it, believe me."

"Hmm, yes. But I suppose you'll be sweeping some of your findings under the rug," Clipper remarked, acerbity audible in his tone of voice.

"Nothing like that, sir," Mallard said, "at least not from the CIA."

Clipper chuckled. "Really? Don't try your angelic do-gooder attitude on me, Agent Mallard. It won't work." He paused and turned his gaze to Gilbert. "I hope you will not be party to any of their hush-hush scheme, Mr. Evans, and that you will see to it that I can take Lizzy home as soon as possible, won't you?"

"I'll do my best, sir," Gilbert replied, standing up as soon as Clipper did.

"Good day, gentlemen," Mr. Leonard Clipper said before walking out of the office.

CHAPTER THIRTY-THREE

Wilma Simpson

SOMETIMES IT IS HARD to be in the present with all the 'things' that are going on around you. The multitude of thoughts that occur tend to take one away from being in the now. Today was one of those days on *The Baroness*. Fortunately Alan's friend, Calvin, must have sensed it. He too was a believer that humor is the best medicine and he was at it again. He had sent a message to Alan when he had heard that the doc had encountered some troubles aboard the vessel.

> Dear Alan, if you feel like you're getting old too fast, here are some tips for you to keep in mind (if dementia doesn't set in beforehand).
> 1. Wear your glasses to make sure Tiffany is actually in the bed.
> 2. Set timer for 3 minutes, in case you doze off in the middle.
> 3. Set the mood with lighting. (Turn them ALL OFF!)
> 4. Make sure you put 911 on your speed dial <u>before</u> you begin.
> 5. Write Tiffany's name on your hand in case you can't remember.
> 6. Use extra polygrip so your teeth don't end up under the bed.
> 7. Have Tylenol ready in case you actually complete the act.
> 8. Make all the noise you want.... the neighbors are deaf, too.
> 9. If it works, call everyone you know with the good news!!
> And please give Tiffany a big hug for me when you see her next. I'll see you guys when you get back.
> Cheers, Calvin

Laughing his head off, Alan picked up the phone on the third ring. "Yes, Gilbert, what can I do for you?" he asked.

"You won't believe this, Alan, but Wilma Simpson is on her way."

"Who's Wilma Simpson?" Alan blurted, still grinning to himself.

"Irene Walter's sister, that's who."

"And you're saying she's in town?"

"Yeah, and on her way to the ship. She'll be wanting to take her sister back to San Francisco."

"Okay. That shouldn't be much of a problem. I think Rivers and his crew will be finished tomorrow before we leave anyway."

"But, Alan, what do I tell her? Have you determined if it was death by misadventure or manslaughter yet?"

"Not my department, Gilbert," Alan replied. "I can only tell you how she died, not if someone did or did not push her over that railing."

"Okay, I hear you. But we can be fairly certain that Chubb pushed her, can't we?"

"Well, as soon as Daniel Richard has confirmed the prints on the knife he allegedly used to attack Babette, Mallard will be able to arrest him and then question him about Ms. Walter's fall."

"Has Rivers come back from Simon's department yet?" Gilbert asked.

"Not here he hasn't, but I only left him a while ago – give these guys a bit of time."

"Yeah, but our captain is jumping up and down right now. He's afraid these guys won't be done before we leave in 24 hours. You know how head office hates delays."

"Don't even go there, Gilbert. I've got enough on my plate as it is and rushing these things could really go against us later on."

"Don't I know it? If we were to miss one piece of evidence or if Rivers was rushed off the ship before he's done, we would be blamed if Chubb goes free on a technicality."

"Besides which, Interpol could have us all fired…"

"Exactly, and I don't fancy spending my holidays searching for another job."

"That said, why don't we leave well enough alone and let Rivers and his crew do their jobs, okay?"

"What about Wilma Simpson – what do I do with her when she gets here?"

"Give her a nice cabin and take her to lunch while she waits for us to release the body – that's the best I can suggest, Gilbert."

"Okay, but I'm sure she'll want to see you."

"Well – I'm always here. Call me if you need me, okay?"

"Sure will, Doc. And thanks for your help."

When Alan hung up, he reclined in his chair and thought about Wilma Simpson. She was a mother with children, but she traveled regularly to various cities across the States. *What was she doing traveling like that,* Alan wondered.

As soon as Rivers entered the sanitation department, he saw a number of yellow tags lining the floor of the metal walkway. Before going any farther and while still fully covered in his bodysuit, he pulled a pair of booties and gloves out of his pocket. He slipped them on and proceeded gingerly to the stairs leading down to the floor where he found Jenny and Daniel busy taking samples from the edge of the tank.

"How is it going?" he asked his two assistants.

"Slow but *steady as she goes*," Daniel replied, lifting his gaze to the pathologist. "We've got traces of blood, hair and even a smear of what looks like gel that's been rubbed against one of the railing pickets."

"Very good," Rivers said, nodding. "What about you, Jenny, anything interesting?"

The forensic assistant lifted her head to her boss. "Nothing out of the ordinary, no, apart from some blood traces on the inside edge of the tank." She pointed to it. "The perp must have pushed her head downward into the tank, rubbing it against the upper rim."

"Have you taken photographs of it all?"

"Sure did," Daniel replied. "And we're about ready to wrap this up."

"Good. But before we go to the victims' cabins, there's one more item that I'd like you, Daniel, to examine."

"What's that?"

"There are some tissue scrapings that we've taken from the wounds on Mrs. Clipper's skull and tibia. I'd like you to determine what sort of weapon was used on the victim, whether wood or metal."

"Have you brought them with you?" Jenny asked.

"No, I left them with Dr. Mayhew. Daniel, you can pick them up later."

"Anything else?" Daniel asked.

"Well, I think there's going to be one more item for you to analyze…"

"Have you found the murder weapon?"

"No, Jenny, not yet – and we're still not sure what that weapon is." Rivers shook his head. "Anyway… as I was about to come down after the autopsy, I got a call from Agent Mallard. Apparently the lady playwright has been attacked while visiting the city."

"Oh wow, is she alright?" Jenny was quick to inquire.

"Yes, thanks to Ms. Sylvan, the entertainment director, who was with her. Anyway, Mallard's got the knife that the perp used in the attack. We should get a good set of prints from it, if nothing else, as long as he was not wearing gloves."

"Okay then, it sounds like we'll be here a while longer," Daniel said, starting to pack up his case. "I'd like to leave all of the tags in place though, until we've had a chance to verify the samples we've collected – if that's okay with Mr. Albertson."

Although nodding, Rivers said, "It will have to be okay, won't it, Daniel?" He chuckled. "By the way, where's the blighter now?"

"Haven't seen him since we got started, I don't think autopsies are his thing," Jenny said. "But I've got his phone number. Should I call him?"

"Yeah, why don't you?" Rivers agreed. "We need to keep this area as is for a few hours and we need to lock this place up when we leave anyway."

Five minutes later, Simon burst through the door and stopped dead in his tracks when he saw the floor littered with yellow tags. "What do you think you're doing?" he shouted in the direction of the three forensic agents waiting for him at the bottom of the stairs.

"Just don't step anywhere, Mr. Albertson," Rivers hollered back,

"These are reference tags where we collected samples…"

"But how could you have collected anything? My guys have wiped this floor every morning since the murder…"

"They have, I'm sure, Mr. Albertson," Daniel said, "but there were a few things we were still able to collect."

"Like what?" Simon demanded, quite annoyed that someone could have found dirt, or anything else for that matter, where he thought there wasn't anything to find.

"Like traces of blood and hair," Jenny replied.

"But…"

Rivers went up the stairs to join the sanitation engineer on the walkway. "Don't be alarmed, Mr. Albertson, we're going to remove all the tags and close the lid of the tank as soon as we've ascertained that our samples are good enough for analysis back in DC."

"And what am I supposed to do in the meantime? I can't very well leave the tank open. The chemicals in there are dangerous when you breathe them."

"We know, Mr. Albertson," Daniel agreed, having joined the two men. "And that's why it will be important for you to keep the entire area under lock and key until we're done."

"And how long are you guys gonna be?"

"Another couple of hours, I suspect. But after that, it'll be all yours again," Rivers said, patting Simon on the back.

"I guess, I could do with some shut eye," Simon said, pivoting on his heels and opening the door. "Are you guys ready to go then?"

"Right behind you, Mr. Albertson," Jenny said, heading out the door first.

Once Daniel Richard had collected the scraping samples from Alan – he had stored them in the medical center's fridge – and the knife from Agent Mallard, he made his way back to their suite. It didn't take him long to scan the prints on the knife with his portable device and send the results to the CIA for comparison. Within minutes, he turned from the desk to look up at Rivers. "The prints are a perfect match with those of Agent Chulbridge, sir," he told him.

"Okay then, let's give a call to Mallard and let him know."

"What will happen now?" Jenny asked. "It's not like we've ever found culpable evidence against one of our own before."

"No, Jenny. When a person, whether CIA, FBI or Interpol is suspected of having committed a crime, he or she has to face the music. And we're not judge or jury; we've simply collected evidence and reported our findings. The rest is up to the powers-that-be."

"Is he going to be arrested then?"

"Well, that's up to the guys in Washington, but I'd say he'll be going back with Mallard and Chalkstone in the morning if they can find him." He paused and returned his attention to Daniel. "Okay, let's leave the scrapings for later and concentrate on verifying the samples you found in Albertson's area. The blighter will have a conniption if we don't close the tank soon." He chuckled. "In the meantime, I'll have a look around Ms. Walter's cabin."

His phone rang. "Yes, Rivers here," he replied, and listened. "Okay, Mr. Evans, I was actually on my way to her cabin right now." He paused. "Yes, sir, we'll be as quick as possible, of course. I'll see you then," he said, closing his phone.

"What was that about?" Jenny asked.

"Mr. Evans was just informing me that Ms. Walter's sister is on her way, and that she'll probably want to pack her sister's belongings and take her corpse back to San Francisco before this ship sails tomorrow night."

"But that's not very much time."

"No, Daniel, it's not much time, you're right, but she's not our prime victim either, is she?" Daniel shook his head. "Okay, I'll leave you two kids to sort the samples and I'll go examine Ms. Walter's cabin. If anything pops up, you call me, okay?"

After receiving a nod from his two assistants, Rivers went to the bedroom of the suite, took off one body suit and slipped into a new one. He grabbed his forensic bag and in a moment was out the door of their suite.

On his way to Irene Walter's cabin, he called Mallard to let him know that the prints on the knife were indeed those of Agent

Chulbridge.

"That's good," Mallard said, "but now the shit is going to hit the fan. I don't relish writing that report, I tell you."

"Well, if it will help, I'll send the print comparison file to the chief tonight and then it's up to them."

"Thanks for that, Rivers. Anything else?"

"Not yet, Ducky. But as soon as I've got something, like the murder weapon – should we be so lucky – I'll give you a buzz."

"Okay then…. Oh, when do you think you'll be done with Ms. Walter's cabin?"

"Shouldn't take too long – I'll let you know."

"Right you are, Doctor. Later then."

Meanwhile, when Gilbert saw the taxi stop at the bottom of the gangway, he inhaled a sigh. He was exhausted. He had hardly slept more than a couple of hours each night since Mrs. Clipper's murder and he was sure he wouldn't see his bed for at least several hours. Lost in thought, he watched the woman make her way up the gangway somewhat distractedly. However, when Wilma Simpson was a few feet from him, he stopped breathing for a fraction of a second. The woman who extended a hand, saying, "I'm Wilma Simpson, and you must be Chief Evans," was the exact carbon copy of her sister Irene.

"Well, yes I am, Mrs. Simpson," Gilbert replied, shaking the woman's hand. "Pleased to meet you. I wish it would be under better circumstances though."

Wilma smiled. "Thank you, Chief Evans, but crying over my sister's demise won't bring her back, now will it?"

"No, you're right…" Gilbert blurted, still shocked at the resemblance between the two sisters. "Why don't you come with me; I'll show you to your cabin where you can relax for a bit. And when you're ready, I'll see you in my office."

"That's fine – thank you," Wilma replied, following Gilbert to the fifth deck.

CHAPTER THIRTY-FOUR

The case of the flaming potty

SINCE *THE BARONESS* WAS DUE to spend another 24 hours at port, several passengers had decided to enjoy a game of golf at one of Antsiranana's best courses. Unlike some of the less than elegant cityscapes they passed en route to the links, the clubhouse of this course was spectacular. It was one of those beautiful remnants of the British Raj that had been maintained over the years and a pleasure to visit. After registering, the two women rented a set of very nice clubs and made their way out, while admiring the pictures of all the famous players adorning the walls of the very well maintained historic surroundings of the clubhouse.

One of the two ladies teed off and watched in horror as her ball headed directly toward a threesome of men playing the next hole. The ball hit one of the men. He immediately clasped his hands together at his groin, fell to the ground and proceeded to roll around in agony. The woman rushed down to the man, and immediately began to apologize.

"Please allow me to help. I'm a licensed massage therapist and I know I could relieve your pain if you'd allow me," she told him.

"Oh, no, I'll be all right. I'll be fine in a few minutes," the man replied. He was in obvious agony, lying in the fetal position, still clasping his hands at his groin.

At her persistence, however, he finally allowed her to help. She gently took his hands away and laid them to the side, loosened his pants and put her hands inside.

She administered tender and artful massage for several long moments and asked, "How does that feel?"

"Feels WONDERFUL," he replied, "but I still think my thumb's sprained."

"Good Lord," the therapist exclaimed, retrieving her hand quickly and her face turning a delightful shade of red. "I'm so sorry... I didn't realize."

"Don't worry about it, Miss...?" the man said, getting to his feet and zipping up his pants.

"Miss Livery, sir, and again I'm very sorry."

"As I said, don't worry about it.... I'm Jason Roberts." He smiled amiably. "Why don't I offer you and your friend"—he nodded in the second woman's direction—"a drink at the club's bar?"

Miss Livery was far too embarrassed by now to respond coherently, however. She blurted a few words of thanks-but-no-thanks to her 'patient' and trotted off in the direction of her friend. Mr. Roberts watched them for a moment and then returned to his mates.

"What did you do?" one of them asked.

"Got a sprained thumb and a rub," Mr. Roberts replied, chuckling but still shaking his hand from the pain. "I think I'll get back to the ship and have this looked at." And with these words, he walked away toward the clubhouse.

Simon was snoring away when his restless sleep took him in a dream back to deck four in the vicinity of the medical center. He was staring ahead of him when he saw a ball bouncing in front of his eyes. He stopped, wiped his brow and face with one hand and shook his head. "I must have breathed a little too much of those chemicals," he said to himself, shaking his head again. When he looked up, the bouncing ball was back, dancing in front of his face.

"Okay, I know who you are," he hollered in his dream, turning around. "Alice told me about you, Mr. Kris Angel – or what ever you call yourself these days – but I won't fall for your tricks." He looked around him – the ball had disappeared. "That's better," he mumbled in his sleep and turned to his side. He opened one eye and looked at the alarm clock.

"Oh shit," he swore, sitting up. "I've got to close that lid." In a bounce he was up and running out of his cabin.

As he opened the door of the sanitation department, the oxygen intake provoked an explosion and a flaming torch flung Simon back all the way to the railing where he fell in a heap. "Bloody hell," he hollered, "who's been smoking around here?"

Having witnessed the scene aghast, a male passenger – Mr. Roberts as it happened – rushed to his aid. "Are you alright, Officer?" he asked, grabbing a swaying Simon by the arm as soon as he was on his feet.

"I'm okay, sir… thank you," the engineer replied, staring at the open door across the deck.

"But your shirt… sir, it… it's burned," Mr. Roberts insisted. "Let me call the doctor…"

"Yeah, why don't you do that," Simon said, shaking the man's hand off his arm.

As Mr. Roberts called the medical center on his cell-phone, Simon walked cautiously to the door of the sanitation room. He peered inside the door only to see the blackened walkway and all the yellow tags piled in a corner near the door. "I hope these guys haven't been lighting a fag around here," he said to himself, walking along the walkway carefully. He was about to reach the tank when he heard Alan call after him.

"Simon? Are you okay?" When he didn't get an answer, Alan proceeded down the walkway to the stairs. What he saw then took his breath away.

"He's dead!" Simon blurted, pointing to the burned cadaver at his feet.

The nylon suit the young man was wearing had melted through his upper body – he was unrecognizable.

"Let's get you out of here, Simon," Alan ordered. "Buddy, you've got some burns on your torso as well. Okay? Let's go."

"But I'll have to close the lid…" Simon tried arguing, as Alan grabbed hold of his arm and led him up the stairs and out the door.

"You'll do that later, when we get back here with Alice, Okay?"

This time Simon nodded resignedly, although throwing a glance over his shoulder a couple of times before the two of them reached the door.

As soon as Gilbert heard from Alan, he called Ekelton. When he had explained what he knew of what had occurred, the staff captain said, "Meet me in the med center and get Dr. Rivers there on the double, okay?"

"Yes, sir." He hesitated. "What about damage control?"

"Don't worry about that for now; I'll have Epstein Silver arrange something special for the passengers at dinner tonight." The staff captain had no idea what their cruise director could do at this point to save the situation. If "three was the charm" then they might have a sliver of hope that nothing else would happen on this trip. Three deaths during one cruise were damning for any cruise ship, let alone *The Baroness* – home office would be afraid that no one would ever climb aboard this vessel again.

"Are you sure it's Daniel?" Dr. Rivers was saying as he entered Alan's office in a rush. "He was only there to gather the tags…"

"Yes, I'm afraid, the body – although burned to the bones – is that of Daniel Richard," Alan replied, watching the pathologist slump down in one of the chairs.

"What could have caused such an explosion, do you think?"

"Dr. Rivers, you know as well as I do that the chemicals used in such a septic tank are flammable under the right conditions. And if someone lit as small a flame as that of a cigarette lighter close to the tank, after being opened for so many hours, such an explosion was certainly probable." Alan paused. "Do you know if Daniel was a smoker?"

Rivers appeared offended at the suggestion. "Absolutely not, Dr. Mayhew. No one in my team smokes. And if I caught one of them with a fag in his mouth, I'd have his hide."

"Sorry, Doctor, I didn't mean to sound offensive, but I had to ask. And since Mr. Albertson is not a smoker either, we have to assume someone else did light something to ignite the gases."

Still nursing his sore thumb, which Alice had put in a splint after the accident, Jason Roberts was now walking toward the bar where he had arranged to meet his mates for a drink. When he entered the premises, he went to sit on a stool between his friends.

"Ah, there he is," one of the two men said jovially, "how do you feel?"

"Better, thanks," Jason replied, showing his thumb. He looked up at Eric. "Rum and coke for me. Thanks," he told him.

Eric nodded and turned away to prepare the drink.

"You will never guess what happened…" Jason began, turning to the man on his left.

"Oh we don't have to guess," the guy replied, chuckling, "do we now, Ivan?"

Ivan shook his head, "We sure don't…"

"I don't mean that Miss Livery giving me a massage," Jason cut-in. "I mean when I got back to the ship…"

"Did the nurse give you another massage before she got to your thumb?"

"Oh stop that, George, will you?" Jason's face was obviously reflecting his concern, because his friends stopped the bantering and stared at him.

"Here you go," Eric interrupted, depositing the rum and coke in front of Jason.

"Thanks," the latter replied distractedly, returning his attention to his expectant mates.

"So what else happened?" Ivan asked.

Jason took a sip of his drink. "Well, just as I was making my way back to the ship, I was routed to one of the lower decks. They were apparently loading some supplies so I obviously had to use the crew gangway. I saw an officer open a door on the lower deck…"

"And…?" George asked.

"And the guy was thrown by a flame torch way to the other side of the deck from the force of the blow and landed at my feet in a heap."

"Was he hurt?" Ivan asked.

"The front of his shirt was burnt and he probably won't need to get rid of his chest hair for a while." Jason smiled.

"Do you know what room it was – was it someone's cabin?"

"Oh no, I don't think so. The officer had to open it with a key." Jason paused. "I think it was the sanitation room. It had a sign on the door and all sorts of warning posters on it."

Unexpectedly Ivan burst out in loud laughter. "That's what I would call *the case of the flaming potty!*"

When Ekelton arrived at the medical center, he rushed into Alan's office and sat down beside Rivers. "You've got my condolences, Doctor Rivers," he said, and he meant it. Losing a young team member under such dreadful circumstances isn't easy for anyone.

"Thank you, Mr. Ekelton," Dr. Rivers replied, looking down to his lap. "But I really don't know what could have caused such an explosion. And that's what I intend to find out."

He had hardly pronounced the last word when Jenny burst through the front door and practically ran into Alan's office. "Is it true?" she blurted. "Is Daniel really dead?" She was appalled.

Rivers got up and offered his chair to his obviously shocked assistant. "Yes, my dear, he's truly gone. And it was probably a very unfortunate accident."

"It's all my fault," Jenny said, as she began crying. "I should have gone and closed that tank. I knew how dangerous those chemicals could be."

"It's no one's fault, Ms. Ashton, as far as we know for now," Alan said, "But as Dr. Rivers said, we will find out one way or another."

"What is there to be done now?" Ekelton interposed. "Do we close the sanitation department down… or…?" He looked at Alan.

"No, Mr. Ekelton, I don't think that will be necessary," Rivers replied for Alan. "I will personally examine the tank and surrounding area and once Mr. Albertson has verified the functioning of the septic system, I should think you'll be able to leave Madagascar tomorrow on schedule."

"Will you be able to determine what caused the explosion by then, Dr. Rivers?" Alan asked.

The pathologist looked down at his assistant. She was wiping her tears with a Kleenex by then. "I think Ms. Ashton and I will be able to give you an answer before morning, yes."

Ekelton got up. "Well, I sure hope so, Dr. Rivers, otherwise, the CIA will have to explain what happened to our head office. The company will not take gross misconduct on the part of your agency lightly, I can assure you." He riveted his gaze on Rivers for a fraction of a second, before turning toward the door.

"I'm sure it won't come to that, Mr. Ekelton," Rivers said. "And if it comes down to assuming responsibility, I'll be the one holding my hand up. Of that you can be sure."

"Let's hope it won't come to that," Ekelton remarked, walking out.

As he opened the medical center's door, Gilbert bumped into him. "Oh sorry, Mr. Ekelton, sorry I'm late," he said. "Is Dr. Rivers here?"

"Yes, Mr. Evans. You go and question him and his assistant – they're both in Dr. Mayhew's office right now. Let me know what you can get out of them before I finish writing my report to head office, okay?"

"Sure will, sir," Gilbert replied, noticing the annoyance and obvious worry in the deepening lines of Ekelton's face. *Another death is all we needed*, he thought.

"Come on in," Alan said to Gilbert as he passed the threshold of his office. "Pull up a chair from the waiting room, will you…?"

Gilbert nodded, went to fetch the chair, put it down beside that of Dr. Rivers and sat down, switching his gaze from Alan to the pathologist.

"Have you been able to talk to Mr. Albertson yet?" Alan asked. "I had told him to go to your office after Alice dressed his burns."

"Yeah"—Gilbert nodded—"that's why I'm running late, sorry."

"And did he tell you what happened?" Rivers asked.

"There wasn't much he could tell me. He went in to close the lid and as he opened the door to the sanitation room, he was thrown by the force of the explosion to the other side of the deck. That's all he could tell me."

"What about finding Daniel?" Rivers pressed on.

"All he could tell me was that he found the body of Mr. Richard at the foot of the tank. He really doesn't understand what could have happened."

"Neither do we," Rivers added, nodding.

Alan had been listening to this exchange with interest. He was trying to reconstruct the incident in his mind when he said, "What I'd like to know is what lit up the gases that had been emanating from the open tank. When Mr. Albertson opened the door, the sudden oxygen intake into the room could have ignited the gases, yes. Yet, you would still need a spark or flame of some sort to provoke such an explosion."

Gilbert frowned. "Are you saying someone was waiting for him to open the door, lighter in hand?"

"Yes. Of course the only other alternative is a short circuit somewhere in the room, which ignited the fumes at the same moment as Mr. Albertson opened the door. But that seems too much of a coincidence to me."

"So, Dr. Mayhew," Rivers said, "what you're suggesting is that someone was laying in wait just inside the sanitation room door and as soon as the person heard the key being turned in the lock and the door being pushed opened, he threw a lit match in front of Mr. Albertson. Is that what you're advancing?"

"Pretty much, yes. But I don't even know if that would work," Alan replied pensively.

"Could we try reconstructing what happened?" Jenny asked suddenly, after she had listened to Alan's suggestion.

"Perhaps we could," Rivers replied, "however, I think we should first see if we can find any evidence of someone other than Daniel being in that room before the explosion."

"But wouldn't that blow-torch have burnt everything in its path?"

"Yes, Mr. Evans, but we wouldn't be looking for evidence in the path of the torch, we would be looking for traces of someone being there – perhaps beside or under the walkway, or even behind the tank itself," Rivers suggested.

"Okay then," Gilbert said, "but I think this time, it would be much better for you both to work with Mr. Albertson, rather than sending him away. He could be of help, don't you think?"

"Yes, Mr. Evans, I believe you're right. Actually, we should have relied on his expertise in the first place," Rivers said ruefully.

"Okay then," Gilbert said, getting to his feet, "I'll leave you guys to it." And on second thought, he added, "What about Ms. Walter's room, have you found anything?" He directed his gaze to Rivers.

"A few things that I still have to understand in my own mind, Mr. Evans. But I'll email you my report as soon as I've got it completed."

"And I'm sorry to be a little insistent, but have you had a chance to examine Mrs. Clipper's room yet?"

Rivers shook his head. "No, Mr. Evans, but Jenny has done a first inspection, haven't you, my dear?"

Jenny nodded. "Yeah. And the only thing I could tell you for sure is that she was not killed in her cabin." She paused and then lifted a finger to Gilbert and shook it. "But Daniel determined that she was probably killed with a wooden cane – no metallic traces were found in the scrapings Dr. Mayhew gave us."

CHAPTER THIRTY-FIVE

Where's Chubb?

WHILE GILBERT AND THE CIA agents were busy with all that was happening aboard *The Baroness,* Chubb returned to the ship, along with some other passengers who had spent the morning visiting Antsiranana, and made his way to his cabin unnoticed. Chubb didn't think anyone could have recognized him in the city, and failing to kill that busybody didn't bother him that much. *Tomorrow's another day,* he thought. *Besides, Dr. Rivers and his team are probably history by now. I wish I had been there to see how that turned out.* He put the knapsack that contained the cloak back in the bedroom closet and went to the bathroom to freshen up.

He was washing his face and changing his clothes when he heard a knock at the cabin's door.

When he opened it, he was slightly surprised to see Agents Mallard and Chalkstone standing on the threshold.

"Look at what the cat dragged in," Chubb said, chuckling. "I was wondering when you would come around for a visit."

Chalkstone and Mallard exchanged a glance.

"I'm Agent Mallard and this is Agent Chalkstone." They pulled their ID wallets out of their jacket pockets.

"Yes, yes I know," Chubb said, waving a dismissive hand in front of them. "I've been informed of your arrival on board. And what can I do for you, fellows?"

"You can invite us in for one thing, Agent Chulbridge, and then we can sit down and have a chat, okay?" Mallard said, stepping indoors.

Chubb closed the door and went to sit in one of the sitting room chairs, while the two agents took a seat on the mini-sofa.

"So, what's happening, fellows?" Chubb asked, switching his gaze from one agent to the other.

"What's happening, Agent Chulbridge, is that we need your help," Chalkstone began. "We've been looking into Ms. Walter and Mrs. Clipper's deaths and…"

"Very disturbing events indeed," Chubb cut-in, shaking his head.

"Yes they were," Mallard said, "and this morning Ms. Babette…"

"Who?"

Chalkstone was losing patience. "You know very well who we're talking about, Agent Chulbridge!"

"I'm sorry, but I don't. Oh, wait – isn't she the playwright?"

"Yes, that's right, Agent Chulbridge, and as my partner was saying, Ms. Babette has been attacked…"

"How, where?" Chubb cut in again, feigning total lack of knowledge of the incident.

"That's what we would like you to tell us, Chulbridge," Chalkstone said. "Where were you this morning between nine and twelve?"

"Right here," Chubb lied, pointing at the open laptop on the desk. "I was writing reports to Interpol. I'm due to meet my contact."

"What if I told you we have evidence to validate that you were off this ship this morning, Chulbridge? It is called a sea pass keycard."

"I'd say, you're wrong and I'd say I'd like to call my lawyer…"

"Alright then…" Chalkstone began saying when Mallard's phone rang.

Visibly annoyed at this latest interruption, he opened the phone and listened for a moment before he said, "Okay, we'll be right up."

Chalkstone and Chulbridge stared up at him as he stood up.

Closing his phone, Mallard said, "Okay, Agent Chulbridge, we're going to leave you for a while now, but we'll be back as soon as we can." Since his partner had not heard any of the conversation Mallard had just had, he threw him a querying glance. "We'll have to lock you in here, of course…"

"What about calling my lawyer?" Chulbridge objected. "I have told you I won't say another word until I've spoken to him."

"We've heard you, Chulbridge. And as soon as we come back, we'll let you make that call." Mallard rose to his feet. "In the meantime, take it easy, okay?"

"How could I take it easy…? I've only done what I was supposed to do. I'm undercover, remember?"

"Yeah, we remember, Chubb. But being undercover doesn't give you the right to attack or kill people at will." Mallard turned to Chalkstone, who was on his feet by now, too. "Let's go," he added, walking to the door of the cabin, opening it and stepping out together with Chalkstone.

"What's happening?" Chalkstone asked, as he locked the cabin door.

"We've got another body – one of our own this time," Mallard replied, walking toward the elevators.

"Who's that? I thought… oh you mean one of Rivers' guys?"

"Yes, Chuck. Richard has been killed with a flame torch…"

"Are you serious?" Chalkstone questioned, google-eyed.

Mallard pressed the elevator button. "Yeah. And this time we can't blame Chubb, or can we?"

"When did it happen?"

"Can't tell you yet. Evans will be able to answer that one, I'm sure."

When they arrived in Gilbert's office, they found Wilma Simpson sitting in one of the visitors' chairs, across the chief.

She and Gilbert stopped talking when the two CIA men entered the room. Wilma turned around.

"Mrs. Simpson, may I introduce you to Agents Mallard and Chalkstone of the CIA," Gilbert said, standing up. "They're the agents who are going to release your sister's body into your custody." He looked up at the two men. "Gentlemen, this is Mrs. Wilma Simpson, Ms. Irene Walter's sister."

Mallard stared into the woman's face. He, too, was taken aback by the resemblance between the victim and her sister. "Pleased to meet you, Mrs. Simpson. Sorry for your loss," he blurted, averting his gaze from looking at the woman." *That's something else,* he thought, *I've rarely seen twins looking that much alike.*

Wilma stood up. "Well, I better leave you to your duties, Chief," she said. She then turned to look at Mallard. "I'll be in cabin 403, if you need me, Agent Mallard. I'm sure you'll let me know when I can disembark with my sister, won't you?"

"Hmm, yes, of course, Mrs. Simpson. But if you don't mind we would like to have a chat about…"

"About what, Agent Mallard?" Wilma demanded. "I've only one thing to say to you and the CIA as a whole – Irene shouldn't have helped any of you!"

Not missing a beat, Mallard asked, "How did you know that your sister assisted our agency?"

"If she hadn't told me that she felt she was in danger, I would have sensed it anyway. When it was time for her to get some help, as she boarded this cruise ship, all she got from you people was a brush off." Wilma was decidedly not messing about. "She told me everything she knew and even emailed me when she had to meet Agent Chulbridge." She paused to stare into Mallard's eyes. "So, I don't think you need any more answers than what I've given Mr. Evans here." She turned to him. "Please give a copy of my statement to these agents, Chief. But for now, I'm going." And with these words, Wilma brushed past Chalkstone and rushed out the door, slamming it behind her.

"Whoa! What was that all about?" Mallard asked Gilbert, taking a seat beside Chalkstone.

"It's about a grieving sister, Agent Mallard." Gilbert sat down too. "And before you ask, I've emailed you a copy of her statement. Apparently your Chubb guy was supposed to get the drugs from Irene, as planned, but when he started asking her to deliver them in Madagascar, and Irene refused, he threatened her. And that's when she wrote to Wilma. She explained the whole thing to her, already fearing for her life. According to the date on that email, Irene died a day later."

"Okay, I'll have a read of that statement and get back to you." Mallard paused. "Now, what about Daniel Richard – can you tell us what happened?"

"Well, once I finally had all the facts straight, the upshot of it all is that we've got someone aboard holding a grudge against your agency."

"To say the least," Chalkstone remarked. "Could you elaborate maybe?"

And Gilbert did. When he finished, Mallard asked, "And is Rivers certain he can find the evidence he needs before the ship is due to leave tomorrow?"

"He was when I last talked to him, yes."

"Okay, Mr. Evans. We will have to contact Washington and see what our chief says about this latest situation, but my guess is that Agent Chalkstone and I will disembark with Chulbridge and leave Mr. Clipper and Mrs. Simpson to take their loved ones back to the States tonight."

"What about Dr. Rivers and Ms. Ashton?"

"I don't know yet, Mr. Evans, but I suspect they'll be asked to remain aboard until they've completed their investigations."

"Okay," Gilbert said resignedly. "You will let me know, won't you?"

"Absolutely," Mallard replied, getting to his feet together with Chalkstone.

Gilbert looked at the two men as they left his office and reclined into the back of his chair. He wished Rivers would be finding an answer to the mystery of *the flaming potty* sooner, rather than later.

Eric knew it wasn't his place to comment on what he had heard at the bar about Simon being thrown across the deck by a flame torch. Consequently, he decided to keep his mouth shut until he had a chance to talk to the "Potty Man" himself. As he entered the crew mess, he was surprised to see Simon sitting at a table with some of his crew hands. They were having a break, Eric gathered.

"Hey, Eric," Gaspar, one of Simon's crew, shouted as he saw the bartender enter the mess, "Have you brought a beer or two for our *Potty Man* here? He's had a shock – and a drink is just what he really needs right now."

"Yeah, I've heard about that. Sorry, Simon, but I didn't bring anything with me." Simon smiled up at Eric as he pulled up a chair and sat down beside him. "But I'm sure Lisa"—he nodded in the direction of the self-service machine—"could get you something stronger than coffee."

"No thanks, Eric, I've got some painkillers from Alice and I don't think a drink is to be added to that prescription." Simon was visibly hurting.

"Why don't you go and have a sleep?" Gaspar suggested. "I can cover for you for a bit, eh, what do you say?"

Simon shook his head, returning his gaze to his half empty cup of coffee. "Thanks, Gaspar, but I've got to go back soon. That Dr. Rivers needs help around the potty room, and it is better for me to be occupied…"

"Are they going to try to find out what happened?" another crew hand asked.

"That's what the doc said, yeah," Simon replied. "But I really don't know what they can possibly find – it's all black down there…"

"You never know," Gaspar said, "you know these CSI guys are pretty smart when it comes to finding evidence…"

"But this ain't a movie, Gaspar," the other man objected.

"Oh you're always looking at the glass half-empty, aren't you, Ari?" Gaspar snapped. "But what I'm worried about is if we'll be ready to go tonight?" He looked at Simon inquiringly.

"All I can tell you, guys, is that if the septic tank is okay and working properly by tonight, we'll leave at 0500 hours. Ekelton is adamant about it. The head office has had enough with the CIA's interference. The Captain is not about to delay the cruise because of what happened."

"Well, that's good to know," Eric piped up, because I don't relish another night of staying at port – like we did on the last cruise I was on. I don't think I slept for three days after that. And you know, when we are in port, our pay is cut even further. It is almost like we are working for free."

"Don't remind me about that last cruise," Gaspar said, "the pax didn't know what was going on and they were putting their noses into everything…"

"Anyways, guys," Simon cut in, getting to his feet, "let's get back to work and get our supplies sorted before we sail, okay?"

Except for Eric, everyone around the table got up and followed Simon out of the mess.

"See you later," Gaspar said to the bartender, waving to him as he closed the door behind the men.

If there had been any other way to tell Babette what had happened in the past few hours, other than to come straight out with it, Edmund would have done so to save her any further anxiety.

"I'm sorry to intrude on your rest, milady," he said quietly when he saw Babette open her eyes. "But I think we need to talk…"

"Sure, Edmund," Babette replied, pulling herself to a sitting position in her bed. "What do you want to talk about?"

"It's about Mr. Albertson, you remember him don't you?" He sat down on the edge of the bed.

"Yes, I do. He's the sanitation engineer, isn't he? Lizzy had swiped the keys for the sanitation room from him, didn't she?"

"Precisely."

"Well…? What happened, Edmund?" Babette peered into the old doctor's eyes. "What is it?"

Seeing concern rising to her eyes, Edmund was quick to say, "Don't worry, my dear, the man is alright, but someone else is dead…"

"Who…?" Babette blurted. "Are Alan and Tiffany okay…?"

"Yes, yes, my dear, they're both fine."

"So, who is it, and why?"

When Edmund finished recounting what had happened, Babette got out of bed without a word and went to the bathroom.

Edmund remained nonplussed where he was. He wondered if his lovely lady was going to be sick. Thinking about it a bit further, he said to himself, *I guess I shouldn't have described how they found the poor young man.*

A few minutes later Babette came out of the bathroom all dressed and apparently ready – *to do what*, Edmund wondered.

"Alright, Edmund, we've got a show to put on in the next twenty-four hours and we better get ready for it!" Her tone left no doubt in Edmund's mind that Babette was all business and nothing but business at this point. "We've got over 200 passengers waiting for the second act of my play, and I've had enough of running scared. I assume Agent

Chulbridge has been arrested, and as far as the boy who's been killed, it's none of my concern. I have a duty and a responsibility toward our fellow passengers and toward Captain Galveston. So, let's find Tiffany and Miss Pilkington and get the rehearsals going."

Edmund only nodded and followed Babette out of her cabin. However, the playwright soon stopped dead in her tracks when she caught a glimpse of a man wearing a cloak rounding the corner toward the elevators just ahead of them. "Get him, Edmund!" she hollered, pointing to where she had seen the figure disappear.

Not waiting for Edmund to return, Babette took her cell-phone out of her jacket pocket, looked for the number she wanted, and opened the line.

Not letting the man speak when she heard him blurt out something of a greeting, Babette said, "Agent Mallard, it was my understanding that you have your 'Agent' Chulbridge under lock and key…"

"Yes, that's right, Ms. Babette…"

"Well, I am sorry to have to inform you that the man is still roaming this ship. I've just seen him near the sixth floor elevator. And before you try arguing the point, Agent Mallard, let me also inform you that if you cannot confirm the man is incarcerated and under guard before you leave the ship with him in shackles, I'll be the first to report your gross incompetence to your director!" And before Mallard could reply, Babette slammed her phone shut and rounded the corner to plant herself in front of the elevator – soon to be joined by Edmund. His face told her immediately that he had failed at locating the cloaked man.

"That's it, the shit is about to hit the fan," Mallard groaned to Chalkstone. Both men were reading Irene Walter's last email to her sister in their cabin.

"What's happening now?" Chalkstone asked, already on his feet and rushing after his partner, out of the room.

"Chubb is on the loose, and Ms. Babette has seen him – or a cloaked man – on the sixth floor."

"You're kidding, right?" Chalkstone argued. "You saw me lock the room didn't you?"

"Yeah, I saw you lock it alright, Chuck. But we've still got to see if he's still in there, haven't we?"

When the two agents reached Chubb's cabin, the door was ajar.

"How the hell did that happened?" Mallard exploded, flinging the door wide open and stepping into the room.

Chalkstone rushed to the desk. "The computer," he blurted.

"What about the computer?" Mallard asked, watching his partner take a seat in front of the open laptop.

"Do you remember Mr. Evans saying that they couldn't open his room even with a passkey back when he found Chubb's reports?"

"Yeah, so what's that got to do with anything?"

"Well..." Chalkstone replied, scrolling down what looked like a complex program, "Chubb has this software that is designed to lock and unlock secure doors... look..." He turned his gaze up to Mallard.

"I don't know much about computers, Chuck, you know that. So, what ever you're showing me right now is gibberish to me." He shook his head. "The long and the short of it is that Chubb has escaped and we've got to find him right now."

"And what's more, we can't be sure that he wasn't the one who messed with the tank, now can we?"

"You're right, so let's go and find him ASAP, shall we?" Mallard said, stepping out of the cabin and closing the door behind him. "Do you think he'll be able to open it again?" He shot an inquiring glance at his partner.

"Why don't we leave it ajar such as he did, and trap him if he returns?"

"Good idea, let's do that," Mallard said, opening the cabin door once again.

CHAPTER THIRTY-SIX

A bomb in the potty!

AS SIMON ARRIVED IN THE sanitation room, he found Dr. Rivers crawling under the walkway and Ms. Ashton examining the back of the septic tank.

"Oh, hello, Mr. Albertson, how are you feeling?" Rivers piped up, coming out from under the walkway.

"I'm okay, Doc, but how you doing? Anything to tell us about the guy who thought I was a marshmallow?" Simon smiled, although he didn't feel like it. His torso hurt and he couldn't breathe properly without feeling his skin and ribs screaming for relief.

"We've collected a few interesting items, yes, and something that would indicate how the explosion occurred."

"You mean like a fuse or something?"

"Yes, Mr. Albertson, that's exactly what I mean." Rivers opened the palm of his gloved hand. "See this?" Simon peered down at a small metallic plate and wire. "This looks very much like part of a remotely controlled detonator."

"Where did you find it?" Simon asked.

"In the door jam, nicely squeezed in between the hinge and the door. As soon as you opened the door the bomb exploded."

"Good grief," Simon said, "but why? Why try killing me?"

Rivers shook his head. "Not you, Mr. Albertson. You only detonated the bomb. But Daniel or Ms. Ashton, or even I, were the targets. You see, I was due to come down to help Daniel, so it stands to reason that I was the one who should have been burned to a crisp along with Daniel."

"But what about the fumes from the chemicals in the tank?"

"They contributed, of course, but I believe we should find the remains of some other combustible material in the tank itself. Do you think we could close the ship's septic system for an hour or so?"

"Let me tell you a little story, Dr. Rivers, before I give you my answer," Simon said, going down the walkway with him. "One day the different parts of the body were having an argument to see which should be in charge. The brain said, "I do all the thinking so I'm the most important and I should be in charge." The eyes said, "We see everything and let the rest of you know where we are, so we're the most important and we should be in charge." The hands said, "Without us we wouldn't be able to pick anything up or move anything. So we're the most important and we should be in charge." The stomach said, "I turn the food we eat into energy for the rest of you. Without me, we'd starve. So I'm the most important and I should be in charge." The legs said, "Without us we wouldn't be able to move anywhere. So we're the most important and we should be in charge." Then the rectum said, "I think I should be in charge." All the rest of the parts said, "YOU?!? You don't do anything! You're not important! You can't be in charge." So the rectum closed up. After a few days, the legs were all wobbly, the stomach was all queasy, the hands were all shaky, the eyes were all watery, and the brain was all cloudy. They all agreed that they couldn't take any more of this and agreed to put the rectum in charge. Today's lesson: You don't have to be the most important to be in charge, just an *ass-hole*."

Chuckling, Rivers said, "Very funny, Mr. Albertson, but what has this story got to do with my asking to shut down the septic system for a while?"

"The septic system is the rectum of this ship, Doctor, and if you shut it down, the legs will be wobbly, the stomach will be queasy…"

"I get it, no need to explain further, Mr. Albertson. But we need to retrieve what ever combustible material is probably left in the tank, so how do you propose we do that?"

"No need to shut the whole system down to do that, Doc. We simply shut off the tank's circulation system for a few minutes and, just like we did when we got Mrs. Clipper out of it the other day, then we go in and rake the bottom of the tank."

Coming out from behind the tank at just the same moment, Jenny piped-up, "I don't think that will be necessary, Mr. Albertson."

"Why not?" Rivers asked, turning his attention to his assistant. "Have you found something?"

"Yes, actually I did. Have a look." She came around the tank, a hand extended. "See, these scrapings came from the floor near the back of the tank. And if I'm right, you're looking at the remnants of nitro-glycerin."

Rivers adjusted his glasses over his nose and peered down at Jenny's opened palm. "I think you might be right, Jenny. And if our perp used nitro as a combustible for making his bomb, there wouldn't be any of it left in the tank. It would have all burned during the explosion."

"But where would he have placed the explosive then?" Simon asked, also looking down at the small piece of evidence Jenny had found.

"Very good question, Mr. Albertson," Rivers said, lifting his gaze to the engineer. Anywhere under the stairs would be my first guess." He took a complex-looking lens with a funny looking light attached out of the bag that he had left standing beside the stairs, and pointed to each of the steps in turn. Suddenly, a blue smear appeared at the edge of the bottom step. "There... that's where our perp placed his explosive device, I'd say."

Both Jenny and Simon bent down to look at the illuminated spot. "But how did he detonate it then?" Simon asked.

"Remotely, I suspect. As I showed you, the detonator was lodged in the door jam and as soon as the door was opened, it sent a signal to the bomb and it exploded."

"But, Doctor," Jenny said, "Why then didn't it detonate when Daniel came in?"

"That I don't know yet, my dear. But once we have inspected the remnants of the device by the door, we'll be closer to an answer."

"Okay then," Simon said, "if you don't need me anymore, I think I'll go and see what my guys are doing with loading the supplies."

"Right you are, Mr. Albertson," Rivers told him. "We'll just collect what ever else we can find around here and get our reports to Mr. Evans as soon as we possible."

Meanwhile, Babette had joined Tiffany back stage in the theater.

"Are you okay to work here for now?" Tiffany asked Babette after she had told her that she had seen the cloaked man roaming the ship again.

"I'll be fine, Tiffany. The man must be demented. That's all I can say. And now, as I said to Edmund here"—she threw him a glance—"we've got a responsibility to our passengers for a show in twenty-four hours. So we better get to work, alright?"

"If you feel up to it, I'm all for it," Tiffany replied, smiling at Babette and Edmund in turn.

Seeing that Babette was in good hands – surrounded by some of the cast members now, so as soon as Sarah Pilkington joined the group back stage, Edmund decided to pay another visit to Chubb. There was something that bothered him. *How could the man have vanished so fast round the corner? It didn't take me but a few seconds to reach the spot where Babette saw him – how's that possible?*

When he reached Chubb's cabin he saw the door ajar. He slipped in and went directly to the bedroom. The closet door was opened slightly. He looked in and found Chubb's knapsack. He rummaged through it and only found the white stocking he had seen the man wear when he caught up with him in the old city. As for the cloak it wasn't there.

As he was about to leave the bedroom he heard someone enter the cabin. He flew to the sitting room to find Chubb divesting himself of the cloak and throwing it on the sofa.

Edmund had enough of this cat and mouse chase. Using his kinetic powers, he lifted the coffee table a few inches from the floor and had it travel to the door, which was now closed. All the while Chubb stood frozen in the middle of the sitting room. "What the hell is going on here?" he hollered, running to grab the table. Edmund was quicker; throwing one of the chairs in Chubb's path and flinging the desk lamp at his head, so hard that Chubb fell at Edmund's feet in a heap.

"Good," Edmund said, "Now that I've got you and your cloak, Chubby, Chubb-Chubb, let's see who had left the door ajar?" He went to sit on the sofa, after he had re-opened the door again, and waited.

It wasn't long until Agent Mallard pushed the door open and stopped. Surprised to see the unconscious agent lying between the chair and the coffee table that blocked the passage into the suite, he blurted, "What happened here?" turning to Chalkstone. "It looks like someone paid our wandering monk a little visit, doesn't it?"

"Yeah," Chalkstone said, as he walked to the sofa, "and he's left Chubb's cloak behind, too."

"You're kidding," Mallard said, looking at the garment his partner was now handling with gloved hands. "Good God! But didn't Dr. Mayhew say that he had searched this cabin at some point?"

"Can't remember," Chalkstone replied, "but now let's make sure he doesn't go anywhere." He dropped the cloak back on the sofa, pulled some nylon straps out of his back pocket and tied Chubb's wrists to his back with them, including one of the legs of the heavy chair. "Do you think we should call the doc?" He looked up at Mallard who was examining the cloak now.

"Yeah, I guess we better make sure he's still alive, I suppose."

"Good Lord," Alan exclaimed when he entered Chubb's cabin, "What happened to him?" He knelt down beside the victim, emergency bag in hand.

"I guess someone else had enough of this character," Chalkstone remarked, chortling.

"And we found his cloak," Mallard added, going to the sofa and lifting the garment with a gloved hand, for Alan to see.

"Well," Alan said, "who ever clobbered our cloaked man has done a tremendous job of it"—he lifted his gaze to see his granddad chuckling—"He's got a mild concussion I suspect." He straightened up.

"What do you want us to do with him, Doc?" Chalkstone asked.

"Let's get the straps off his wrists first and then get him on his bed…"

"But, Doc, we can't trust that he won't try to escape again," Mallard objected.

"I understand that, Agent Mallard, but my first duty is to this patient, and he needs to lie down on a bed. And then you can strap his ankles and wrists to whatever you want – like maybe the toilet?"

While they were transporting the unconscious agent to the bedroom, Edmund whispered in Alan's ear, "You better have a look in the closet." Alan looked up at his great-grandfather. "The stocking he wore this morning is in the knapsack."

Alan only nodded as a reply and followed the CIA agents to the bedroom.

As they were re-strapping Chubb's wrists in front of him this time and securing his ankles, Alan opened the closet door and took out the knapsack.

"And what have we here?" he said, pointing to the white stocking.

"What have you found?" Mallard asked, rounding the bed and looking down into the open bag. "Wow! Isn't that what the perp was wearing over his face when he attacked Ms. Babette?"

"From her description, I think it is," Alan replied.

"That's strange," Chalkstone said suddenly from behind them.

"What is?" Mallard asked.

"Look for yourself – he's not wearing any signet ring – it's not there!"

"Miss Pilkington," Edmund said for Alan to hear, vanishing suddenly.

"I think there's something you should know, Agent Mallard," Alan said, looking down at Chubb on the bed, "I've got a confession to make."

"Don't tell me you're the second cloaked man," Mallard uttered jokingly.

Alan shook his head smiling, and then proceeded to tell about his encounter with Sarah Pilkington and seeing her wearing a ring with the initial E. C.

"And how do you account for Ms. Sylvan seeing Chubb here wearing that same ring this morning?"

"That I don't know, Agent Mallard, but somehow Ms. Pilkington is involved. And since she's working with Ms. Babette, I think you would do well to maybe have a chat with her?"

"Okay, Doc, as soon as Chubb comes around, we'll go and find her. I suppose she's in the theater right now?"

"Yes, I think Ms. Sylvan is there as well." Alan looked down at his patient. "I think I would prefer if you were to lock this man where he wouldn't be able to open any doors or portholes."

"You got it, Doc. We'll ask Mr. Ekelton to open one of the secure cabins that you guys use as a brig," Chalkstone answered.

"Okay, I'll leave you to it then, and when he wakes up, call me, okay?"

Mallard assured Alan that he would do so while he walked the doctor to the cabin door. "Who do you think attacked him like that?" he asked Alan.

"I don't know, Agent Mallard, but I believe this man has rubbed quite a few people the wrong way for quite a while. Maybe one of them paid him a visit when he came back from roaming the ship again."

Mallard nodded. "Anyway, I'll call you, Doc. See you later."

As Alan walked away, he wondered why Ms. Pilkington would be involved with Chubb. On the other hand, he wanted to talk again with Dr. Sigmund, the psychiatrist he had met earlier on this cruise. Chubb's behavior had all the trademarks of a DSM-IV diagnosis of schizophrenia. *And this latest concussion won't help matters either,* he thought.

CHAPTER THIRTY-SEVEN

Sarah Pilkington...?

GEORGE AND HARRIET DECIDED to celebrate their last hours in Madagascar by going on shore and staying at a five-star famous old hotel. They knew they would have to be back aboard *The Baroness* before midnight, but a few hours of luxuriating in one of the hotel suites beforehand was just what they needed. Steeped in tradition with wood panels and chandeliers abounding, when they entered the hotel and registered, a sweet young woman dressed in a very short skirt became overly friendly. George brushed her off.

Harriet objected, "George, that young woman was being so nice, and you were so rude."

"Harriet, she's a prostitute."

"I don't believe you. That sweet young thing?"

"Let's go up to our room and I'll prove it."

In their room, George called down to the desk and asked for "Delicia" to come to room 217. "Now," he said, "you hide in the bathroom with the door open just enough to hear us, okay?"

Soon, there was a knock on the door. George opened it and Delicia walked in, swirling her hips provocatively.

George asked, "How much do you charge?"

"$225 basic rate, plus $100 tips for special services."

Even George was taken aback. "$225 in Madagascar! I was thinking more in the range of $50."

Delicia laughed derisively. "You must really be a hick if you think you can buy sex for that price."

"Well," said George, "I guess we can't do business. Goodbye."

After she left, Harriet came out of the bathroom. She said, "I just can't believe it!"

George said, "Let's forget it. We'll go have a drink, then eat dinner."

At the bar, as they sipped their cocktails, Delicia came up behind George, pointed slyly at Harriet, and said, "See what you get for $50?"

"And she was so rude," Harriet added to George's comment about Delicia later that evening.

"Yes, our sweet Delicia wasn't that sweet after all, was she?" George concluded, lifting his gaze to a young woman who had just entered the restaurant. "But this one is a classy woman." He nodded in the direction of the elegantly dressed lady.

"Don't tell me she's another prostitute."

"No, Harriet, that's Ms. Pilkington. I've met her at the bar a couple of times. She works in the theater apparently."

"Did you talk to her then?" Harriet asked, a tinge of jealousy lacing her words.

"Well no, not directly. We've never been introduced but I heard her commenting about something at the dress rehearsal…"

Harriet's face brightened up suddenly. "Wasn't that just a perfect show?"

George nodded, throwing a glance in Ms. Pilkington's direction. She had taken a seat at the far end of the restaurant.

"And we can look forward to tomorrow night…"

"Why?" George asked distractedly, twirling his spoon in his coffee.

"They're putting on the second act of the play tomorrow night, that's why."

Meanwhile, Babette and Tiffany were coming out of the theater after the dress rehearsal was over, when they saw Edmund appear before them.

"Is Ms. Pilkington still with you?" he asked.

Babette and Tiffany exchanged a curious glance.

"No, she left as soon as the rehearsal started," Tiffany replied.

"We didn't need her anymore. The costumes didn't need anymore adjustments," Babette added helpfully. "But why would you want her?"

"Because, my dear lady, Ms. Pilkington has been wearing the signet ring..." was all Edmund offered as an explanation, vanishing before the two women's eyes as quickly as he had appeared.

"What do you think that is all about?" Tiffany queried, walking out of the theater with Babette to the foyer.

"I really don't know, my dear. But I can tell you one thing; Sarah Pilkington has always been a mystery to me."

"What do you mean by that?" Tiffany asked, pressing the elevator button.

"Well, she approached me out of nowhere one night in San Francisco and told me she had heard that I needed a dresser for my next production, which was true." They stepped in the elevator as its doors opened. "And when I looked through her resume," Babette went on, "I thought, why not. I've got no one else. My regular girl was due to deliver her baby in two weeks. So, I hired her on the spot."

"And she had worked in the theater before?"

"Yes, Tiffany, she had. She had worked on a couple of the plays I did on Broadway years ago. Otherwise, I wouldn't have taken her on so readily. But other than seeing that she's got the knack for altering garments quickly and expertly, I don't know anything about her."

While Babette and Tiffany were discussing Sarah Pilkington's unexpected arrival on the scene, so to speak, Edmund was scouring the city searching for the "missing" dresser. When he arrived at the Alhambra, the hotel where Sarah was having dinner, he exhaled a sigh of relief. *Now, how do I get her back to the ship,* Edmund wondered. Seeing that she had only just sat down to eat, Edmund decided to call on Alan for help.

He arrived at the medical center a few minutes later to find his great-grandson typing away on his computer keyboard. *This is not a way to live a doctor's life,* Edmund remarked to himself, *he's going to waste his talent writing reports, and then what?* He shrugged. This was not the time or place for this sort of discussion. He hollered instead, "Come with me, son."

Alan practically jumped out of his skin and stared up at his granddad, when he said, "We've got to get her back."

"Who? Who are you talking about?"

"No time to explain, Alan. Follow me – and quickly – now."

"Knowing that his granddad wouldn't be interrupting him for the mere fun of it, Alan got to his feet and said to Evelyn, before exiting the center, "Hold the fort for a bit, please. I'll be back as soon as I can."

"What is it, Doc? Do you need me…?" Evelyn called back at the closing door. She shrugged and returned to her duties. *This cruise has been a crazy one for sure*, she thought.

A half-an-hour later Alan was entering the Alhambra following his great-grandfather to the restaurant, when the latter said, "Get her back to the ship, Alan. There's something wrong with her."

Alan couldn't answer since the maître d' came to him and asked, "Would you like a table, Officer?"

"No-no. Thank you. But I need to talk to one of your guests." He jutted his chin in Sarah's direction. She had her back turned to him. "I won't be but a moment."

"Go right ahead, Officer," the maître d' replied, smiling amicably.

When Alan reached Sarah's table, he stood beside her. "Ms. Pilkington, I'm very sorry to interrupt your dinner, but Ms. Babette needs you urgently. It seems that one of the costumes has been damaged and…"

"Damaged? How?" Sarah questioned, visibly taken aback.

"That I don't know, Ms. Pilkington, but she's asked me to escort you back to the ship as soon as possible."

Obviously annoyed, Sarah took her napkin off her lap, gulped her glass of wine empty and said, "Alright then, let's go, Doctor," getting to her feet.

They went to the bar counter, where Sarah paid her bill, and then she followed Alan out of the restaurant.

As they were leaving, Harriet said, "There's something happening, George. Did you see?"

George nodded. "I hope she's okay – she's such a fine looking woman."

"And not a $50 session either," Harriet concluded, grinning.

"What's going on, Doc?" Sarah asked, as soon as they were in the hotel lobby.

"I think we better get back, Ms. Pilkington. I'm sure Ms. Babette will be able to explain." He led her by the arm out of the hotel.

"Oh stop being so cryptic, Doc," Sarah erupted, as Alan was about to hail a cab to return to the pier. "I know there couldn't possibly be any damage to any of the costumes. So, what's going on?"

Alan suddenly decided to open up. "Listen to me, Sarah. I know that you're not the person you claim to be…"

"How could you possibly know that?"

Alan took her left hand and held her little finger in front of her eyes. "This ring, Sarah. Whose is it?"

She bowed her head. "Can we discuss this somewhere else?"

"Sure, let's get back to the ship where it'll be more comfortable to talk about Edward Chulbridge, shall we?" And with these words, Alan flagged a cab.

While Alan and Edmund were ashore, Evelyn was taking a count of the medical center's supplies that had just been brought aboard earlier that afternoon. She was opening the last box when Gilbert rushed in and shouted, "Where is he?"

Stunned, Evelyn raised an annoyed face to him. "What's the matter now?" she demanded, putting down her tablet and putting her hands on her haunches. "If you mean Doctor Mayhew, he's not here, Mr. Evans." She walked up to him, as he was about to pivot on his heels to leave. "Hold on a minute there. Could you tell me what's going on with everybody tonight? I mean it's like you've all been bitten by something…"

"It's nothing that should concern you, Miss Evelyn. It's just that we've got a bit of a problem…"

"Another one!" Evelyn exclaimed. "We've got corpses lining up in the morgue like sausages on a rack and now, as if that wasn't enough, everybody is running in and out of here like they have their tails on fire."

Staring at the nurse, Gilbert bowed his head for an instant and then raised it to shake it with a grin on his lips. "Apart from our sausages in the morgue, Ms. Evelyn, we've got an Interpol agent going absolutely bonkers in the brig…"

"Who's that?"

"Never mind…" Gilbert said, chuckling now while looking at Evelyn's unsmiling face. "Just tell me if the doc has gone ashore or if he's aboard… please?"

"I have no idea, Mr. Evans. He only asked me to hold the fort when he left." She paused to peer into the chief's eyes. "Do you need my help?"

"I guess… maybe, I mean, do you have any bed restraints or something like that in your storeroom by any chance?" Gilbert resounded.

"You were not joking, were you, when you said you had one of the agents going bonkers?" Gilbert shook his head yes in Evelyn's direction. "Well, don't that beat all? As a matter of fact, yes, we do have some bed straps along with an injection of valium or lithium that should do the job." Evelyn turned around and over her shoulder, she added, "I'll call Alice. She's better than I would ever be at that sort of thing…"

Gilbert stayed planted where he was and waited.

Brandishing a small emergency bag, coming out of the storeroom, Evelyn said, "Okay, these should be just what you need." She handed him the bag. "And if you tell me which secure room the guy is in, I'll call Alice and tell her to join you there as soon as she can, okay?"

"That's tremendous. Thanks, Miss Evelyn," Gilbert said, hurrying out.

Looking at him as he was leaving, Evelyn shook her head and took her cell-phone out of her pocket.

On his way to the lower deck, Gilbert tried calling Alan on his cell again. *Where the heck is he? I just hope nothing's happened to him,* he thought, *that's all we'd need, the doc being abducted. In that case, this ship won't move anywhere tonight or until a replacement Doc would be flown in, and corporate would be livid.*

"I'm on my way to your office..." Alan said as soon as he opened the line.

"Where were you?" Gilbert queried, sounding rushed. "I've tried..."

"Never mind that, Gilbert, I've got 'Ms.' Pilkington with me and we need to talk."

"That's great, but we don't have time for chatting, Alan..."

"What's happening?" he asked, leading Sarah up the gangway.

"Chubb is having a fit of some sort and he's gone insane... I don't know..."

"Are you with him?"

"No, I'm on my way to the brig now. I've got some bed straps and a syringe of medicine that Evelyn gave me..."

"Okay, I'll be down there as soon as I can. Where are the two CIA agents now?"

"They're with him. When I left they were trying to hold him down before he destroyed the furniture, walls, windows, and them."

"Doctor?" Alan heard Sarah say behind him as the two of them reached the deck. "Sorry, I couldn't help but overhear what you both said." She took in a breath. "Who are you talking about?"

"Edward Chulbridge, Sarah. Why, what exactly do you know about him?"

"Hello...? Alan, are you still there?" Gilbert hollered over the line.

Alan replaced the phone to his ear. "Which cabin, Gilbert?"

"105."

"Okay, I'll be there in a minute." Closing his phone, Alan peered into Sarah's eyes. She was on the verge of tears. "Well, who is he to you, Sarah?"

"My father."

CHAPTER THIRTY-EIGHT

Chubb doesn't remember

"WHAT HAPPENED TO HIM?" Sarah asked Alan while they were on their way down to the cabin where Chulbridge was being held.

"I should ask you the same question, Sarah. He's under suspicion of having committed two murders and an attempted murder on Ms. Babette. Does he have a history of mental illness?"

Sarah bowed her head and then nodded yes. "But not insanity really. He was diagnosed with a form of schizophrenia shortly before he accepted this assignment with Interpol." Sarah didn't have time to expand on her explanation for the moment. She and Alan had reached cabin 105.

Everything seemed quiet inside, *which is a good sign,* Alan thought before he knocked on the door.

What he saw when they entered the cabin took his breath away. Chubb was tied to the bed with the emergency restraints Evelyn had given Gilbert. His face was showing signs of severe bruising while his lower lip was bleeding. Chubb looked haggard and didn't seem to be aware of what was going on. A moment later he closed his eyes and fell asleep.

Gilbert was the first to speak after he had opened the door for Alan and Sarah. "What is Ms. Pilkington doing here?" he asked, shooting a disapproving glance at Alan.

"She's with me," Alan replied curtly. "But what I'd like to know is what happened to Agent Chulbridge? Did you have to beat him into submission?" He directed his query to Chalkstone who had taken a seat at the edge of the bed.

"I'll answer that," Mallard piped up. "The only way we could deal with the guy was to knock him out, Doc. That's the long and short of it."

Both Chalkstone and Mallard looked as if they had been in a catfight, their faces and necks were scratched and had bleeding lacerations.

Alan turned to Alice, who had remained quiet since Alan came in. "What injection did you give him?" he asked.

"Valium, Doc. Since I wasn't sure of the diagnosis, I thought that was the best choice."

Alan nodded. "Okay then"—he looked around him—"I want you two out of this cabin," he ordered, glaring at the two CIA agents.

"But, Doc…"

"No buts, Agent Mallard, you and your partner go and wait outside."

"What about Ms. Pilkington…? Do you want her here?" Chalkstone demanded.

"Yes. And please don't ask me why. You'll have all the explanations you want once I'm done examining the patient."

"What about me?" Gilbert asked, his voice pleading.

"Perhaps you should stay as well, Gilbert. Maybe you can witness this conversation with our patient." He looked at Alice next. "Would you mind going back to the center and finding Dr. Sigmund's number on the passengers' list. Then call him and have him come to this cabin."

"Sure, Doc, right away." With these words, Alice went to open the cabin's door and shouted, "Come on, you two, get out and let the doc do his job."

Dumbfounded, both agents nodded. They threw a last glance at Chulbridge before Alice closed the door behind her.

Once the three of them had gone, Sarah finally spoke. "Is my father going to be okay?" She looked at Alan while going to sit beside her dad.

"He's going to be fine, Sarah. But for the time being I don't think he'll be up to answering any questions. He's probably had a mild concussion and the Valium Alice gave him will have him under sedation for a while."

"And what can I do in the meantime?" She looked from Alan to Gilbert.

The latter was still puzzled. He had heard Sarah call the man laying on the bed her father. He was trying to process this new information when Sarah repeated, "What do you want me to do?"

"Why don't you explain how you came to take this cruise with your father," Alan answered for Gilbert.

"That's a bit of a long story, Dr. Mayhew…"

"We've got all night," Gilbert interposed, "so go ahead."

"Okay," Sarah said, nodding and taking her father's hand in hers. "My dad has been with Interpol for a number of years now, but on his last assignment – the one he took before this one – he was in a car accident apparently and after that he was 'not all there'."

"What do you mean by that?" Alan asked. He was still standing his back to the wall.

"Well, first he seemed to lose track of time. We always had an arrangement by which he would call me on Skype once a week from where ever he was and he usually arranged to call me at the same time on Sundays. But he started forgetting the day or confusing the days and time. He would call me on Tuesday and tell me that it was Sunday. At first I thought he might be in the middle of a sticky situation – I don't know – but I didn't want to argue. Anyway, when he came back, he began calling me Elizabeth, my mother's name. Then there were times he couldn't remember what he had been doing the day before…"

"And that's when you sought medical attention for him and had him diagnosed, was it?"

"Well, I couldn't even mention the word 'psychiatrist' without him throwing a fit. So, I waited until he started calling me Elizabeth again and then went on with the pretense. We went to a doctor in Washington and that's where I learned of his condition."

"But why did you let him come on this assignment then, being aware of his condition?" Gilbert asked.

Sarah turned to the chief. "Have you ever tried dealing with Interpol as a mere mortal, Mr. Evans? They would hardly listen to me."

"But didn't they notice something was wrong with his behavior?" Alan queried.

"I guess not. And you've got to understand my father was an expert in his field. He could take on any personality they wanted. If they told him to be a baker, he would be the perfect baker. He was an exceptional undercover agent, Dr. Mayhew. And that is what's so sad about this whole situation."

"I'd say it's much more than that, Ms. Pilkington," Gilbert remarked. "Your father is now under suspicion of committing no less than two murders…"

"I know, I know, Mr. Evans. And right now I have no idea how I can help."

"Why did you take the ring from him?" Alan asked.

"I was trying to divert attention to me, but I guess I still have women's looking hands, don't I?" She released her father's hand and put both of hers on her knees.

"Did you tell your father about your sex change at any point?"

Sarah shook her head. "I couldn't. I was going to tell him, believe me. But when he began losing it, I didn't see the point. I felt that it would have confused him more."

"Okay, Sarah," Alan said, pushing himself off the wall against which he had been leaning. "I'm waiting here for Dr. Sigmund and I'll explain the situation to him."

"Who is he?" Sarah asked, lifting questioning eyes to Alan.

"He's an eminent psychiatrist and if there's one person on this ship who could see your dad through this ordeal it's this man."

"Will he go to prison you think?" Sarah switched her gaze to Gilbert.

"He'll probably be incarcerated for life." Gilbert looked down at his notepad. "Why don't you and I go to my office? I'll need a formal statement from you. Okay?" He stood up.

Sarah got to her feet. "Thank you, Dr. Mayhew." She hesitated. "Does Ms. Babette have to know about any of this?"

"I don't think she'll want to know, Sarah. As long as you don't tell her, she probably won't ask. Yet, the truth will have to come out some time, I hope you realize that?" Sarah nodded. "Oh, one more thing," Alan added, "Would you mind if I take the ring back from you?"

"No-no"—she took it off and handed it to the doc—"here, please keep it safe. It's the last thing we have from my mother."

"I'll be sure to do that, Sarah." Alan shot a glance in Gilbert's direction. "But I think it will be evidence in court."

"As long as I can have it back, that's fine," Sarah said, stepping to the door.

"I'll see you later, Doc," Gilbert said, exiting the cabin with Sarah.

A few minutes later Alan went to open the door to Alice and Dr. Sigmund. "Come on in, Doctor. Thank you for sparing some time," Alan said and then asked Alice, "Where are the two agents?"

"I cleaned up their wounds and sent them on their way," she replied, closing the cabin's door. "I think they said they were going to check with Dr. Rivers."

"Okay then," Alan said while returning his attention to Dr. Sigmund. "I'm sorry, Doctor, but we've had a bit of a situation…"

"No need to explain, Dr. Mayhew, your nurse gave me a run down of what has occurred on the way down here." He looked at Chulbridge. "Is that our patient?"

"Yes, but I think I better give you a summary of what happened to him before you question him at a more appropriate time."

"Why the restraints? Has he demonstrated some violent behavior?"

"Yes, he did. But I suggest he had no idea at the time where or who he was."

Sigmund nodded, and sat on the chair that Gilbert had vacated upon leaving the cabin. "Okay, tell me what you know of this man's behavior with as many details as you can."

While Alan recited Sarah's account, Alice busied herself cleaning Chubb's face and hands. She dressed the superficial lacerations on his forehead and mandible and sat down beside the patient. *Diseases of the mind are the worst,* she thought. *This poor man will probably never remember what he has done and will never walk the street of his hometown again. An awful fate indeed.*

As soon as Mallard and Chalkstone arrived in front of Dr. Rivers' cabin, they knocked on the door, shaking their heads. "We're not flying home tonight," Chalkstone remarked as Rivers opened the door.

"I guess none of us are, Chuck," Rivers said, letting them in.

"Why do you say that?" Mallard asked, stepping indoors.

"Because we found the remnants of a detonator in the sanitation room…"

"Yeah, you told us about that," Chalkstone interrupted.

"Okay, Chuck," Rivers uttered, obviously annoyed. "Why don't you sit down anywhere you like and listen, okay?"

Both agents nodded and sat down on the sofa. Rivers took a seat, facing them. "As I said we found pieces of a detonator and after we examined the items, Ms. Ashton and I came to the conclusion that the device must have been detonated remotely…"

"How?" Mallard cut-in to Rivers visible displeasure.

"By a cell-phone, Ducky. The arsonist or murderer must have ignited the device by pressing a digit on his cell-phone."

Mallard and Chalkstone exchanged a glance, stood up and rushed out.

"I bet they forgot to get the cell from Agent Chulbridge, didn't they?" Jenny Ashton said from the doorway to the bedroom, a wry smile drawing on her lips.

"That would be my guess. You're right on, my dear." Rivers then turned to her. "What about the nitro, any idea where he could have procured it?"

"No, sir. We don't have the instruments right here to determine the nitro's provenance. All we can do is bag it and take it back to Washington for further analysis."

When Mallard and Chalkstone arrived in front of the secure cabin, they banged their fists on the door. "Ouch," Mallard yelled, shaking his injured hand from the pain.

"You shouldn't have punched him so hard," Chalkstone said, a smirk on his lips.

When Alan heard the banging, he nodded to Alice. She strode to the door decisively. She was not about to let anyone interrupt the two physicians' conference.

"What else do you want?" she blared at the CIA agents as she opened the door wide.

Chalkstone didn't hesitate and tried pushing past her. Alice was so quick that the next thing anyone noticed was the agent stretched on the floor at her feet. "I said: what else do you want?" Alice repeated, grabbing the man by the collar of his jacket and standing him up.

Mallard, although stunned, said, "I'm sorry, Ms. Muller, but we need to find Agent Chulbridge's cell-phone.

All the while, Alan and Dr. Sigmund had gotten to their feet and only smiled. That until Sigmund said, "An able nurse under many circumstances, I see."

"Yeah, that she is," Alan agreed and then added, "Why would you want his cell-phone, Agent Mallard?"

"Because he's most likely detonated the device in the sanitation room with it, that's why."

"Have you searched his cabin?" Alan asked.

"Not thoroughly, no, but I'd say he's got it on him…"

"Okay, fellows, why don't you go and have a thorough look in his room first. I'll search him in the meantime, okay?"

"Okay, Doc," Mallard said resignedly, grabbing Chalkstone by the arm and leading him out of the cabin.

"But…"

"No buts, Chuck, let's go," Mallard said to Chalkstone's objection.

In a minute they were gone. Alan shook his head. "Again, I'm sorry, Dr. Sigmund, but dealing with the CIA is never easy."

"Don't worry, Dr. Mayhew. My interest is only in this patient"—he nodded in the direction of the bed—"and although he's probably going to see prison bars for a while, as soon as I return to Washington, I'll take him under my care – with his daughter's consent of course."

"That's all I could ask, Doctor, and thank you for any advice you may have in this case. As soon as Agent Chulbridge wakes up, I'll let you know."

"Fine, you do that," Sigmund said, turning a musing gaze to Alan. "But in the meantime, I also suggest keeping an eye on Ms. Pilkington. There is something about the explanation she provided about her father's condition that doesn't sound quite right to me."

"What, for instance?" Alan asked, all the more curious now.

"If the man suffered from dementia, I would understand his confusing days and times, but schizophrenics generally – and I stress generally – have black outs but when they come out of these, they are quick to regain their bearings. They cannot remember what or who they were during these black out periods, yes, but they function normally and only assume the personality that occupies their minds at the one time."

"I see," Alan said. "I thought it was something like that. Anything else?"

"Irrational behavior, Dr. Mayhew. Ms. Pilkington said her father called her Elizabeth; again, I would associate such behavior more to dementia than to schizophrenia. You see what I mean?"

"Yes, and as you recommended, I will talk to her and keep an eye on her." Alan paused and hesitated to ask, "Would you be willing to have a specific conversation with her in the near future?"

"Yes, absolutely. In fact, I was going to ask if you would permit me to do so."

Alan smiled. "Okay then, Doctor, I will call on you again after we leave in the morning. And thank you…"

"You've got me exercising my brain again, Doctor, so it's me who thanks you. I will take pleasure in analyzing these cases, believe me."

CHAPTER THIRTY-NINE

Where is the cell phone?

WHILE ALAN HAD RETURNED to the medical center, hoping to finish his reporting to the head office, Gilbert, at long last, had authorized the release of Mrs. Clipper and Irene Walter's bodies to their respective family members. The coffins rolled off the ramp in the middle of the night under the watchful eyes of customs officers and baggage handlers. Gilbert had watched the procedure from the lower deck and was now ready to hit the sack. After taking Ms. Pilkington's statement, he only wanted to have a bite to eat before he finally returned to his cabin.

When he entered the officers' mess, he noticed that George Phillips, one of the crew from the engineering department had rejoined the cruise after being hospitalized for suspected bowel cancer and then sent home for a well-deserved vacation. George had noticed some rectal bleeding and Alan had sent the man ashore at the next port following the bleed, during a previous cruise. A confirmatory FOBT test had also been positive. With a typical Scottish sense of humor, George was now recounting his adventure.

Gilbert took a seat beside the man and said, "Hey, Georgy-boy, good to see you back, mate. How was the trip?"

George turned to the chief and replied, "Interesting!"

"Is that it?" Lynn, another engineer asked. "Come on, mate, let's have it, okay?"

"Well," George began, "As soon as I was on shore, Doc Alan had gotten me into see a specialist so I didn't have to wait 16 hours in the emergency room. In Dubai, when I was on the M.V. Princess Flame, I waited 14 hours to be seen by some 15-year-old guy in a white flowing robe who called himself a doctor. I wish Doc Alan had been there. I had lost so much blood from a GI bleed, they tell me I was yelling, "Jesus, save me". Anyway, this time, the gastroenterologist that I saw made an appointment for me to have a test two days later. Since we were scheduled to be in this Mexican port for another couple of days, all was well. The doctor was actually very good about explaining all about colonoscopies to me. He showed me various pictures and reassured me about the procedure and how it was going to be done. I was given some home instructions and a prescription, which I filled in the local Mexican pharmacy for "SuperPrep". This stuff comes in a box large enough to hold a microwave oven. And I tell you right now, we must never allow it to fall into the hands of terrorists or any other of our country's enemies."

Gilbert and Lynn chuckled. "That bad, eh?" Lynn said.

George only nodded and went on, "So, I brought it back on board and opened the darn thing.

"In accordance with the instructions, I didn't eat any solid food that day, just some fluids. Then, in the evening, I took the SuperPrep. "

"It said that you mix two packets of powder together in a one-liter plastic jug, then you fill it with lukewarm water. Then you have to drink the whole jug. This takes about an hour, because SuperPrep tastes – and here I am being kind – like a mixture of cow piss and urinal cleanser, with just a hint of lemon. The instructions for SuperPrep, clearly written by somebody with a great sense of humor, state that after you drink it, 'a loose, watery bowel movement may result'. This is kind of like saying that after you jump off a roof, you may experience contact with the ground."

Both Gilbert and Lynn had a hard time keeping a straight face. They could see the big guy reading these instructions....

"The SuperPrep is like a "nuclear laxative"," George went on, "there are times when you wish the commode had a seat belt. You spend several hours pretty much confined to the bathroom, spurting violently. You eliminate everything. And then, when you figure you must be totally empty, you have to drink another liter of SuperPrep.

"In the morning, Dr. Mayhew sent me in a cab to the gastroenterologist. I was very nervous. I was not only worried about the procedure, but I had been experiencing occasional return bouts of SuperPrep spurtage.

"Even in Mexico, I had to sign many forms acknowledging that I understood and totally agreed with whatever the Spanish forms said, which I didn't. I wish Dr. Mayhew had been there to translate. Then they led me to a little curtained space and I put on one of those hospital garments designed by sadist perverts. These are the kind that, when you put it on, it makes you feel even more naked than when you are actually naked.

"Then a nurse put in an I.V. and in trying to make the situation lighter, told me that some people put tequila in their SuperPrep. At first I was ticked off that I hadn't thought of this, but then I pondered what would happen if you got yourself too tipsy to make it to the bathroom. You'd be staggering around in full *fire hose mode*. You would have no choice but to burn your cabin."

"Was the nurse good looking at least," Lynn asked, between bursts of laughter.

"Not bad, but not my type," George replied with a light chuckle. "Anyway, when everything was ready, I was wheeled into the procedure room, where the doc was waiting with a nurse and an anesthesiologist. I was seriously nervous at this point. The nurse had me roll over on my left side, and the anesthesiologist began hooking something up to the needle in my hand. There was music playing in the room, and I realized that the song was 'Dancing Queen' by ABBA. I remarked that, of all the songs that could be playing during this particular procedure, 'Dancing Queen' had to be the least appropriate. Then I fell asleep and woke up in a very mellow mood. Afterward, the doc told me that it was all over, and that my colon had passed with flying colors!

"Dr. Mayhew had told me before I left for the examination that colonoscopies are no joke; and that they are an effective way of discovering if there are cancerous polyps or other abnormalities in the colon. A Proctologist physician friend of his claimed that these are actual comments made by his patients (mostly male) while he was performing their colonoscopies." George pulled a piece of paper out of his shirt pocket and passed it to Gilbert. "Have a look, Chief. I don't know which is mine, but I could have said them all."

1. "Could you write a note for my wife saying that my head is not up there?"
2. "Find Amelia Earhart yet?"
3. "Can you hear me NOW?"
4. "Are we there yet? Are we there yet? Are we there yet?"
5. "You know, in Arkansas, we're now legally married."
6. "Any sign of the trapped miners, Chief?"
7. "You put your left hand in; darned... Doc, you take your left hand out..."
8. "Hey! Now I know how a Muppet feels!"
9. "If your hand doesn't fit, you must quit, promise!"
10. "Hey, Doc, let me know if you find my dignity."
11. "Take it easy, Doc. You're boldly going where no man has gone before!"

Once the laughter around the table had died down, George said, "Thanks for listening, guys, but now I think it's time for my colon and I to get some rest." He got up.

After another round of chuckles, George's mates left Gilbert to his late supper. *So glad to see the big guy is back,* he thought, *maybe now Simon will have time to heal his chest.* Although he doubted it somehow.

Once Alan had closed the files and sent his reports to head office, he decided to take another look at what he could find on the Internet's medical social media websites for Emergency Medicine and Family Physicians regarding a couple of specific mental disorders. Although it was late, he wanted to take the opportunity of still being in port for the next few hours and getting a decent Wi-Fi signal. Tomorrow, at sea, the satellite Internet connection would be sparse to nil. What he found out definitely put another slant to Chubb's mental diagnosis. He promised himself to have another chat with Dr. Sigmund in the morning before the man would have his interview with the Interpol agent.

When Alan ultimately reached his cabin that night, he looked at the clock on the nightstand and swore under his breath. It was nearly 2:00 am. *Well,* he thought, *two or three hours' sleep is better than none.* As a resident and intern, he had long learned how to sleep at the 'drop of a hat' and to go into deep REM sleep immediately. As soon as his head hit the pillow he fell asleep. Edmund, for his part, watched him for a little while and then returned to Babette's cabin. He had been listening to Alan's conversation with Dr. Sigmund and was indeed troubled by what he had heard. He sensed there was more to Sarah Pilkington's story than she let on. For one thing, she had not told Alan which psychiatrist she and her father had supposedly visited in Washington. Schizophrenia was not a well known malady in the 1850s, even so, Edmund felt sure Dr. Sigmund had been right. Older folks displayed signs of dementia all the time and being confused about days and people's names was generally one of the most distinguishable symptoms of deterioration of brain cells.

He sat down in the sitting room of Babette's suite for a while and then after ensuring the dear lady was indeed fast asleep, Edmund decided to have another look around the ship and in particular, Ms. Pilkington's cabin. When he first searched her cabin, all he was looking for was her ring. But now, he wanted to find anything that could resolve his qualms.

As for Dr. Rivers and Miss Ashton, they too had left the ship. There was no need for them to stay aboard. All their work would need to be done in labs in Washington. Moreover, there was an autopsy to be conducted on their colleague's corpse, which they would accompany during its journey home.

"I really hope they'll lock him up for life," Jenny remarked as they watched Daniel's coffin come down the gangway ramp of the vessel.

Rivers nodded. "I have no idea how I am going to tell his parents that their boy died during an explosion."

"You know, the Romans had it right," Jenny said, "guys like Chubb, once caught, were sent to the arena to fight lions before the animals would feed, on their remains, of course. No tax dollars going to jails with Internet and TV."

"Perhaps, he's not totally responsible," Rivers mused, turning his face to his assistant.

"What do you mean by that? Have you found something that would indicate Chubb didn't detonate the bomb?"

"I don't know that he did, Jenny, that's the point." Rivers paused as they saw the coffin of their companion being loaded in the hearse. "Let's get him aboard the flight and I'll explain, okay?"

Jenny nodded, and climbed in the back seat of the government car that had been dispatched to transport the three of them to a private airport lounge. They would leave in a couple of hours aboard a US government aircraft.

Meanwhile Mallard and Chalkstone had resigned themselves to the fact that they would spend several more days aboard *The Baroness* while the ship would be making her way to the next port of call – Cape Town, South Africa.

"And we haven't found the darn cell-phone yet," Mallard remarked, slipping under the cover of the lower bunk of their cabin. These cabins, alongside the crew cabins, were for entertainers, corporate computer techs, specialized mechanics, representatives for certain equipment on board that 'only they could repair', onboard speakers, and for the occasional inspectors.

Climbing to the upper bunk, Chalkstone said, "I bet Chubb never had it in the first place."

That comment had Mallard prop himself on his elbows, almost hitting his head in the process. "What do you mean?" he demanded, stretching his neck to look up at his partner.

"The time line, that's what we need to look at, Mallard. But for now, let's get some shut-eye, okay?"

"That's easy enough for you to say. I don't think I can sleep now," Mallard said, lying down again. We've got to find the cell and…"

"Shut up, okay?" Chalkstone yelled. "If you can't sleep, do it in silence, okay?"

Mallard didn't answer but groaned, punching his pillow into submission instead.

CHAPTER FORTY

A near normal day

ALL OFFICERS WERE ON DECK for *The Baroness*'s departure from Antsiranana. It was only five o'clock in the morning and the sun hadn't made its appearance over the horizon yet. Even so, it seemed that half of the city's population had come to attend the elegant ship's sailing. She sounded her horn twice, saying goodbye to the ones who had lost their lives aboard and to one of the most troubled parts of this cruise, or so Alan hoped. There were quite a few problems still to be resolved, but after what he read last night on the Internet, Alan felt confident solutions or answers were near at hand.

As soon as Babette opened her eyes, the first thing she saw was Edmund looking down at her. "Good morning, milady," he said, a broad smile drawing on his lips. "How did you sleep?"

"Like a log, if one could ascribe sleep to a piece of wood," Babette answered, propping herself to a sitting position. "What about you, have you roamed the ship all night again?"

"Ha-ha-ha-ha," Edmund laughed, sitting on the edge of the bed. "Not really, dear lady, I just went for a look around Sarah's cabin."

"Sarah? What for? Is she alright?"

"Oh yes, she's just fine. But to tell you the truth, I think there's a lot more to Ms. Pilkington than meets the eye."

"I knew it!" Babette exclaimed, flinging the covers aside. "I was saying the same thing to Tiffany yesterday when you vanished after saying her name. So, have you found more about her? Anything I should know?"

"The one thing we can be certain of is that she is Agent Chulbridge's daughter..."

"Say what?" Babette burst out, reaching for her robe.

"I just said..."

"I heard you, Edmund. I'm sorry. I'm not used to hear such news this early in the morning. How did you find out?" Babette asked, but then lifted a hand in front of Edmund's face. "Don't say another word. I need to freshen up first and order some breakfast, alright?"

Edmund only smiled and nodded.

A half-an-hour later, sitting in front of a scrumptious breakfast tray and a cup of her favorite tea, Babette asked, "Okay, now you can tell me what you found out about my dresser and how you did so." She took a sip of her tea.

Edmund watched while sitting across from her in the sitting room. "It all happened yesterday evening when I left the theater after I realized that Sarah was the link..." Edmund then went on recounting the events of the previous night to his captivated audience of one.

When he finished his recital, Babette put her cup down in the saucer, took another croissant from the basket, buttered it, and then raised her gaze to Edmund. "What am I supposed to do now? I've got a show tonight and if there is any possibility that she had anything to do with her father's action, am I supposed to dismiss her?"

"No, Babette. As I said, there's no indication at this point that she's done anything but try to prevent her father from pursuing people in his madness. So, I would suggest, you say nothing to her and go on as if you know nothing of what I told you."

Babette didn't respond and continued eating her croissant in silence.

She then said, "Although I have been working in the theater for all these years, and acting would come naturally to me if I were to take on a role, I am not good when it comes to pretending or straying from the truth, Edmund. I don't think I could lie to Sarah's face, or pretend that I didn't know anything about her father if the subject ever came up."

"May I then suggest that you refrain from talking to her, except when you are discussing costume alterations, wouldn't that be better?"

"I suppose so. I'll be so busy from now until the curtain rises on the second act tonight that I will not have time to think about Sarah Pilkington anyway."

A couple of hours after *The Baroness* sailed away from Madagascar, Alan made his way to the breakfast café on the upper deck where he had invited Tiffany to join him. She was waiting for him. As soon as she saw him rounding the corner from the deck, she waved – a smile on her lips.

"I missed you, Tiff," were Alan's first words as he sat down and took her hand in one of his. "I just hope we can return to some degree of normalcy for the rest of the cruise." He squeezed her hand.

"I missed you too, sweetheart," she whispered. "How are you anyway?"

"Tired. Too many unanswered questions. Too many routine examinations I couldn't perform. Too many deaths." He got up from his seat. "I'll get myself a tray. Do you want something else?" he asked, looking down at the bowl of cereal, toast, juice and coffee in front of her.

"No, thanks. I'm fine," Tiffany replied.

"Okay, I'll be back in two ticks," Alan said, already making his way to the counter.

As he was putting the last of his breakfast items on the tray, he heard a familiar voice behind him.

"Good morning, Dr. Mayhew."

Alan swung on his heels and smiled. "Just the man I wanted to see. Good morning, Dr. Sigmund. A bit early for you isn't it?"

Sigmund chortled and shook his head. He then grabbed a mug from the stack on the counter, filled it with coffee and replied, "Sleep doesn't come easy to those who have too many things on their minds."

Taking his tray off the counter, Alan said, "Why don't you join us," jutting his chin in the direction of the table where Tiffany was sitting.

"If you're sure I'm not intruding?"

"Not at all, Doctor. I think our entertainment director will be most interested in what we have to discuss."

"Very good. Then I accept."

"This is Dr. Sigmund, Tiffany," Alan said as they reached their table. He deposited his tray and turned to the psychiatrist. "Ms. Tiffany Sylvan, Doctor."

"Very nice meeting you, Ms. Sylvan. And before you say anything, let me congratulate you on the superb set of entertaining soirees you've organized for this cruise. Absolutely splendid!"

Blushing now, Tiffany replied, "Thank you, Doctor. And compliments should really go to the staff and cast of our shows. I just put artists and cast and passengers together at the same time."

"And you do a very nice job of it, too." Sitting down now, Sigmund smiled and sipped on his coffee quietly. A moment later, he asked, "What did you want to discuss, Dr. Mayhew?"

"I'd like to go over what I found out last night…"

"Do you want me to leave you two alone," Tiffany interrupted, thinking the two physicians were about to discuss medical matters.

Alan said, "Oh no, please, Tiffany. What we need to talk about will probably concern you as well."

"Me? How?"

"Well, apart from being acquainted with Ms. Sarah Pilkington, I'd like to have a woman's insight on what we're about to discuss."

"Okay then," Tiffany agreed. Her curiosity aroused now. "As long as you don't mind me eating while I'm listening."

"No-no, go ahead. I'll do the same"—Alan turned to Sigmund—"if you don't mind, Doctor?"

"I don't mind at all. Just give me the gist of what you thought about Mr. Chulbridge's diagnosis, and I'll think about it while you two eat away."

"Drug induced mental state," Alan replied, taking a spoonful of his yogurt and putting it in his mouth. He swallowed. "And it's more than a thought, Doctor; it's actually a strong possibility."

Sigmund nodded. "Yes, as you said it's a strong possibility."

"You mean Agent Chulbridge could have been drugged?" Tiffany piped-up after she ate the last bite of her toast.

Alan nodded, but didn't reply and continued eating. Sigmund

retreated to the back of his chair and continued sipping on his coffee. He looked pensive.

A few minutes later, when both Alan and Tiffany had finished their breakfast, Sigmund said, "Yes, mental conditions could be – and often are – induced by the side effects of ingesting certain drugs."

Alan pushed his chair back from the table, took a folded sheet of paper out of his shirt pocket and crossed his legs. "Here are my thoughts, Doctor." He handed the sheet to Sigmund. "As you will read, there are several possibilities that should be examined before we reach a conclusion, or draw a picture of what may have happened to Agent Chulbridge."

Sigmund took a pair of reading glasses out of his summer jacket pocket, adjusted it on the bridge of his nose, unfolded the sheet of paper and began reading.

> While still in port in Papua, Sarah may have gone to one of the local healers and ostensibly gotten a combo of herbs that were supposed to give energy to the recipient, but instead resulted in a bit of memory loss and decreased concentration, and related symptoms. The combo of herbal medicines could have comprised any or all of the common ones given by local healers there like: St. John's wort, ginkgo biloba, kava, valerian, and ginseng among others. The series of potential interactions between the herbal combo and the conventional drug therapy he was perhaps taking – Chantix – could have resulted in an adverse drug event (i.e. driving Chulbridge crazy.) With this combo of drug and herbs, you can go pretty well anywhere with symptoms. Chantix itself can have adverse effects of a mental nature. Add to that some of these herbs used for depression etc., and you have a combo that could explain pretty well any behavior. The herbs could be either in a tea, tincture or capsules.

> Chantix – to keep him from smoking – has its own side effects of psychosis in some patients. There was recently a meta-analysis of

some of these herbs. They, on their own, really could make one crazy (with memory loss and decreased concentration) and related symptoms. At first perusal, there are some 28 articles that describe interactions between these herbal concoctions (St. John's wort, ginkgo biloba, kava, valerian, and ginseng) and conventional drug therapies. It is even worse if you are older.

Sigmund took his glasses off, folded the sheet and handed it back to Alan, saying, "Very good, Doctor Mayhew. However, before we can determine if the cause of Agent Chulbridge's psychotic behavior was the result of drug ingestion or side effects from taking Chantix, we need to do two things." He paused while Alan passed the piece of paper to Tiffany. "First, I'd like to have you draw some blood from our patient and have some tests run on it to determine if there are residues of any drug or herbs in his system, on the off-chance that the levels are high enough to still be in his system."

"Yes, I was going to do so this morning, although I'm not sure the tests I can run at the medical center will be conclusive. At least we would have some indication of the presence of drugs in his system. I'll courier a few samples to a reference lab in Canada that I know does some specialized tests."

"Yes, a very good idea, if you could do that, Dr. Mayhew. And the second thing will be for me to have a conversation with our patient. He must be awake and alert by now, I suspect."

"I believe he is. My nurse checked on him this morning. He only asked for something to eat and she gave him some dry toast and milk."

Tiffany coughed lightly after she read Alan's summary. "I'm sorry to interrupt, but if Sarah was giving her father herbs – or this combo you mentioned – how could she have done it? I mean it's not like Agent Chulbridge seems like the kind of man to accept being spoon-fed anything he didn't want to eat or drink. Besides, do we know he was trying to quit smoking? Does he have a girlfriend he was trying to be sexually potent for? Was he body building?" She looked at the two physicians in turn.

"All very good observations, Ms. Sylvan, and that's the reason I want to have his blood tested before we advance anymore theories about Ms. Pilkington having drugged her father. We need to be careful with advancing accusations before we have evidence in hand." Dr. Sigmund sounded as if he had done this sort of thing before.

"Have you been examining patients before they faced the courts , Dr. Sigmund?" Alan asked.

"Too many to recall, actually. And evidence of psychosis is probably the hardest to prove. Psychotic behavior can be witnessed easily enough, yet, the origin of the symptoms or their ensuing results is difficult to ascertain."

"What about schizophrenia, Dr. Sigmund…"

"Please call me Gabe – short for Gabriel…"

"Sure if you call me Alan, okay?"

Gabe smiled benignly and then replied, "Faking schizophrenia is not easy, much less provoking it. However, considering the mixture that Ms. Pilkington could have procured in Papua, when added to Chantix and then given to him in the form of a "health tea", Agent Chulbridge definitely could have suffered from psychotic events. These, in turn, could have provoked a change of personality." Gabe paused for a minute and then added, "The fact that he was allegedly exacting justice on people he felt were either preventing him from doing what he needed to do, such as killing Mrs. Clipper or attempting to eliminate the forensic crew trying to discover how he killed…"

"…is what made him initially sound schizophrenic, but it all could be explained with the drug combo he might have ingested," Alan finished for Gabe.

"Precisely, Alan. What's more, there is still something that doesn't sit right with me – two things actually…"

"What's that?" Alan asked eagerly.

"First I doubt that Ms. Pilkington actually took her father to a psychiatrist in Washington, DC as she claimed. Second, fabricating a detonator then planting nitro-glycerin in the sanitation room and ultimately detonating the bomb remotely doesn't sound like the work of a schizophrenic or even a person suffering the side effects of a drug. Killing Mrs. Clipper the way he was supposed to have done it, yes, that's a possibility, but the second murder, I would have to say, I certainly doubt he acted alone."

Tiffany, who had been listening attentively to Alan and Gabe's exchange, decided to ask, "Would you then say that Sarah Pilkington had a hand in the killing of the forensic agent?"

"Too soon to tell, Ms. Sylvan, but we may arrive at that conclusion, unfortunately."

After a moment of silence, Alan said, "Well, it looks like we've got some work ahead of us before we can offer our CIA agents some sort of answer, doesn't it?"

"Absolutely," Gabe replied. He stood up. "But now, if you'll excuse me, I think I'll go down to join my friend, Dr. Lanugos." He fixed his gaze on Alan. "You do remember him, don't you?"

"Oh yes I do. Please give him my regards, will you?" Alan said, getting to his feet as well.

"I'll be sure to do so." Gabe then turned to Tiffany. "A pleasure meeting you, Ms. Sylvan. And if I may suggest, since you're working with Ms. Babette and Ms. Pilkington, that you remain quiet about this conversation. If Ms. Pilkington is unstable, the mere mention of her father's troubles could provoke a reaction you would not want to witness."

"I'll be sure to keep my mouth shut, Doctor. None of us aboard this ship want to see anymore killing, to be sure."

"Very well then," Gabe said, smiling at Tiffany. "Will I see you tonight?"

"Absolutely, Doctor. I'll be backstage but I'll make an "appearance" during the intermission, I'm sure."

"Okay." Gabe turned to look at Alan. "Why don't you call me in my cabin when you are ready to attend my meeting with Agent Chulbridge?"

"Will do, Gabe," Alan replied, watching the psychiatrist walk away.

"Well, wasn't that interesting," Tiffany said, standing up too, as soon as Gabe was out of earshot.

"Yes, interesting, Tiff, but possibly a very grim diagnosis, in the end."

CHAPTER FORTY-ONE

Before the curtain rose

AGENTS MALLARD AND CHALKSTONE woke up late. "Shit!" Mallard expostulated when he looked at the clock on the table beside his bunk bed. "Why didn't you wake me up?" he hollered to his partner as the latter came out of the bathroom. "Do you realize what time it is?" He flung his legs out of the bed and banged his head on the edge of the upper bunk as he sat up.

Chalkstone chuckled. "I wanted the shower all to myself and you were sleeping and snoring like a baby. I didn't have the heart to wake you."

Rubbing his forehead, Mallard said, "We've got to get our hands on that cell-phone. That broad may have already chucked it overboard." He stood up and strode to the bathroom, lightly caressing the naked bum of his partner.

Chalkstone shrugged and got dressed. He looked at his attire with a degree of disgust. Since he hadn't expected to stay aboard *The Baroness* more than a couple of days, he hadn't brought an extra change of clothes. *Oh well, it will have to do for another day,* he thought. But then he shouted to the bathroom door, "Do you know if they will take care of our laundry?"

He heard a grumble through the door and shrugged again.

As soon as Mallard came out, he asked, "What were you saying?"

"I was asking if they are going to wash our clothes. I don't even have a change of briefs …"

It was Mallard's turn to laugh. "Well, I guess, if you get lost, I could always follow your scent, couldn't I?"

"Cut it out, will you? But I'm being serious, do you think we could ask…"

A knock at the door interrupted their bantering.

"Yes, what is it?" Chalkstone inquired, opening the cabin's door wide.

"I'm Lim, your cabin steward, sir. Sorry, so sorry, sir. I could come back later … after your partner has put some clothes on"

"No-no, Lim," Chalkstone said to the diminutive Chinaman, "Glad you're here actually. Do you know if we could have our laundry cleaned?"

"Oh, yes, yes, of course, sir. You give me laundry bag…"

"Laundry bag? Where?" Mallard asked, his eyes traveling around the small cabin.

"Right here, sir," Lim replied, pointing to the closet drawer. "If you put dirty clothes in, I bring back clean this afternoon."

Chalkstone and Mallard exchanged a quick glance, opened the drawer, grabbed a bag out of it and filled it with their dirty laundry and handed it to Lim on the spot.

The latter took it and promptly deposited it at his feet. "I will take bag when I finish clean the cabin, okay?"

"Okay, Lim," Mallard replied. Just let me get dressed and we'll let you have the cabin all to yourself, okay?"

"Very good, sir. I wait outside." And with these words, Lim dropped the fresh set of towels he had been holding down on the lower bunk and walked out.

Not two minutes later, Mallard and Chalkstone exited their cabin, briefly holding hands and giving a sly smile at Lim as they walked away.

Sarah had left her cabin early that morning. Edmund, who had been keeping a very close eye on her after he had heard Alan's conversation with Dr. Gabe Sigmund, decided to have another look around her cabin. He did so the previous night, but in the dark, he hadn't been able to search her room thoroughly. As soon as he penetrated the cabin's door, he looked for bags of herbs, medicine bottles or anything that resembled those things Alan had described in his summary. He was in the bathroom when he heard the cabin door being opened. He stood silent and waited. A moment later, he looked into the bedroom to see the two CIA agents crawling on hands and knees, apparently looking for something. Edmund stood his back to the wall and watched them.

"Where would she have put it?" Mallard asked. "I told you, she might have already thrown it overboard."

"No one throws a cell-phone overboard," Chalkstone replied, while rummaging through the dresser. "All she has to do is replace the SIM card, and Bob's your uncle."

Confused, since he didn't know what a "SIM card" was, let alone who Uncle Bob was, Edmund decided to ask Alan. He flew out of the cabin and soon landed in the medical center. His great-grandson was listening to a crewmember that was obviously undergoing a physical examination. Edmund stood by the door quietly and watched.

The crew was telling Alan, "...then Marvin walks into the ship gift store, buys a condom, then walks out of the store laughing hysterically. The store manager thinks this is weird, but, hey, there's no law preventing weird people from buying condoms. Maybe it's a good thing. The next day, Marvin comes back to the store, purchases another condom, and once again he leaves the store laughing wildly. This peaks the interest of the store manager. What's so funny about buying a rubber, anyway? So he tells his clerk assistant, "If this guy ever comes back, I want you to follow him to see where he goes." Sure enough, the next day Marvin is back. He buys the condom, starts cracking up, then leaves. The manager tells his clerk to go follow this character. About an hour later, the clerk comes back to the store. "Did you follow him? Where did he go?" asks the manager. The clerk replies, "The cabin you and your girlfriend stay in."

Amid Alan's laughter, Edmund said to himself, *"There's another word I haven't heard before. What's a condom?"*

"Okay, Jillian, everything looks fine," Alan said. "You're in good health as far as I can see, enough to keep working for *The Baroness*. I'll just ask Evelyn to draw some blood, and you can be on your way."

Jillian, a mountain of a man, muscles bulging all over the place, slipped into his shirt and pants quickly, saying, "You just have to watch the medical center's free condom distribution, Doc," laughing.

"I'll be sure to do that, Jillian," Alan answered, turning around and now noticing his granddad waiting for him in his office.

Jillian had his blood drawn and left and Alan sent Evelyn to draw some blood from Chulbridge, under Gilbert's watchful eye. Then he joined his granddad, sat down at his desk and said, "I bet you've listened to the conversation I had this morning with Dr. Sigmund, didn't you?"

Edmund nodded. "Indeed I have, son. Very informative. But that's not why I am here."

"And why are you here? Is there something wrong?"

"Not really. After I heard what you and Dr. Sigmund discussed, I went to search Sarah's cabin in quest of herbs or medication that could prove your theory…"

"And did you find anything?"

"Not yet. I was interrupted in my search by the two CIA agents…"

"What were they looking for, do you know?"

Visibly getting annoyed with Alan's interruptions, Edmund said, "Alright, Alan, I know you're not given to listen to anyone quietly, but would you do me the favor of hearing me out before you ask questions?"

Alan nodded and remained silent.

"Alright then. As I was saying, Agents Mallard and Chalkstone were searching Sarah's cabin for her cell-phone. When I left they had not found it yet. But it is something they said that brought me here." Alan raised an eyebrow, but once again didn't utter a word. "Yes, not only is the cell-phone obviously significant but Agent Chalkstone said that she would only have to "throw the SIM card overboard and Bob's your uncle". Could you enlighten me as to what it all means?"

Alan erupted in laughter under Edmund's reproachful gaze.

"I'm sorry, Granddad, but I should explain. A SIM card is a little memory card that retains the information contained in any mobile device. If you remove it, the cell-phone becomes inoperable, for one thing, but when you throw away the SIM card, all phone calls or communication records will thereafter disappear."

"I see," Edmund said concertedly. "But who's Bob the uncle then?"

Alan couldn't help but snicker. "It's an expression meaning that you have resolved the problem at hand. There's no Uncle Bob to add to our list of persons of interest. Don't worry."

Edmund fell silent for a minute before he asked, "What about this condom that your crew mentioned – what is it?"

This time Alan cracked up. "That one…" he said between spurts of laughter, "I'll have to show you. Come with me."

They went to the storeroom. When Alan ripped a condom packet open and showed the item to his granddad without explanation, Edmund said, eyebrows arched, "What is this? It looks like a section of cat gut…?"

Alan shook his head. "No. Look…" He stretched it in front of his pelvis. "What does it remind you of?"

Still visibly puzzled, Edmund said, "I couldn't readily say, son. It still looks like what one cuts up for suture material…"

"It is a form of contraceptive, Granddad," Alan cut-in. "Men put it on their penises to prevent their sperm from spreading inside the women's fallopian tubes during intercourse, thus preventing conception."

Edmund stared at the condom and then asked, "Are men really using this thing? Do women really want to prevent pregnancies?"

"Oh yes, Granddad, they are. Every doctor on the planet these days recommends the use of condoms not only to prevent unwanted pregnancy, but to prevent either party from contracting sexually transmitted diseases, like syphilis, gonorrhea, and HIV, for example."

"Incredible!" Edmund exclaimed. "I wish I would have had access to these condom devices in my time, son. Truly, I would have been able to save dozens of lives. Are they made out of cat or sheep gut?"

"Well, originally yes, now we make them out of rubber or plastic. Technology has made huge progress in every direction, Granddad, but we are all thankful to physicians such as yourself for their original teachings and theories, which we later were able to use or refine."

Edmund nodded and moved out of the storage room. Alan followed him back to his office. "Are you going back to search Sarah's cabin now?" he asked.

"Perhaps I'll leave that task to the CIA agents for the time being, son. Since we know what they're looking for and why…"

"Why, did you say?" Alan blurted. "Do you know why they're looking for the cell-phone?"

"Oh yes. Didn't I mention that the explosive device in the sanitation room was activated by a cell-phone?"

"Did Dr. Rivers determine that such was the case?"

"Yes, I heard him mention it to Miss Ashton when I followed them to the airport."

"You did? It sounds like you've had a busy night."

"Undoubtedly, son. You see, I first wanted to search Sarah Pilkington's cabin but the nightlight wasn't enough for me to complete my quest. So, I thought I would accompany the young Daniel Richard to the airport, before he made his ultimate journey to Heaven."

"Thank you, Granddad. That was thoughtful of you. I wish we could have had a memorial aboard *The Baroness* for those who lost their lives here. But, unfortunately that is not something we could do, under the circumstances."

"Keeping it all hush-hush, eh?" Edmund remarked.

Alan nodded.

"Talking about keeping matters quiet, I think I better go to the theater and watch over Babette. Sarah Pilkington will be there, too. Although I believe my dear lady will refrain from letting the 'cat out of the bag', as they say in this century, I would prefer being there in case someone forgets to keep their mouth closed."

"I think that's a grand idea, Granddad, and in the meantime, I think I'll have an interview with Agent Chulbridge."

"Alright, son, I will be seeing you later then." And with these words, Edmund flew out of the medical center under the caring gaze of his great-grandson.

A half-hour later and after he had called Dr. Sigmund to let him know that he was on his way to see Agent Chulbridge, Alan entered the secured cabin in the company of the psychiatrist.

Chulbridge was now sitting in a chair beside his bed with straps around his wrists. He was still dressed in the shirt and trousers he had worn the day before when he had been apprehended. Fortunately, he looked a lot better. His face sported a couple of Band-Aids that Alice had applied over his lacerated chin and forehead. His lower lip was still swollen, too, but apart from that, the man looked and acted alert and cognizant of his surroundings.

"Good morning, Agent Chulbridge," Alan said cheerfully.

"If it is, then yes, same to you, Doc," Chubb replied, throwing a glance at Dr. Sigmund. "And who's that? You've brought in reinforcements?"

"Not really, Chubb. This is Dr. Sigmund." Alan turned to Gabe. "He's going to help me determine what went wrong with you, okay?"

"Hi, Doc. Nice meeting you," Chubb said, cracking a smile. "Are you a ship's doctor too?"

"Oh no, Agent Chulbridge. I'm a psychiatrist practicing in Washington D.C."

"So, you think I've gone crazy, do you, Doc," Chubb asked Alan.

"I don't think anything at the moment, Chubb. I just thought you would appreciate a second opinion." Alan smiled. "Why don't we grab some chairs, sit with you for a bit, and have a conversation. Is that okay?"

Without being asked, Gabe pulled the two chairs on both sides of the desk and brought them by the bed to face Chubb. The physicians sat down.

"That's okay with me, Doc. But really I don't know what I can tell you. All I really remember is getting on board this ship and asking our Interpol contact to get the cocaine to Antsiranana..."

"Do you remember the name of your contact?" Alan asked.

"I've been thinking about that when I woke up here"—his eyes traveled around the cabin—"this morning, and I think her name is Irene Walter."

Alan then asked, "Did she agree to go with you, do you recall?"

"No, Doc. I mean I only remember talking about it with her one morning ...or was it one night?" He shook his head. "I really can't remember. Sorry."

"That's normal after a concussion," Sigmund remarked. He then took a small MP3 recorder out of his pocket. "Would you mind very much if I were to record our conversation, Agent Chulbridge? My memory fails me at times, too." He clicked the device to "record" and placed it on the bed near Chulbridge.

"I don't mind, as long as in exchange you two explain to me why I'm locked in here with hand-straps around my wrists."

"Do you remember what happened to you yesterday?" Alan asked.

"I remember a few things here and there, but I tell you, frankly, what I do remember seems absolutely idiotic to me. It's like when you wake up from a bad dream and you shake your head because you don't believe what you've done in that dream."

Sigmund crossed his arms over his chest. "Could you tell us those idiotic things you remember?"

"Well, one of them is me painting something on a mirror…"

"Do you remember what you painted?"

"Not really, Dr. Sigmund. I think it was a warning of some kind."

"Okay," Sigmund went on, "what else?"

"The other thing was me running through some back alley wearing some kind of cloak, something like a brown monk habit."

"Right. And do you know if you have ever worn a cloak on any other occasion?"

Chubb burst out laughing. "I know I've done some silly things in my time, Dr. Sigmund, but I don't recall ever wearing a monk's cloak, no."

"Do you remember any other of your idiotic dreams apart from those you just mentioned?"

"Well, there was one that I can't really understand…"

"What's that?" Alan queried.

"I'm in this room and there's some sort of vat – like the ones you find in a brewers warehouse or something – and I'm dropping a woman in the vat."

"Do you recall if the vat contained beer or wine perhaps?" Sigmund asked, thinking that the smell emanating from the septic tank might have tweaked the patient's memory.

"I'm sure it was neither beer nor wine, Doc. It was some green soup of some kind and it smelled terrible."

"Do you know why you dropped the young woman in there?"

Chubb shook his head emphatically. "No, Doc. I couldn't even tell you who she was."

"Any other incidents that might have stayed with your memory?"

"No, nothing right now, Dr. Sigmund, I'm sorry." Chubb looked down at his lap. Then raised his gaze to Alan. "Come on, Doc, can you please tell me what's going on?"

"All we can tell you at this point is that someone – a man dressed in a cloak – has murdered two people and attempted to murder another aboard this ship. The reason you're in here is because we need to protect you…"

"Protect me? From what? Do you think I've seen this cloaked guy for real and he's after me now?"

"That's a possibility, Agent Chulbridge, yes," Sigmund said, keeping his poker face in check.

"Why the straps then?" Chubb asked. "It's not like I've attacked anyone… or is it?" His eyes searched the two doctors' faces.

"Well, yesterday you got into a fight with two CIA agents – that's why your face is all cut-up – and we thought it would be prudent to strap you until you calmed down."

"What about now? It's not like I'm going to jump anybody coming through this door, is it?"

"That's unlikely, but if you don't mind being handcuffed for another twelve hours or so, I think after that we'll be able to convince the two CIA fellows to cut off the straps."

"I guess that should be fine." Chubb paused and then asked, "Could you ask your nurse or the steward to bring me something else other than dry toast? I'm starving and need some real food."

Sigmund chuckled. "Absolutely. I think you'll need to restore your strength and some nice soup might just do it." He took the MP3 off the bed, switched off the recording and slipped it back in his jacket pocket.

"Well, thank you for your cooperation," Alan said, getting to his feet.

"And I'll make sure Evelyn or Alice bring you a full meal for lunch, okay?"

"That'll be just great. Thanks to you both," Chubb said. And then as an afterthought he added, "Could you ask someone to bring me some clean clothes too? I think these will stand on their own in another day."

"By all means, Agent Chulbridge. We'll make sure you've got everything you need."

As the two physicians were making their way to the medical center, Alan asked, "Why didn't you ask about his daughter?"

"That could be the trigger to another psychotic episode, Alan. At the moment he has no idea what happened. He truly can't remember what he has done. And until we've got the blood work results, I'd like to keep it that way."

"Okay, that's what we'll do then. And thanks again for your collaboration, Gabe. I couldn't have gone this far with this patient if you hadn't been there."

Sigmund only smiled amiably in modest reply as the two men went up the elevator.

CHAPTER FORTY-TWO

A Cat Named Hoodoo Voodoo
ACT II

THE FOYER OF THE THEATER was vibrant with expectancy. Passengers and officers alike had been waiting for the curtain to rise on the second act of Babette's play for several days, and their impatience was obvious.

Captain Galveston was in attendance, of course, and was the first to approach Alan as soon as he saw him come off the elevator.

"Ah, Dr. Mayhew, nice to see that you have been able to spare a few hours to attend the performance. How are you?"

"Thank you, Captain, and I'm fine. Apart from trying to catch up with the crew's regular physicals, we seem to have returned to some normalcy."

"Good to hear, indeed, Doctor. But I meant to ask you; have you been able to complete the blood tests from Agent Chulbridge? Mr. Evans has kept me informed, as you well know I'm sure, and I was wondering if the results indicate that the man has been drugged."

Alan looked down at the floor beneath his feet before replying, "The results are not conclusive yet. I still have to courier another sample to Toronto to have the lab run some specialized tests. And although the results will be confidential, since we're looking at a murder investigation, I will say that Ms. Pilkington will have questions to answer."

"Very good, Doctor. And do you expect that Dr. Sigmund will be able to get to the bottom of her story?"

"I would hope so, Captain. He's apparently interviewed suspects in an official capacity on several occasions, so I think he will be able to draw some conclusions from interviewing her."

"Well then, let's hope we can close the book on the dramatic part of this cruise sooner rather than later," Galveston concluded, walking with Alan toward the theater doors as they heard the bell ring.

Once everyone was seated, unexpectedly, Babette, dressed in a gorgeous black gown with a rose corsage pinned just below her left shoulder, walked from the stage apron to address the audience.

"Captain Galveston, Officers and Ladies and Gentlemen, thank you for returning to our theater..." She was interrupted by a wave of applause. "Thank you, dear friends," she went on, "Since you have been waiting for many days to see the second act of *A Cat Named Hoodoo Voodoo*, I thought I would refresh your memory of the events that occurred as Marie Laveau, our main protagonist, takes her first steps into the practice of voodoo. Her cat, named Hoodoo Voodoo, has become her able assistant. She becomes romantically attracted to and involved with Louis De Glapion, a rich heir from a powerful family in New Orleans. So, without further ado, let's return to Marie's home and see what's going to happen next.... Thank you."

As Babette was about to turn toward stage right, she seemed overwhelmed for a moment by the audience's applause. Tiffany came to her aid immediately and led her toward the back of the stage.

Alan had noticed his dear friend flinch for a fraction of a second and it worried him. He excused himself to the first officer sitting beside him and exited the theater to check on her before the curtain rose.

A CAT NAMED HOODOO VOODOO – ACT II

(There is a knock on the door. Marie is crying. She wipes her eyes and goes to the door. Louis Christopher de Glapion enters.)

DE GLAPION: I knocked. I thought nobody was home so I was just going to put your cat in the house.

MARIE:	(Grabs cat) Hoodoo Voodoo, oh my darling, where have you been? Are you all right? (Notices de Glapion) I'm sorry; I was just so thrilled to see Hoodoo Voodoo. Please come in and tell me where you found her. (Motions him to sit down.)
DE GLAPION:	(Sits) Only for a minute; just to tell you about your cat. I found the poor thing way out of town, running down the road at great speed. Out of nowhere, two enormous dogs started in hot pursuit. I followed to hopefully intervene when suddenly Hooo…
MARIE:	Hoodoo Voodoo.
DE GLAPION:	She turned, and with those intense blue eyes, looked directly at those dogs. It was the strangest sight I'd ever seen. She neither spit nor attacked, just fixed her gaze on them. I tell you it was an eerie thing to see those two dogs run away, howling, tail between their legs. That is some cat you have, Madame.
MARIE:	Did you do all that? Poor baby.
DE GLAPION:	I tried to coax her, the cat I mean, but she looked at me, then she seemed to blink and slowly walked away, as if to say, "Coming?" And step-by-step she led me to your door. What kind of a cat is she?'
MARIE:	Very special, aren't you, Hoodoo Voodoo. How can I ever thank you?
DE GLAPION:	Where did you get such a name for her?
MARIE:	She was named before she came to live with me.
DE GLAPION:	What's Hoodoo…?
MARIE:	New world blacks who perform magic and or witchcraft are referred to as hoodoos. . Voodoo is more African and elsewhere it's rather tied to native religions. As a matter of fact, Hoodoo

	Voodoo lived with a witch.
DE GLAPION:	(crosses himself. Stands)
MARIE:	If you're thinking I'm a witch? The answer: is no, no. I couldn't be one and be a Christian at the same time, and I'd rather be a Christian all-the time. .
DE GLAPION:	That's a relief. You seemed to read the question I had on my mind.
MARIE:	Did I?
DE GLAPION:	Do you do that quite often?
MARIE:	May I offer you some tea?
DE GLAPION:	No, thank you. My coachman will report me missing. We couldn't have that (starts to stand)
MARIE:	You said, Mr. de Glapion that Hoodoo Voodoo was far out of town. Where was she?
DE GLAPION:	Do you know where the clearing is for duels?
MARIE:	I've heard of it.
DE GLAPION:	Perhaps she was there hunting.
MARIE:	Perhaps (smiles).
DE GLAPION:	Do you live here all alone, I mean, is there anyone else besides Hoodoo Voodoo?
MARIE:	(shakes head) just the two of us (smiling).
DE GLAPION:	Isn't that a bit unusual, a pretty girl living all by herself?
MARIE:	There's a reason for it. I'm a widow.
DE GLAPION:	My commiserations.
MARIE:	And I do not have a lover.
DE GLAPION:	I wouldn't have asked that.
MARIE:	But you would think it.
DE GLAPION:	Only because . . . there you go reading my mind again. I'd best stop thinking when I'm around you.
MARIE:	That could be very dangerous for you, Mr. de Glapion
DE GLAPION:	Please call me Louis. (Hands her his card)

MARIE:	Louis Christopher de Glapion. Very impressive. I see Louis. You are from a titled family
DE GLAPION:	(Shrugs his shoulder) May I call you something else than Madame?
MARIE:	(Hands him her card) You are the first person to have one of my cards. My new cards. Tell your friends about me.
DE GLAPION:	Certainly, but few of my friends use a lady hairdresser.
MARIE:	Oh, I am sorry (takes back the card) those were my old cards. Here is the new one. Please read it.
DE GLAPION:	(Reads) Queen, Marie (bows) queen of?
MARIE:	Queen of all gris-gris in New Orleans
DE GLAPION:	Were you born to that position, or...?
MARIE:	No, I fought my way to the top.
DE GLAPION:	I don't understand.
MARIE:	Every time I wanted to move up, I beat up the other queen who stood in my way (laughs). Come, I'll show you. Tell me the name of the lady that you would like to have fallen passionately in love with you. I can verify it, you know.
DE GLAPION:	There is no lady.
MARIE:	An enemy then...?
DE GLAPION:	No, thank you, I don't care to have my enemies fall passionately in love with me.
MARIE:	You don't believe me?
DE GLAPION:	I do. And if you couldn't, Hoodoo Voodoo could.
MARIE:	You're making fun of me (lights some candles).
DE GLAPION:	I'd never do that... I don't know why I've stayed so long. I must go.
MARIE:	(starts to hum to Hoodoo Voodoo, all the while staring at Louis).

DE GLAPION: You have strange eyes, I can feel them penetrating. They seem to burn deeply into my very soul. And your hair, your beautiful, long hair. As it moves it hypnotizes-me I feel that I must tell you all about myself. O, yes, yes, I have-just returned from abroad, from France. My parents wanted me to be politically involved but I care nothing for politics. In fact, the entire operation of politics bores me. My mother, please, understand me. She is still beautiful and very much the aristocrat. She has titles to her name as does my father. He has a very important title abroad. I found out all about him, why he left home and came to Louisiana, would you believe my distinguished father had a scandal with a woman? He did, and so the family banished him. He came here with a small fortune. As a gentleman painter, he turned his small fortune into an even bigger fortune. Now he has money and influence. With this, he hopes to put me up as a politician, par excellence. (Pause) Why do you want to know all about my family and my love life? There's nothing to tell about my love life. A woman here and another there. I love beautiful and interesting women I especially enjoy. dancers and actresses. My last association was with a hot-tempered Corsican. Of course, my family disapproved. They needn't have. I had no intention of marrying her. In fact, I hold no ideas of getting married for a long, long time. (He's holding Marie's hair.)
And I would not care to give up my inheritance. It's quite a fortune, and it will make living easy.

MARIE: (snaps her fingers.)

DE GLAPION:	I beg your pardon; your lovely hair is irresistible. But I assure you I hadn't the slightest intention of touching it or you. It's just that some hair, your hair, got caught on the button of my suit. Here, I'll show you (tugging at his buttons)
MARIE:	Keep your button on your shirt or your mother's maid will be angry with you for having to sew it on. Did you tell such button stories to your fiery Corsican?
DE GLAPION:	Who told you? You know that too?
MARIE:	(laughs and looks at the cat).
DE GLAPION:	Forgive me, I'm always so proper. I don't know what got into me. (Picks up his hat. Kisses her hand) I always know when to leave, that is one of my virtues. I hope I haven't overstayed my welcome.
MARIE:	(sees him to the door) not at all, come again.
DE GLAPION:	You may count on it (exits).

The curtain for the intermission then fell under the thunderous applause of the audience. The play had truly captivated the spectators. Some even remarked that it must have been written under a spell. Or maybe the passengers were "spellbound", so to speak. But no matter what the comments were, the play was an absolute success.

CHAPTER FORTY-THREE

Intermission

GILBERT HAD NOTICED Alan leave his seat before the play even started but since he didn't want to alarm anyone unduly, he had remained seated until the intermission. As soon as the passengers had filed out of the theater, he rushed back stage to see what had happened.

There, he found Babette, Tiffany, Alan and Edmund sitting in one of the dressing rooms. As he entered, after knocking softly, Babette said, "Nothing's wrong, Mr. Evans, don't worry. According to Alan here"— she turned her gaze to him—"I must be overly tired – exhausted actually – and it's nothing that a good night sleep won't cure."

"Well, I'm sure glad to hear it, Ms. Babette. Once again you've outdone yourself with this play; no wonder you're tired."

"And would anyone know where I could find Ms. Pilkington?" He looked at Alan and then shot a glance toward Edmund.

"I think she's gone back to her cabin to change. She left a while ago," Tiffany interposed. "She should be back after the intermission."

Edmund didn't appear to agree with Tiffany, for he said, "Why don't you follow me, Mr. Evans, I think I know where we can find her."

Alan, who had listened to the exchange wondering what his granddad was up to, only shrugged his shoulders.

"Okay, lead the way then," Gilbert said. But before leaving, he added, "Break a leg, Ms. Babette!"

"Well, thank you, Mr. Evans, I sure hope I don't – not really I mean."

Babette laughed as Gilbert closed the dressing room door.

"Where are we going?" Gilbert asked Edmund before they reached the foyer.

"To your office, Mr. Evans."

"My office, but why? I thought Ms. Sylvan said…"

"I know what she said, Chief, and I'll explain once we get there."

"Okay, no problem," Gilbert replied, shaking his head.

Once in the foyer, he shot a glance overhead to see Edmund fly above the crowd. Silently he wished he could do the same.

Thirty minutes later the bell rang again, calling the passengers back to their seats. Before the curtain rose, Captain Galveston joined Alan before the two men returned to their seats.

"Is Ms. Babette okay," Galveston asked in Alan's ear.

"Yes, sir. She's fine. But I'd like to make sure she has a long rest after this play is over. She's exhausted."

"Well, we'll make sure she's not disturbed for the rest of this cruise. You have my word, Doctor."

"Thank you, Captain, much appreciated," Alan said before going to his seat.

ACT II (cont'd)

MARIE: (Picks up cat) Hoodoo Voodoo (whirls, swings around in a circle with the cat in her arms, dances, sits with Hoodoo Voodoo on her lap. Then, in deep concentration, chants and whispers to the cat), bring Isabelle to me. Go, my darling Hoodoo Voodoo.
I'll need some love powder, not peace powder. Love has to be a bit stormy to be interesting; to fight, then make up. That's the best part. I think I'll keep the anger powder out of the mix. Who needs that? I won't need any lucky water this time. When I get Louis I'll be lucky enough. But

I'll need some 'follow me' drops and a pinch of sacred sand. My religious figure and greens (puts ingredients into a little sack, She kneels before a statue, and sings as she picks up three green peppers and charms, a wax figure, then some other greens. She puts the peppers in her mouth. She then draws a circle with a piece of chalk and chants.) Love, love, beloved, be mine (three times) She writes: Louis, Christopher de Glapion with the chalk and quickly says his name, then writes it again faster yet. She mumbles his name as she writes.)

ISABELLE: (Enters on a dead run. Falls down on her knees next to Marie, touching her) Are you all right?

MARIE: I'm fine.

ISABELLE: I had this feeling that overpowered me. There was no way I could do anything. Every time I'd start something, the idea of you would flash across my mind so strongly that I'd find myself shaking from head to toe. Then I saw Hoodoo Voodoo and it became too much for me, and I followed that cat over lawns, hedges....

MARIE: I hope not over fences and rooftops.

ISABELLE: Here's where Hoodoo Voodoo stopped and so did I. What do you want from me? And why?

MARIE: I have made a gris-gris.

ISABELLE: I don't want any part of it.

MARIE: Yes, you do, or I'll...

ISABELLE: On second thought, I'm delighted to help. Tell me what I must do?

MARIE: I want to test Louis.

ISABELLE: Never, not Louis Christopher de Glapion. I'm not getting mixed up with that big important family.

MARIE: Then I shall have to talk to Hoodoo Voodoo.

ISABAELLE: Why me? You have the cat. Let the cat do it.
MARIE: Cats can only work so long. Then they must rest quietly, in front of the stove: or in the sunshine. Haven't you ever seen a cat resting?
ISABELLE: Sometimes I wish I were a cat. You don't mind my working all the time.
MARIE: What tricks you turn are your business. All I want you to do is sprinkle this love powder on Louis' food. Be sure it's only one little sprinkle at a time
ISABELLE: How do you propose that I manage that?
MARIE: Do it in his kitchen, before his dinner, then after dinner…
ISABELLE: There is more?
MARIE: You are to try seducing him.
ISABELLE: I thought you were in love with him.
MARIE: Listen to me: I am. (She is hypnotizing Isabelle and she pantomimes) Very, very quietly tonight, I see you sprinkling this potion on Louis Glapion's food. You are very quick, like a cat.
ISABELLE: (Sniffs, switches her nose like a cat).
MARIE: (Chants) Love, love, love. Quiet down, my little one. Not Your usual enthusiasm for men. Tonight you think of only one man, Louis. My Louis. When he leaves his home, before he enters his carriage, you are to be waiting for him dressed in a flimsy negligee and a beautiful fur coat. You are to open your coat, let him have a good look. Close the coat securely and then hop into a carriage that you will have waiting for you, and allow his carriage to follow yours. You will lead him to my door – my door only – understand. You must then depart quickly and go about your own sordid business of love and money making. Under no conditions are you to

	return here until I send Hoodoo Voodoo for you. One more thing, Hoodoo Voodoo will be waiting in your carriage and will give Louis de Glapion the eye from the back of the carriage window. That is all. When you awake you will be in a great hurry to go. (Snaps her fingers)
ISABELLE:	(Opens her eyes) where is my purse? I don't want to appear (looking for it under the bed) ungrateful for your hospitality, but I do have to go right now. I'm in a great hurry.
MARIE:	(puts money in Isabelle's purse).
ISABELLE:	(exists hurriedly).
MARIE:	Hoodoo Voodoo (gets the cat) and now my lovely, my darling, you are to do a very important task (whispers and then hums and sings to cat)
	(BLACK OUT – to denote time)
MARIE:	(In negligee, on the bed).
LOUIS:	(Rushes on stage) Marie, where are you?
MARIE:	Here, my darling, waiting for you (arms open).
LOUIS:	You knew I'd come (over to bed).
MARIE:	Of course.
LOUIS:	How beautiful you are, how I love you and only You.
	(LIGHTS dim and up fast)
LOUIS:	Say something.
MARIE:	Yes.
LOUIS:	Keep talking. I don't care what it is. I just want to hear your voice again.
MARIE:	You are in love with my voice?
LOUIS:	No, no, I'm not in love with your voice, I am in love with you. You know that, don't you?
MARIE:	I feel your love and I am pleased with it (kisses him again)

LOUIS:	I can hardly describe how I feel. Yes, I feel hot and cold at the same time. I feel suspended, in time. Yet, I feel as if I am in some sort of hypnotic spell. That I am sort of spellbound -- spellbound together. You and I could make such magic.
MARIE:	magic?
LOUIS:	Could this beautiful magic we have, can it last forever and ever?
MARIE:	Look at me, my darling, if we believe, we can!! we can keep this love we have…
LOUIS:	I want to marry you.
MARIE:	When? Just tell me when.
LOUIS:	Not tomorrow or the next day.
MARIE:	When?
LOUIS:	Do you know I never felt like marrying anyone? The thought of going to bed with the same woman night after night would be very monotonous and boring, but with you, I would look forward to it – and to our marriage.
MARIE:	When?
LOUIS:	When? When I leave you now I will ask my father. Come sit there like my very stern father sits, no, scowl more as if it was painful to sit and be bored at whatever I tell him. That's better. "Papa, may I marry the most beautiful woman in the world? She will bear you many beautiful grandchildren." How could he say no?
MARIE:	When?
LOUIS:	Great, he would say. No, I will say that I am going wed a lady who has utterly bewitched me (Goes to kiss her… She pulls away).
MARIE:	No. If you are speaking of me, I'm not a witch.
LOUIS:	"Papa, I love Marie…"
MARIE:	That is simple and truthful. I like that.

LOUIS: It is settled, I will tell papa and mama. Immediately (exits)
(LIGHTS OUT and then turn on to denote time)

MARIE: (Singing, then stops and calls the cat) Hoodoo Voodoo (letting the sound carry. Gets the cat} we must celebrate you and I, for we have cast such a love potion on Louis that he will be bound to us forever.

LOUIS: (Enters) (Marie rushes into his arms) My little kitten, I love you so much

MARIE: Look at you, you look like you've been through a war, are you sick?

LOUIS: how perceptive of you, yes, I've been through a war. (Sits on the bed).

MARIE: I have herbs to make you well.

LOUIS: Too late, nothing will heal what is wrong with me.

MARIE: (Goes to Louis, sobs in his arms)

LOUIS: Come, little kitten (sits her on chair, takes out hanky, dries her tears.) I love you above all women. I will never feel less for you than when I professed my love for you. Help me. This is very difficult for me.

MARIE: And for me.

LOUIS: Where do I begin?

MARIE: With your father.

LOUIS: My stubborn, pig headed father. I told him how much I adored you. . He seemed delighted as he counted on having grandchildren, his posterity, and then he asked me your name. I told him (Pause) you were a queen…

MARIE: A queen of gris-gris and of…

LOUIS: Queen, all right? I wish I had never mentioned that word. He went down all the thrones of

	Europe, then' said where, what country? What's her name? He knew all about you.
MARIE:	Of course, I have a good reputation in my profession.
LOUIS:	To be rather blunt about it, he doesn't approve of who your parents were, who you are, and what you do.
MARIE:	Being part black – he doesn't approve of mulatos?
LOUIS:	I'm sorry. It pains me to repeat this to you. We cannot get married – not ever. My family is a true 'hide your head in pillow' type of aristocrats. They think more of what people think than what they would think for themselves.
MARIE:	I can't and won't understand.
LOUIS:	Think of it this way – as if I were a pureblooded poodle dog.
MARIE:	(Under her breath) True, you are acting like a dog.
LOUIS:	So, I, the pure blooded poodle…
MARIE:	Dog.
LOUIS:	Got mixed up with a dog of unknown ancestry.
MARIE:	You are calling me a bit…
LOUIS:	I said nothing like that.
MARIE:	(Very angry) You and your hemorrhoidal old father. Let him sit wherever he can. As for you…
LOUIS:	I will call on you every day. We can go right on with our Love making as if nothing ever happened.
MARIE:	But it did! Now, I have something to say…
LOUIS:	anything. I feel better for having gotten it off my chest.

MARIE: You are the dog. About that you are right. And I (opens door) the queen of gris-gris and Hoodoo Voodoo is chasing you out of her house.

LOUIS: (Looks at Hoodoo Voodoo. Picks up his things, puts on his hat)

MARIE: Go now! (Starts to, sing)

LOUIS: Good day, Madame (exits).

MARIE: (Picks up cat. Sits with cat) He won't marry me because of my mother. Oh, Hoodoo Voodoo I do love him (sobs).

(LIGHTS DIM to denote time)

MARIE: (Is preparing to pray. Lights a candle, then chants, holding candle and sings while walking in a circle. Ends with...) Love, love, love is the strongest element of all. Keep Louis loving me forever. Make me the only love in his life.

ISABELLE: (Enters stage left) Marie, Marie, I am sorry; I didn't know you were...

MARIE: I have finished (blows out candle).

ISABELLE: Not yet. Light the candle. Do something...

MARIE: About what?

ISABELLE: Your Louis...

MARIE: Is he dead? Or ill? Or ...what? (Marie is shaking Isabelle.)

ISABELLE: If you don't stop shaking me, I can't tell you.

MARIE: (Stops shaking her) see, I've stopped. Talk then...

ISABELLE: I forgot...

MARIE: Liar.

ISABELLE: (Gets down on her knees) didn't I help you before?

MARIE: And it worked. Yes, you can help. Take this basket. Put into it one black cat. Leave it in Louis' room. He will put the cat outside. Then

ISABELLE: Wait, I have better tricks...
MARIE: No, he is impressed by my tricks. So away with the white cat in the basket. Now, Hoodoo Voodoo will take its place.
ISABELLE: Okay, but what good will it do?
MARIE: It will bring Louis to his knees before me (She bends herself over).
ISABELLE: You are ill?
MARIE: No. Hurry, the basket and cats, at once. Hoodoo Voodoo knows what to do and what gris-gris to take (she crawls to her bed and lies down. Calls out...) Hoodoo Voodoo, hurry, bring Louis... Hurry, Hoodoo Voodoo.
(BLACK OUT – then lights back on)
LOUIS: (Enters. Goes to her & kisses her gently.) Sorry I woke you...
MARIE: you came back.
LOUIS: With your Hoodoo Voodoo, the blue eyed one. (Takes her hand) you taught me a great lesson (brings basket with Hoodoo Voodoo) she never ceases to amaze me. But that's not important. But my love' is what's important.
MARIE: I'm so glad you understand because I have something wonderful and important to tell you.
LOUIS: mine first.
MARIE: I'm pregnant with your child. I told you it was wonderful. Now, what are you going to say?
LOUIS: Something not so wonderful. My father still doesn't understand. The baby, oh, Marie, I will always love it and I will take care of both of you.
MARIE: Don't worry about the money; let your father disown you. I'm doing very well with my gris-gris. We will manage nicely.

LOUIS:	I said I would take care of you and the baby. But I am not ever going to be disinherited. I will come and be with you always. But I can't, and won't marry you, not ever!
MARIE:	But you love me, don't you?
LOUIS:	Yes, I do love you and will only love you.
MARIE:	(Snuggles in his arms.) You had something else to tell me. What is it?
LOUIS:	Not so important, I forgot (kisses her)... Oh, yes, now I remember. I'm engaged to be married.

As the curtain came down, the audience was on its feet. "Bravo! Bravo!" could be heard along with appreciative whistles from passengers and officers alike. Amid the deafening noise, Babette came to the forefront of the stage and waited for the applause to die down before she said, "Thank you so much.... You've been a fantastic audience and since you obviously liked the play so far, I think, just maybe, I'll let our wonderful cast entertain you one more time with the next act of *A Cat Named Hoodoo Voodoo*..." The audience interrupted her once again with another ripple of clapping hands mixed with laughter. "So, we'll be seeing each other again in three days' time." She paused, smiled and then added, "Thank you," and walked backstage under roaring applause.

CHAPTER FORTY-FOUR

The witch's potion

AS SOON AS THE TWO MEN reached Gilbert's office, he noticed the door being slightly ajar.

"What's going on here?" he asked Edmund. "Do you know anything about this?"

"I think you'll find your answer once you get in," Edmund replied.

"And where are Raphael and Stephan?" Gilbert asked, rushing to the security center. The two men had abandoned their usual position on the chairs in the entry to the department.

Gilbert ran back to his office, pushed the door open and at first didn't notice anything wrong. But when he stepped farther indoors and went around his desk, he gasped. "What the hell...?" he blared, kneeling down beside Sarah's unconscious body. He raised his gaze to Edmund. "Did you have anything to do with this?"

"Not really."

"What do you mean by 'not really?'"

"I just moved a few things and she fainted when I threw your paperweight at her beautiful head."

"But why? What was she doing here anyway?" Gilbert asked, taking his cell-phone out of his pocket.

"If you are calling your two fellows, they're gone to have a rest, I believe."

"How? I mean they're not supposed to leave their posts."

"You'll have to ask that question of Ms. Pilkington when she regains consciousness. When I arrived, she was having a coffee with your two employees and as soon as they felt sleepy, she sent them toward their cabin, but not before taking the safe deposit box keys from Raphael's waist belt."

His cell-phone to his ear now, Gilbert heard the ring at the other end of the line and then the communication went to voice mail. He hung up, shaking his head. "And what do you suppose she wanted with the keys?" he asked Edmund.

"By the looks of things, I would suggest Ms. Pilkington was about to open your safe…"

"But why?"

Edmund then turned his gaze to the safe.

"Don't tell me, she was after the cocaine."

"I'm sorry, Mr. Evans, I don't know much about such things, but according to my great-grandson, it would appear that raw cocaine is very valuable in this century. Isn't it?"

Gilbert stood up and nodded. "Let's find my crew, and then I think we should transport Ms. Pilkington to her cabin…"

"I'll find Raphael and Stephan before you, if you allow me, Mr. Evans. And once I do, I'll come back to tell you where they are."

"Okay . . . go, go. In the meantime, I'll call my other guy," Gilbert said, waving a dismissive hand toward Edmund.

It didn't take long for Edmund to find Raphael and Stephan a few steps from their cabin, sleeping under the nearby stairs.

That woman and her witch's potions need to be stopped, Edmund decided, as he flew back to the security office. There, he found Gilbert and another crew lifting Sarah's inert body and hoisting it over the man's shoulder. When they were outside, Edmund told Gilbert where he could find Raphael and Stephan and then flew back to the theater where he was on hand when the curtain came down on the second act of *A Cat Named Hoodoo Voodoo.*

Once Tiffany and Edmund had accompanied Babette back to her suite, Edmund flew to his great-grandson's cabin. He sat in the chair by the desk and waited for Alan to come out of the shower.

Only clad in a towel around his waist, Alan stopped at the bathroom door when he saw his granddad. "I don't suppose you're here to wish me good-night, are you?"

Edmund shook his head. "Unfortunately not, son."

"Okay, what is it? Did you and Gilbert find Ms. Pilkington?"

"Oh yes. And I think you should have a look at her…"

"Where is she? What happened?" Alan asked in a rush.

"She's in her cabin, I believe, and she's sustained a nasty bump on her head, thanks to Mr. Evans's paperweight…"

Alan was staring at his granddad by now. He shook his head. "I don't think I want to know how Gilbert's paperweight made contact with Sarah's head." He paused, still staring. "I suppose I'll have to get dressed again…"

"You supposed right, son, unless, of course, you want to make an obscene display of yourself in the glass elevator…" He chuckled heartily.

"Okay, okay," Alan grumbled, grabbing his discarded uniform and getting dressed quickly.

A few minutes later, Edmund and his great-grandson were on their way to Sarah's cabin when they ran into Chalkstone and Mallard on the upper deck.

"What are you doing here already, Doc?" Chalkstone asked. "Has Mr. Evans called you?"

"No, but I wanted to make sure Ms. Pilkington was in her cabin…"

"Why?" Mallard asked suspiciously.

"Gentlemen," Alan said, "I can understand that you have a job to do, but I don't think I should have to account for my movements at this juncture, and I doubt the CIA gave you guys any formal medical training."

"Okay, okay, Doc, don't get your knickers in a knot. Ms. Pilkington is in her cabin all right. She's been clobbered over the head and as soon as she comes to, we want an explanation, get it?"

"Oh I get it, gentlemen. And I'll leave her in your capable hands as soon as I'm sure she's okay medically." He peered into their gazes. "So, if you'll excuse me, I'll be on my way." He squeezed between the two men and hurried to Sarah's cabin.

Mallard and Chalkstone looked after the doc. "Mark my word,"

Mallard said to his partner, "Him and that Sigmund guy have more answers than we've got questions."

Chalkstone nodded. "At least if we were in Washington, we would be able to interview all the players properly."

"Not only that, but we could decide who has access to our suspects," Mallard added.

"Maybe we should have stayed with the witch and asked her where she's hidden her concoctions and her dad's cell-phone…"

"Nothing doing, Chuck," Mallard countered, shaking his head. "Even if she woke up while we were alone with her, it wouldn't have done any good. She'd probably have twisted her story into another series of lies that would have had us chasing another rabbit for nothing but an empty hole."

"What do you think she wanted with the cocaine?"

"I can't tell you that, Chuck, but I guess we'll find out sooner or later."

Meanwhile, Gilbert and another crew went to the spot where Edmund had told him he would find Raphael and Stephan.

"Okay, Ivan, let's put these two idiots to bed, shall we?"

"Right on, Chief. What do you think got them to fall asleep like that?"

"A witch's potion," Gilbert replied.

"You mean like in that play they're showing in the theater tonight?"

"Exactly like that, Ivan. We've got a mean witch aboard *The Baroness*, but we've caught her now before she's able to drug anymore people."

While Ivan was dragging Raphael to the cabin's door, Ivan asked, "Is the witch Ms. Pilkington?" He took in a deep breath. "I think Raphy here needs to lose some weight; he's too heavy for his own good."

"You're right about that," Gilbert replied. "Here, let me help you," he added, going inside the cabin and holding the heavy door open for Ivan.

Minutes later the two men watched Raphael and Stephan sleeping soundly – snoring actually – in their bunks.

"Okay, now, let's you and I go to Agent Chulbridge's old cabin,"

Gilbert suggested as he closed the door on the two sleeping men.

"Chubb's cabin, but why? I thought that Doctor Rivers had taken everything out of there before they left last night. Didn't they?" Ivan shot an inquisitive glance at Gilbert.

"So did I, Ivan. But I have to check if Chulbridge's laptop is still in there. I should have asked the CIA guys if they took it," he remarked as if talking to himself. And then he added, "Apparently, the agent had a software program that can override the electronic door openers on this ship…"

"Are you serious, Chief?"

"Dead serious, Ivan. And I'm beginning to think Ms. Pilkington has a lot more than a witch's role to play in this production."

"Let's hope Dr. Rivers had taken the laptop then," Ivan stated concertedly.

"Besides which, we've got to find that cell-phone."

"You mean the one that detonated the bomb that hurt our *Potty Man*?"

"…and killed a CIA forensic agent, don't forget," Gilbert added as they arrived in front of Chubb's old cabin.

The security chief opened the cabin's door carefully and looked around it before both men stepped inside. The cabin was empty and spick-and-span clean.

"I just hope Ms. Pilkington hasn't got the same software on her laptop," Gilbert said, closing the door.

When Alan had examined Sarah and diagnosed that she indeed sustained a mild concussion from the heavy blow she received above the left temple, he asked, "How are we going to explain that one, Granddad?" He straightened up and flung his stethoscope around his neck.

"Maybe Mr. Evans could find an explanation," Edmund suggested, bowing his head.

"Not likely, Granddad. Gilbert would have overpowered her rather than hit her. And although she's a suspect in a double murder, I don't think he would allow himself to harm a passenger by throwing a paperweight at her head." He paused and shrugged. "Anyway, she'll come to very soon I suspect..."

At that very moment, the cabin's door burst open and Gilbert rushed into the bedroom – Ivan in tow. "Did you notice a laptop in this cabin?" he asked, turning to Alan after quickly looking through the dresser's drawers.

"Sorry, Gilbert, but no, I didn't notice any laptop when I came in. Why?"

Gilbert didn't reply but turned to Ivan. "You stay right here, while the doc and I go for a walk, okay?"

"No problem, Chief." He hesitated before he asked, "Shall I put her in handcuffs?"

"Better safe than sorry, so, yes, Ivan. I think you'd do well to secure one of her wrists to something heavy, otherwise, she's liable to fight her way out of here when she wakes up."

"Why would you think that, Chief?" Alan asked.

"I'll explain outside, Doc. Just come with me, okay?"

While replacing the stethoscope in his medical bag, Alan nodded and then followed the chief out of the cabin.

As soon as they were outside, Gilbert said, "Why do you think none of us could find her cell-phone?" Alan frowned. "And why do you think no one has found any potions or meds in her cabin?"

"Because she's using another cabin," Alan replied as if a light bulb suddenly came aglow over his head. "But how did she open the cabin or lock it...?"

"Think, Alan."

The doc shook his head. "Of course; the same way her father opened or locked his own cabin door when my granddad found the reports in his cabin."

"Exactly. And now, we need to find out which cabin is supposedly empty or has been unoccupied since the beginning of this cruise. And I'm quite sure we'll find our answers there."

"Do you want to do this tonight?" Alan inquired, sounding too tired for his own good.

"Not "we", Doc. Me and your granddaddy"—he looked around him—"if he's still available."

"You called, Chief?" Edmund said, descending from the bridge to land before the two men.

"Yes, Edmund. And if you've heard what we've talked about with…"

"Yes, yes, Mr. Evans, I have a fair idea of what you intend to do. And I am at your entire disposal. This will be sort of like an old fashioned crew cabin inspection, just for the two of us." Edmund bowed under the smiling gazes of his great-grandson and friend.

CHAPTER FORTY-FIVE

Is there a vicious witch in our midst?

WHEN ALAN WOKE UP the next morning, he felt as if he could have slept another ten hours. Of course this was not a totally unknown feeling for a ship's doctor. Being on call 24/7 and having all these bloody reports to do for home office rarely left enough time to sleep. Add to this, a few murders, and sleep deprivation was the obvious diagnosis. His first thought went to Sarah Pilkington. He wondered why an intelligent woman, and a beautiful one at that, would go down the road of murder and deceit so easily. *Perhaps not as easily as that,* he reflected, getting out of bed. *Her actions must have been based on a revenge of some sort against her father. But then why kill other people and not her father?* He shook his head and went to take a shower – a cold one this time. He dearly needed to wake up and it was going to take more than a couple of cups of coffee.

An hour later Alan was back in his office, looking at the physical examinations' schedule. He breathed a heavy sigh. He couldn't think straight it seemed. But he had a job to do and the crewmembers would soon come in for their physicals. Shaking himself once again, he turned on his computer and went to check his emails. He smiled when he saw another message from his friend Calvin. *Anger Management* had been typed on the subject line. Instead of reading what looked like a long story on the screen, Alan printed it and then sat back and read:

<u>Anger Management</u>
When you occasionally have a really bad day, and you just need

to take it out on someone, don't take it out on someone you know, take it out on someone you don't know, but you know deserves it. I was sitting at my desk when I remembered a phone call I'd forgotten to make. I found the number and dialed it. A man answered, saying "Hello." I politely said, "This is Chris. Could I please speak with Robyn Carter?" Suddenly a manic voice yelled out in my ear, "Get the right damn number!" And the phone was slammed down on me. I couldn't believe that anyone could be so rude. When I tracked down Robyn's correct number to call her, I found that I had accidentally transposed the last two digits. After hanging up with her, I decided to call the "wrong" number again. When the same guy answered the phone, I yelled, "You're an asshole!" and hung up. I wrote his number down with the word "asshole" next to it, and put it in my desk drawer. Every couple of weeks, when I was paying bills or had a really bad day, I'd call him up and yell, "You're an asshole!" It always cheered me up. When Caller ID was introduced, I thought my therapeutic "asshole" calling would have to stop. So, I called his number and said, "Hi, this is John Smith from the telephone company. I'm calling to see if you're familiar with our Caller ID Program?" He yelled, "NO!" and slammed down the phone. I quickly called him back and said, "That's because you're an asshole!" and hung up. One day I was at the store, getting ready to pull into a parking spot. Some guy in a black BMW cut me off and pulled into the spot I had patiently waited for. I hit the horn and yelled that I'd been waiting for that spot, but the idiot ignored me. I noticed a "For Sale "sign in his back window, so I wrote down his number. A couple of days later, right after calling the first asshole (I had his number on speed dial) I thought that I'd better call the BMW asshole, too. I said, "Is this the man with the black BMW for sale?" He said, "Yes, it is." I then asked, "Can you tell me where I can see it?" He said, "Yes, I live at 34 Oaktree Blvd., in Fairfax. It's a yellow ranch style house and the car's parked right out in front." I asked, "What's your name?" He said, "My name is Don Hansen." I asked,

"When's a good time to catch you, Don?" He said, "I'm home every evening after five." I said, "Listen, Don, can I tell you something?" He said, "Yes?" I said, "Don, you're an asshole!" Then I hung up, and added his number to my speed dial, too. Now, when I had a problem, I had two assholes to call. Then I came up with an idea... I called asshole #1. He said, "Hello." I said, "You're an asshole!" (But I didn't hang up.) He asked, "Are you still there?" I said, "Yeah!" He screamed, "Stop calling me" I said, "Make me." He asked, "Who are you?" I said, "My name is Don Hansen." He said, "Yeah? Where do you live?" I said, "Asshole, I live at 34 Oaktree Blvd., in Fairfax, a yellow ranch style home and I have a black Beamer parked in front." He said, "I'm coming over right now, Don. And you had better start saying your prayers." I said, "Yeah, like I'm really scared, asshole," and hung up. Then I called Asshole #2. He said, "Hello?" I said, "Hello, asshole," He yelled, "If I ever find out who you are..." I said, "You'll what?" He exclaimed, "I'll kick your ass." I answered, "Well, asshole, here's your chance. I'm coming over right now." Then I hung up and immediately called the police, saying that I was on my way over to 34 Oaktree Blvd., in Fairfax, to kill my gay lover. Then I called Channel 7 News about the gang war going down on Oaktree Blvd. in Fairfax. I quickly got into my car and headed over to Fairfax. I got there just in time to watch two assholes beating the crap out of each other in front of six cop cars, an overhead news helicopter and surrounded by a news crew. NOW I feel much better. *Anger management really does work!*

After he had a good laugh and as Alan was about to place the sheet of paper in his "funny folder" with the other jokes he had been saving, Tiffany came through the door of the medical center, talked to Alice for a moment and then came into Alan's office – all smiles.

"How's my favorite doctor this morning?" she asked, going around his desk and planting a kiss on the top of his head.

Alan looked up at her and took one of the hands that was massaging his shoulders. "I'm still tired, but this"—he handed her Calvin's email—"really cheered me up almost as much as seeing your smiling face."

Tiffany took the sheet and went to sit in the visitor's chair across from Alan.

He observed her while she was reading. *She is such a gorgeous lady,* he mused. *She must be as exhausted as all of us, and yet she looks as if she just came back from vacation.*

Tiffany raised her gaze to "her favorite doctor" when she came to the last line of the email. "I'll try to remember not to irritate Calvin when we go back," she said, "or I'll have to expect "asshole calls" from someone not too pleased with me."

Alan chuckled and said, "I am quite sure Calvin wouldn't do a thing like that to my favorite lady, otherwise, I'll be the one making "asshole calls" to him."

With a nodding smile, Tiffany said, "talking about trouble, do you know why Sarah didn't turn up for rehearsal this morning?"

"Oh, you don't know do you?" Tiffany shook her head, fixing her eyes on Alan's face. "Well, last night Granddad found her sniffing around Gilbert's office after she had drugged two of his crew…"

"Good gracious, what on Earth did she want in Gilbert's office?"

"I'm not positive, Tiff, but according to Granddad, she was about to open the safe when he clobbered her with Gilbert's paperweight."

"Oh no, did he really?"

"Oh yes. And I'm due to check up on her this morning before Dr. Sigmund interviews her."

"Is she alright?"

"Yes, she's suffered a mild concussion, but other than that, she's okay."

Tiffany looked down at her folded hands in her lap. "I guess Babette is going to be told, isn't she?"

"Unfortunately, yes, Tiffany. Is there anyone else who could adjust the costumes for the last act?"

"I have no idea, Alan." Tiffany lifted her eyes to Alan again. "But you know, this whole thing has been so hard on the lady, she'll need to be left in peace as soon as this play is over."

"That's exactly what I said to Galveston last night after he saw her flinch when she finished introducing the second act."

"And what did he say?"

"He's promised me to keep everyone away until the end of the cruise."

"Thank goodness for that."

"You said it, Tiff. And Babette is not the only one who needs a rest. I think half of the crew has been running ragged since we found Mrs. Clipper in the septic tank..."

"By the way, how's Simon?" Tiffany cut-in. "How's his chest?"

"He should be okay in a couple or three weeks, but now that George Phillips is back, I think Simon will have a chance to heal while he's delegating some of his duties to George."

"Burn-victims are the worst, aren't they?" Tiffany seemed concerned.

"If you mean they endure more pain than victims of other injuries, I would say burns are probably reaching up there to the top of the list of painful recovery, yes." Alan paused to look into her face. "Why do you ask?"

"It's just because I thought of the victims' injuries, Alan. It seems to me they were all designed to inflict enormous pain." She advanced her body to the edge of the chair while putting her elbows on her knees. "When it came to Irene Walter, the intent wasn't probably to kill her, but to paralyze her..."

"But the culprit didn't know she would break her neck in the fall, did he?"

"Was her neck broken as a result of falling against the rowing bench of the rescue boat, or was it broken beforehand?"

"Well, I can't answer that question, Tiff, since I only did a preliminary autopsy. But maybe, you have something there. Go on," Alan encouraged.

"Then the next victim, Mrs. Clipper, she was caned in the leg so badly to break a bone before being viciously whacked over the head. That's pure viciousness, Alan. If she was conscious even for a few minutes before she was dumped into the tank, she would have been in horrible pain." Alan nodded. "And then we've got this explosion that not only killed Daniel Richard in the most horrible possible way, but left Simon still suffering from his injuries, and that for weeks to come." She paused and went to lean against the back of the chair again. "All I'm saying is, if Sarah is really guilty of these crimes, which were perpetrated on her behalf, by her father, she is a really vicious witch."

"And let's not to forget the attack on Babette," Alan added. "The way Chubb attacked her was brutal, to say the least." He paused. "That reminds me; I should have a look at her back. When you described the way she was slammed to the floor, she may have injured one of her lower lumbar vertebrae in the fall."

"And remember that she's not one to complain. You heard what she said last night: "…nothing that a good night sleep won't cure", didn't you?"

"Yes, and that's why I will need to run a complete physical on her, once things have calmed down around here."

Tiffany got to her feet. "And now, my prince, I shall have to go back to the theater and see what we need to do."

"Okay, but please don't do too much yourself, alright?"

"Why, do you expect me to fall asleep in your arms before we have a cuddle next time we have a chance to spend a night together?" She grinned. "Do you?"

Alan laughed. "Yeah, something like that."

Tiffany nodded and turned toward the door of his office. "That's what I thought," she replied, tittering as she closed the door behind her.

Alan reclined in his seat and reflected on what Tiffany had described as the viciousness of the crimes that had been perpetrated on Sarah and Chubb's victims. *Yeah, I think I'll mention this aspect of their mindset to Gabe before he talks to Sarah.*

An hour later, Dr. Sigmund and Alan were about to enter Sarah Pilkington's cabin when the psychiatrist stopped him. "Before we go in," he said to Alan, "I want to ask you, not to be surprised by the answers you might hear coming out of our patient's mouth. This is a very troubled woman. All I want to know is why she induced her father to commit the crimes and why she chose to do all this in the confines of a cruise ship."

"I've been wondering about that myself. And I can assure you I won't interrupt this interview. I am an ER doctor with Family Medicine training that only included a couple of months at the psychiatric hospital in Halifax. I've got way too much to learn yet to try intervening."

Sigmund smiled. "Okay then, let's go in and see what answers we can extract from the 'lady', shall we?"

CHAPTER FORTY-SIX

A vengeful witch

ALMOST AS SOON AS ALAN knocked on the door Ivan opened it wide. "Thank goodness you're here, Doc. Next time I'll go and watch over a hungry tiger at the zoo rather than a witch like her. She's just all claws..."

"Okay, okay, Ivan," Alan cut-in soothingly as he and Sigmund went past the security officer to enter the cabin. "You just relax now and have a seat in the sitting room while we have a talk with our tigress, okay?"

"Sure thing, she's all yours, Doc, claws and all." Ivan shot an inquisitive glance at Sigmund.

"This is Dr. Sigmund, Ivan," Alan said. "He's going to conduct the interview."

"Please to meet you, Dr. Sigmund," Ivan replied, shaking hands with the psychiatrist.

"Same here, Ivan. But tell me, did Ms. Pilkington show aggression toward you as soon as she regained consciousness or was it something you said to her after she woke up?"

"Can't rightly remember, Dr. Sigmund. But I think it was the fact that she was unable to get out of bed that made her angrier than anything."

"Did she want to have access to the bathroom, is that the reason?" Alan asked.

"Oh that's another story altogether, Doc. Going to the bathroom wasn't that much of a problem. I checked and removed potential weapons in there, and let her do her thing. When I had to get her out of there and put the handcuffs on her again, she had all her claws out, as I said..."

"Okay, Ivan, I get the picture. Thanks." Alan turned to Sigmund. "Shall we go in then?"

"Sure, better now than later, I think," Sigmund replied, walking in the direction of the cabin's bedroom.

"I'll be right here if you need me," Ivan said to their backs as the two men were about to enter Sarah's bedroom.

Sarah, her hair frazzled, her dress wrinkled and sitting at the edge of the bed, seemed all done-in. She raised her head as soon as she heard the door open.

"How long do you think you can keep me handcuffed to my bed, Dr. Mayhew? I'll have my lawyers on you and this cruise company so fast; it'll make your head spin..."

"I'm sorry, Ms. Pilkington, but the handcuffs were necessary according to ship protocol, since you were found breaking and entering the security office..."

"What are you talking about?" she shouted at Alan and then stopped abruptly as if she had realized for the first time that someone else was in the room. "And who's this joker?" She threw a derisive glance at the psychiatrist.

"This is Dr. Sigmund, Ms. Pilkington."

She snickered. "Two doctors. My, I must really be sick." She glared at Sigmund. "And what kind of doctoring are you doing?"

"I am a psychiatrist, Ms. Pilkington. I practice in Washington..."

"Oh, I see, another DC spy are you? Any relation to Freud?"

Suddenly Sigmund grabbed the chair beside the dresser, planted it in front of Sarah and sat down. "How about we talk a little about your Dad, shall we?" he said, fixing his gaze on her face, three inches away.

Alan noticed her reaction. She shrank as if she was about to receive a beating. He took the other chair, set it down on the other side of the bed and sat down, too.

"Okay, Sarah. May I call you Sarah?" Sigmund went on. She nodded, putting her free hand to her forehead and brushing her hair back. "Well then, Sarah, can you tell me where your dad is right now?"

She pulled on her handcuffed wrist. "Can you get that thing off?"

"You don't like being handcuffed, do you, Sarah?"

She shook her head. "That's the way I'd like to see him," she answered.

"Who's that, Sarah?"

"My dad. He's the one who's done all those horrible things to me. And now he's done it to my friends…" Her voice trailed off while she pulled on her wrist again. "And I want *him* to suffer. I want *him* to be handcuffed. I want *him* to pay…"

"To pay for what, Sarah?" Sigmund asked. "Apart from you and your friends, has your dad hurt anyone else?"

"What do you think?" she shouted. "My mom…. He killed my mom, don't you know?"

"No, I don't know, Sarah. Why don't you tell me?"

As Sarah fell silent, Sigmund threw a quick glance at Alan. The latter had his arms crossed over his chest. He had to admire the psychiatrist. The man had geared the conversation to the crux of the matter with just a few questions. He smiled at Sigmund.

Sarah passed her fingers through her hair again. "She was so beautiful, my mom was."

"I am sure she was, Sarah. And how did she die? Do you remember?"

"He killed her, I tell you," she said, her voice raised a couple of decibels. "He pushed her around every time she'd ask him a question about his job, and then one time he put her head in the toilet. She almost drowned." She started sobbing and then screamed, "*I hate the bastard. He's nothing but a clown that hurt my mom all the time.*"

"And how did your dad kill your mom," Sigmund asked once more.

"He burned her, don't you know?"

"No, I don't know, Sarah, I wasn't there, remember?" He paused to let her recall the scene, Alan supposed. "So, tell me how did it happen?"

She sniffled and wiped her nose with the back of her hand. "I wasn't there either. I was in college," she replied quietly. "And then the police called me saying that there had been an accident and that my mom had died during the fire."

"Was your house burned down then?"

Sarah nodded. "She died because of *him*," she yelled. "He's got to be caught. Don't you see? It's the only way he's gonna pay for what he did to her."

"Yes, I see that, Sarah," Sigmund agreed, nodding. "And is that why you made him do all those things on this ship?"

"*Yes, yes,*" she shouted. "I had to show everybody what he's like. He's a monster."

"But why have him do all those things on this ship? Wouldn't it have been better to do it in your neighborhood, so everyone who knew your mom could see how bad he was?"

That was a long question, Alan thought. *I wonder if she'll understand the implication...*

But apparently Sarah did, for she replied, "Oh that's easy. See, Dad is a master of disguise and he knows how to disappear when he needs to. So, on this cruise, he couldn't escape, now could he?" She laughed now. "Unless he jumped overboard. Don't you see?"

"Yes, Sarah, I see what you're saying." He paused before asking, "Would you like to take a little break now?"

"Yes," Sarah retorted decisively. "I want to go to the bathroom again and then I'd like to order some lunch. I'm just famished."

"Okay then. Why don't we ask Dr. Mayhew to take you to the bathroom and then we'll order some lunch. How's that sound?"

"Just perfect," Sarah replied and then turning to Alan, she asked, "Why don't you do the honors, Doctor."

"I'll do that," Alan said, "just as soon as Dr. Sigmund gets me the key to get your handcuffs off." He got up and noticed that the psychiatrist had already gone to fetch the key from Ivan.

As soon as Sigmund returned, he handed the key to Alan and softly said, "Just be careful you don't get hurt," throwing him a conspiratorial glance.

Alan understood immediately. The moment Sarah was free, she could pounce and really do damage. Yet, he knew that she wouldn't have much of a chance against two men – three if need be.

Alan let Sarah go into the bathroom by herself after he had taken her hand to lead her around the bed. She seemed docile enough but he was ready for anything. He was far from trusting her. A minute or so later, Alan and Gabe heard the toilet flush and then a furious shout escaped Sarah's mouth before she flung the bathroom door wide open and tried grabbing Alan's face. Her eyes blazing with untold fury, she roared, "Where did you take my meds? You've got no right to take my meds. They're mine. *Do you hear me?*"

Alan had clasped his hands around her wrist by this time and had forced her arms down. His face was only inches from hers when he said, "I have not taken your meds, Sarah. None of us here knows where they are. Only you can tell me where I can find them. Do you understand me?"

As suddenly as Sarah had transformed into a snared animal, just as suddenly did she calm down. Alan thought it was an extraordinary behavioral display, but didn't take the time to dwell on it.

As he turned, leading Sarah back to the bed, he cracked a quick smile at Gabe, who had been observing the whole incident while preventing Ivan from intervening.

Once Sarah was handcuffed again, Alan went to the phone to order a big salad and some mineral water to be brought to the cabin.

It was only after he had replaced the receiver in its cradle that Sigmund waved for Alan to follow him to the sitting room.

Ivan asked, "Shall I go back and watch her?" nodding in the direction of the bedroom.

"No, Ivan, that won't be necessary," Sigmund answered. We'll let her be for a while and then resume our interview after she's had lunch."

"Okay then," Ivan said. He then asked, "Do you mind if I get someone to relieve me, Doc?" He looked at Alan.

"No-no, go ahead, Ivan," he replied, "you've been up with her half the night, so go and ask Mr. Evans to send someone in about an hour." He turned his gaze to Sigmund. "Will that be enough time?"

"Sure. Besides, I prefer to have a strong man on hand while I'm conducting this type of interview."

"Alright then," Alan said to Ivan, "You go, and don't go back on duty until you've had some sleep, okay? That is a medical order, my friend."

"Sure thing, Doc," Ivan replied, already opening the cabin door.

"Thanks," he added, walking out.

"Let's sit down for a moment," Gabe suggested, plopping his plump body into one of the plush sitting room chairs.

Alan sat on the sofa and put his elbows on his knees. "Did you record the interview?" he asked, looking up at the psychiatrist.

He tapped on the breast pocket of his jacket. "Oh yes. It's all there." He smiled. "Did you notice the switch in behavior?" he asked Alan.

The latter nodded. "She's obviously reliving some of her experiences while her mother was alive. And then there's that demonstration of aggression when she couldn't find her meds…"

"Precisely, Alan," Gabe cut in. "You see, I believe Sarah has suffered some form of abuse at the hands of her father, and her mother died under some kind of terrible circumstances. She not only attributed her mom's death to her father, but she also wants to plant revenge on him."

"And I noticed something else that was interesting about her account…"

"What's that?" Gabe asked.

"Three things actually. First, she said her father pushed her mother all the time. Irene Walter was pushed to her death. Next, she mentioned her mom almost drowning in the toilet. Elizabeth Clipper died in the septic tank. And last, Daniel Richard died in the same way as her mother did."

"Very good observations, Alan. And, yes, she provoked her father into doing to other people exactly what she perceived he had done to her mother. That was probably the reason she was able to have him perpetrate the crimes in question."

"How?" Alan asked, leaning into the back of the sofa.

"When a person is coaxed into doing something, it's better if the victim is already known to the person." Gabe shook his head. "I'm afraid I'm not explaining this very well. Say I wanted to induce you to kiss a woman,"—Alan had to smile—"and although you would have been sufficiently induced to do so, it would be better if I were to convince you that the lady in question was a person you have already kissed."

"Oh, I see what you mean now. If Agent Chulbridge thought he was pushing, or drowning or burning his wife to death, he would accept the mission much easier than if he were told who these people really were."

"Precisely, Alan. Let's assume that Sarah had succeeded in drugging her father sufficiently so that he became susceptible to her suggestions, all she had to do was to tell him that he would be facing her mother – that horrid woman who made his life a misery."

"But what about Ms. Babette, why would he have knifed her the way he attempted to do?"

"We'll see about that recollection this afternoon. I'll try inducing Sarah into revealing why she wanted her father to knife someone. But it may have also been a reaction to the agent's own recollection or desultory state. He may have been making one of his visions a reality." Gabe paused. "I'll have to analyze that part of the agent's behavior once I get him back to Washington."

"What about Sarah; what do you think is going to happen to her?"

"She'll probably be deemed criminally insane and interned for life. And not solely for what she induced her father to do, but for what she did herself."

"You mean detonating the bomb, right?"

"Exactly," Gabe replied at the same moment as the steward knocked on the door.

Alan let him in and asked him to leave the tray on the coffee table. As soon as the young man had left the cabin, Gabe got up from his seat and said, "Let's get her that food before we continue, shall we?"

CHAPTER FORTY-SEVEN

Is there another bomb on the ship?

TWO HOURS LATER Alan and Gabe came out of Sarah's cabin satisfied with the information they had obtained from her. One, they now knew where the herbal potions and drugs were kept. Two, Sarah had told them that her father did, in fact, try to quit smoking and that he took Chantix regularly, and that she knew what the interactions would be with the herbs. Unfortunately, there was still one troublesome question Sarah had refused to answer, when asked where she had placed the second bomb on the ship.

"Wouldn't you like to know?" she had answered, smiling at Sigmund's face.

"Alright, Sarah, if you won't tell me now, maybe we'll have to play a little game of "hot-and-cold" with you. Would that be alright?"

"No. I don't like games," she had snapped back. "You just get my dad's cell-phone from where I've hidden it, press the "Go" app and *Poof*, you'll have your answer."

"But wouldn't you like your dad to do that?" Sigmund had then asked.

"NO! I want to see for myself when it goes *Poof!*"

And after that, there hadn't been any way to shift her from her position.

"So, what do you suggest we do now, Gabe?" Alan asked, as the two men were about to take the elevator to the café to have some lunch.

"We'll need to find the cell-phone first. If it's where she told us it should be, then I'll have to induce her into revealing where she'd like to go to watch the bomb go *Poof*."

"And how do you propose to do that?" Alan asked, obviously puzzled.

"Hypnotic trance, Alan. As soon as I have ascertained that she's sufficiently tired, I'll try hypnotizing her to reveal where the bomb is placed."

"I sure hope you can do it, otherwise, we'll have to advise our captain and he'll probably order a Code Charlie…"

"What's that?" Gabe inquired, coming out of the elevator now.

"It's a drill that allows crew, staff and officers to search for a dangerous item throughout the ship. By law, everyone is then authorized to search every room, cabin and common areas of the ship."

"And is it generally successful?"

"Absolutely. You can imagine some two hundred crew, staff and officers being able to rummage through every nook and cranny of the ship – it's very effective. Nothing is private. That's how we managed to find Mrs. Clipper so quickly. Otherwise, her body would have been entirely dissolved by the time we reached Madagascar – or sooner."

"But I imagine the passengers would be in a state of panic if you were to reveal what we were looking for in this instance, wouldn't they?"

"Yes. And that's why most of the time we try avoiding this sort of search. It's something we do as a last resort. If possible, we do not identify what the danger is up front. It keeps down the myocardial infarct rate that the medical department has to attend to."

Once they had finished their lunch, Alan left Gabe to transcribe Sarah's interview on paper and the psychiatrist promised to inform the CIA agents of their findings. Sarah would obviously be arrested along with her father and detained in a secure cabin until *The Baroness* reached Cape Town in three days' time. As for finding the bomb – if there was one, which Alan doubted somehow – he would wait until Gabe had hypnotized Sarah that evening before he would take the necessary steps and alert Captain Galveston. Nevertheless, he decided to inform Gilbert of the possibility of another explosive device being hidden aboard ship. Since the CIA agents probably would now be in possession of the cell-phone, they could disable it and "Bob's your uncle". Alan smiled when he recalled his granddad not knowing who Uncle Bob was.

When he arrived at the medical center, Philip Granger was waiting for him. Philip was one of the passengers who worked for the insurance company that insured *The Baroness.*

Philip had been on board before all the trouble, and Alan liked the fellow as a person. He was pleased to medically help him out with his sore shoulder, and continued to treat it even while they were in the midst of all the issues affecting the ship and its current problems.

"And how's my favorite doctor?" Philip asked, shaking hands with Alan before going into his office.

"Just peachy," Alan replied sarcastically. "We're heading for Cape Town, leaving three bodies in our wake, and two prisoners in secure cabins. Apart from that, I'd say the cruise was a success so far."

Philip guffawed. "Yes, I've heard from my head office and they were curious as to what they can expect – if anything – regarding civil actions against your company."

"I shouldn't think there will be any, Philip. The CIA and Interpol are primarily responsible for the mess, and I don't think the victims' families would want to make waves at this point. If either of them wanted to sue our company, they'll have a hard time proving that we, aboard *The Baroness,* had anything to do with this entire affair. We were the bystanders, so to speak, who took the brunt of the attack while trying to protect more than four hundred people from harm."

"Yes, I can see your point, Alan. Besides I can certainly vouch for the fact that none of the passengers have been disturbed in any way during this part of the cruise. You've kept it all well under wraps, haven't you?"

Alan chuckled. "Yes, we've tried," he agreed and then paused. "And now, how's that shoulder of yours?"

"It's okay, I suppose. It hasn't been bothering me lately, but since I'd like to return to playing some tennis, I just want to make sure my shoulder will accept the added effort."

"Have you been exercising it?"

"Sure have. Every morning, "She" goes with me to the gym, without fail. I will not stand any crying on "her" part. No way Jose!"

"Okay then," Alan said, laughing, "let me get your file…"

"While you're doing that, I've got another story for you from our company files. You're going to like this one."

"Have you now?" Alan queried while looking at his computer screen.

"Before this cruise I was told of a lawyer who purchased a box of 24 very rare and expensive cigars, then insured them against, among other things, fire, loss, theft, etc. Within a month, having smoked his entire stockpile of the cigars, the lawyer filed a claim against my company. In his claim, the lawyer stated the cigars were lost in a series of small fires." Alan mentally flashed to a few of the lawyers *The Baroness* had had to deal with in the past.

"Our insurance company refused to pay, citing the obvious reason, that the man had consumed the cigars in the normal fashion."

"The lawyer sued – and won!"

Alan's eyes went wide. "How could that happen?" he asked.

"Well, let me tell you – this is good. Delivering the ruling, the judge agreed with my company that the claim was frivolous. The judge stated nevertheless, that the lawyer held a policy from our company, in which it had warranted the cigars insurable and guaranteed against fire without defining what is considered to be unacceptable 'fire'. Consequently, we were obligated to pay the claim.

"Rather than endure the lengthy and costly appeal process, my company accepted the ruling and paid $15,000 to the lawyer for his loss of the cigars that perished in the 'fires'.

"Now for the best part: After the lawyer cashed the check, we had the guy arrested on 24 counts of *Arson!* With his own insurance claim and his own testimony from the previous case being used against him, the lawyer was convicted of intentionally burning his insured property and was sentenced to 36 months in jail and a $45,000 fine." Philip laughed. "How do you like them apples?"

"I might have to check if my lawyer smokes cigars," Alan remarked, laughing together with Philip while he was printing his latest treatment e-file.

Meanwhile, now that Mallard and Chalkstone had been advised that the cell-phone, herbal concoctions and medicines were hidden in one of the upper decks' vacant cabins, they had gone directly to the cabin in question and had found the items hidden in behind some spare towels inside the bathroom vanity cabinet.

Mallard was about to check the cell-phone for messages, when it flew out of his hand unexpectedly, and landed on the sofa of the sitting room.

"What the hell?" Mallard shouted, unable to contain his surprise.

Although Dr. Sigmund had advised the agents that there was possibly a second bomb aboard the ship, Mallard thought he would check the phone anyway.

Yet, as far as Edmund was concerned, it wasn't a recommended action to take, until Dr. Sigmund had verified the existence of the bomb and its location later that evening when he hypnotized Sarah.

When Chalkstone attempted to grab the phone off the sofa, it moved away from his hand so fast that the agent gasped.

"Don't tell me that witch's put a spell on the darn thing," he shouted angrily, trying again to grab it.

Seeing that neither Mallard nor Chalkstone would give up on the idea of touching the cell-phone, Edmund decided to take more serious actions against these two idiots. He lifted the lamp from the bedside table and had it chase Mallard all the way to the door of the cabin until he opened it wide and ran for cover somewhere on the promenade deck – Chalkstone in tow.

As soon as the door had been opened, Edmund dropped the lamp and re-directed his kinetic powers to the cell-phone, which he carried, so to speak, all the way to the medical center.

When he arrived, he was lucky, for the door opened to let Philip out. The cell-phone passed over the insurance agent's head unnoticed and landed on Alan's desk. Edmund sat in the visitor's chair and waited.

Unfortunately, Alice had come out of the storeroom in the interim and had observed the phone's air-travel, agape.

When her mouth finally returned to moving, she yelled, "Dr. Mayhew, the guy is at it again…"

Alan emerged from the examining room, stared at his nurse, and then turned his gaze to where she was pointing.

"He's at it again, I tell you, look there Doc. Look."

Alan rushed into his office, where Edmund was laughing his head off by now.

"Come on, Alice, what did you see?" he asked her as she stepped in the office cautiously.

"That . . . that . . . that phone," she babbled, "I saw it fly into your office. I tell you, that magician will have me interned in some asylum soon, if you don't stop him."

"Calm down, Alice," Alan said soothingly, trying very hard not to laugh. "Mr. Granger probably left it here by mistake."

"But, Doc, I'm sure I saw it fly in here," Alice insisted.

"Okay, okay, Alice," Alan said, sitting down, "I'll go and have a talk with the magician and make sure he understands that his tricks are not welcome, here in the medical center."

"You'd better, Doc, otherwise, I'll go see him myself and give him a piece of my mind that he won't soon forget!"

Alan nodded. "But for now, I think we should get back to whatever we were doing. We've got another three crew scheduled for their company physicals this afternoon. So, if you're okay, I suggest you get the trays ready for three more sets of blood tests, cardiograms, etc." He looked at her. Alice didn't seem convinced, but finally shrugged and turned on her heels.

Once she had closed the door, Alan frowned and looked at the cell-phone. "Is that Sarah's cell-phone?" he asked his granddad quietly.

"Yes, son. I had to bring it here before those two CIA nincompoops had time to press the wrong button and have the bomb explode."

"So, you were there during Sarah's interview, were you?"

"Oh yes my son, and although I love a good prank anytime I am allowed, having *The Baroness* going *Poof* on my watch isn't something I would contemplate, or allow with you and Babette aboard, even in my wildest dreams."

Alan bent down and put his head under the desk before he allowed himself to laugh out loud. *The Baroness* going *Poof* conjured up more than one image in his mind, and he couldn't help but laugh until tears were menacing to fall from his eyes.

When he finally dared come up for air, he saw his granddad smile while keeping a deadpan face. "You like the inference, did you, son?" he asked benignly.

"Yes, absolutely, Granddad, but this is no laughing matter, is it?"

"Precisely, Alan. And that's the very reason for which I brought the cell-phone to you. You probably know how to disable it, since you mentioned that retrieving its SIM card would render it inoperable, correct?"

Alan nodded. "Yes, I did say that, Granddad, however, it might have a self-igniting digit, which would detonate the bomb in the wrong hands."

"Sarah is really a vengeful witch, isn't she?"

"Witch maybe, Granddad, but she certainly is a very sick woman. She must have been abused – badly abused – during her childhood and now all that bottled up anger is coming out in the worst possible manner."

"What about her father?"

"What about him?"

"Well, when Dr. Sigmund questioned her about his attack on *my* poor Babette, she had no answer, did she?"

"No, she didn't. And from the lack of an answer to that question, I can only deduce that Agent Chulbridge must have been drugged to the point of having delusions of power, or something like that."

"So you think he'll be incarcerated in a mental institution, too?"

"That or a state prison, yes. But it will be up to the jury to decide. We won't have anything to say about his punishment in our justice system…"

At that moment, the door of the medical center burst open to let Mallard and Chalkstone rush inside.

They pushed past Alice and flung Alan's office door open without knocking. Edmund got out of his chair, all smiles, and went to perch himself on top of the filing cabinet in the corner of the room. *I'm going to enjoy this,* he thought, grinning at the two agents, who obviously couldn't see him.

"Well, why don't you come in, gentlemen, since you've already burst past my door," Alan suggested sternly, while shuffling some papers over the cell-phone. "Just tell me what you want and be on your way. I'm busy!"

"We've seen things move around the witch's cabin and we want an explanation," Mallard blurted.

"Yeah, and the cell-phone's disappeared, too," Chalkstone added. "And we want it back."

"And what makes you think I would know where the phone is, or have an explanation for 'the witch moving it around'?" Alan asked, feigning indifference.

"I don't know," Chalkstone said, shrugging. "You've interviewed the witch, so you know more about her tricks than we do…"

Alan had enough. "Okay, Agent Chalkstone, I've had about all I can take from your insinuations, and I would advise you to call our passengers by their names and give them the respect they're due. Ms. Pilkington is under my medical care, and until further notice, she'll remain in a secure cabin until she is surrendered to the authorities in Cape Town. Until then, whatever she divulges to me or to Dr. Sigmund is confidential."

"But the shrink…"

"There you go again, Agent Chalkstone, calling a respectable physician and the person you have to thank for finding the cell-phone before a disaster occurred; a shrink. That is an insult to our profession." Alan stood up. "And now if you'll excuse me, I've got patients to see and reports to write…"

"Just tell us if you've got the phone or if you know where it is at least. Please?" Mallard pleaded. "It's our necks on the block, Doc. And we wouldn't know how to explain the phone disappearing the way it did."

"Okay. I can tell you, the cell-phone is in a safe place and will remain there until Dr. Sigmund has conducted his last interview with Ms. Pilkington tonight."

"Could you sign a statement to that effect…?"

Now Alan exploded, "Get out of my office, right now and don't come back until I call for you! You've had your answer, so get out!"

"Okay, okay, Doc. Sorry," Mallard said, grabbing his partner by the arm and leading him out of the medical center without another word.

CHAPTER FORTY-EIGHT

Broccoli, 49 cents a pound

AS GILBERT WAS RIDING the elevator on his way to see Alan, an elderly woman dressed in her best came in. Everyone was well dressed to attend and delight in the High Tea the Chef and cruise director had arranged for that afternoon. When a young and gorgeous woman got into the elevator, smelling of expensive perfume, she turned to the old woman, who was sniffing the air, frowning, and said arrogantly, "*Romance* by Ralph Lauren, $150 an ounce!" On the next floor, another young and beautiful woman stepped onto the elevator. The elderly lady sniffed the air again. Noticing this, the second woman, also very arrogantly, turned to the old woman, saying, "Chanel No. 5, $200 an ounce!" About two floors later, the elderly lady reached her destination and was about to get off the elevator when she turned around, looked both attractive women in the eye, then bent over, farted and said, "*Broccoli*, 49 cents a pound!"

Gilbert had a hard time keeping from laughing. He put his hand over his mouth and nose not to inhale the curious scented mixture of *Romance, Chanel No.5* and *farted broccoli*. When he finally got off the elevator and rounded the corner to take the stairs down a few flights in the direction of the medical center, he burst out in loud laughter under the curious gazes of some passengers passing him by at the same moment.

He was still chuckling when he stepped into Alan's office. "You'll never believe what happen *on my way...*" He burst out in another round of laughter.

"Were you on your way *to the theater* by any chance," Alan asked, chortling.

Gilbert shook his head, trying to regain his composure. He did so with some difficulty since Alan wasn't helping.

"Anyway," he said at long last, "You said you've got the cell; do you want me to keep it?"

"No, Gilbert, I don't think that will be necessary. It's in my safe now and I think it's better if it stays where it is until we find out *where the bomb is.*"

Gilbert's mouth dropped open. "Did I hear you correctly? Have we got another bomb on board? You've got to be joking, right?"

"No, I'm afraid not."

"How did you find out? I mean is that what Ms. Pilkington told you when you interviewed her this morning?"

"Well, if we can believe her, she did say that she planted another bomb on the ship, yes, but she wouldn't tell Dr. Sigmund or me where it is. She did divulge how she intended to detonate it."

"How?" Gilbert asked, dead serious now.

"Apparently there is an app on the phone marked "Go" that will detonate the bomb if anyone presses it."

"Did you tell anyone about this, apart from our snooping CIA guys I mean?"

"I rue the moment I opened my mouth to them, truth be told, Gilbert. When they learned where to find the potions, meds and cellphone, and located the items, they were trying to manipulate the phone when my granddad took it away from them."

"And that's why it's in your safe now, right?"

"Right. But I don't know how to manage these two. They are snooping everywhere. And if there is a bomb on board, I don't want to alert anyone unduly until we ascertain where it is. It's not like we've got a bomb disposal unit on hand, have we?"

Gilbert nodded. "I see your point, Doc. But when will we know one way or the other?"

Alan looked at his watch. "In a couple of hours Dr. Sigmund will try hypnotizing Ms. Pilkington. Hopefully she will reveal where she put the explosive."

"But what if it explodes when someone opens the wrong door, like what happened to Simon?"

Alan shook his head. "Let's put it this way, Gilbert; if there is a bomb somewhere, I believe Sarah Pilkington will want to witness the explosion. She said as much during the interview this morning."

"Yes, maybe," Gilbert said, sounding unsure, "But which ever way you look at this problem, if we don't say anything to Galveston, and something happens in the meantime, we might as well kiss our jobs goodbye."

"I know what you're saying, Gilbert. And if you feel you should report what you know to Mr. Ekelton or the captain, you should do it."

Gilbert remained silent for a moment before he asked, "Two hours you said?"

"Yes, that's when Dr. Sigmund will put Sarah under. If he succeeds, we'll have an answer soon thereafter."

"Okay, I'll buy that. But if our CIA guys go and blab to the cap beforehand, what do we do?"

"Somehow, I think they'll keep their mouth shut. They're as scared as anyone else who knows about the bomb, believe me."

"Well, let's hope so, for all of our sakes," Gilbert concluded, getting up. Then as an afterthought, he said, "Even though I have yet to see the meds and potions properly bagged as evidence and locked in my safe, I wouldn't mind locking up the infamous laptop…"

"Ah yes; that was something else I meant to ask you," Alan said, "How did these two agents gain access to the cabin where Sarah had stashed the evidence? Did they find the laptop, do you know?"

"One question at a time, Doc. First, when they called to ask me to open that cabin, I sent Raphael to open it for them. He left them to search the room, but I don't know if they found the laptop. Did they mention finding it?"

"No. All they were worried about was the cell-phone falling in the wrong hands, other than their own that is."

"Okay then, I think I'll go and find them and see what they did with the laptop; unless Dr. Rivers took it with him after he cleaned up

Chulbridge's cabin."

"Yes, that's possible," Alan agreed. "But I think we're not talking about Chubb's laptop. Sarah had another laptop with the same software as her father did. And that's the one we need to locate."

Gilbert sat down again. "If Mallard and Chalkstone do not have it, where do you think it is?"

"If my assumptions are correct, I think the laptop is probably the bomb itself."

"And you concluded this how?" Gilbert asked, eyebrows arched.

"Because of how Sarah described the explosion. She didn't say it would go "bang" or "boom" as most people would, she said it would go "poof"." Alan tilted his head to one side. "I know it's a long shot, but if you've ever seen a laptop sustain a strong short-circuit, you would have noticed how it would go up in a "puff" of smoke."

"Okay, I'll bite. But where do you think it might go "Poof" then?"

"I am not sure, Gilbert. But, the only person she or her father hasn't managed to eliminate is Babette…"

"Good God, Alan, do you realize what you're saying?"

Alan nodded. "Yes, of course I do, and that's why I've sent Granddad to the theater to search for the laptop. If he finds it, he should be back here any minute now."

"I think I'm somehow glad he can't touch it. Can he "transport" it somewhere safe do you think? That is, if he finds it?"

"Yes, I believe he can. And what's more, I don't think the explosion is designed to do grave damage, but to kill with poisonous gas emanation."

"You mean like one of those terrorists' Sarin chemical gas bombs?"

"Yes," Alan answered before standing up. And looking at his watch again, he added, "Why don't we take a stroll to the theater and see if Granddad has found anything. Shall we?"

Gilbert was already out of his seat and preceding Alan out of the medical center. *Our doc must be tired,* he reflected. *"Taking a stroll" indeed, when you're looking for a bomb!*

"Why didn't you mention this before, Doc?" Gilbert asked while they were hurrying to the elevator now. "I think it's the first thing you should have said when I came in."

Alan shook his head as he pressed the elevator button. "No, Gilbert. All of what I said is only pure conjecture on my part. Sarah may have just left the laptop in the costume room backstage, not expecting to be collared before the curtain came down on the second act."

They stepped into the elevator. The odd aroma of perfume mixed with broccoli still lingered. Alan sniffed the air and smiled. "I see, I mean I *smell* what you mean," he said to Gilbert.

When they arrived at the theater, everything was quiet except for some faint noises coming from backstage. The two men rushed in that direction and found Babette, Tiffany and Edmund in deep conversation, sitting around a small sewing table at the back of the costume room.

"Ah, here you are," Edmund said to Alan, "I was about to come and find you…"

"Have you found the laptop?" Gilbert asked by way of a reply.

"Patience, Mr. Evans, is a virtue. So, please use some of it and hear me out."

Gilbert nodded. "Okay, Edmund, I'm sorry. But I really don't want anyone to get hurt…"

"No one is going to get hurt, Mr. Evans," Babette interposed. "We found Sarah's laptop and it was Tiffany here"—she threw her a smile—"who told us not to touch it."

"Okay then, Granddad," Alan said, "Do you think you can "transport" it out of here and to Mr. Evans's office?"

Surprisingly, Edmund shook his head. "I'm afraid I cannot do that, Alan." He raised a hand in front of his face. "And before you say anything, I'll let Ms. Tiffany explain why that is."

Gilbert and Alan exchanged a glance.

"I'm sorry, Alan," Tiffany said, opening her mouth for the first time since Alan and Gilbert entered the costume room. "I'm the one who stopped Granddad from transporting the laptop anywhere." She paused and smiled at Alan's frown. "You see, Granddad uses kinetic power to move things, and kinetic power is nothing more than well-directed magnetic energy – mostly energy. So, I figured if he were to direct the amount of energy it would take to lift and transport the laptop anywhere, it might short-circuit the signal and detonate the bomb inside it. That's why I didn't want to let him do anything with it."

Alan nodded and bowed his head in acknowledgement. "I should have thought of that myself. I'm sorry, Tiff. You may have just avoided getting everyone in this room killed."

"Oh don't be so hard on yourself," Babette exclaimed, getting off her chair and going to pat Alan's shoulder. "You've just saved our lives. Yes, that's what you did," she said, peering into the doc's contrite face. "Enough of that, you hear? Let's figure out a way to get this laptop out of here safely. Okay? Besides, as Edmund explained, without the cell-phone, the bomb is harmless, right?" She turned to her ghostly friend.

"Absolutely, milady," he replied.

"Alright then," Gilbert said, "can you tell us where it is then?" He looked up at Edmund.

"Yes. Let me show you," he answered, floating to the sewing machine table. "It's lodged inside the table. If you lift the sewing machine cautiously, you'll find it."

Alan was about to touch the machine when Gilbert grabbed the doc's arm and pulled him back. "Please, Doc. We'll need you to resuscitate me and others if anything happens, but no one will need me anymore, okay?"

Reluctantly, Alan said, "Okay, but why don't you lift the machine just a bit so I can look inside the bin?"

"Alright, we'll go with that," Gilbert replied, while putting his hand around the neck of the sewing machine and lifting it gently.

"Okay, I see it," Alan said, looking through the crack between the table and the machine. "But how did you see it, Granddad? Did anyone lift the machine for you?"

Without answering, Edmund pointed to the transformer on the floor and the wire leading to the plug in the wall. "Ms. Tiffany told me about the electrical wires and the fact that the sewing machine would only need one electrical cord, not two. So, the second cord was obviously for something else."

Alan smiled as he straightened up and Gilbert let go of the machine, cautiously replacing it in its slot.

Babette and Tiffany had come around the corner to watch the three men, and Tiffany then asked, "What do you think would happen if we unplugged it?"

"The battery would die in a couple of hours I should think," Alan said and then stopped talking abruptly. "That's an excellent idea, Tiff. Absolutely brilliant!"

"Where there's no power, there's no *Poof*," Gilbert said, grinning. "Is that what you're thinking?"

"Exactly, Gilbert," Alan replied, bending down to "pull the plug" on the bomb – literally. And then holding the cord up, he added, "And in a couple of hours we'll know if we were right."

CHAPTER FORTY-NINE

It won't go "Poof"!

TO ENSURE THAT NO ONE entered the costume room before Dr. Sigmund interviewed Sarah that evening, Gilbert asked Raphael to sit outside the room for the next two or three hours. The chief did not explain why he was assigning the young man to this mundane, if not boring task, but Raphael was happy enough to relax and read his book for how ever long it would take until Stephan would relieve him.

Meanwhile, Alan had gone back to the medical center and had continued typing his reports for the day. He had also called Dr. Sigmund to inform him of their discovery in the costume room.

"That's marvelous, Alan," Gabe exclaimed when he learned that the laptop had been disconnected. "But I still want to hear from Sarah on that score, you understand? It's important that she confirms the location of her laptop and if it is indeed the explosive mechanism we think it is."

"Absolutely, Gabe," Alan replied. "I wouldn't have it any other way. But there is one more thing we need to know before we close the file on this case…"

"What's that?" Gabe asked.

"Gilbert and I would like to know why Sarah wanted to have access to the safe. As you know, that safe still contains several packages of cocaine. It would be good to know why she intended to take them out, and the ultimate purpose for doing so. Do you think she will talk about that willingly?"

"I would say yes, Alan. You see, Sarah, in her demented state, has demonstrated a narcissistic trait. That's the reason she would not divulge where the bomb was and why she wanted to see it go "Poof". So, if she had some grand-plan for the cocaine, perhaps she'll be only too glad to tell me what the plan was."

"That's good, Gabe." Alan hesitated. "Would you like me to attend the interview again?"

"It will not be necessary for you to be present, but if you'd like to see how hypnosis is done, by all means I wouldn't mind the company."

"Okay then, Gabe, I'll be there at seven o'clock – no problem."

And as agreed, at seven o'clock sharp, Alan was waiting for Sigmund in front of Sarah's secure cabin. Only a couple of minutes later, he saw the psychiatrist make his way down the corridor.

"Ah, good to see that you could make it, Alan. I am glad for the company. I've also asked for one of Mr. Evans's men to stand outside the door while I interview Sarah. I never know how a patient might react when under hypnosis, especially since she hasn't been medicated. She has not been under my observation for that long, so there may be other aspects to her psyche we do not know about as yet."

As Alan was about to answer, the two men saw Stephan come down the corridor.

"Good evening, Dr. Sigmund," the blonde, distinguished-looking young man said politely. "And to you, too, Doc." He looked at Alan, who smiled his greeting, and then the security man returned his gaze at Sigmund. "My name is Stephan, Dr. Sigmund. You just tell me what you expect me to do and I'll be at your disposal."

Sigmund nodded and smiled. "Actually, Stephan, I only want you to stand or sit outside Ms. Pilkington's cabin, right here"—he pointed to the door—"and if you hear me call your name, you come in and help me restrain the patient. Do you think you'll be able to do that?"

"Sure thing, Doctor. And will you stay out here, too?" Stephan asked Alan.

"No, I'll be in the cabin with Dr. Sigmund. And if we need you I'll come out and get you, okay?"

"Okay then, Doc. I'll be right here," Stephan replied, leaning his back against the opposite wall to Sarah's cabin.

"Shall we?" Sigmund invited, opening the cabin with its key card.

The room was in total darkness, but from the light streaming through the open door, Sigmund and the doc could see a very uncomfortable scene before their eyes.

Alan didn't hesitate; he turned on the light switch and went to kneel down beside Sarah's body. He palpated her neck to check for a pulse and couldn't find any. The woman on the bed was dead!

Sigmund seemed to be frozen on the spot for a moment, but finally spoke in an undertone as he closed the door of the cabin. "You think she is dead, do you?"

Alan nodded, stood up, took the bed cover and pulled it over her body. "I think she's been dead for a couple of hours only. Rigor mortis hasn't set in yet. And I would bet my bottom dollar that she killed herself."

"What makes you say that?" Sigmund asked, visibly dumbfounded.

"She knew the game was up, Gabe. And when Agents Mallard and Chalkstone transferred her down here, they probably told her as much."

"Those two always wanted to have the upper hand, didn't they?" Sigmund remarked. "But how could she have done it?"

"My guess would be that she swallowed a strychnine pill which she had probably hidden in her bra."

"But where could she have procured such a deadly pill?"

"I have an idea that we'll find the answer in the signet ring," Alan replied. "Her father was a spy on his way to meet the head of a cartel in Madagascar. And if he was recognized for what he really was, a CIA operative, he would have swallowed the pill himself."

"How dreadful," Sigmund said, bowing his head. And then looking up at Alan again, and added, "What do we do now?"

"Let's go back to Mr. Evans's office and tell him what we found. I'll ask my nurse to come down with a body bag so that she and Stephan can transport the corpse to the morgue."

"What about the laptop then? Are you sure it's the bomb?"

"As sure as anyone can be, Gabe. But I think, we can resolve that issue as well."

"Well then, let's get the wheels in motion, shall we?" Sigmund suggested, turning to the door.

"Yes, but before we go, I'd like to ask you not to speak about what we found here to anyone, Gabe." Alan's tone of voice was definitely denoting the importance of his request.

"Absolutely, Alan. I'll write my report and send it to you as soon as it's done. And after that, I'll resume my leisurely vacation until I get back to Washington."

"Very well, and once again, Gabe, let me thank you for all your help."

"Don't mention it, Alan. It's been my pleasure." He paused. "Actually, I've received an offer for the chair of the Department of Forensic Psychiatry from Stanford University…"

"That's sounds fantastic. Are you going to accept it?"

"Yes, I think I will. This idle life is not for me really. And if I can help other doctors, such as you, understand their patients' a little better; I think I would do well to accept the offer. Besides, there is sunshine all year round in Palo Alto, California and I won't miss the East Coast winters, I can assure you."

After Gilbert had joined Raphael at his post backstage, he explained to the young tech what he needed done – if at all possible?

"How long since you've disconnected it?" Raphael asked.

"About two hours. Do you think that is sufficient time to empty the battery?"

"I don't know until I see the laptop, Chief. Some newer ones can run ten to sixty hours without being connected."

Gilbert exhaled a worrisome sigh. "Well, all we can do is to have a look, right?"

With only a nod as a reply, Raphael followed Gilbert into the costume room. And once Gilbert had lifted the sewing machine high enough to enable Raphael to grab the laptop, the latter said, "That's an older model, Chief. The battery should be dead alright." He took the laptop gingerly out of the cavity and went to deposit it on the nearby table. "You see this little clip on the side here?" He pointed to what looked like the head of some paperclip jammed between the lid and the keyboard of the laptop.

"Yes. Is that the detonator?" Gilbert asked.

"It should be," Raphael answered. "And when the signal from the cell reaches the clip, the pressure from the explosive on the keyboard would simply open the lid to release the gas inside."

"But shouldn't there be some sort of envelope or canister inside…"

"I don't know that it would take that much, Chief. Just a thin capsule or even something as small as a stamp would release enough gas to kill the person whose head was over the laptop. But we should know more once I carefully open it."

"Oh no, you don't, Raphy. We've had enough dead people on this cruise," Gilbert retorted. "You just take this to the ship's vault in the security room, and they can do what ever they want with it once we get to Cape Town, okay?"

"Okay, Chief, no problem. But let's take the service stairs to transport it. I wouldn't want to have a passenger bump into me in the elevator, okay?"

"I'm with you on that one, Raphy. Lead the way and I'll follow."

That night, Alan and Tiffany decided to accept Captain Galveston's invitation to have dinner with him, Robert Ekelton, and Gilbert Evans.

"Why hasn't he invited Babette to have dinner with us, I wonder," Tiffany asked as they were riding the elevator to the dining room.

"I think he's saving the congratulatory dinner for another night – after Babette's play."

"Oh, that will be fantastic for her. She needs to forget all of the turmoil and concentrate on what ever she wants to do from now on."

"And what do you think that is?" Alan asked.

"I don't know for sure, but she mentioned something about going to Luxemburg after this cruise."

"You know, Tiff, I would love to be a fly on the wall when she meets her family." Alan smiled at the thought as the elevator doors opened to the dining room floor.

CHAPTER FIFTY

───────────────────

A Cat Named Hoodoo Voodoo

ACT III

IN THE WAKE OF SUCH a troublesome part of the cruise, *The Baroness* was finally treading the waters of the South Atlantic Ocean with some renewed vigor it seemed. It was with anticipation that everyone on board was looking forward to attend the third act of *A Cat Named Hoodoo Voodoo* that night and perhaps none as much as Roger. A young buck in his mid-twenties, Roger was the sort of hunk girls dream about. His dark hair and enticing chestnut eyes were nothing short of captivating. He had captured the heart of a lovely young passenger named Isabelle. That afternoon, Roger decided to buy an expensive locket at the ship's jewelry store. Once he had chosen the piece which he thought would please her, the store manager asked him if he'd like to have it engraved. Roger thought about it for a minute and then replied, "Yes, that's a great idea. Thanks for suggesting it."

"Not at all, sir. And to whom shall I make the dedication?" the jeweler asked.

"Why don't you engrave it with: *To My One and Only*, that way if things don't work out I could always give it to someone else."

By 7:30 that evening, the foyer of the theater was already crowded. Passengers were mingling and having an early drink of champagne before the bell was to ring at about eight o'clock.

"I never thought I would say this," Mallard was saying to Alan, "but I'll be glad to see Washington again."

"You mean you didn't enjoy cruising aboard one of the most elegant ships in the world?" Alan's voice was derisive. "I wouldn't have thought that you and your partner would have had many opportunities to conduct an investigation aboard a cruise ship, or am I wrong?"

"Oh no, you're not wrong, Doc. But I never encountered so many problems when it should have been a simple matter of getting Agent Chulbridge off the ship."

"You know what they say: The best laid plans," Alan remarked, turning to see Gilbert come off the elevator to join them.

"Good evening, Agent Mallard. How are you?" Gilbert asked.

"Fine, Mr. Evans, thanks." He paused. "Do you know when we're due to arrive in Cape Town?"

"Not before the morning I'm told, why?"

"Well, it's because I don't think I can stand another night of my partner snoring the night away, like he does."

Alan smiled and shook his head. "Perhaps you should ask him to sleep on his side. It generally helps."

"Yeah, I know. And I've asked him every night, believe me. But as soon as he's asleep, he turns on his back and then the freight train starts going through the cabin. Impossible, I tell you."

And that's when the ringing of the bell calling the audience to their seats interrupted everyone.

As soon as the passengers and officers were seated, Alan turned around to see if the theater was full. And it was. Not one seat was vacant; people were even standing against the back wall – three rows deep. *Incredible,* he thought. *I wonder if Tiffany and I will go to Broadway one day and see one of her plays in one of the famous theaters there. That would be such a treat.*

Not even a minute later, the curtain rose on a dance – love, potions and fertility being the theme. Alan was in awe. It was simply spectacular.

A dancer leaped into the center of the circle, turned and turned, falling towards the floor as he got dizzier and dizzier, then collapsed. There was a scream off stage, then another scream.

(Marie is lying on her bed with baby)

LOUIS:	(bending over bed, picks up baby) She is so little.
MARIE:	She is more white than black, but she will live with my people and me.
LOUIS:	She's another Marie. I shall call her Marie. Please name her Marie.
MARIE:	If you wish. Won't you stay long enough to see her baptized?
LOUIS:	I don't want to go, but I have to.
MARIE:	You don't have to if you don't want to.
LOUIS:	We've been all over that more times than I care to mention
ISABELLE:	(enters) am I on time? I was asleep when Hoodoo Voodoo licked my cheek and I came right away.
MARIE:	The baby came, here do you want to hold her?
ISABELLE:	Did Hoodoo Voodoo make the baby too?
LOUIS:	No one is to ever know I am the father.
ISABELLE:	That's not fair!
LOUIS:	I am her father. I will be her father and love her, but I cannot give her my name
ISABELLE:	Hoodoo Voodoo is a lovelier name (takes baby in arms and rocks her).
LOUIS:	No one is to know, no one.
MARIE:	I understand. There is some champagne on the table. It's a very fine vintage. Louis brought it over for us.
LOUIS:	Yes, you must have a glass with us; to celebrate the baby's arrival (opens the bottle, pours three glasses.
MARIE:	(Takes out a potion & when Louis brings the

	glasses, she puts the potion into Isabelle's glass). I'll take the baby, this is your champagne; It might make you a bit dizzy, but don't worry. It's such good quality that it might give you a little kick.
ISABELLE:	(Gulps it down in one gulp) Could I have another glass, please? (Louis pours another. She drinks it and exits) I'll be back.
MARIE:	It is fixed. She won't remember anything.
LOUIS:	Is anyone else coming?
MARIE:	The religious leader is coming, Father CYRIL, to baptize the baby.
LOUIS:	Please stop him.
MARIE:	But my baby is to be baptized.
LOUIS:	Well and good, but not here and not with me present.
MARIE:	Whatever you say, Louis, then I will take her to your church and have her baptized.
LOUIS:	What name will you use?
MARIE:	Marie Laveau's, she will be princess Laveau of the gris-gris
LOUIS:	Fine, fine, but how are you going to manage it in the largest, most pompous and elite cathedral of New Orleans?
MARIE:	You . . . you will manage it through your mother. She is a lady of great wealth and influence, and if you can't, Hoodoo Voodoo will.
LOUIS:	(opens his mouth, she looks at him with her intense blue eyes.) I will speak to my mother right away.
MARIE:	(kisses Louis) you look mighty handsome today. Where are you going?
LOUIS:	To a wedding.
MARIE:	Who's wedding?
LOUIS:	My wedding (takes out his pocket watch) I'm

	late, so late, in fact, she's already been waiting for me for over an hour. Darling, I must go now.
MARIE:	What is this "darling" I must go now, to what darling's wedding?
LOUIS:	Believe me, it is only a formality. You are my only love.
MARIE:	Whom is the lady being wed? Louis?
LOUIS:	I will explain it to your satisfaction later, promise.
MARIE:	That is the only truthful thing you've told me so far. I'm sure you will be able to explain it to my satisfaction. Just answer my question now, or by all saints, I'll call Hoodoo Voodoo.
LOUIS:	My parents have arranged a marriage; for me. But I swear by all that is holy, that I shall be faithful to you. I'm coming back to you tonight (walks towards exit).
MARIE:	Ten minutes of your time. Keep her waiting ten minutes longer. If not, you will lose me forever. Go, Hoodoo Voodoo, quickly and…
LOUIS:	(Looks at watch) ten minutes, only.
MARIE:	(Drags out a statue, catholic incense and holy water). Kneel, Louis.
LOUIS:	I cannot betray my God. I am a Christian…
MARIE:	So am I.
LOUIS:	But you are adding hoodoo to the service
MARIE:	Now we begin (lights a candle. Ties Louis to herself. Throws incense) I burn this incense to bring you sweetness, which I pray shall be in your marriage. And may this union be as pure as this holy water that I sprinkle on both our brows. May the seriousness of this marriage be implanted by the holy water that will penetrate our minds, to believe as Christians, but to, share in the love that has for generations been known

by the hoodoos. Louis, as we are tied to one another in love, so may no one ever undo our love and devotion to one another (takes rose petals). I take these rose petals as a symbol of sweetness" may our union be blessed by the arrival of many buds . . . Our 'babies to be', will share in the joy of our lives. With this knife I cut you and I cut myself (places two small cuts together) let our blood flow together and be one in our hoodoo marriage, bless God, bless us, bless our baby and the hoodoo.

LOUIS: (kisses her)
MARIE: (Takes a sweet and puts it in his mouth)
LOUIS: You are free to go now, and return to me as I am your first and only wife until death do us part.
LOUIS: (Starts to go) we are bound so together.
MARIE: By our vows, I shall loosen the string that binds, but I can pull you back whenever I choose. Go now, my love, and God go with you.
LOUIS: (Exits)
MARIE: (Gets Hoodoo Voodoo's basket) You did very well, Hoodoo Voodoo. He is ours forever and ever. Now, I must mix this anti gris-gris. This is for Louis' aristocratic bride (Goes to bottles) a pinch of this and a pinch of, that... (Holds her nose) hold your breath, Hoodoo Voodoo... it is done (puts it in a bag). Now, Hoodoo Voodoo, do no other bidding but mine. You must take this gris-gris to Louis' bride. She is at the great cathedral. As she walks down the aisle, bite into the bag that holds the magic potion that I have given you. Release the powder that goes poof, and scat very quickly for home. But do not fail to hold your breath. Go, 'my beloved Hoodoo Voodoo. (Puts basket outside) come lightning,

come thunder, for the queen of Hoodoo Voodoo has spoken. May that bride of Louis keep sneezing at the church. May she continue to sneeze the whole night through (she dances around and around making the circle dance. Then the vulture (dancer) jumps into the circle and dances. He tries to capture Marie, she runs screaming...) Hoodoo Voodoo, where are you? (She gets hold of Hoodoo Voodoo, holds her up to the vulture that backs off and runs away. She hugs Hoodoo Voodoo). Thank you Hoodoo Voodoo.
(Dimming of lights to denote time)

ISABELLE: What are you doing? Don't go away until you hear what I have to tell you. Your princess Marie is to be baptized in the great cathedral.

MARIE: I know.

ISABELLE: You know everything what's the use of me telling you anything?

MARIE: Tell me what?

ISABELLE: Louis' wife sneezed all through the wedding.

MARIE: What else is new?

ISABELLE: All those important people are coming here.

MARIE: What important people? And why are they coming here?

ISABELLE: To speak to you. It seems that a young man from the most distinguished family in all of Louisiana...

MARIE: Yes?

ISABELLE: This family's son has been arrested for a crime and the evidence seems so strong against him, that there is no hope, no chance to save him from hanging.

MARIE: They should go to church and pray and also, get a good lawyer. Better yet, get the very best

ISABELLE: lawyer.
They've done all that, and now the boy's father is coming here to see you, to have you save him.
MARIE: Did you tell them I could save him?
ISABELLE: I wasn't the only one. All the servants from all the big plantations ~ the first families told the parents *about* you. Every fine lady who comes to you for charms and love potions spoke highly about you. The boy's father has said that if you save his son. There will be a very, very handsome reward for you. The whole world knows that the queen of Hoodoo Voodoo is the only one left to save him. I'd like to help him.
MARIE: You always help, only for money.
ISABELLE: This time it is different. I'd kind of know the boy...
MARIE: By reputation?
ISABELLE: Sort of. My great auntie Jasmine worked for his parents. She raised the boy, and I played with him when we were very little. So I have a personal interest in him.
MARIE: Call all the servants from the plantations, from the city, and my people from the Bayou. We will dance. After the dancing we will search the minds of each person and put all their secrets together. I shall go to church and pray each day. Hoodoo Voodoo will bring my potions. When you finish calling everyone, comeback here and watch the princess.
ISABELLE: I'm not a nursemaid.
MARIE: You wanted to help. This is the way you can. So do it right away.
ISABELLE: What are you going to do?
MARIE: First, I will pray at St. Louis cathedral, then I shall mix my potions and when the day of

	sentencing arrives…
ISABELLE:	It is tomorrow.
MARIE:	Why do they always wait until the last moment before they call me? On second thought, I'll do my gris-gris before they come to my ceremony. (Lights, candles and dances in between the candles occur on center stage.)
On apron:	Drummers enter, then the dancers. In the center stands Marie chanting and singing. Soon men and women come to dance in and around the candles. Marie is directing the dancers with arm movements and chants then she takes a snake out of a basket. She wraps it around her shoulder and does an eerie, twisting, snake-like dance. One by one, dancers fall down exhausted. Marie chanting holds the potions while the drums keep beating. She dances and slowly stops.
MARIE:	Hoodoo Voodoo, these potions are to be put under the judge's chair just before he enters the courtroom. I shall be at the St. Louis cathedral for several hours after the sun comes up to pray. There I shall meet the judge. He, of course, will not notice me but I will be in position to see him quite well (laughs) we will make eye contact. Then it is up to you, Hoodoo Voodoo. You must hurry to the court and hide under the judge's chair. (Beating of drums and lightning)

CURTAIN

The applause was deafening. Everybody was on his/her feet. Yet, when the lights dimmed again – much to the audience's surprise – the spectators sat down again.

EPILOGUE

(Stage is dark – thunder and screams – lightning strikes)
(Music continues)

DR. JOHN: (Standing at the pole as in the prologue. He is dressed as a vulture.) You know me. I am Dr.John and the spirit the vulture. I have news for all of you on this beautiful ship. The court set the accused free and the grateful father presented Marie with houses and wealth. Marie bore Louis fifteen children. True to his word, he never married Marie Laveau but was always by her side
- and in her bed. As time went on, her daughter,
- the young Marie took her mother's place at ceremonies. No one knows when Queen Marie actually died.

Today, over one hundred years after it was announced that she had died, there are thousands of people who gather at her tomb every year in the cemetery in New Orleans the Queen of gris-gris.

If you should ever meet the descendants of Hoodoo Voodoo the cat, you'll know because she has patches of grey and white. You can look into her blue, blue eyes, and whisper Hoodoo Voodoo and she will respond. But I warn you, treat this cat very well for she is a very special cat who is most loving ~ you will be privileged to know her

(Flash of lightning & thunder)

FR. CYRIL: You remind me of a photo of one Dr. John. Or, I think it is but a large vulture…? You know the

Christian church does not approve of hoodoo voodoo, gris-gris or these ceremonies such as you have seen tonight. The beginnings of hoodoo came with the slave ships to America. And the slaves developed these practices as their religion. When they adopted Christianity, the church benevolently allowed them some of the innocent procedures as they stepped toward faith. Again, Christianity has and will always frown on hoodoo, voodoo and cults. However, it is here with us and we should be aware of it. It is my opinion that there was not only Marie but also her daughter and her granddaughter that carried on her hoodoo, voodoo and gris-gris for so many years.
(Flash of lightning)

DR. JOHN: God is good
CHORUS: Amen
DR. JOHN: God is love and don't hurt nobody.
Do good as you please, God don't hurt you, but do bad and the spirits (Thunder) will get you for sure. (Lightning)
CHORUS: Amen
DR. JOHN: We need not worry but we try to keep on the good side of him.
(Thunder & lightning)
FR. CYRIL: (Lights up as he crosses the stage with a cat, Hoodoo Voodoo, in his arms). Poor kitty, what were you doing out in this storm? And why did you pick Marie's grave of all places – very strange.
DR. JOHN: (Screams) Hoodoo Voodoo lives!
Dances in a circle. Vulture dances.
Cat comes in and chases him in the circle
FR. CYRIL: Holds up a cross. Vulture drops in the circle.

	Dancer picks up Hoodoo Voodoo and exits.
CHORUS:	(Off stage): there will always be Hoodoo Voodoo.

CURTAIN

(Drums quiet down)

Amid waves of applause, appreciative whistling and words of congratulations, Babette came out on stage. This time dressed in a delightful blue gown, she bowed and then addressed her adoring audience, saying, "You have been wonderful, my friends, and I couldn't have presented this play if it weren't for the able assistance of our entertainment director, Ms. Tiffany Sylvan." She extended an arm in the direction of stage right. "Come out, Tiffany, I won't bite, I promise," she added to the crowd's titter and laughter.

When Tiffany stepped from behind the curtain, she held an enormous bouquet of red roses, which she gave to Babette as soon as she reached her.

"Oh my goodness, Tiffany," Babette said, "What am I supposed to do with these?"

"I suggest putting them in water," Tiffany quipped, winking at the audience.

"Of course, of course," Babette said, quite taken aback by the gesture. "But you know, these should go to our cast – they're the ones who made this play what it had to be." She looked in the direction of stage left. "Come, all of you," she said, "It's time for one last bow…"

Ten minutes later, the audience filed out of the theater – none without a smile on his or her face – the show had been a memorable one.

CHAPTER 51

Crabs or Crabs?

WHEN THE SUN ROSE over the eastern range surrounding the city of Cape Town, Alan was standing near the railing of the promenade deck, lost in thought. He hadn't seen South Africa in a long time and was looking forward to getting ashore for a few hours with Tiffany. He wanted to take her hand and travel through the market lanes, walk down a beach, and have a fantastic meal at a terrace restaurant.

As *The Baroness* reached her berth, and the gangway was lowered, he immediately noticed someone waving his arms about and speaking loudly to the customs' officer. He wondered who this older-looking gentleman could be. He didn't give the incident another thought until later that afternoon when Gilbert came into the medical center to see if Alan would be free to have a coffee with him on the upper deck, now that most passengers had disembarked and were on their way to a day safari or had made plans to visit some of the diamond jewelers in town.

"So, are you coming, or should I ask Ivan to unglue you from that seat," Gilbert demanded as he walked into Alan's office.

"Be right there," Alan said, logging out of his report program. He stood up and shook his head. "These reports will be the death of me," he added, following Gilbert out of the medical center."

"Speaking of death, not that it's one of my favorite subjects," Gilbert said on their way to the elevators, "Have you been able to do a preliminary autopsy on Sarah Pilkington yet?"

"Sure. A very cursory one, mind you," Alan replied.

"And do you know if it was strychnine that killed her?"

"Unless I have her stomach content analyzed, I can't answer that question, Gilbert. But she showed all the symptoms of strychnine poisoning when I found her. Why do you ask?"

"It's just that I'd like to have all my soldiers in a row before I wage war with the lawyers, the CIA and the other letters of the alphabet in the next day or so."

"Are they coming to the ship or are you meeting them in town?" Alan asked as they arrived at the café.

"Only one of the MI5 lawyers will be traveling with us back to San Fran. He's supposed to interview everyone who's been involved, even remotely, with this case."

While they were helping themselves to a mug of coffee, Alan recalled the gesticulating gentleman he saw come aboard that morning. "Would he be an older fellow with grey hair and a white suit, by any chance?"

"Yes," Gilbert said, taking a first sip of his coffee, "I mean that sounds like a good description of the man, why?"

The two men sat down. "Well I saw him wave arms and hands at the customs' officer…"

Gilbert burst out laughing and then shook his head. "Yeah, that must be our guy. But let me tell you the story behind his verbal attack on the customs' officer."

Alan was all ears now. "Okay, I'm listening."

"Well, I'll tell it the way the officer told me." He paused. "Okay, here it goes," Gilbert went on. "En route to join our ship, the stiff upper lip solicitor with an attitude to boot, boarded the airplane in Heathrow with a box of frozen crabs and asked a blonde stewardess to take care of them for him. She took the box and promised to put it in the crew's refrigerator.

"He advised her that he was holding her personally responsible for them staying frozen, mentioning in a very threatening manner that he was a solicitor, and proceeded to rant at her about what would happen if she let them thaw out.

"Needless to say, she was annoyed by his behavior. Shortly before landing in Cape Town – 14 hours later – she used the intercom to announce to the entire cabin, "Would the gentleman who gave me the *crabs* in London, please raise your hand?"

"Not one hand went up. So she apparently took them home with her."

"Are you serious?" Alan asked, unable to contain his laughter.

"Absolutely. And he wanted the officer to alert the police and have the city turned upside down to find his crabs. Of course, it wasn't the customs' problem and when I asked the officer if the man had any hope in finding his crabs, he just laughed and said, "Unless he sues the airline for the loss, I don't think he'll ever see them again".

"And where is the dear man now?"

"We've put him in Sarah's old cabin," Gilbert replied. "Maybe he'll suffer from some spell she left behind or sea-sickness once we get at sea…"

"Oh don't you call on that devil, Gilbert. I've got enough on my plate without having to deal with a wave of mal de mer, gastroenteritis or Norovirus for the rest of the cruise."

"Okay, I hear you. But I hope the Chef won't serve crab tonight, otherwise I can hear Mr. Brighton Esq., already," Gilbert said, drinking some more of his coffee. "Are you going ashore tomorrow?" he then asked.

"I hope so. I've asked Tiffany to come with me. We both officially got a day off – not that there is such a thing for me. Evelyn and Alice insisted that I take off tomorrow. Apparently they don't want to see my face all day tomorrow." Alan chuckled.

"And you guys are coming to the Captain's Table tonight, aren't you?"

"Wouldn't miss it, Gilbert. I think it will be the least we can do for Babette. She's been through so much on this cruise; a dinner is just a very small token of our appreciation in comparison to everything she's done."

"And that play – wasn't that something?"

"You said it, my friend. It's the best I've seen yet."

EPILOGUE

THE REST OF THE JOURNEY was spent in relative tranquility for the passengers and crew of *The Baroness*. Mr. Brighton, Esq. never saw one claw of his lost crabs, but delighted in being served lobster and tenderloin at every opportunity.

Alan had to admit the gentleman wasn't that bad after all. They spent quite a few hours together discussing the case, and Mr. Brighton writing and dispatching reports to the various authorities involved in the demise of the smugglers aboard *The Baroness* or what was affectionately named the *Case of the Flaming Potty* by the crew.

As for Babette, she was very sad when the day came to say "au revoir" to Edmund. Yes, it was only an "au revoir", since Alan promised both of them that they would find each other again once they came aboard another cruise.

"Okay, Granddad, are you ready?" Alan asked him as they were preparing to disembark in San Francisco.

"Yes, son, as ready as I'll ever be, I suppose." He looked at Babette, who was trying to hide the tears that were menacing to course down her cheeks. "Don't worry, my dear. I know my great-grandson is good to his word and we'll be together again very soon."

Alan then took the frame of the photograph out of its box and rubbed it gently. Seconds later, Babette, Alan and Tiffany saw Dr. Edmund Netter fly back into the picture to re-appear in it, a smile adorning his gentle face.

Tiffany took their friend in a big hug and whispered in her ear, "You'll be seeing each other very soon, I'm sure."

Babette nodded, stepping back from Tiffany's embrace. "I'll book my next cruise as soon as I've heard from you and Alan," she said. "I definitely want to travel with Edmund some more. He's such an inspiration for me."

"No problem, Babette, we'll let you know," Alan replied, giving the playwright a hug, too. "But didn't you say that you intended to go to Luxembourg at some point soon?"

"Oh yes, that's on my bucket list as well, Alan, but I'll have to see when the most opportune time to meet the Grand Duke, Henry would be. Anyway, I'll keep in touch."

As for Gilbert, he was glad this trip was over. He definitely needed a vacation, as did Simon Albertson and all the people who had been involved in this affair. None of them would ever forget this cruise and its septic tank---the flaming potty.

When Agents Mallard and Chalkstone finally returned to Washington they met with Dr. Sigmund. The latter had a lot to say about their conduct aboard *The Baroness*. "They were impervious to the consequences of their actions," Sigmund reported to their CIA supervisor. "If Dr. Mayhew hadn't prevented them from touching the cell-phone; for example, none of us aboard would be here to account for our involvement in this affair."

Some time later, listening to Dr. Sigmund's comments during one of his lectures at Stanford University, a young student of Italian descent bent over to his companion sitting beside him and said, "That reminds me of a story…"

"Okay, I'm listening," the other student said as quietly as he could.

Unfortunately, Dr. Sigmund had heard the whispering. "Mr. Calvin, since you're so keen in sharing your experience with your colleague, why don't you share it with all of us?"

Franco Calvin hesitated but then said, "Okay then, Doctor Sigmund I was just telling my friend about an old Italian Mafia Don who was dying. He called his grandson to his bed. "Grandson, I want you to listen to me. I want you to take my 45 automatic pistol, so you will always remember me."

"But, Grandpa, I really don't like guns, how about you leaving me your Rolex watch instead."

"You lisina to me, some day you goin a be runna da bussiness, you goina have a beautiful wife, lotsa money, a biga home and maybe a couple of bambino, some day you goina come hom and maybe finda you wife in bed with another man. Whata you gonna do then? Pointa to your watch and say, "TIMES UP"?"

It took several minutes for the laughter to die down, but when it finally did, Dr. Sigmund said, "Now I know why I've accepted giving these lectures. I'll make sure *my time is never up*!

Dr. Paul Davis trained in mainstream western medicine in Canada, the United States and England (Family Medicine, Occupational Medicine and Emergency Medicine). During his 35-year career, he has spent extended periods of time doing volunteer work and being a consultant in Asia, India, South & Central America and the Middle East. Dr. Davis uses his insider knowledge, as his novels are based on his ten-year career as a cruise ship doctor. He currently lives in Canada and is the director of a medical specialty group.

Look for these books by the author:

CRUISE SHIP CRIME MYSTERIES
A Medical Murder Mystery (Vol. 1)
The Curious Cargo of Bones (Vol. 2)
The German Intrigue (Vol. 3)
Murder in the Northwest Passage (Vol. 4)
The Ghost of Dr. Edmund Netter (Vol. 5)

NON-FICTION
Baby Boomer Longevity:
Strategies to Transform Your Health

Visit his websites at:
http://www.cruiseshipcrimesite.com
http://cruiseshipcrime.wordpress.com

Dr. Paul Davis is available for lectures and readings. For information regarding his availability, please contact Skye Wentworth, Publicist: skyewentworth@gmail.com.

Made in the USA
Monee, IL
09 August 2024